The Man Who Made it Rain

A true story based on the experiences of J.Dietrich Stroeh

The Great Marin County Drought of 1976-77, Our Looming Climate Crisis and the Future of Water in the State of California

By
Michael McCarthy

This is a work of fiction based on the true experiences of J. Dietrich Stroeh. Some names, places, physical descriptions and other particulars have been changed. For that reason, readers are cautioned that some details in the text may not correspond to real people, places or events.

Although the author and publisher have made every effort to ensure the accuracy and completeness of information contained in this book, we assume no responsibility for errors, inaccuracies, omissions, or any inconsistency herein. Any slights of people, places or organizations are unintentional.

QUM 10987654321
Printed in the United States of America

Library of Congress
Catalogue-in-Publication-Data:
McCarthy, Michael
The Man Who Made It Rain/Michael McCarthy
Library of Congress Control Number: 2005936995
ISBN: 0-9772371-052495

Book Design by Focus Design
www.focusd.com

Published by:
Public Ink
314 Sandpiper Court
Novato, CA 94949
themanwhomadeitrain@sbcglobal.net
www.themanwhomadeitrain.com

Contents

Chapters

INTRODUCTION

I was a U.S Congressman from the North San Francisco Bay Area when the events in this book took place. The 1976-77 drought was a wake-up call to a population that took water for granted. People in California, as in most developed countries, tend to forget that water is a precious and essential resource. Many people assume it is their right to use as much water as they want, whenever they want.

When Marin County, one of the most affluent counties in California, ran out of water during the drought of 1976-1977, it took the combined efforts of my office and of numerous local and regional agencies to turn the tap back on. Unfortunately, a quarter of a century later, we still haven't learned the lessons of this book. Struggles over water continue at the forefront of political debates and battles — not just in California, but throughout the world.

The most popular lesson of this book is that people, when educated to understand what is at stake, will respond. Water consumption was reduced by 65 percent. A spirit of cooperation existed not only through the neighborhoods of Marin County but also through all the local, state and federal agencies who collaborated on the solution – a pipeline over the four-mile-long Richmond-San Rafael Bridge.

Droughts come and go, and people forget their lessons and go back to their wasteful ways. That must change. Water conservation and recycling should be second nature, not just a crisis response. There should not be water "haves" and "have-nots." The hard work and planning that solved the crisis in the 70's should be used to solve today's water dilemmas. The kinds of unconventional cooperation that sent water across a bridge could help us find ways to equitably allocate enough water among everyone's competing demands by creating the model for a genuinely sustainable water management program anywhere. This book is a cautionary tale that reminds us that with vision, creativity and cooperation, we can make the impossible work.

John Burton
Former State Senator and U.S. Congressman

EPIGRAPH

By Michael McCarthy

Sometime around 1930, according to old tribal lessons, several traditional Hopi Indian leaders crafted a message to the world. In effect, their message said that there was a rising danger that mankind's lack of spiritual attention to the planet was going to lead to disaster.

The Hopi leaders said that this disaster would take the form of violent storms and trigger many forms of disruption that would eventually threaten all human beings. This had happened before, they warned, and all signs, including ancient prophecies, indicated it was going to happen again.

Their prophecy may be right. Since then, the air temperature in Alaska has risen seven degrees. Glaciers there are retreating at a rate of 20 feet per year. The Arctic permafrost is melting and no plans were made for this when the Alaska pipeline was built. Climatologists estimate that in 50 years there will be no glaciers left in Glacier National Park.

The seas are rising. Great storms batter the planet. Weather records of all sorts, of heat and cold, flood and drought, have been broken in every region of the world. Weather forecasters predict much more of the same yet to come . . .

The 20/20 Factor

Whiskey's for drinking, water's for fighting about.

~ Mark Twain

A simple rule governs all commodities. The law of supply and demand says that the less there is of any commodity, and the more demand there is for it, the higher its price will be. If that commodity is essential to maintaining life, in times of scarcity people will pay any price for it and do whatever is necessary to obtain it. That's how wars start.

The most essential component of life is water. People can do without food but we cannot live long without water. Oil may make the world go round, but we can survive without it. Water — fresh, clean drinking water — is about to become a very hot commodity in the world. Water is the new oil.

There is a subconscious assumption that the amount of water in the world is infinite. We all know about the water cycle. Rain falls from the sky, it flows into the seas and rises through evaporation into clouds, and the cycle repeats itself endlessly. At the same time there is another assumption that the amount of water in the world is adequate to meet the needs of the world's population. Historically, as the world's population has grown, the challenge has been to move fresh water to the people, usually in the form of reservoirs and canals. But when you start guarding, measuring and selling it, God's gift to mankind suddenly becomes a commodity.

Since the Industrial Revolution, much of the world's fresh water supply has become polluted. Our aging water infrastructure is also springing leaks. The world's underground aquifers are being drained and it will take thousands of years to replenish them. Population growth in America has meant poor people moving to desert communities in search of cheap land and rapidly emptying aquifers. Fancy desert resorts and retirement communities are springing up in the deserts, where golf courses and swimming pools suck back fresh water like sponges.

Ninety-nine percent of the world's water is found in the oceans, but it contains salt and is not drinkable. Most of the world's fresh water is preserved in a frozen form, either in glaciers or in the polar ice caps. Many of the glaciers in the world are rapidly melting due to climate change. That fresh water eventually ends up in the ocean, mixing with salt. The snows that replenish these frozen reservoirs are now often falling as rain instead, leading to early runoff from reservoirs. All water that runs off to the sea is wasted for drinking and irrigation purposes.

Several glacier-fed rivers have dried up completely in recent droughts, eliminating drinking supplies to cities. In such circumstances, unforeseen consequences can ensue; nuclear reactors are shut down because there is no water available for cooling. Cities dependent on nuclear power can experience blackouts and the ensuing economic consequences.

Some cities located next to coastlines have been able to construct desalination plants to purify salt water, but only if they have direct access to abundant sources of cheap energy. All power plants burning fossil fuels emit vast quantities of carbon dioxide, accelerating climate change. Those looking to modern technology for energy solutions may not be aware that technology itself is causing the problem in the first place.

California's water system might have been invented by a Soviet bureaucrat on an LSD trip.

~ Peter Passel, The New York Times, February 27, 1991

Most of the world's dams and reservoirs that can be built have already been built. In California, for instance, every inch of Sierra Nevada snowmelt is already being stockpiled, while most of the state's underground aquifers are being sucked dry. Meanwhile, California's population has greatly increased, along with the rest of the world's. In California, estimates are that the population could rise to as many as 48 million people as soon as 2020. While there may be efficiencies in irrigation, no more fresh water will be created for these millions of new residents.

Water wars are starting to erupt around the world. In California, farmers, fishers and environmentalists are already skirmishing over access to the same rivers. Don't forget the natives and the emerging outdoors and recreational industries either. River rafters, hikers, birders and anglers like their water too. In fact, there may be less. Urban communities are starting to fight agricultural interests in court over fresh water and will soon be competing against other urban communities for the same supply. The political ramifications are overwhelming and the economic results will be far-reaching. Already, huge agricultural interests have defeated activists trying to save the environment, but in turn those agricultural interests have lost major court battles to metropolitan districts that possess far greater political power.

The price of this most precious commodity will rise in direct proportion to increasing demand and declining supply. To chart the changes and predict the future, let's draw current water consumption, and its rising cost, as a line shooting upward on a steeply accelerating curve. Draw the expected population increase as another line, shooting upward as well, but on a conflicting path. It is theoretically possible to estimate a time when the two lines will intersect. It's less easy to predict what repercussions will result when that collision occurs, but it certainly won't be harmonious.

Since the population in California could reach 48 million by the year 2020, and given that the state's finite water supply will have increased in price by a relative amount during the same time frame, and given that many powerful interests involved will be fighting over the same supply, we have a formula for disaster.

Let's call this formula "the 20/20 factor." Using this phrase allows us to quantify a focal point and see when the ever-growing state of California will finally run out of water. Imagining the world's sixth-largest economy without sufficient water for all its needs is a difficult thing to do. Yet history teaches us that catastrophic weather-related events have ravaged California in the past. Carbon dating of ancient tree rings clearly indicates that California experienced several killer droughts long before the arrival of European settlers.

A drought can be defined as a period when it doesn't rain at all, or when far less than the usual precipitation occurs, or when less rain falls than is needed to support the population. Extended droughts, some up to 200 years in duration, have not been uncommon in California's pre-settler history, but that's not public knowledge, yet. Currently the entire state's water supply, stored in lakes and reservoirs and moved by pipelines and aqueducts, can only serve a thirsty public's demand for water for a period of 2 to 3 years. After that, the well runs dry.

Modern research also shows that the 1850s to 1880s, when we first started keeping weather records in California, were some of the wettest years in the state during the last several millennia. The data that we have been using as a yardstick for over a century may prove useless for future precipitation projections.

The future, according to some scientists, will be exactly like the past, only far more expensive.

~ John Sladek, science fiction author

As an example of what the future of water in California may look like, we have to go back only a few years. Marin County, located just north of San Francisco, is beautiful country with several reservoirs positioned to catch the bountiful winter rainfall. Marin enjoys one of the highest per capita incomes of any county in America, but during 1976 and 1977 Marin County went 25 months without rain, and its wealth didn't provide any magic solutions to the drought. Money does not make it rain. In fact, some very strange events occurred.

Marin County, because of its normally bountiful rainfall, is not connected directly to the state aqueduct system. During the Great California Drought of 1977, while much of the western United States suffered badly from a severe lack of rain, wealthy Marin County came within a prayer of disintegrating into dust. Some of the most expensive real estate in the world blew away in the wind. Lawns, gardens, parks and public lands died, as did livestock and wildlife. It's not just human beings that can't live without water.

Human nature being what it is, everyone looked for someone to blame. Local bureaucrats and water officials were cursed and threatened. Strict water rationing was imposed, rain dances were held, and bizarre plans were formulated to tow icebergs from Antarctica or to fly in snow from the frozen East Coast. Other water districts had some spare water but they refused to share. Every water district was on its own, nobody seemed to be in charge, anger and blame didn't provide any solutions, and nobody knew what to do. After all, only God can make it rain.

Panic set in. Prayers went unanswered. Prices for water went haywire. Finally, somebody took charge and a miracle occurred. No, the heavens didn't open and rainbows emerge like in the Land of Oz, but water finally came to Marin County. It's a story of political maneuvering, the foibles of human nature, and brilliant engineering.

Bitter lessons were learned about the nature of drought, but they were soon forgotten. In the fullness of time, people went back to their water-wasteful ways. You have to wonder if anyone was paying any attention. As the old saying goes, those who ignore history are doomed to repeat it.

This is a true story of "the man who made it rain." Some of the story lies in the past, some in the present, and the rest in an imaginary future. Only time will tell what will happen next, but history has taught us one thing: When you fight the laws of nature, the law always wins.

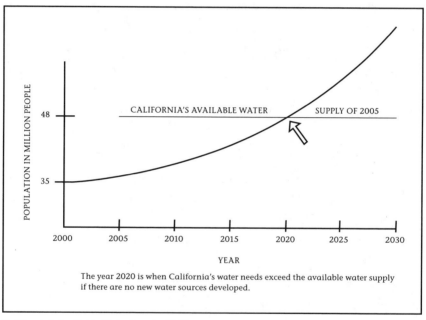

California's Available Water Supply, 2005

1 / Tingsang-La Pass, northern Nepal

We do not inherit the earth from our ancestors, we borrow it from our children.

~ Native American proverb

Nepal, late May, 2010

"Wow, like I feel like I'm 90 years old. Or something worse. Man, like I am dying here."

Breathing the rarified air at 12,000 feet is like sucking on discount oxygen, some sort of cheap "two for one" deal that turns out to be no deal at all. You breathe twice, three times, maybe you suck in one good one. Two miles high in the sky, the air is thinner than a Nepalese rupee. You want to know how it feels to be very old, or very sick, go climb a steep Himalayan mountain pass for the first time, sit down, and wait for your head to explode.

"My skull is like killing me, and I can't breathe right."

Dave Moore was panting, just sitting down and complaining.

1

"Damn," he wheezed, under what was left of his breath, "I thought this was supposed to be a stinkin' vacation, not some sorta death march."

But he said nothing to the rest of the group sitting 20 feet away. They had pitched their tents not far from the top of the pass, behind a cluster of rocks out of the wind. Sitting on the rocks just above Moore were co-trekker Will White Jr., expedition leader Bob Walsh and five porters. The view was terrific from the top of Tingsang-La, in the Dilakha region of the Himalayan mountain range in northeastern Nepal. Directly to the north, dozens of 25,000-foot mountain peaks pierced the sky like a giant's picket fence, their peaks glistening pink and silver in the setting sun. Mount Everest was only 30 miles away to the east, just another in an endless array of gigantic peaks.

But Moore wasn't enjoying the fabulous view at all. Not being able to breathe properly was only part of his unease. A much bigger pain was his trekking buddies' stupid dinner chatter, all about assorted looming disasters.

"This is a stinkin' nightmare," thought Moore. "We're all going to die up here and they'll never find our bodies."

Chowing down freeze-dried dinners while the porters warmed up their own meager meal of *tsampa*, barley dunked in Tibetan tea, the trekkers were having a chin wag while watching the mind-boggling sunset over the Himalayas. They were also conversing about the end of the world and other useful topics. Moore, sitting just behind the group out of the stiff late afternoon wind, was not enjoying the drift of the conversation at all. With a dinner of freeze-dried curried chicken stuck in his craw, the temperature starting to fall rapidly, a vicious headache and the conversation getting weird, Moore was starting to seize up.

"So what's a GLOF?" asked trek leader Bob Walsh, washing down his own dinner with a cup of hot chamomile tea. "Is that like a yeti?"

"You a trekker and you don't know what a GLOF is?" responded Will White, chewing on a mouthful of beef stroganoff. "Hey Pema, what's a GLOF?

Pema Behadur was a sherpa, the group's *sirdar*, or leader of the porters, and a local trekking guide. He thought for a moment and answered. "You hit ball with stick."

"Ha ha. No, it's science jargon for glacial lake overflow flood," said Walsh. "Happens when a lake made from melting glaciers, hanging maybe 15,000 feet in the air, suddenly overflows its boundaries and like a million tons of water fall out of the sky. Boom, like a nuclear bomb going off. Wipes out everything downriver within a hundred miles."

"Oh, yeah," replied Walsh, "I heard of something like that happening down in South America once, like back in the 1940s. Took out an entire town in 30 seconds."

"I think I've heard enough," thought Moore. He got up and dusted himself off. "Hey, I've had a tough day, guys," he called out, getting up and stretching. "I'm bagged. I think I'll pack it in and see ya in the morning."

"See ya, big guy," said Walsh. "Grab some Z's. Big day again tomorrow."

"Watch out the GLOFs don't getchya," said White.

Moore turned and ducked into his tiny mountaineering tent. Digging in the bottom of his daypack, he found the satellite phone he had stashed in the bottom along with some spare socks. He turned it on, pointed the antenna at the northeast sky, and whispered softly.

"Day seven," he said, peering through the tent flap to make sure no one was listening. "Note to Big Daddy. Ask the Home Boys to check out current status of Tsho Rolpo Lake and Trakarding Glacier. Approximately four miles northeast of village of Beding. Get satellite reconnaissance to check the exact lake levels. Look for possible imminent breach, south end of the lake. Get data on flooding possibilities in the Rolwaring Valley to the south of the lake. Immediate response requested."

Outside the tent, the rest of the group started singing, the Nepalese porters laughing while trying to follow the words of an old Beach Boys song led by White. "Ba ba ba, ba ba baran," went the refrain, carried off by the endless wind into the gathering darkness.

3

"What the hell is going on?" Moore thought to himself, putting the phone carefully away in the bottom of the pack and rooting around for a box of Advil. "My head is killing me. I'm coming down with altitude sickness. This was supposed to be like some holiday, watching out for the President's one and only crazy son. Not some stupid disaster that's gonna kill everybody within a hundred miles. Why wasn't I briefed on this GLOF junk anyway?"

Nepal, late May, 2010

The sun shone brightly and a soft wind caressed the thin high mountain air. Bob Walsh led the expedition, striding strongly up the valley, Moore following and Will bringing up the rear, lagging badly. Will was named after his father, the current President of the United States. His mother called him "Will do" for his determination, and he was "Wild Willie" to the media because he did whatever he wanted to despite strong presidential contradiction and occasional intervention. But even using his willpower, Will was totally exhausted.

The porters carried the group's mountaineering gear, except for each trekker's daypack and water bottles, but at this extreme height the hike was hard slogging for the Americans. Will had to stop every few hundred feet to grab his breath. As soon as he was rested, he began to hum, a fatigue-quelling device he had learned cramming for exams in college.

Will always hummed old rock-and-roll songs. He hummed and tapped his fingers, an endless bundle of energy always needing a release. Blue-eyed and bearded, with long blond hair hanging below his collar, at 6 feet 4 and 200 pounds of solid muscle, Will looked like a rock star or football quarterback. In Nepal, where he towered above the tiny porters, Will was a true mountain man. With his handsome Hollywood looks and famous name, he commanded immediate attention wherever he went in

America. Here in Nepal, Will was a giant, but size or no, at high altitude the porters could walk circles around him all day long despite carrying huge packs almost half their weight.

"Man, I gotta get in better shape," he thought. "These little dudes are embarrassing me."

There were eight hikers in the expedition. The leader was Bob Walsh from High Mountain Adventures out of Denver, plus Will, Dave Moore, sirdar Pema Behadur and the Nepalese porters. At this extreme elevation, all three Americans were going so slowly that every few hundred yards, the porters would rest their heavy loads on a rock and wait for them to catch up.

The expedition had met on the first day back in the capital, Kathmandu. They gathered first at an inn in the Thamel district that international trekkers favored, then spent a day checking out the ancient city's markets and streets while buying more supplies. They met Pema, their sirdar, who had worked for High Mountain on previous treks in eastern Nepal. Pema selected four porters he knew from previous expeditions he had led, and Walsh bought them new sneakers for the trek.

Will thought Moore and Walsh seemed to be pretty good guys, the same age as himself. He knew that Moore was probably another damned bodyguard ordered by his father to keep watch, even though Moore called himself a student. Will couldn't go anywhere without some Secret Service guys hanging around in the background, part of the price of being the son of the U.S. President.

"Davey-boy, do me a favor," he shouted to Moore, just above him in the line of trekkers. "Dial up a pepperoni and sausage pizza, will ya? I'm gettin' kinda peckish back here."

Aside from security surveillance, Will was usually under constant media watch too, which was a good reason to head out on expeditions where the media couldn't follow. He requested total privacy on his own personal affairs and excursions, but that was a luxury he never seemed to get, although he had shaken off the paparazzi in New Delhi by switching

5

planes. At age 22, a university scholar and adventurer, he was both a popular figure in the public eye and the apple of his father's eye. But no matter what, it seemed he could never be let alone.

"Sure dude," shouted Moore into the wind. "Ya want anchovies and olives on that?"

By 2025, 52 countries, with two-thirds of the world's population, will likely have water shortages.

~ National Rivers System

By day three, the expedition had driven two Jeeps, loaded down with all the necessary equipment, to the trailhead to start what was planned as a 20-day trek. At a mere 2,500 feet, the town of Barabise was low enough in elevation that none of the hikers was going to suffer any ill effects from altitude, so they set out immediately for their first campsite at Dolangsa, beyond which lay the first mountain pass.

At Bigu they rested a day, then trudged slowly on to Laduk and a night sleeping on the wooden floor in the relative luxury of the tiny local schoolhouse. The next day they slowly trudged on to Simigaon and the Shakpa Pass at 7,000 feet, up to Dalldung-La at 11,500 feet, on to Ramding and finally down into the district capital at the little village of Beding. For any lover of high mountains, it was the trek of a lifetime.

After Beding, they would hike up to a summer yak encampment the local herders called Na, the last trace of human habitation in the district, and one of the highest inhabited places on the planet. Then would come the highlight of the trip, a quick detour that Will had specially requested, up to the rarely visited Trakarding Glacier and Tsho Rolpa glacial lake.

By day 15 the expedition would end up at Namche Bazaar, the famous trekking village that is the gateway to Mount Everest, to spend several days in the region. From there, the party would trek south to Lukla where, at just under 10,000 feet, a precarious high-altitude landing strip clings to the edge of the mountain. With luck and good weather, after three weeks trudging in the highest mountains on earth, the expedition would then board a plane and fly back to Kathmandu.

High Mountain Adventures usually led recreational treks for rich American hikers looking for "off the beaten track" experiences, but Will was keen on reaching one of the Himalayan glacial lakes he'd been researching. If the newest environmental warnings were accurate, many Himalayan glaciers were shrinking quickly, thanks to global warming. They were like the proverbial canary in a coal mine. Will thought that proving glaciers in the world's highest mountains were disappearing might possibly convince his father that global warming was no longer just a theory, but a proven fact. If even the highest places on the planet were melting, thought Will, maybe his Dad would finally take some action on combating climate change. And of course a hike through the highest mountains on earth, without hordes of paparazzi following him around, would be a blast.

According to a report from the Swiss-based World Wide Fund for Nature, the rate of retreat of glaciers in the world's high mountains had recently accelerated up to 100 feet per year in some instances. As glaciers melt, they sometimes leave behind glacial lakes, usually constrained by nothing more than natural dams formed by buildup of glacial moraine, a loose fill of rocks and ice falling off the mountains that form temporary, and very unstable, holding pens. When a glacial lake suddenly breaches its moraine dam, which can be caused by a variety of factors ranging from earthquakes to heavy rains or simple collapse from water pressure, very bad things are known to happen. A few million tons of lake poised high up in the sky, ready to explode into a catastrophic shower of boulders and a river of water, can be hazardous to anyone living below.

Water is nine thousand times heavier than air. If conditions are right, the sudden meltdown of a glacial lake falling out of the sky can have the impact of a nuclear bomb. Within minutes, millions of tons of debris will race downstream, sweeping away everything in its path like a giant tsunami. Best not to be underneath when one blows.

According to Will's best research, Tsho Rolpa Lake had expanded greatly in the past three years from glacial melt, and was expected to breach, sooner or later. A small research station had been built at the 15,000-foot elevation of the lake's shoreline, and a sluiceway constructed to let the glacial melt slowly drain through the moraine dam. It could be years before the lake fell out of the sky, if it ever did, but Will wanted to see for himself what a glacial lake with impending GLOF actually looked like. And, of course, any excuse to hike the high mountains of the world was an excuse he would always make, extreme dangers or not. Hey, especially if there were dangers.

"Hey guys, wait up," yelled Will at the porters far ahead. "You're dealing with an old man here. I can't keep up."

Because we don't think about future generations, they will never forget us.

~ Henrik Tikkanen, writer

The hiking party reached the top of the Shakpa Pass, crossed and descended 1,000 feet or so. They settled down for the night at a rock hut that had been built in the lee of the wind as an emergency shelter for hiking groups such as this. The Americans rested while the porters quickly prepared the evening meal. Over another dinner of freeze-dried beef stroganoff, Walsh hit Will with questions about the detour he wanted to make to look at Tsho Rolpa Lake, a unique geological feature Walsh had never seen on any of his treks.

Although Walsh would also call himself an environmentalist ("Hey, we all have to breathe the same air, don't we?") he was far more adventurer than scientist. Blond and bearded like Will, but short, thin and wiry, Walsh was an indefatigable climber. His High Mountain Expeditions would take any trekkers to any destination in the Himalayas they wanted to go, but most of his clients were simply wealthy tourists who wanted to trek to exotic places while traveling in relative luxury. This was the first quasi-scientific expedition Walsh had led, and he was interested in Will's theories. At rest stops all along the trek, he peppered Will with questions.

"This research I'm doing here in the Himalayas is really all about drought," said Will, between bites of food. "I'm gonna write a book on it. You see, glacial meltdown's main threat isn't really about water, it's more about the lack of water that you get as an end result."

"OK, now you got me confused," answered Walsh, sipping from a Thermos of hot tea. "I thought you said back in Kathmandu that sometime soon there was going to be a great, almighty mother of a flood happening in some of the highest mountains of the world. Like here in the Himalayas. You said it'll be like Noah's Ark, part two. Major meltdown. I thought this is all about flooding. So, what part of drought are we talking here? No comprende, padre."

"Yeah, first comes the almighty flood," said Will, holding a bottle of filtered water up to the late afternoon sun, watching its dying rays bounce off in multiple colors. "What happens is, a lot of these gigantic mountain glaciers are rapidly melting as the planet gets hotter, right? And the glacial lakes that sometimes result from the melt are expanding, and what's holding them back? Not much. One day soon one of these suckers is gonna blow its banks, and then look out! We're talking like billions of gallons of water blasting downhill. When it blows, anything and everyone below that lake is gonna be wiped out for like hundreds of miles, dude. Major floods, complete disaster."

"I still don't see how that causes any drought," said Walsh, draining the last of his own bottle of filtered water. "Flooding sounds like a lot more water, not less."

"Not the way it works out in the long run, bro," replied Will. "A GLOF only happens, like, once in a blue moon. Very rare. What will happen all over the world is, increased glacial melting will mean a lot more water flowing into rivers, which means lots more flooding downstream, but only initially. Like, for a decade or so, until all the ice is gone."

Will got up and pointed south, toward the plains far below.

"For instance, way down there in Bangladesh, at sea level, which is already flooded during the monsoon season every year anyway," he said, "with a lot more flooding, now you're looking at the whole country being about seven feet under water. Comes a big monsoon, with all the increased rainfall, maybe 50 or 100 million people will need evacuating. The lucky ones make it to high ground, the rest end up dog paddling in the Indian Ocean."

"Well, Bangladesh is already kinda messed up big time anyway, isn't it?" butted in Moore, who so far hadn't said a word. "They already have major floods every year, and typhoons and monsoons and stuff. Where's any drought fit into the big picture? Sounds like a drought would be good for them."

"Hey dude, you're only looking at the small picture," replied Will, sitting down and resuming his meal. "You got to look at the entire global situation. Its not just Bangladesh getting flooded, it's not just the Himalayas. They got glaciers in America too, and Canada, and South America and Europe. All over. What happens is, after the ice all melts, the initial flooding will be over. Gone, kaput. All that nice fresh water ends up way out in the ocean, mixing with the salt water, and you can't drink that. After the glaciers have disappeared, there won't be any melt water coming down from the mountains. Gone, dude. So, first the floods, then comes the drought."

Will wandered over to the edge of the ridge, and looked up to the range of mountain peaks glowing red and pink in another gorgeous Himalayan sunset.

"Besides Bangladesh, anybody living at sea level anywhere is gotta be worried. A few trillion acre-feet of water flooding into the world's oceans? Seas are gonna rise a lot. Waterfront property at Malibu? Gone. The French Riviera? Say goodnight, Dick. And places like the Maldive Islands are gonna be under water permanently. Like very soon, along with anyone else living at sea level," he said. "The sea level is going to rise a lot."

"OK," said Moore. "I get it. Land dry, sea wet, major problems."

"What about Florida?" asked Walsh. "And the Gulf Coast? They got whacked by Hurricane Katrina a few years ago. They goin' under too?"

"Yeah, it's not just expensive oceanfront property where the rich folks live," continued Will. "First the water level in all the rivers fed by melting glaciers will drop, and all the people who depend on that fresh water from those rivers will have to move somewhere else. Hundreds of millions of people depend on water from the high mountains. So what we are talking about is like a global water crisis, dude. No more easy water. That's the drought I'm talking about."

"You see that mountain?" he said, pointing to Mount Everest, some 30 miles to the east, glistening in the quickly dying light. "It's famous because it's the highest mountain in the Himalayas and the highest in the world, right? This whole mountain range, and the glaciers in Tibet, they feed the biggest seven rivers in Asia. Some of those rivers are going to dry up, at least to some degree, over the next few decades."

"Let's see," said Walsh, getting up and following Will to the edge of the trail. "I know this area of the world pretty good. You got the Ganges, the Indus, the Bhramaputra, the Mekong, the Salween, Yangtze and Yellow rivers, all major rivers flowing downhill out of Tibet. So we're talking massive floods in Nepal, Bangladesh, India and China, just for starters?"

"Yeah," responded Will, walking over to the edge of the trail and looking down. "Then after the flooding is over, we are talking like serious

11

water shortages for about 500 million people, and that's just in Asia. Last week I read that the minister of the interior in China said they got 180 million people they know they got to move eventually. They know there won't be enough water in western China in a few decades, when the rivers start to dry up."

From the trail, Will turned and pointed a finger way down toward the Gangetic plains, on which hundreds of millions of people have survived for centuries.

"Take just India and Bangladesh. You start messing with a billion people," he said, "you got a few problems on your hands. Wars have started over a lot less. I wouldn't want to be in charge of controlling all that mess, not for all the tea in China."

"How about your dad, then?" asked Moore, a look of curiosity spreading across his face. "Have you talked to him about all this? What's he say?"

"Of course we talk, whenever I see him. He said global warming is just a theory, and he doesn't make political decisions based on theories. He also said he isn't going to be President of the United States by the time all this crap happens," answered Will, clearing his throat and spitting into the void, "so he says he doesn't care about it. Not his problem, so why should he care?"

2 / Before the deluge

And it never failed that during the dry years the people forgot about the rich years, and during the wet years they lost all memory of the dry years. It was always that way.

~ John Steinbeck, "East of Eden," 1952

Marin County, late May, 2010

While the trekkers were watching the sunset in Nepal, halfway around the world in northern California, J. Dietrich Stroeh, retired civil engineer and grandfather of seven, was bustling around the kitchen of his country house. The Stroehs, Diet and wife Margaret, lived in the rich countryside outside of Novato, 25 miles north of San Francisco. Marge was washing and Diet drying dishes from the evening meal. Novato, a prosperous town of 50,000 residents in Marin County, was a pleasant country town, a nice mix of suburban American middle-class houses surrounded by hobby farms, horse ranches, and fields of green. No glacial melt, no floods, no drought in beautiful Novato.

13

Novato is comfortably situated at the northern end of magical Marin, a stunningly beautiful slice of semi-rural real estate comprising low rolling hills and lush valleys, deep groves of old oak trees and redwood forests, waterfalls and chattering creeks, and sandy beaches on the ocean. With its wonderful weather and gorgeous topography, Marin County may be one of the most beautiful places in the world.

The Stroehs have lived in their country home for over three decades, since the days back in the 1970s when Diet was general manager of the Marin Municipal Water District. Dietrich, or Diet ("Deet") as everyone called him, still worked occasionally at CSW Stuber Stroeh and Company, the civil engineering firm he founded when he left the MMWD. The company's offices were located in a small one-story building in what passed for "downtown" in Novato, really nothing more than a few square blocks of retail stores and light industrial warehouses just off Highway 101, the six-lane freeway that runs south through the county down to the big city of San Francisco.

The Stroeh house was hidden away in the Verissimo Hills, a couple of miles west of Novato. Back in the early 80's, after he left the water district, for $50,000 Diet bought eleven acres, which, at that time, was nothing more than empty farmland way out in the country. People thought he was crazy to spend that kind of money for a place where nobody would ever want to live. Then he sold off all but two acres, enough space for seven lots on which he built seven luxury homes. It always pays to plan ahead. Population growth is inevitable. Engineers are practical people who think of things other folks might not, like urban growth.

Diet built his own home on one of the lots, down by a little creek that ran through the valley, right next to a big grove of old oak trees. Designed after the General Vallejo house, named for the Mexican military leader who founded Northern California's first town at Sonoma over 150 years ago, the Stroeh home was built in a style that can be called "early Californian," with sweeping wooden balconies all around the exterior to block out the hot summer sun. To an engineer, every detail was important, especially practical details such as keeping out the sizzling summer heat. Every inch bore his handiwork.

The phone in the Stroeh living room rang. Diet, a sturdy and stocky man just above average height with a thick mop of blond hair gone gray, moved with the quickness of the amateur boxer he once was way back in high school. His wrist was bandaged from a fall off a fence the previous week, the result of an overeager job of landscaping. At age 74, he was still a workaholic, an active, high-energy, no-nonsense kind of guy who left no task undone for long.

On the second ring, since none of the grandchildren watching TV in the living room made a move to answer the phone, Diet picked it up. In a gruff voice, left over from smoking cigarettes during the tense years when he was managing the water district, he answered.

"Who is it?"

"Hello, is Megan there please?" Megan was Diet's granddaughter from his daughter Christina, now in her 40's and over for a visit from her own home on the other side of Novato, over at Black Point on San Pablo Bay. Tonight was a bit of a family reunion. Megan, 10, a slim blue-eyed beauty with a red barrette holding back her long blond hair, was sitting in front of the television along with her sister Erica, age 8, a constant bundle of energy. Cousin Alex was also over, at 12 the senior citizen and wise old owl of the pack. None of them bothered to look up when Grandpa walked into the room. There was a special show on TV about climate change, not normally something the kids would watch, but Megan had a geography project she had to finish for homework.

"Megan," he said, striding into his study with the cordless kitchen phone in his hand, "it's for you. I think it's Britney Spears looking for a backup singer. She's calling Earth from outer space on her special interplanetary rocket ship, so I think you should answer."

Megan made a face; Grandpa had a wicked sense of humor, usually a bit saltier when there were no little girls in the vicinity. She reached for the phone, keeping both eyes glued to the screen. On the TV, meteorologist Joel Bartlett, an old friend of Grandpa's from back in the old days, was explaining something about the jet stream and how it affects Marin's weather. Bartlett had been a staple of Bay Area weather forecasts for over 30 years, way back to the Great California Drought of 1977, and his weather forecast was taken as gospel.

"The Sierra Nevada snowpack this past winter was down about 50 percent from normal levels," explained Bartlett, pointing to a computer graphic on the screen. "That means state reservoirs are also down about 50 percent, which means that we can expect serious rationing across the state later this summer."

Phone calls when the TV was on were a major irritation, but Megan took the phone and wandered out of the room, talking absently, the way 10-year olds are likely to act when on the phone or doing anything more complicated than chewing gum.

"Well kids, what's my old pal Joel up to today?" said Diet, settling into the chair vacated by Megan. "Last time I watched, he was telling us that the end of the world is coming. Did I miss it? Are we going to have another drought, or what?"

Over 25 years since leaving the water district, he still had water on the brain. Fresh water, salt water, floods and droughts, tsunamis in southeast Asia; if anybody knew the importance of water to the planet and its thirsty inhabitants, it was J. Dietrich Stroeh.

"As part of this special program on climate change," said Bartlett, "we take you now to Janet Spalding at our New York headquarters."

New York City, late May, 2010

Janet Spalding was the rising star of the network, a striking blond woman in her early 50's who, thanks to the magic of Botox and cosmetic surgery, appeared to be no more than 35. Stunningly dressed in a silk blouse with matching scarf, Spalding looked every bit the major network news anchor. The first female to head a major network news division, Spalding was tough, seasoned and sexy but with an icy demeanor that put chills down the backs of old-fashioned political hacks and smart-mouthed media pundits alike.

"This just in from Washington, D.C," said Spalding. "President William White has just called a news conference at the White House for tomorrow to deal with the growing crisis over the drought in the western states, the worst crisis since the late 1970s. We have just learned the President will be making a statement in connection with the news coming out of Phoenix, that Arizona will not be able to meet its commitments to allow downstream water out of the Colorado River. There simply is not enough water to share. This is the first time they have been unable to keep their commitment to Mexico."

"The news making the rounds at the White House, according to staff that we've spoken with, is that the President is finally willing to reopen talks with the European Community and take immediate steps to counteract global climate change," said Spalding. "That will certainly be a historic moment. The United States, both under this and previous administrations, has always refused to sign any treaties acknowledging that climate change or global warming even exists."

"It's obvious that the President needs to do two things. First, he has to keep his traditional support from the energy sector," Spalding continued. "Second, he needs to find some new votes from the middle, where a lot of people are coming to agree that climate change is going to have a huge impact on the economy if some action isn't taken soon. The President simply can't continue to stonewall about climate change like he has in the past, and he knows it."

Politics is supposed to be the second-oldest profession. I have come to realize that it bears a very close resemblance to the first.

~ Ronald Reagan

"Grandpa," said Megan, who had wandered back into the room and was watching the TV, "is climate change like the same as global warming? Our teacher says that global warming is a terrible threat to the future and the United States is the biggest polluter in the world."

"Well kids," said Diet, leaning forward and giving her a big wink. "I'll tell you what it is. In fact, if you are really good and promise not to squabble, I'll make a big vat of popcorn and tell you a really good story about it."

"Yea!" shouted the kids in unison, jumping on the couch and huddling together. "Grandpa's going to tell us another bedtime story."

"You want to know what climate change means, kids?" he asked, once they were settled. "It sounds pretty dull, but actually it's pretty exciting. Once upon a time, long ago and far away, like way back in 1976, long before you were born, there was a magic kingdom called Marin County. In this magic kingdom, in those days, there were no traffic jams, everybody had a nice little house, and the weather was always perfect."

"Every day was a sunny day, even in the winter," he continued. "It never rained, ever. It was very nice weather for a very long while and then one day people realized that it had stopped raining entirely. Just like that. It never rained, week after week, month after month, even in the winter, and people began to worry when it would rain. Everything turned to dust and blew away in the wind and everybody wondered if it was ever going to rain ever again. I was the manager of the water system, you see, and it was my job to make sure everybody had water, for drinking and watering their plants and lawns and gardens. So, what happened was, eventually, everybody turned to me, and asked me if I could make it rain, pretty please . . ."

We should all be concerned about the future because we will have to spend the rest of our lives there.

~ Charles F. Kettering, electrical engineer and inventor

---

3 / In the beginning

A perfect summer day is when the sun is shining, the breeze is blowing, the birds are singing, and the lawn mower is broken.

~ James Dent, author

Marin County, December 18, 1975

On December 7, 1975, Billy Compton signed a deal with Fantastic Records for a nifty $50,000 signing bonus and a nice slice of the royalty pie. Hey man, that's what happens when you send two gold records to the top of the charts back-to-back, right? To sweeten the deal, Fantastic even threw in a 1958 Sunbeam Tiger sports car. OK, it was a used Tiger, but they stopped making them like 20 years ago, and it came with twin carbs and white racing stripes down the side. Billy used to take the beast out for Sunday drives from his home high above Kentfield in Marin County, which he had bought from the sales of his first album, which happened to go gold. He kept a Rolls Silver Cloud in the garage, only to be used for ceremonial purposes like weddings and funerals. Lately the funerals seemed to exceed the weddings by a 2-1 ratio, but hey, that's life in the rock music biz.

On December 18, reeling from a harsh two weeks of savage partying, Billy felt the urgent need to commune with nature. He had perfected several ways he could do this, some of which were even legal. Jumping into the Tiger, he roared down Crown Boulevard to Magnolia Avenue down by the college and headed west out Sir Francis Drake Boulevard. That was a fancy name for what was really just a two-lane country road, which he drove all the way out to Point Reyes National Seashore, where the vibes were always right and there were no fuzz or narcs to drag you down over details.

Today the sun shone in an endlessly blue sky. No clouds, no sign of rain, not even any weekend hikers. Arriving at the Point Reyes seashore after a leisurely hour's drive, Billy slowly walked the long sandy beach, looking for spiritual inspiration for his next song. Billy watched some whales spouting off the shoreline on their annual migration from the Arctic Ocean to the shallow bays of Baja California in Mexico, and wondered whether life was really as simple as it seemed.

"Man, this is tolerable," he thought dreamily. "I could retire here and do, like, nothing. Forever."

After a suitable period of time, when musical genius failed to thrust itself upon him, Billy drove back home. On the way, he took a little detour to Phoenix Lake, on the slight chance that karmic inspiration might be lurking at the lake rather than the ocean. He parked the Tiger in the tiny lot at Natalie Green Park just below the lake, a mile from his home, and walked up the fire road. On his left, the concrete spillway that drained excess water from the lake during the rainy season stood empty. During many Decembers the spillway roared into action and became an instant waterfall, hurling tens of thousands of gallons of pure water down into Ross Creek far below. A sign warned walkers to stay away from the floodgates, but today the spillway was dry.

Drifting around the shore of the lake in a daze, Billy stumbled into another man, an older gentleman walking his dog on a leash. Percival F. Walton was Billy's neighbor and a serious pain in the ear hole. Pompous, spectacled, always wearing suspenders and sporting highly polished wing tip shoes, his thin white hair combed forward over his bald spot, old Percy was a nightmare from another generation. Immediately upon Billy's arrival in Kentfield, Percy had complained bitterly to the neighbors about the "riffraff" that had recently moved into the neighborhood, i.e. rock-and-roller Billy G. Compton. Billy wasn't sure what cheesed Percival off more, the fact that a rowdy rocker had moved in right next door, or the fact that Billy made more money in a week than Percival did in an entire year, and did so without actually "working."

Percy Walton was really only a glorified bookkeeper with a fake British accent, picked up on his annual budget vacations to England where he sponged off relatives in Oxfordshire, and carefully polished like a bowling trophy. Percy had inherited the family home and accounting business a few years back when his ancient mother finally passed away. He was property rich but cash poor, and his poverty in comparison to others in his neighborhood was a sore point that flared into anger whenever he saw longhaired hippies such as Billy, especially longhairs with lots of money. Percy didn't like hippies whatsoever, and verbalized that opinion whenever offered the opportunity.

"Hey Perce, how's it hangin'?" said Billy, as he came nose to nose with his obnoxious neighbor. "Groovy weather, ain't it?"

"What are you doing down here at the lake?" replied Percy, in his affected manner, while his dog Roscoe tried to sink his nose into Billy's crotch. "I wasn't aware that you had any affection for exercise, or a penchant for any sort of recreation that required either effort or clothing."

"Well, I come down here to the lake from time to time to, uh, meditate," said Billy, "and today's just one of those days."

"Have you seen the level of the water in the lake?" inquired Percy, pulling hard on Roscoe's leash. "There is almost no water left in this lake. It had better rain soon or we are going to be in trouble with our water supply."

"Whaddya mean? So, like this is where the county's drinking water comes from?" asked Billy, taking a quick glance at the lake. Normally the water in Phoenix Lake filled the banks right up to the brim, and in winter there was usually lots of overflow roaring down the spillway. Billy noticed that the lake was less than half full, and that reeds and other plants were sticking up through the surface in some places.

"No, actually the rain falls from the sky and we stick out our tongues and catch it like turkeys," replied Percival, in his snottiest voice. "Then we put it in pipes and it leads to your kitchen, where you turn on the tap and out it comes as water. Unless all you drink is beer, which apparently is what some people do."

"So, when was the last time it rained?" asked Billy, refusing to take the bait and thinking wistfully of finishing his smoke. He had only moved to Marin from Haight Ashbury in San Francisco recently and lacked essential local history about such things as drinking water and rainfall patterns.

"I don't remember exactly," said Percival, over his shoulder, walking away while Roscoe strained on the leash, still interested in Billy's crotch. "Certainly it didn't rain much last spring, at least not enough to remember. I guess maybe last winter about this time was the last time."

"Wow," said Billy. "So Marin has, like, the best weather in the world, right? I mean, I've been here six months and it hasn't rained at all. Man, compared to Seattle, which is like living in a carwash, this place is like heaven."

"Do they have any droughts in Seattle?" snapped Percival, as he walked away. "What do they do in Seattle when they have a drought? Bathe in Budweiser?"

You can observe a lot just by watching.

~ Yogi Berra

"What a moron," said Percy, trudging up the steps to his modest home on Crown Avenue in Kentfield, with lovely views of Phoenix Lake far below. "If it didn't rain for 10 years that silly hippie would be happy. These longhairs wouldn't know a desert from a dessert, even if it were a cream Danish."

Percy picked up his mail from the box at the top of the stairs.

"What's this then?" he thought, opening a letter from the Marin Municipal Water District. "A rebate from the last water bill, I hope?"

Grim-faced, Percival read the letter and his anger began to grow. Unless it rained soon, warned the letter, restrictions would be imposed on the use of water throughout Marin. Also, of more importance to Percy, water rates might have to be raised.

"Bloody bureaucrats," he swore, "always out for other people's money. Stealing is what it is. My rosebushes! I haven't worked for years on my garden to let it be harmed by simple bureaucratic foolery. We'll see about this."

He slammed the door behind him, catching Roscoe's tail. Roscoe began to howl, and his howl was almost as loud as Percy's. Percy picked up the phone and dialed the MMWD number listed on his bill. When the receptionist answered, he was ready with a barrage of questions.

"What in the world is this bloody notice I have just received in the mail?" he blustered. "This isn't a notice, this is a threatening note. I'd like to talk to the general manager, please."

One fifth of the world's freshwater fish — 2,000 of 10,000 species identified — are endangered, vulnerable, or extinct. In North America, the continent most studied, 6 percent of all mussels, 5 percent of crayfish, 4 percent of amphibians, 3 percent of fish, and 75 percent of freshwater mollusks are rare, imperiled, or already gone.

~ NJAWWA.com

After Percy left in a huff, Billy Compton stood on the edge of Phoenix Lake, where reeds peeked through the mud in the nearly empty reservoir, and poked the mud with a stick. He was lost in thought, or "meditating" as he would have said, if someone asked. His manager was suggesting that he and the band go out on the road to support his new album, and his promoter had offered the chance of a big festival right in Golden Gate Park, but his latest girlfriend wanted to go to Paris. Ah, choices, choices.

The boys in the band were still partying from the new record deal, and radio stations were playing up the album heavily. Billy just wanted to relax and enjoy the winter, then hit the beach and do nothing. He was lost; there were so many things to think about, and not enough concentration to go around.

A soft wind sighed and waves rippled over what was left of the lake. High above, the blue skies were completely free of clouds. There was no sign of rain. "Man, what a beautiful place," thought Billy. "I have finally arrived. It's like I have died and gone to heaven."

Billy hopped back in the Tiger, and headed back home, lost in a dream, thinking about a rhythm that was running through his head. Over and over, the music riffed through his brain, while he tried to think of words that matched the rhythms.

"I know where that vibe comes from," he thought to himself. "It's just like that mid-section bridge from that Jefferson Airplane song, the part about feeding your head. It builds up and up, and then right there at the end it's like you are going to rip your own head off and feed it to the mushroom monster. I wonder if I can take that section, and then maybe switch it from voice to guitar, and add some organ behind it?"

Billy roared up the steep hill in Kentfield, cut hard left onto his own street, and pulled the Tiger into his driveway, narrowly missing Roscoe, who was sitting in his favorite spot for basking in the sun, which was Billy's driveway. Billy hit the horn and Roscoe bounded up and away in just the nick of time, barking furiously.

Percy jumped off his front porch, where he had been tending his rosebushes, and yelled at Billy. "Hey, watch where you are going, you imbecile!"

But Billy was in another world, where syncopated rhythms were building up to a crescendo, and didn't hear a word. His tape deck was cranked as loud as he could crank it, and he was howling along to the music on the radio. "Feed your head . . ."

4 / In the classroom

Berkeley, California, September 2006

Good morning, class. Welcome to the college campus here in Berkeley. Please find a seat and sit down. My name is Professor Constance Klein. Here in the Geography Department, we'll be studying Earth System Science for the next few semesters, particularly as it applies to water here in the Bay Area and the State of California. Earth Sciences is an interdisciplinary field that describes the cycling of energy and matter between the different spheres of the earth system. Water will be our primary focus.

For those students who have already asked, yes, one subject we'll be discussing is global climate change. Or "global warming," for those who prefer that phrase. But not just yet. We'll start with an overview of the interactive processes that result in the mosaic of environments on planet Earth. Environmental change will be explored in a variety of ways so as to distinguish between natural and human-induced climatic changes.

For those so inclined, later on we'll also present a class in climate dynamics, with an emphasis on California. That will examine how various components of the climate system — the atmosphere, ocean, and land — interact together. We'll take a look at surface energy balance, the hydrologic cycle, and the role of the ocean in the world's weather. Yes, we will include computer modeling of the current global climate.

For those who are planning to speciaize later on in glaciology, we'll start with a review of the mechanics of glacial systems. Then we'll move on to glacial flow mechanisms, hydrology, temperature and heat transport, global flow and response of ice sheets and glaciers. We will examine glaciers as geomorphologic agents and as active participants in climate change.

First, I'd like to welcome to the campus all those students who are new to the Bay Area, especially those of you who have already asked about the fabulous fog we see outside our window this morning. The Bay Area is famous for its microclimates. It may be foggy here on the campus, and hot and sunny just over the inland mountains. Every few miles the weather changes.

I quote the poet Carl Sandberg: "The fog creeps in on little cat feet. It sits looking over harbor and city on silent haunches and then moves on." Actually, in my opinion, San Francisco's fog does nothing of the sort. It squats on the city like a heavy blanket, summer and winter, and only sometimes does it actually move on. But really, San Francisco's famous fog is one of the most amazing weather phenomena in the world.

It's our unique geographic location, as you can see on the map, tucked away between the cool waters of the Pacific Ocean and the hot inland deserts of California, which generates the fabulous fog. As we all know, heat rises, so the heat of the inland deserts acts as a giant convection oven, sucking in cooling air from the waters of the Pacific Ocean through the Golden Gate and various nearby mountain passes. The fog is like Mother Nature's very own air conditioner.

On a hot summer day the fog gets so thick around the Golden Gate that the air temperature can be 50 degrees cooler than the inland valleys just behind us, a few miles away. The hotter it gets outside the city, the thicker the fog grows along the coast. It's very weird.

Personally, I live in Marin County, which is over in the North Bay. While we wait for the last stragglers to come in, let me tell you a little bit about the weather where I live. As beautiful as San Francisco can be on a summer day, there is really no place on the planet like Marin County.

We're finally going to get the bill for the Industrial Age. If the projections are right, it's going to be a big one: the ecological collapse of the planet.

~ Jeremy Rifkin, World Press Review, December 30, 1989

For me, crossing the Golden Gate Bridge and driving through the Waldo Tunnel into Marin County is like falling down the rabbit hole in Alice in Wonderland. The instant you arrive on the other side of the tunnel into Marin, everything is different. The fog lifts and the sun shines.

The weather in Marin, along with a few other regions of the Northern California coast, has been described as being Mediterranean in nature. That means the weather is characterized by mild temperatures, dry summers with cool evenings, soft springs and warm falls, and a short winter with often intense rains that fill up the county's reservoirs and lakes.

Marin County is really just a peninsula totally dominated by the mighty mountain at its center, Mount Tamalpais. Depending on which side of Mount Tam you are on — or which time of day, or which season — the weather may be completely different. At 2,571 feet, it's not a huge mountain, but its influence on Marin and the Bay Area weather is fairly significant. Located right next to the Golden Gate, the mountain affects the winds and fog in the Bay Area a great deal, and it certainly affects Marin County.

It always seems to be sunny on some part of the mountain, but you can also get fog in every season of the year. The west side, where fog comes through the Golden Gate, gets some of the coolest summer temperatures in all of North America. The north side, protected by the summit, can be free of fog at the same time, with temperatures up to the 90's, depending on which ridge or valley you're in. In the late fall or early winter, the Pacific High Pressure Zone retreats north up the Pacific Ocean, with the jet stream following, and suddenly the six to eight months of our endless summer in Marin is gone, and we get big storms, from either Hawaii or Alaska, depending on circumstances that we'll discuss later.

During the winter, radiation fog often covers parts of the mountain, especially the north side. Radiation fog occurs when the ground gets saturated from the storms, and sometimes in the morning temperatures are low enough that the moisture condenses into thick fog in the valleys. Then, as soon as it gets warmer and sunnier, the radiation fog disappears and it's like summer again, even in the winter. You have to live in Marin to appreciate the crazy weather. The weather in Marin County is just like everything else in Marin. In a word, it's pure magic.

The coldest winter I ever spent was a summer in San Francisco.

~ Mark Twain

The Pacific Ocean weather phenomenon known as El Niño affects the entire California coastline, so it also affects Marin County. Warming of the deep ocean off the coast of Chile changes the weather patterns in the entire Pacific Ocean, producing warm, intense storms all along the California coast. In January of 1982, an El Niño storm dropped so much water on much of Marin County that entire downtown areas were under water. There are old photos of people kayaking through the main street of San Anselmo. Another deluge flooded much of the county in 2006.

On the north side of Mount Tam, Lake Lagunitas averages 52 inches of rain per year, which is double the rainfall of downtown San Francisco, just 20 miles away. The highest recorded rainfall in Marin was in the winter of 1889, when a phenomenal 109 inches of rain deluged the county. Yet Marin can also suffer from severe droughts, as we'll discuss later.

Marin County is comprised mainly of hills, ranging in height from 200 feet to 2,000 feet at Big Rock Ridge in the county's northern reaches, and separated by pleasant wooded valleys. Each valley has its own weather. Not only can the weather differ from valley to valley, and at different elevations, and at different times of day, but the weather from one house to another in Marin can differ too. In summer, a house on a ridgeline facing southwest toward the sun will bake in the heat. Its next-door neighbor, on the other side of the same ridge, may be quite cool, enjoying the natural air conditioning provided by the wind or fog.

Call me prejudiced because I live in Marin, but there is really no place like it anywhere. If not for the occasional flood or drought every decade or so, the weather would be perfect.

Weather forecast for tonight: Dark.

~ George Carlin

---

5 / Warning signs

God forbid that India should ever take to industrialism after the manner of the West... keeping the world in chains. If our nation took to similar economic exploitation, it would strip the world bare like locusts.

~ Mahatma Gandhi

Nepal, June 1, 2010

While Will and the trekking party slogged through the high mountain passes, just a few miles to the east in the yak herders' *yarsa* of Na, the morning sun had risen. The few inhabitants rose to a new day, waiting patiently for the monsoon to come and bring the blessed rainfall that would water the crops down in the valley below.

High on a ridge above the small scattering of huts that comprised the tiny village, young Sumita Magar reached down and grasped a handful of old tree branches hidden behind a large rock. Carefully she put them into her basket, along with the twigs and shrubs she'd already collected on the barren hillside.

"No one has been this far up the hill," she thought. "I thought maybe there were some bits of wood still to be found here." On the ridgeline above, a handful of dead, twisted pine trees huddled together like bent old men in the endless wind. The alpine forest that once stood in the valley below had long since been cut down for fuel. Foraging for firewood meant scrounging any sort of plant or twig she could find.

Above, in an azure blue sky almost purple in its intensity, a punishing sun radiated brilliantly, with a few hazy clouds climbing up from the valleys far below. At 13,700 feet in the high Himalayas, the morning air was cold, even in the summer sun. High above towered Kang Nachugo, at 22,096 feet the highest peak for miles around. Na was nothing more than a few huts in a high pasture, inhabited only in the summer yak grazing season. In the savage cold of the long winter, the few herders of Na returned to the sherpa village of Beding, a small community of two hundred families living in stone houses a few miles down the valley.

Beding, at 12,000 feet, is the capital of the Dalakha district, a typical tiny sherpa village nestled between the Rolwaring River and the mountains above. Its stony village grounds included many rock walls that surrounded small potato and barley fields. Not many people remained in Beding full-time anymore. The few old men left in the village attended their animals in the fields. Most of the young men had left to go to Kathmandu and work as porters on well-paying trekking expeditions operated by wealthy American outfitters. The women and children left behind in the village did household chores.

Smoke from burning yak dung drifted upward from the hut in Sumita's yarsa, swirling in the constant wind that drifted down the steep ravines from the mountains far above. With wood mostly gone, yak dung was all the Na villagers had to use for fuel, but yak smoke is foul and acrid and burns the eyes. Sumita's mother, now an old woman at 42, could no longer forage the hills for firewood and had gone back down to Beding, so Sumita made the long climb up the steep hill every morning alone to forage after her first household chores were done.

Sumita was only 19 but already a widow. Her husband had died on a mountaineering trek in the Everest region two years before, falling into a crevasse. His body had never been recovered. Although her skin was burned a deep brown by the scorching sun, Sumita was a beautiful woman for a poor Nepalese peasant, with high cheekbones and a vivacious smile showing perfect white teeth. Dressed in Nepalese peasant costume of red woolen cap, knitted sweater of yak wool and baggy pants, she was a lonely but lovely sight, leaning forward against the mountain wind.

Gathering twigs was women's work. Sumita's father, a decrepit alcoholic nearing the end of his life at 45, sat by the door of their hut pretending to grind barley into tsampa for their meals. His job was to mind the chickens, but most days he would stay in the hut and ferment barley into beer to get drunk. Sumita's two older brothers had long since left the village to seek work as porters in the trekking trade.

Behind the boulder Sumita found what she was hoping for. She eagerly grabbed the few sticks of wood and put them in her bag on her back. She headed slowly downhill, carefully stepping along the tricky narrow footpath that led down the mountain. In the valley below the village, the Rolwaring River danced like a thin silver sword in the bright mountain air. "Perhaps I should walk down to the river before the noon meal," she thought, "and get a pail of water."

As Sumita passed the hut to drop off the meager bag of twigs she had gathered, her father called out to her from his perch in the doorway. "Look at the sky, you foolish child," he said in a rough voice choked by bidis, the cheap Indian cigarettes he smoked. "Clouds are coming. The monsoon is soon here. It will rain before long."

On the foothills way down near the Indian border, thick, dark cumulonimbus clouds were starting to drift up from the Gangetic plains. The summer monsoon was coming, very early this year.

We forget that the water cycle and the life cycle are one.

~ Jacques Cousteau

Trudging over yet another in an apparently endless series of mountain passes, every time they paused for a rest break, Will answered his trekking buddies' questions about life as the President's son, and his research into global warming. Already Dave Moore had learned more about the weather in Nepal than he knew about the weather in his hometown.

"The ancient Arabs called the monsoon the Mausin," said Will to Walsh, as both sipped on a bottle of filtered water. "That means 'season of winds' in Arabic. The monsoon is everything to people in this part of the world. Without all that water getting dumped on their heads, there wouldn't be billions of people living in southern Asia.

The monsoon is a complex and fascinating weather phenomenon. If it weren't for the vast amounts of rainfall it produces and drops over Southeast Asia, flooding the land and irrigating crops and providing drinking water, hundreds of millions of people would starve to death. Every year Asians look to the sky and pray for the rains to come, not only for the moisture it brings but also to interrupt the deathly heat that builds up over the subcontinent in the spring months.

"So what kind of heavy precipitation are we talking about?" queried Moore, just out of curiosity. "What's the record, anyway?"

"The record is 37 inches of rain that fell on Mumbai in one day back in July 2005," answered Will. "Mumbai you probably know as Bombay. That's three feet of water in one day, so you get the idea how much it can rain."

"Wow, that's more than my hometown gets in an entire year," said Moore. "When did you say this annual deluge is set to commence?"

"Usually the monsoon starts around the beginning of June, way down at the foot of India," replied Will, swigging from his water bottle, "and it slowly moves on northward, until it finally hits the Himalayas. Which is normally around mid or late June, but this year it looks like it will be early. Like, very early."

"Well, let's get a move on then," said Walsh. "We don't want to get caught in any 37 inches of rain, that's for damn sure."

Berkeley, California, 2006

Thank you to the student who brought in the newspaper headline this morning about the death and destruction in India caused last week by the monsoon. We'll be studying global weather later in the semester, but let's talk a minute about the unique weather phenomenon of the monsoon.

The key ingredients for creating a monsoon are a hot land mass and a cooler ocean. In the Indian subcontinent, for instance, the huge land mass absorbs heat faster from the scorching sun than does the surrounding Indian Ocean. This causes air masses over the land to heat up. As the land heats, the air expands, and rises. As the air rises, then the cooler, wetter and heavier air from over the neighboring ocean rushes in to replace it. In the Indian subcontinent, which is an enormous place, this damp, cool layer can be gigantic. It's a sight to behold. Some clouds can be several miles high, and as they become denser with moisture from the ocean they turn black with rage.

Monsoon flooding is a major issue in this part of the world. In the wake of the 1998 monsoon, two-thirds of Bangladesh was completely inundated and remained under water for two months. Scientists in Bangladesh say they have found a link between the devastating floods and global warming.

Vast amounts of soil are washed down from the Himalayas through erosion, which causes soil to pile up on the low-lying floodplain and helps rivers to overflow their banks. A recent United Nations report estimated erosion currently affects 2 billion acres in Bangladesh, or 25 percent of all agricultural land.

In many areas of steeply sloping land in Asia — for example in neighboring Nepal — erosion caused by deforestation is severe. Lack of any other sort of fuel has caused villagers to cut down most of the ancient forests in the mountains of Nepal. In the next few years, the Himalayas could also experience even more intense flooding as mountain lakes overflow from melting glaciers. Many mountain lakes in Nepal and Bhutan are so swollen from melting glaciers that they will soon explode over their banks and cause devastation to many Himalayan villages in their path.

Let's take a close look at the map. One such lake is Tsho Rolpa in the Dolakha district of Nepal. When records were first kept about 50 years ago, the lake was only one-tenth of a mile long. Today Tsho Rolpa is five times bigger. The Trakarding Glacier, which feeds the lake, is retreating at a rate of at least 65 feet a year. In the last decade, glacial erosion in the Himalayas, thanks to warmer air temperatures, has reached up to 350 feet per year in some locations.

Between earth and earth's atmosphere, the amount of water remains constant; there is never a drop more, never a drop less. This is a story of circular infinity, of a planet birthing itself.

~ Linda Hogan, Northern Lights, Autumn 1990

6 / Pulling the plug

Journalists aren't supposed to praise things. It's a violation of work rules almost as serious as buying drinks with our own money or absolving the CIA of something

~ P.J. O'Rourke

Marin County, July 30, 1975

At the Marin Municipal Water District offices in late July 1975, crippling drought was not the first thing on Diet Stroeh's mind. The skies were blue, the days were warm, the birds were singing and everybody was very pleased with the summer weather. Yes, very pleased indeed. The beaches were packed, the golf courses were full, and gardeners were at work in the gardens, and all seemed well with the world.

Marin County may very well have the most pleasant climate of any place in the world. For instance, it seldom rains in the summer in Marin County. You can make your camping and summer holiday plans well in advance, knowing you won't get soaked. Oh, once in a rare while there are a few sprinkles in the summer, but Marinites mainly rely on the summer fog to keep the county moist. From June to October there is never anything more than a trace, and sometimes it doesn't rain in October or November either, producing one of the longest and loveliest summer seasons to be found anywhere in the world.

Things were starting to get very dry in Marin by July. The last time there had been a downpour was back in March, when 11.95 inches of rain had fallen. February had been its usual rainy self too, with 18.06 inches of rain soaking the ground. But the fall and winter months of 1974 and 1975 had been exceptionally dry. If it weren't for those two wet months you could have called it a drought.

As it turned out, thanks to those two wet months, Marin hit 51.04 inches for the 1974-75 rainy season, right on its average. So nobody was even thinking of drought. The MMWD, however, under the direction of new gung ho manager Diet Stroeh, was already planning ahead for possible future water shortages. The county's population was growing, and history showed that Marin was prone to a serious drought every once in a while, although with a smaller population in the past there hadn't been any real crisis, yet.

While those with the good fortune to have the day off work were out and about in shorts and sandals basking in the warm summer sun, Diet was in his back office at the MMWD headquarters poring over rainfall figures and wondering about the future. Would this winter be wet enough to fill the county's reservoirs? What else could be done to plan ahead for possible shortages?

"Diet," his secretary, Marge, buzzed through from the front lobby, "straighten your tie. Those people from the media are here to see you."

"Hi there," he said, opening his door to the TV crews. "Come on in. Let me explain how we are going to fit a dozen people into Harry Dennis's bathroom."

We abuse land because we regard it as a commodity belonging to us. When we see land as a community to which we belong, we may begin to use it with love and respect.

~ Aldo Leopold, A Sand County Almanac

Berkeley, California, 2006

Today, class, we are going to talk a little about our water history here in the Americas. There are plenty of people in the United States, and some I suspect in this very class, who think that the western world's history begins in 1492. When Christopher Columbus discovered America he realized that the world wasn't flat, and that there were lots of other people living in the "new world." As a European, he typically dismissed the native Americans he met as savages, probably because they didn't have any modern technology, like armor and guns and other good stuff.

The fact is, well before drive-in burger restaurants and high-speed freeways, a sophisticated culture had long since been established in the Americas. The Incas in South America had engineered a system of public works including roads and canals that provided them with ease of transport and access to water. Yet the fact is that by the time that Cortez the Killer and his band of merry men from Europe appeared on the scene to reduce the surplus population, the Incan empire had already begun to disintegrate.

While the overthrow of the Incan Empire is often credited to modern technology — the Spanish had muskets that went "bang" and the Incans only had clubs and knives — recent theories hold that the Incan, Mayan and Aztec empires dwindled away because of an endless killer drought. No matter how intricate the irrigation system you have built, if it doesn't rain for an extended period of time then there is no water to move around.

For instance, between the years 750 and 1100 AD, the Anasazi Indians had created a thriving culture in what is now known as Colorado. At Mesa Verde the Anasazi had built elaborate reservoirs and irrigation canals to capture and channel any rainwater that fell.

Scientists have recently discovered that one of the worst drought periods in modern American history commenced around 1130 and ran to about 1180. In South and Central America, and the south and central areas of what is now the United States, the land still bears scars from this period. Sand dunes along the South Platte River in eastern Colorado, still standing, date back to that period. In 1275 another drought hit the American west that lasted until 1300. During these two droughts, for up to 50 years there was insufficient water from which to grow crops.

Although the Anasazi had thrived on Mesa Verde for many centuries thanks to their genius at water management and transfer, even their elaborate system of reservoirs and canals couldn't withstand a drought lasting several decades. Although their magnificent cliff houses and canyon edifices still stand to this day, the Anasazi simply disappeared from the face of the earth.

A recent study of ancient tree rings in the western U.S. by scientists shows that there may have been a similar drought in the 1600s in California, lasting over 30 years. In fact, recent research shows that the entire western U.S. has a history of extended droughts occurring on a regular basis every few centuries.

Water can only be moved from one place to another if there is any water to transfer. Although the state of California today resembles an elaborate jigsaw puzzle of reservoirs, canals and aqueducts transferring water all over the state from its main source — chiefly the snowpack in the Sierra Nevada — the fact remains that if no precipitation falls from the sky, there is no water to transfer. Ergo, you have a problem with living in places where it doesn't ever rain. Which may very well be where we in the western U.S. are headed.

Marin County, early August 1975

Old-timers remember that 1975, except for one wet month, was a very dry year in Marin County. They also remember it as the year that Harry W. Dennis of Corte Madera became famous for his toilet. But before Harry entered the picture, Diet Stroeh and the Marin Municipal Water District had already been experimenting with various ways to reduce water consumption.

The MMWD started an informal survey of restaurant managers, trying to get a sense of how many would buy into a voluntary water saving plan. Most who replied said they were willing and interested, but of course not all complied immediately. Bit by bit, though, the MMWD staff worked with restaurant managers and their staffs to bring about changes in service, especially the habit of automatically giving a customer a complimentary glass of water.

MMWD staff designed an attractive poster that explained new water policies and respectfully solicited everyone's cooperation. Decals were also affixed to mirrors and other surfaces, with messages urging staff and customers never to leave the taps running. The MMWD staff also designed "table tents," small cardboard devices that advised patrons of the reasons why they had to ask for a glass of water. Each one contained a brief water conservation quiz with thought-provoking questions like: "How many gallons of water does the average person use every day in Marin?" (Answer: 148 gallons.)

While MMWD staff was attempting to educate consumers about the need for water conservation, consumers responded with their own water-saving ideas. The newspapers printed some of the ideas sent in by readers. Elderly Andy Somerville of Novato, for instance, had some dandy observations that he shared with the local paper. Why, the 78-year old gentleman had been saving water all his life.

"A person washes his hands about four times a day after using the bathroom," calculated Andy. "For a family of four that's 16 times a day. The average wash takes 30 seconds. If you cut the flow from six gallons a minute to one and a half, that's 36 gallons a day saved, or 13,000 gallons a year per family."

Or, of course you could simply not wash your hands at all after using the bathroom, but neither the MMWD nor any letter writers were advising that. At least, not yet. Things would get more desperate later on. But after Harry Dennis displayed the proper use of toilet facilities and Navy-style showers to the media, events began to heap up.

No news is good news. No journalists is even better.

~ Nicolas Bentley, 1930s English writer and artist

Within a year Diet Stroeh was so inundated with media people from around the world asking him about the drought that he would be forced to hold daily media conferences, but July 1975 saw the first electronic media coverage in Marin of what would eventually become a daily soap opera. Of course local Marin newspapers had already been all over the story of MMWD's new conservation strategy like flies on a dead dog, but at this point in time — before they became a major headache — TV and radio crews from San Francisco were actually a welcome novelty in rural Marin.

In order to get the biggest bang for their buck, the MMWD Board of Directors had decided that instead of blowing their entire budget on advertising, maybe obtaining free publicity was a better — and cheaper — course to follow. So they hired a big-name public relations firm, Hoefer Amidei of San Francisco, which in turn created a plan sure to get attention, and summoned the mainstream media, and verily the media came. Dozens of radio and TV reporters appeared, all eager to crowd into Harry W. Dennis's little bathroom on Flying Cloud Course in suburban Corte Madera. Toilet humor is always a big seller.

Marin County, as small as it is, has become internationally known over the years — perhaps due to the ingenuity and creativity of its talented and highly educated citizenry — for creating new social trends or inventions, especially those pertaining to the environment. Hot tubs, mountain bikes, the chardonnay-sipping Bohemian Bourgeois lifestyle, the "green revolution" — all these hot trends evolved out of hip, progressive and rich Marin County.

Because its own water supply was so limited, Marin was among the first regions in the country to implement water-saving devices and programs, such as conserving water when flushing toilets. During the ensuing Great California Drought of 1977, a new phrase was coined: "If it's brown, flush it down. If it's yellow, leave it mellow." For the Bay Area media in 1975, this sudden trend toward water conservation spelled news.

Although water conservation has slowly become a normal daily practice for most Americans these days, drought or not, back in 1975 ecologically aware Marin County was considered "quaint" for trying to launch a public awareness campaign, especially one based on toilets.

Since wealthy and progressive Marin County had already gained a reputation as the unofficial hot tub capital of the world, the big-city television crews all wanted to film Harry W. Dennis in his bathroom taking a shower. That is, an official MMWD water-saving, scanty Navy-style (get wet quick, turn off the shower fast, soap up even faster and rinse really fast) shower. And, having agreed in advance to hype the fun, 77-year-old retiree Harry W. Dennis was quite eager to show them how it was done.

Radio reporters with tape recorders, newspaper reporters with notebooks, television camera operators with bulky cameras, sound men with microphones, television directors with funny hats and suspicious facial hair all showed up at the MMWD offices, where Diet herded them over in a big cavalcade to Harry's house. It was a precursor of things to come the following year, the mainstream media having fun with upscale Marin.

San Francisco television channels 2, 5, 7 and 9 were there with bells on, and KNBC-TV even flew in a crew all the way from Los Angeles to shoot prime-time footage for national television anchor John Chancellor. What fun! The crews stood around on Harry's front lawn, dozens of them admiring his flowers, simultaneously mocking Marin County while very happy to get such a slack assignment.

On cue, two college students hired by the MMWD to give away showerheads to the public went up to Harry's front door and rang the bell. Harry, a slender and diminutive fellow, was immediately blocked out from view by a crew of burly cameramen fighting over the best angle. Cameras rolled.

"Hi there, come on in."

Dozens of camera people, reporters and directors trudged into

Harry's living room, bumping into each other while shooting footage of the furniture and walls.

"Mind the dog," shouted Olga, Harry's wife of 30 years.

The crowd pushed and stumbled its way through the doorway into Harry's tiny bathroom. The little two-bedroom rancher had been built back in the days when people didn't hold soirees or press conferences in their bathrooms, and they didn't need 7,000 square feet of living space to hold all the loot they had acquired through a consumer lifestyle, so there was only room for one burly camera person at a time.

"Who goes first?" asked the camera operator from Channel 2.

"We'll take turns," offered the director from Channel 7.

"Me first," said the camera guy from Channel 5, and pushed right in.

Harry did his thing, holding up the low-pressure showerhead to the camera and displaying its low flow, a less than manly trickle. This was a historic moment in American television news. Until then, no self-respecting, manly American would have ever considered taking a low-flow shower. Why, that would be like eating a tofu hamburger. Times were tough, and water might be short in Marin, but no one knew things were so tough that you had to cut back on a long, leisurely shower.

"Can we get you to demonstrate the three-minute Navy version, Harry?" laughed the editor from Channel 5, a real wisecracker. "That bathrobe has got to go."

"Can you show us how the low-flow toilet works, Harry?" smirked the camera guy from Channel 2. "But keep your pants on though."

Soon the crews were done with their fun and filed out, taking pictures of everything that moved in the Dennis home but careful not to take pictures of each other taking pictures. The main media assembly headed north along Flying Cloud Course, filming the college kids as they knocked on every door along the street, handing out free showerheads. Other reporters rang the neighbors' bells, perhaps hoping for a more photogenic shower model.

And so it was that the Dennis bathroom was all over the national TV news at 6 o'clock, perhaps the first time many people in America had ever heard of Marin. Within a year, camera crews would come from all across America, Canada and as far away as Australia to film the ongoing soap opera of The Rich Little Town That Was Running Out of Water! The next day's Marin newspapers were all over the story too. "Straight Flush a Winning Hand," ran one headline. Everybody thought it was a good joke. Ha ha, little did they know.

The average person in the United States uses 80 to 100 gallons of water each day. During medieval times a person used only five gallons per day.

~ NJAWWA.com

---

7 / The good old days

And Man created the plastic bag and the tin and aluminum can and the cellophane wrapper and the paper plate, and this was good because Man could then take his automobile and buy all his food in one place and He could save that which was good to eat in the refrigerator and throw away that which had no further use. And soon the earth was covered with plastic bags and aluminum cans and paper plates and disposable bottles and there was nowhere to sit down or walk, and Man shook his head and cried: "Look at this Godawful mess."

~ Art Buchwald, 1970

Marin County, January 5, 1976

"Let's see now. If our projections are accurate, we can save 300 million gallons," said Diet during a staff meeting, looking out the window of the MMWD boardroom at the weather outside. "That would translate into annual savings of approximately 935 acre-feet, which would mean . . ."

The summer and fall of 1975 had gone by without any rain. Christmas came and went and still no rain. Early January was far too early in the winter to start worrying about rainfall, but engineers are seldom given to capriciousness when it comes to future planning. Depending when winter storms started to roll in off the Pacific, Marin County could start seeing rain as early as October in wet years, as late as January in others. It always rained in February and March in Marin, so there was plenty of time for it to rain. Nonetheless, the previous year had also been very dry, and the county's reservoirs were no longer full, so Diet had his calculator out to estimate if and when the county would need to start thinking about a few more water conservation methods.

In the summer, the MMWD had started its conservation movement with the goal of reducing water usage by as much as 300 million gallons annually throughout the county, by offering water-saving devices to the public free of charge. The low-volume showerheads and half-gallon plastic bottles designed for insertion into toilet tanks had being picked up by lots of customers and were being used in many homes. Based on MMWD research, Diet figured an average family of four could save as much as 15,000 gallons of water per year just from the low-flow devices.

If the MMWD projections were accurate, 300 million gallons would translate into annual savings of approximately 935 acre-feet. Given that the public's current annual usage was much the same year to year, the district could be in a position to deal with any rainfall shortages simply through these water conservation techniques. That was assuming, of course, that it began to rain soon and in amounts sufficient to catch up with the annual winter averages. But everybody knew it always rained in Marin in the winter, usually in a couple of heavy storms, so there was no panic yet.

It could be said that gambling is not a characteristic of civil engineers, who always like to have their figures exact and planned well in advance, and gambling was certainly not a weakness that could be ascribed to Diet Stroeh. Meticulous might be a better word to describe him, a characteristic of his personality that went all the way back to his youth. These days, many critics describe California culture as "slack," but growing up a country boy in the old days, Diet knew the value of hard work. Diet was never a slacker.

Ironically, rural America has become viewed by a growing number of Americans as having a higher quality of life not because of what it has, but rather because of what it does not have!

~ Don A. Dillman, Annals of the American Academy of Political and Social
Science, January 1977

He was a natty dresser. Unless he was at home in his vegetable patch digging weeds, he never wore shorts and sandals. As always, whether at work or a social function, he was impeccably dressed in a three-piece suit with matching vest, polished shoes, and his trademark black plastic aviator glasses. Even though he had shaved off his moustache when he was promoted to the position of General Manager, with his thick head of straight blond hair cut in a sixties-style Beatle haircut and his stylish clothes, Diet looked more like a rock music mogul than a civil engineer, but those who knew him well understood that "do your best in everything you do" was his trademark, and those high standards certainly extended to his dapper personal appearance.

Meticulous behavior was a characteristic of the whole Stroeh family. The family emigrated to California from Germany after World War I. Father Otto Stroeh settled in the country outside of Los Angeles, where he started a chicken farm. The hard-working senior Stroeh moved to Marin County in 1940, with wife and 3-year-old son Joachim Dietrich firmly in hand, and the family settled again in the countryside, this time in the rural splendor of Novato. Soon the Stroeh family began to prosper.

The Stroeh kids played in the creek behind their home in the fields near what eventually became the San Marin neighborhood. There wasn't a high school in the little town, so Diet commuted south daily on the bus to the city of San Rafael for his studies. He played a lot of football, boxed a bit, and ran track. His father thought that the young man would develop some toughness through boxing and football, and he was right. Although he presented a polished image through his fashionable clothing and charming demeanor, behind that façade was a tough, no-nonsense competitor who always wanted to win. In sporting parlance, Diet Stroeh was cut out to be the quarterback of the team.

Diet was a fairly good student, although his grades didn't compare to those of his sisters, who were dedicated scholars. Nonetheless he graduated from high school with good marks and went on to attend College of Marin, where a car crash and creeping boredom temporarily derailed his engineering studies.

"I didn't think I was getting anywhere at college, and I guess what I really wanted to do was 'find myself,' as kids are prone to do at that age," he said much later in an interview with local newsweekly The Pacific Sun after it named him "Marinite of the Year" in 1978. "But back in those days you 'found yourself' by going out and getting a job, not by getting high. So I went to work as a surveyor for the California Division of Highways, working on the freeway between Petaluma and Santa Rosa."

This was well before the hippie era hit Marin in the late 1960s. Diet, a quick learner, soon found the meaning of life without the assistance of any metaphysical gurus or hallucinogenic drugs. He deduced that hard work without accompanying professional training is not always sufficient to succeed financially in life.

"It dawned on me very early that there were guys 20 or 30 years older than me and they were only making the same amount of money as me, and me a kid," he said. "And I thought there was no way that I'm going to be in that sorry position in the future. So I quit my day job and went back to school."

He completed his civil engineering studies at the University of Nevada and returned to Marin in 1960, where he applied for a job as a junior engineer with the water district. His first assignment was working on the design and construction of the Nicasio Reservoir, but after three years the restless and ambitious young man realized that his career wasn't blossoming fast enough, so he quit the MMWD and took a job in private construction. It was there that he realized that professional skills and demeanor are not always found in every profession, especially in the construction trades. So he returned to the MMWD in 1964, where he acquired another job as an assistant engineer.

"Suddenly things started moving for me with the water district. I don't know why, maybe I was at the right place at the right time," he said later. He was soon promoted to associate, senior and then principal engineer. He was named manager of the engineering division in 1971 and then promoted to acting General Manager. In 1974 he competed against 150 applicants, many older and far more experienced, from all across the country, for the position of General Manager of the Marin Municipal Water District. He was hired quickly, described by the Board of Directors as "hands down, the best candidate." Diet Stroeh was only 37. Good thing too; with what lay ahead he would need all his youth, energy and ideas.

8 / River deep, mountain high

The control man has secured over nature has far outrun his control over himself.

~ Ernest Jones, "The Life and Work of Sigmund Freud," 1953

Nepal, June 6, 2010

Will paused and caught his breath. In the distance loomed a magnificent sight. Kang Nachugo stood like a sentinel high above the Rolwaring Valley, at 22,000 feet the highest peak for miles around, with Mount Everest hidden in the clouds some 30 miles to the east. It had been a hair-raising, long and tiring trek to get here, carefully following a narrow path along vertical rock faces hanging above steep drops to valleys far below.

From their last camp at the village of Ramding at 10,000 feet, the trekking party slowly trudged uphill, along a miserable trail requiring intense concentration, finally arriving at the provincial capital of Beding at 11,000 feet. Hanging off a steep mountainside, with the Rolwaring River running right beneath the village, Beding was really only a collection of small, whitewashed stone houses with peaked roofs made of slate.

Beding boasted a large *chorten*, or Buddhist shrine, and a small *gompa*, or monastery, where the party would stay for the night. The chorten, with its bright, whitewashed base topped by a pointed needle painted in gold, looked to the trekkers like a snowman wearing a pointed hat. Colorful red, white, orange and blue prayer flags fluttered from the chorten and the roofs of most of the buildings. The sun shone brightly in a sky almost purple in its intensity.

"Wow, looks like we're almost at our destination, gentlemen," said Will, panting as always, as the trekking party staggered into the village. "What a beautiful sight this is."

The Rolwaring Valley was seldom visited, well off the beaten track of most mountaineers, who usually headed for Everest, 30 miles to the east. Some of the villagers at Beding were familiar with trekking expeditions, and some of their children had served as porters on the rare expeditions to the Tsho Rolpo glacier. Today, the few villagers not up in the hills foraging for wood or herding yaks stared at the rare sight of strangers outfitted in colorful nylon parkas and heavy hiking boots.

"We'll stay here one night and then head up to the glacier tomorrow," said Walsh. "It's a half-day trek up to Na, where there are a few yak herders' huts and that's about it, and then we're there. We'll be at the glacier tomorrow noon."

Directly above the village, Kang Nachugo stood like a sharp white knife piercing the heavens. Dark puffy clouds tumbled down the valley from the high peaks, drifting over small potato and barley fields circled by stone fences. It was late in the day and another glowing red sunset started to form like a firestorm in the sky above the peaks.

"I wonder what the chances are of getting some fresh food in this village," mused Will, looking at the chickens pecking in the stony dirt. "My stomach is starting to cave in on itself, and this freeze-dried muck is starting to wear on my nerves."

"I'm starving too," grumbled Moore, "and my headache is back again. I can't get used to this altitude."

There's so much pollution in the air now that if it weren't for our lungs there'd be no place to put it all.

~ Robert Orben, humorist, screenwriter and editor

Hikers on treks such as those in the Himalayas can often face serious problems from high altitude sickness, a condition associated with the lack of oxygen. More serious conditions such as high-altitude pulmonary edema and high-altitude cerebral edema, usually experienced above 15,000 feet, can be lethal.

Altitude sickness is usually caused by a too-rapid ascent or poor physical condition. It can, however, strike at mountaineers even in optimal physical condition who have high altitude experience. It is first evidenced by gloomy behavior that can sometimes evolve into unremitting depression. The only remedy for a serious attack is to descend to a lower altitude as soon as possible, although drugs like azetazolamid can combat some of the mildest symptoms.

The usual plan for any expedition to high elevations, say above 12,000 feet, is gradual acclimatization, approximately one week for every 3,000 feet of elevation gain. The High Mountain Adventures expedition had spent over a week arriving at this height, but heavy exertion above 10,000 feet tends to bring on some degree of mountain sickness.

Psychologists speak about three physiological phases associated with altitude sickness. The first phase is the so-called "blinker stage," where the hiker simply ignores symptoms such as headaches. This appears in altitudes up to 15,000 feet, a physical and psychological condition blamed on bodily stress. The first symptoms are physical tension including backache from heavy packs and steep trails, harsh weather, and bad food, often exacerbated by subconscious fears about higher altitudes yet to come.

The next phase is the "champagne cork" stage, which occurs above 15,000 feet. At this height normally well-balanced and peaceful personalities can experience remarkable irascibility attacks, outbursts of fury formed out of thin air. The phrase refers to people figuratively blowing their cork. Doctors say diminishing amounts of oxygen begin to affect brain cells and affect the mood, somewhat like a killer tequila hangover.

"I'm getting a little whacked out from this elevation," said Moore. "Don't mind me if I bite someone's head off, but my own head is coming off."

"Relax, dude, we'll spend some time here before we climb up to the glacier," said Walsh. "I'm not feeling so great myself. That's 15,000 feet up there. I don't want anybody going off the deep end when we get way up to that altitude."

Washington, D.C., June 6, 2010

Only Americans can hurt America.

~ Dwight D. Eisenhower

While on the other side of the planet his son's trekking party was suffering from altitude sickness, in Washington, D.C., William White Senior, President of the United States of America, was in a very bad mood himself. His filthy mood had nothing to do with high altitude, although at 30,000 feet, high altitude would be a problem if he were not sitting behind his desk aboard plush Air Force One.

"What do you mean the votes aren't there?" he demanded in a tough tone of voice. "I thought you said it was a slam dunk!"

White was on the line with Rudolph Helmsley, his negotiator at the latest round of talks to deal with climate change, meetings sponsored by the United Nations. White wanted nothing more than to position his government as progressive in the ongoing fight against global warming, even though oil and gas companies had been among the biggest contributors to his successful campaign for the presidency. Like his predecessors in the White House, he'd fought any changes to mileage efficiencies in American cars and trucks. His new public position, which he wanted to unveil as soon as possible, was to have the United States appear to be leading the charge to sign a new global accord on climate change. Only he wanted a new accord that allowed Americans to continue on with a style of living that allowed conspicuous consumption, a difficult political trick to pull off, even with the best spin doctors in the world at his command.

White knew that negotiations for any new accord would probably take the entire length of his presidency, but he thought that beginning the discussions now would also allow his government to go forward with exploration of oil and gas reserves in Alaska, and perhaps even off the California coast, if he could line up the votes. It would also buy some time to allow oil and gas companies to secretly acquire more and more small alternative energy companies for the inevitable time when the general public of the United States started to cry out for a climate policy that entailed something other than heating the planet to boiling point.

"Well, you tell Pastow that he won't be getting any support for his autumn election run unless he gets the California votes lined up the way we want them," said White, slamming his desk in anger. He turned to his press secretary and handed him the phone.

"You call the network and tell them we won't be participating in that stupid TV special they're putting together," he said. "Tell them we will have nothing to say for a while yet."

Turning to his wife, Claire, sitting in the next seat aboard the jet, he smiled. "Next time you talk to Will, tell him to call me. I'll explain what I'm up to," he said. "He'll love it. I'm going to commit the United States to lead the fight against global warming, one way or another. It'll just take a bit more time than I had promised him."

One of the first laws against air pollution came in 1300 when King Edward I decreed the death penalty for burning of coal. At least one execution for that offense is recorded. But economics triumphed over health considerations, and air pollution became an appalling problem in England.

~ Glenn T. Seaborg, Atomic Energy Commission chairman, speech, Argonne
National Laboratory, 1969

Berkeley, California, 2006

We all know that the Kyoto Accord, which aimed to curb the emissions of greenhouse gases blamed for global warming, was a historic agreement reached in 1997 after extensive negotiations between senior bureaucrats representing dozens of governments. We all know it failed because the United States and Australia refused to sign the accord on the theory it would harm their economies.

The Kyoto Accord would have required all participating countries to reduce carbon dioxide and other greenhouse gas emissions by 5 percent by the year 2012. We in the United States are responsible for 25 percent of the fossil fuels emitted into the planet's air, mostly by large automobiles with low mileage standards, so we refused to sign the treaty. Our administration said that the agreement was fundamentally flawed because each country involved could set its own pollution reduction goals according to its pollution levels. That allowed certain developing countries, such as newly industrialized China and India, to be outside the rules. China and India are buying up oil at a record pace, and soon will be chasing us here in the United States as the world's biggest consumers and worst polluters, so that was a big problem with Kyoto.

It's important to know that it's not just we Americans who are polluting the planet. Every year almost 7 billion tons of carbon dioxide is released into the atmosphere, mainly through the burning of fossil fuels. Fossil fuels remain in the atmosphere for at least a century, trapping the sun's heat, and raising the planetary temperature. Factories in China and India, and the burning of the world's rain forests, are also a big part of the problem.

Before what we call the Industrial Age began a few hundreds year ago — largely dated back to the invention of the steam engine by James Watt in the early 1800s — the carbon dioxide level in the world had stayed steady for centuries at around 280 ppm. When the Kyoto Protocol was finally drawn up in 1997, the carbon dioxide level had reached 368 parts per million. By 2004, levels were at 379 ppm and rising rapidly. In the last few years alone, concentrations have risen by an astounding 3 ppm per year. We are in trouble, kids, unless we deal with this. We're gonna melt.

Rising levels of carbon dioxide mean rising temperatures, which mean climate changes such as floods, droughts, storms and rising sea levels. Predictions of a global disaster are based on the planet's pollution rising to a concentration as high as a mindboggling 550 ppm, a figure likely to be reached by the second half of this century if serious action isn't taken soon.

It gets worse, though, class. Listen to this: Melting ice caps and changing ocean circulation take a long time to stop, so that means global weather changes will continue onward for centuries even if carbon dioxide levels stop rising at the 550 ppm mark.

If carbon levels are somehow kept below 450 ppm, there still will be huge changes in the planet's weather. Many people say that 550 ppm is a more likely figure because many governments are refusing to take action now while it's still possible. The lower figure would still see our global air temperature increase up to 5 degrees. At that figure, sea levels could rise up to 12 feet by 2100, and perhaps up to 40 feet over the next thousand years. This is where Noah's Ark would come in handy.

Just to remain at the 550 mark, global emissions of greenhouse gases have to peak by 2025. Achieving that figure, as damaging to the climate as it will be, will require a lot more than just reducing emissions from automobiles. Factories around the globe will have to find new and clean sources of fuel, but even that will not be nearly enough. To get to a zero carbon mark will require huge changes to the global energy industry. In short, the days of burning fossil fuels must come to an end, soon, or we won't recognize the planet.

Changing the entire world's energy industries sounds like an impossible job, and as American officials pointed out when they refused to sign the Kyoto accord, it will be horrifically expensive. Most economists agree that it will be extremely costly, but they also note that doing nothing will be far more costly. It seems that many oil and gas companies have already realized that fact, because they are quietly investing in alternative energies now. Whatever happens, the planet as we now know it is never going to be the same again.

This is a beautiful planet and not at all fragile. Earth can withstand significant volcanic eruptions, tectonic cataclysms, and ice ages. But this canny, intelligent, prolific, and extremely self-centered human creature had proven himself capable of more destruction of life than Mother Nature herself . . . We've got to be stopped.

~ Michael L. Fischer, environmental cosultant, Harper's Magazine, July 1990

Nepal, June 6, 2010

Secret Service agent Dave Moore was not at the Beding gompa with the other trekkers. While the sherpas prepared a hot meal and the hikers washed up, Moore wandered away to the edge of the village, where he hunkered down behind a stone fence. Pulling out the contents of his pack, he reached for the satellite phone stowed away down among his socks. Pulling out the phone, Moore quickly dialed a number in Washington. The satellite picked up the signal and bounced it onward to the White House.

Waiting, Moore looked up at the darkening clouds in the darkening sky, as a firestorm sunset of reds and wild pinks danced above the high peaks along the Himalayan massif above the valley.

"That's all we need, a cloudburst and a lake overflow," he thought. "Things are starting to get a little dicey. I think it's time we all get out of here. Maybe the President can take some action, and talk to his crazy son. He sure won't listen to me. What does he think, that because he's the President's son, he can part the waters?"

The phone beeped, and a voice came on. Moore listened intently. "You've hired a chopper to stand by? Great, that's all I need to know. OK, I'll call again if it starts to look dicey. Over and out."

Moore put the phone back in the pack and wandered back to the gompa. "Well, guys, what's for dinner? Not that damned freeze-dried stuff again! What about a nice yak steak?"

9 / Not in my backyard

Everybody talks about the weather, but nobody does anything about it.

~ Mark Twain

Marin County, January 22, 1976

"Well, looks like we're in the news again," said Diet to his staff at the weekly meeting. "The papers have finally used the 'Big D' word. Looks like it's time for us all to panic. We're gonna have a big turnout to the next public meeting, that's for sure."

That morning the dreaded "drought" word was used for the first time in a Marin County newspaper. The local daily quoted Richard Norton, assistant director of the Sonoma Water Agency, who pointed out, "Half of the normal rainy season in the North Bay still lay ahead and so there was no drought and therefore no real need for panic." So there it was; the word "drought" used for the first time in decades. Everybody laughed, and hunkered down to wait for the usual February deluge.

Other Sonoma and Marin water officials were confident that there would "certainly be rain" before the end of the rainy season in May, and that the public water supply would certainly be adequate for the upcoming summer. So, relax dear citizens, relax. No problems, no worries about a drought.

That sunny prediction came as news to some people well versed in the history of the local land and weather, such as rancher Boyd Stewart of West Marin. Some rain had already fallen in West Marin over the winter, but only in the form of intermittent dribs and drabs, nowhere near enough for dairy farmers. Temperatures pushing into the balmy 60 to 70-degree range every day, in what was supposed to be winter, were already turning the fields brown. Under the surface, the earth was as hard as a rock.

Newspaper reporters did not seem to realize, as ranchers and water officials certainly did, that a minimum of five or six inches of rain was needed in a big storm, just in order to saturate the ground and create runoff into creeks and ponds. Scattered rainfall made the pastures look nice and green, but it sure didn't provide any stored reserves for the future.

"A lot of cattle are not in very good shape," said Boyd, interviewed in the local paper about the drought, but few people were listening.

Meanwhile, fisheries officials were also speaking words of warning. For the first time in 65 years, salmon were not able to make it up local creeks from the Pacific Ocean to their spawning grounds. Game Warden Alfred F. Giddings reported that salmon already had serious problems.

"The salmon are gathering at the mouths of creeks," said Giddings in a newspaper interview, "and they are swollen with roe, waiting for water levels to rise." If the salmon didn't make it back to their spawning grounds, they would die and leave unfertilized eggs at the mouth of the creek, essentially wiping out the entire salmon run that had spawned in Marin creeks for millennia.

California Department of Fisheries staff was waiting for some rain before restocking any creeks with fry. Giddings also reported that ducks and geese were crowding Marin County shorelines because the ponds they normally used in the Sacramento Valley were also dry. Deer were also reported wandering all over Marin towns and villages in search of any moisture.

The only rain of the year had been .31 of an inch on January 9, not enough to wet your whistle. Weather experts, at that time without the aid of satellites, laid the blame entirely on what they called "an unusually strong high-pressure zone firmly planted along the California coast," a weather pattern that was shunting winter storms north to Oregon and Washington. Nobody knew if or when the high-pressure zone would move, or when it would rain, or even if it would rain at all. But, hey, it always rained in the winter in Marin, right? It always had, or at least as long as public records had been kept, which was over a hundred years. Why, it could rain tomorrow, people said. Ya never know.

"I think we'd better call a planning session," Diet said to his staff. "It's going to be an interesting meeting. Maybe we'd better get more chairs."

Suburbia is where the developer bulldozes out the trees, then names the streets after them.

- Bill Vaughn, writer and editor

While the big city media in San Francisco made fun of the "richest county in America without enough water for its hot tubs," and sent out reporters to film people like Harry Dennis in their bathrooms, local media within Marin County had a different agenda. Making fun of your own readers isn't an angle that sells newspapers. Local media was focused on doing what local media normally does, which is report mundane civic issues such as urban planning, housing and future land development. There is no issue more important to land development in the western states of America than water. Without access to water there can be no development, and for various reasons (does the term "self interest" ring a bell?) the idea of no development suited a lot of folks in Marin County just fine.

Starting in the early 60's, as the population started to surge in the Bay Area, property developers had proposed building new housing on various "empty lands" within Marin County. Local environmentalists had fought tooth and nail to keep any "ticky-tacky boxes" out of Marin. Where developers saw handsome profit in building new homes to accommodate the future spillover of growth from booming San Francisco, environmentalists saw ruined valleys and growing urban sprawl in their little slice,of paradise. Differences between developers and those who eventually became known as environmentalists soon led to hand-to-hand combat over every square inch of real estate.

The Golden Gate Bridge connecting Marin to San Francisco wasn't built until 1937, and until that time any commuter traffic was limited to ferries that sailed from Sausalito, mainly to the financial district of San Francisco. That lack of easy access to the big city really slowed the growth of rural Marin County which, until the building of the bridge, largely consisted of dairy farms and little villages. Little towns like Fairfax, San Rafael, San Anselmo and Mill Valley had originally sprung up around the stations of the railroads built in the late 1880s to haul lumber and agricultural products down to Sausalito for shipping, but otherwise there wasn't much urban development.

Even after the completion of the Golden Gate Bridge, various events conspired to keep urban development from occurring in Marin. World War II was a major intervention, with many able-bodied young men who otherwise might have become property owners going away to war. Following the war, much of the development in Marin during the 50's was in the southern regions such as Sausalito and nearby Mill Valley, where commuting distances to the big city were tolerable. It was only during the early 60's, when Highway 101 was constructed through Marin to join

Sonoma County to the north, that development in Marin really began to take off. Baby-boomers were looking for affordable housing close to their jobs, and beautiful Marin fit the bill perfectly.

In the Pacific Northwest, over 100 stocks and subspecies of salmon and trout have gone extinct and another 200 are at risk due to a host of factors, dams and the loss of riparian habitat being prime factors.

~ Water Facts.com

Huge suburban developments were being built all over America in the 60's, made feasible by the construction of high-speed freeways. Several rural areas of Marin were targeted. Developers eyed the lush San Geronimo Valley west of Fairfax and imagined thousands of little ranch-style houses. One grandiose housing proposal suggested an entire town be built atop the Marin Headlands, the area of Marin closest to San Francisco and now a national park.

One obvious drawback to building any development atop the Marin Headlands was its complete lack of fresh water. Another serious drawback was the fierce opposition of local hippies, environmentalists, and "no growth" property owners who gathered together to gird their loins for an epic battle against the developers, whom they saw as agents of the devil and despoilers of paradise.

It was to the frustration of the land developers, and the long-lasting gratitude of future Marinites, that the battles between the two groups took place in the 60's. A decade earlier and the developers would have cut a swath through Marin like a farmer through a cornfield, but Marin by the 60's was a completely different community.

In the 60's and 70's the hippies and radicals arrived, mostly driven out of San Francisco by rising rents and the "back to the land" movement. Artists, musicians, writers, activists and squatters descended on Marin County. Unlike many other counter-culture folks who fled big American cities during this time, many were talented and successful people who had made some serious money in music and the arts. Many of these activists had the sophistication, experience and willpower to stop the development of their little piece of paradise.

The activist community fought pitched battles and actually won many of the political skirmishes, so by 1976 a lot of the land in Marin was protected from development and preserved as parkland. Much of the rest of undeveloped Marin subsequently became subject to environmental impact reviews, restrictions on development, or other legal devices intended to ensure that development was slow and subject to the strict wishes of the local residents.

Till now man has been up against Nature; from now on he will be up against his own nature.

~ Dennis Gabor, "Inventing the Future," 1964

Since all battlegrounds have two fronts, the other side of the war against urban sprawl soon showed its ugly face. While many people in Marin were against tacky development and all in favor of such fine ideas as affordable housing, old age homes and rental apartments, they just didn't want these fine amenities built in their own neighborhoods. The Not In My Back Yard syndrome is hardly unique to Marin, but clever Marinites soon refined the practice of nimbyism into a fine art. One of the best ways of controlling growth is by establishing a moratorium on new water connections. Obviously, if you can't get access to a connection to public water it's pretty hard to build a residence or commercial development. So access to water connections became a fight.

While a moratorium on water connections instituted in May of 1973 had served its purpose of restricting urban growth, it also had the adverse affect of preventing any new water reservoirs from being created. Demand for water in Marin as of January 1976 averaged 32,000 acre-feet per year. (An acre-foot is enough water to cover an acre of land one foot deep.) Available supply from local reservoirs constituted only 26,000 acre-feet during normal rainfall years, necessitating the importation of some 6000 acre-feet of water from various sources outside the county.

Back on October 23, 1975, MMWD staffers had recommended the construction of a dam in the Soulajule area of West Marin, which would add 5000 acre-feet to the county's water supply by 1979. Along with an intertie pipeline into the North Marin Water District that would create another 4000 acre-feet of water, and assorted conservation methods being undertaken that could save up to 7,000 acre-feet, a total of 16,000 new acre-feet of water would be created. These new sources would help ease Marin's chronic water shortages. These new developments would also help lead toward lifting the moratorium on new water connections.

Besides these developments, a general plan for allocating water supplies in the county over the next 20 years had been prepared for the MMWD by CH2M Hill, a San Francisco-based consulting company. That plan would allow for "systematic annual growth" in the water district as new water supplies became available over the next two decades.

The CH2M plan called for "tying the amount of water to be allocated in each area of the county to the county's planned growth projections for that area." However, it did not specify any yearly amounts or percentages. Any annual percentages would have to be evaluated at the beginning of each year to adjust for any changes in growth patterns and for any changes or delays in the water supply program. The water district would divide the annual amount of new water supply among cities, unincorporated communities and county planning areas. All in all, at the time the CH2M plan seemed a reasonable compromise.

The report also suggested that if the MMWD directors were to consider lifting the moratorium on water connections, they should "also consider the risk of rationing in dry years." It did not predict when those dry years would be, or how dry those years might be. Who could? After all, who can predict the weather?

Growth for the sake of growth is the ideology of the cancer cell.

~ Edward Abbey

---

10 / No growth is good growth

It is obvious that many projects justified by cost-benefit analysis do result in the predictable loss of life. This is true for any projects that increase air or ground traffic, radiation exposure, or air pollution, for example. What allows cost-benefit analysts to "justify" such projects? It is essentially the fact that we never know in advance the identities of the specific people who will be killed. The result is that we never have to compensate anyone for his certain loss of life but instead we must compensate everyone for the additional risk to which he is exposed as a result of the project.

~ Herman E. Daly, "Steady-State Economics," 1977

Marin County, January 22, 1976

The Marin County Civic Center meeting hall was jammed with over 150 people. Spectators stood in the aisles and in doorways and spilled out into the hallways. The topic was simple, but the audience was steamed. Was an Environmental Impact Review (EIR) needed before water was made available to any new residential or commercial connections in the county? What would be the effect on Marin's vaunted quality of life if thousands of new people moved in? After all, a moratorium on new water connections had just been passed back in 1973, so many people were asking why any change should be allowed now.

But in 1974 there was a brand new board of directors, with fresh faces and a new attitude, and the new board had already voted that an environmental review was not needed, voting 4-1 against it. Approximately 1,500 single property lots on existing water mains throughout the county could be connected if a decision were made to go ahead. Since this was beautiful Marin County, 1,500 new connections would inevitably mean 1,500 new houses being built. So while the public debate was ostensibly over the environmental impact of any new water connections, in effect the question was whether or not to invite a few thousand new members into the increasingly exclusive country club that Marin was already becoming. And there was always the added benefit that, given the law of supply and demand, fewer new citizens meant that property values would rise for those who already owned real estate in Marin.

When the meeting began, Mayor Priscilla Gray of Fairfax was the first on her feet to fire a salvo.

"We have 288 vacant lots in Fairfax," she said, "and relaxing the current water connection ban would have a severe impact on our community. It would be more than we can handle. The town council has already voted on the issue, and we want an impact statement before we go any further."

But feelings among the audience were mixed. Noting that there was a large financial cost associated with launching any such environmental review, taxpayer Theodore C. Wellman from Kentfield was on his feet with a quick response. "To bring the full weight of an environmental review process to this problem would be like using a Howitzer to kill an elephant."

At this point Diet Stroeh rose to his feet and made a few observations about his own calculationsthat had not been previously reported in the media.

"First of all, I have to point out that not all 1,500 lots are buildable, for one reason or another," he said. "But let's project that a house will be constructed on each and every lot that becomes connected to the water mains over a period of the next 20 years. The total amount of water required to service all these houses amounts to 780 acre-feet per year. The North Marin intertie, now under construction, will bring approximately 4,000 acre-feet of water to the district annually. So water supply really isn't the issue."

It was left to Board President Pamela Lloyd to make the definitive statement of the meeting.

"Quite frankly, I am appalled by the number of speakers here tonight who have told us that the cities and councils of Marin don't have any controls for planning and growth and that somehow the water board should make those decisions for the whole county. I feel they are asking the water board to do their planning for them, and that's not our function."

With that statement upon which to reflect, the meeting ended, and everybody went home to ponder the issues. There was still no sign of rain in the forecast.

Berkeley, California, 2006

Well, class, already we have an argument forming over my use of the phrase "global warming." I'm not going to argue whether global warming exists or not, because that's a waste of time. The planet is heating up, and glaciers are melting, and you can describe that process any way you want.

Actually, I think "global warming" is a benign phrase that evokes warm and cuddly images, something like curling up with a puppy and a good book in front of a nice fire. The real story is something different. Perhaps a different phrase is needed to bring the urgency of the situation to public attention. "The end of the world" is a tad dramatic a phrase, but it sums up the situation rather well. Even a 1-degree rise in global temperature will cause enormous change in global weather patterns. Already, records for high temperatures, droughts, storms and floods have been broken all over the world during the last decade. Most scientists predict much greater temperature increases than a mere 1 degree. A 5-degree rise in global temperatures doesn't bear thinking about, but many scientists are predicting exactly that.

As we all know, the first attempt to bring this looming global crisis to public attention, and to take appropriate action, ended in failure. The Kyoto treaty called for reductions of greenhouse gases by a modest 5.2 percent below measurable 1990 levels. A less ambitious global treaty was introduced at an international climate change meeting in Bonn, Germany, in 2002, to take effect in 2008. All signatories, including the world's 39 industrialized countries, would have much easier emission reduction targets to achieve than in the original Kyoto accord. The Bonn treaty was a very complex agreement with several innovative ideas that allowed for flexibility on the parts of signatories. For instance, it would allow industrialized countries to buy "emission credits," rights to emit carbon, from a poor country that had no industry or couldn't afford to burn fossil fuels. The original Kyoto treaty called for a 5.2 percent reduction in emissions of the six main gases believed to be causing global warming, but the new agreement scaled that down to a mere 2 percent.

Another report, titled Meeting the Climate Challenge, written in January 2005 by a wide consortium of concerned global scientists, proposed a different, reasonable long-term objective. That report called for actions to prevent the average global surface temperature from rising by more than 2 degrees Celsius (or 3.6 degrees Fahrenheit) above its pre-industrial level.

That report said that beyond this 2-degree temperature rise, the risks to human societies and global ecosystems would grow significantly. For instance, it would put huge numbers of people at risk of drinking water shortages. It would also create permanent damage to important ecosystems around the world. If the global temperature rises above the 2-degree level, accelerated and highly damaging climate change will likely occur, including melting of the west Antarctic and Greenland ice sheets, and the shutdown of the entire Gulf Stream that provides Great Britain and parts of northern Europe with a tolerable climate.

Global warming may also mean dry regions of the world getting drier, wet regions getting wetter, dry regions becoming wet and wet areas becoming dry. Scientists are uncertain what may happen in California, but some forecasts say that global warming may result in a warmer and wetter California.

While at first a warmer and wetter California may sound promising, the reality is that much of the precipitation that currently falls on the Sierra in the form of snow in future would fall instead in the form of rain. While ice slowly melts over the course of months, gradually filling reservoirs, rain immediately runs downhill toward the sea. Reservoirs built to hold runoff will spill early, and much of California's fresh water supply will disappear into the Pacific Ocean, where it will become salt water.

Spring floods will also strike the fragile delta basin levees and flood control devices with much greater power. A recent breakage of a single levee in the delta caused over $100 million in damages. Estimates are that up to 250,000 new homes may be built on the interior flood plains of California in the next decade, all of them protected by levees built to a 100-year flood level. With a warmer climate, all of those proposed homes would be under a serious flood risk.

Washington, DC, June 6, 2010

"Well, dear, what's the latest with our boy Will? Has Dave been keeping a close eye on him?

"Yes, sweetheart," answered William White, Senior, his side of the bed covered in reports. "I can assure you that Moore is never more than two steps away from Will, and has his back covered. From everything that the Secret Service has told me, there is no Maoist activity in the region, and all trekkers are safe as milk."

"How is Dave getting his reports sent out? By yak or horseback?"

"You know that new satellite phone I showed you a few months ago? They are so small these days they fit right into your hand," answered the President. "All Moore has to do is point the antennae in the right direction, and bounce the signal off the satellite, and it's over to my Chief of Staff's office. They keep me informed daily."

"I'm so pleased that Will has somebody there to watch over him, just in case. Does Dave have a gun, too?"

"Not with him, I'm afraid. The Nepalese government had some objections, and there doesn't appear to be any threat."

"Do you really think that Will wants Dave around?"

"No, I'm sure he doesn't, but he's used to it by now."

"Well, dear," said Claire, taking off her glasses and putting them on the headboard. "I'm going to sleep, but I'm pleased that Will is in such good hands. I worry about him all the same, though."

When some high-sounding institute states that a compound is harmless or a process free of risk, it is wise to know whence the institute or the scientists who work there obtain their financial support.

~ Lancet, editorial on the "medical-industrial complex," 1973

Berkeley, California, 2006

I'd like to point out now, kids, that the rich and abundant state of California, the envy of the modern age and breadbasket for the world, has not experienced a really serious drought since our initial settlement about 150 years ago, in 1849 during the Gold Rush.

Wait a minute before you argue with that statement. A drought can be defined as an "extended period of time without sufficient rain to replenish sufficient supply to meet current demand." California has had several such cycles of low rainfall during several consecutive years during the past century, but those drier periods do not constitute what I call a serious drought. A real drought is when it doesn't rain in sufficient volume to fill our reservoirs for a long time. A real, ongoing drought has serious consequences.

Currently the reservoirs and storage systems of California contain only enough fresh water to meet demand for a period of about two years. Maybe three years if the drought is recognized early and we all make conservation efforts. Even a "minor" drought, let's say of a decade or so, would completely eradicate the intricate system of water supply upon which the entire population of 36 million people — predicated to soon reach 48 million — is entirely dependent.

Although extensive irrigation has transformed much of California into a breadbasket, especially the great inland sea that we know as the San Joaquin Valley, in fact much of California is really an arid desert where little rain ever falls. Most of the rain that does fall anywhere in California does so only in winter and spring along the northern coast from San Francisco to Eureka and a few miles inland. Plus we get a lot of snow in the Sierra. Southern California historically has received very little rain, and if it weren't for the rare winter storms it would be a total desert.

California's arid climate is due to its geographic location on the west coast of America and its proximity to the Pacific Ocean. The Pacific is just that, a relatively stable mass of water where the surface water and air temperature rarely changes. Land masses like the continent of America, however, are subject to heating and cooling, so while the interior of the United States can get blisteringly hot and freezing cold, the air temperature in the Pacific stays much the same the whole year. As a result California remains fairly moderate in its yearly temperature.

The warm, wet mass of air that swarms over California on an occasional basis in winter, and provides the south of the state with much of its rainfall, is often referred to as the Pineapple Express, since these air masses emanate from the direction of tropical Hawaii and flow eastward to reach California. Actually, the fact is the Pineapple Express does not actually come from Hawaii, but originates much farther west. Wet winter storms that hit the California coast can be traced all the way back to their origin, which happens to be in the Indian Ocean.

The scientific name for these warm and wet storms that hit California in winter is the "Madden-Julian Oscillation," a global weather pattern named for the two scientists who first identified it in the 1970s. Clouds and rain form over the Indian Ocean and move east. By the time they reach the Pacific Ocean they form a massive, slow-moving atmospheric "wave" that influences tropical rainfall patterns and changes the path of the jet stream over the Pacific.

By the time that the MJO reaches Hawaii in the central Pacific, it has pushed the jet stream east toward California, creating a pathway for tropical Asian moisture to reach all the way to America. This results in dramatically increased precipitation that dumps heavy rain over much of the state and warm, wet snow on the Sierra. The MJO is the force behind the occasional record winter floods for which California is famous.

Marin County, January 25, 1976

Water, water, everywhere,
And all the boards did shrink.
Water, water, everywhere,
Nor any drop to drink.

~ Samuel Taylor Coleridge, The Rime of the Ancient Mariner, 1798

Percy Walton tied Roscoe to the signpost outside the gate and strode through the front door of Kentfield Garden Nurseries with a scowl on his face. In his hand he held a notice he had received from the Marin Municipal Water District, warning of impending water restrictions.

"I say, old chap," said Percy to Dennis O'Shea, a longtime acquaintance and the clerk working the checkout counter today, "what do you make of this nonsense? Have you seen this notice? Have there been people popping by to inquire about replacing their foliage with plants requiring less watering?"

"Yep, we've seen the notice, of course," replied the clerk. "You're not the only person that has been in here asking about their garden. If it doesn't rain soon, we're all up the creek."

"But what will happen to my lovely rosebushes?" inquired Percy.

"Same thing as happens to all plants," answered O'Shea with a smile. "They'll die."

"I have given loving care to my garden for many years, and I shall be most distraught if damage should come to it just because of a minor thing like a temporary drought," said Percy. "Are there not plants that can live with very little water?"

"Sure, you can replace all your imported plants with native plants that are adapted to the desert," said O'Shea. "Like cactus. They don't need much water at all."

"Cactus?" said Percy, scowling. "That's rather a barren thought, Dennis. And what do you mean about 'imported' plants? Roses are as American as apple pie."

"What I mean is, before European settlers moved to California, we didn't have all the plants we do now," explained the clerk. "Did you know there were no trees in San Francisco, for instance, until settlers arrived? It was all barren sand dunes."

"What? No trees?" asked Percy. "What about here in Marin County?

"Well, much of what you see in Northern California has been planted by settlers. Eucalyptus, are actually Australian They were planted as windbreaks, but they're a bad fit for California."

"I know eucalyptus are from Australia. Lovely smell to them. Why are they a bad fit?" said Percy.

"Because, for one thing they're full of oil, and when they catch fire they explode like giant firecrackers," replied the clerk. "Not so good during fires."

"What shall I do about my roses?"

"I'd hand-water them if I were you, Percy," said O'Shea. "Or buy one of these fancy drip feeders. They dispense water very frugally, but they do the job."

"I'm afraid I'm waiting for some year-end accounting jobs to come through at this time," said Percy, "so money is a bit tight at the moment."

"Well, you know, if this drought goes on, a lot of people are going to lose their gardens, and their lawns too," said O'Shea. "Lawns and gardens are strange inventions anyway. The British created them. Eighteenth century, I think."

"Yes, the British have had something of a civilizing effect on the planet, don't you think?" sniffed Percy. "Impose a little order on things. I think I'll impose my thoughts to the district about this water bill."

Berkeley, California, 2006

It seems we have some students in the class this year that have a meager understanding of California's weather, and how it is driven here by the jet stream. What are referred to as "jet streams" are really only high-speed rivers of air racing through the sky. Understanding the jet streams is the key to understanding global weather, and the key to understanding the weather that hits the California coast, producing both storms and drought.

American B-52 bombers flying to Asia over the Pacific Ocean during World War II first created the term "jet stream." They discovered westerly winds in certain areas over the ocean far higher in speed than they had expected. These were invisible rivers way up in the sky that nobody had ever detected before airplanes were invented.

Typically a jet stream is found at the top of the troposphere, about 20,000 to 40,000 feet high in the atmosphere. They can be as much as four miles high and three hundred miles wide. A jet stream can average about 50 miles per hour in summer and 100 miles per hour in winter, although wind speed can rise to 250 miles per hour at times.

The planet's atmosphere, as you all know, comprises five levels. The troposphere lies closest to earth, followed by the stratosphere, the mesosphere, the thermosphere, and the exosphere. For all intents and purposes, only the troposphere has anything to do with our weather. This is where nearly all clouds are formed.

The troposphere acts like a kind of giant air conditioner fuelled by the sun. Air is heated by close contact with a warm landmass that radiates heat. Heated air rises and is replaced by cooler air underneath, causing winds. At the top of the troposphere is a layer known as the tropopause, once thought to be continuous all over the planet. Recent studies have shown the tropopause to have several breaks or plates in it, giving it an overlapping structure. Jet streams form at these overlaps, particularly at the Arctic and tropical tropopauses, thanks to the sharp temperature contrasts found there.

The number of jet streams around the planet varies a great deal from season to season and even from day to day. Typically jet streams blow toward the east, with areas of minimum and maximum strength. In the winter over North America there are usually three jet streams: one over northern Canada at the Arctic break, one across the United States and one over the subtropics.

Science is a wonderful thing if one does not have to make one's living at it.

~ Albert Einstein

Jet streams are created by moving streams of air, known as low and high-pressure zones. These zones are created by various factors. For instance, down here at sea level, air weighs 14.7 pounds per square inch. This weight is known as "air pressure," which varies according to factors such as air temperature and altitude. Warm air is lighter than cold and rises upward.

Cold air is heavier and descends. Because of that, a cold air region is described as a high-pressure area; a warm region is a low-pressure zone. Just like water, air tends to equalize its area, so it moves from high-pressure to low-pressure zones, causing winds. Warm air is able to hold more moisture. When it begins to cool off, it forms clouds or fog. Air moving from the warm, wet Pacific Ocean tends to cool off when it reaches land, causing rain.

Air across the northern Pacific Ocean moves from left to right, or clockwise (the opposite happens in the southern hemisphere). This is known as the Coriolis Force, after the French meteorologist who discovered it. The winds that emanate from the Pacific and arrive in California are known as "westerlies," which are greatly intensified in the spring and often affected by the Pacific High.

The Pacific High is a mass of air that presses down on the Pacific Ocean about a thousand miles off the California shore, about halfway to Hawaii. Some years the Pacific High does not move as far north or south, causing variable weather in California. As the sun warms up the earth in late winter and early spring, the weather in California, and especially in Marin County, can be highly erratic. It produces record rainfall, and drought as well. In very rare years, like 1977, it may not rain at all.

At least 123 freshwater species became extinct during the 20th century. These include 79 invertebrates, 40 fishes, and four amphibians. Freshwater animals are disappearing five times faster than land animals.

~ Department of Environmental Quality, Louisiana

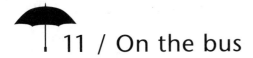

11 / On the bus

When the well is dry, we know the worth of water.

~ Benjamin Franklin

Marin County, January 30, 1976

"Well, folks, is everybody comfortable?" said Diet. "How about you in the back?" The bus bounced its way along the dirt road. It was a hot and dusty day. The rented bus was full of MMWD water board officials, concerned citizens, a few journalists and a young member of the Marin County Board of Supervisors named Barbara Boxer who recently had been an aide to local Congressman John Burton. This was the third stop of the day for the cavalcade, and everybody was getting pretty tired. Looking for new sources for water storage means getting out in the country and riding old buses on dirt roads. That can be hard work for folks used to sitting behind a desk.

In fact, there were three buses bouncing around the back roads of Marin looking at possible sites for a new reservoir. Each bus was crammed with 60 people, making for a total of 180 city folks, many nicely dressed in suits and ties, wandering the Marin countryside. Not only were MMWD staff along for the ride, but various civic officials, key business people and environmentalists had decided to come along too. It wasn't simply that finding a new supply of water was a big deal; it was. No, more than that, the future development of the whole county was at stake, and everybody had a definite opinion about that.

Diet had decided that the best to way to convince all concerned parties of the best site for a future reservoir was to take them to the various possible locations in person. In fact, Diet had already been to all the properties himself, and had talked to the various owners. He had a good idea of what site was best for the county's purposes, but of course you always need to create the illusion of democracy to counteract the inevitable individual dissent.

In what became known as the Soulajule Reservoir when it was later built in western Marin, a small dam already existed that had been built for a scuttled property development. Diet knew this was the best site for any new reservoir. He also knew that no matter what site was chosen, there would be strong opposition from someone, but he thought a deal could be struck to acquire that particular property. The other properties might require court battles, on top of other opposition from many people who objected to any new reservoir being built at all.

Being general manager of any large organization entails a certain understanding of human nature, and Diet knew that as the new guy he needed to get large scale buy-in for his plans rather than just telling people what he had decided. The key question, of course, was how to manipulate the buy-in.

"How much longer now, Diet?"

The voice asking the question was bigger than the woman who voiced it. Boxer had been a personal assistant to John Burton, and was to become a powerful Democratic Senator from California, her rise through the ranks due to her energetic and combative style and her determined support of liberal and environmental causes.

"We've got one more stop on the itinerary today," replied Diet. "San Antonio Creek. We'll be there in two minutes."

"That's nice," replied Boxer, "because my back is killing me."

You go into a community and they will vote 80 percent to 20 percent in favor of a tougher Clean Air Act, but if you ask them to devote 20 minutes a year to having their car emissions inspected, they will vote 80 to 20 against it. We are a long way in this country from taking individual responsibility for the environmental problem.

~ William D. Ruckelshaus, former EPA administrator, New York Times, 1988

Before the 1960s there was no such word as "ecology" in the popular culture and only a few scientists knew what the word "environment" really meant. Fresh water was abundant in much of America, and pretty cheap, so that you didn't care about the price. More importantly, there wasn't widespread degradation of the water supply. The word "pollution" hadn't made it to the headlines just yet. The air was fairly clean, at least in Marin County. Timber companies were still harvesting trees all over America without any great concern for the future, and urban gridlock hadn't been invented yet. All in all, life was pretty good.

As far as urban planning was concerned, a few key strategies for protecting the environment were being discussed. Sewage treatment was mandatory, and clear cutting of forests was no longer allowed, but completing an "environmental review process" was something that still lay in the future. Nonetheless, the golden state of California was growing rapidly and population growth alone forced authorities to take a look at planning processes. In 1970 California became the first state in the country to require an Environmental Impact Report (EIR) before any major development project could be approved.

Even without substantial population growth, the county of Marin was already looking for new sources of water. Long-term residents were well aware of dry years in the past, and planners were starting to look toward the future. The fact that Marin had no water connection to the outside world was a matter of concern and by the mid-60's had become a matter of public debate.

Marin residents had long discussed the possibility of becoming attached to the state water supply system, probably through a pipeline. Some residents favored the idea, others didn't, but as long as the cost of water remained reasonable it wasn't a matter of urgent concern. Many residents favored increasing Marin's own water supply system by building more reservoirs. Unspoken, as in any community, was the obvious fact that increasing the water supply would attract new development. Restricting water connections kept new development to a minimum. A lot of folks liked things just the way they were in Marin, mainly rural and agricultural, with just a few pockets of urban development. Advocating that Marin become a part of San Francisco suburbia was not a popular position to take, and no politicians ever ran for office based on that platform.

During the 60's several options to develop new water supplies were debated. Connecting to the state aqueduct was an option, but Marin had long developed a reputation for going it alone, a reputation for aloofness that would only grow over the years. A reservoir in rural West Marin was proposed. Connecting to the Russian River in Sonoma County, just to the north, was another option. Even at that date some folks were ruminating about the possibility of building a desalination plant.

In 1970 a bond issue was put on the ballot to improve the distribution of water within Marin, and to create a possible pipeline intertie with the North Marin Water District, whose own pipeline dipped into the Russian River in a deal they had with the County of Sonoma to the north. The ballot passed but a subsequent vote to expand Marin's pipeline to the Russian River failed miserably by a 9-1 ratio. In 1972 that proposal was scaled back but still failed on another ballot. The anti-growth faction was still in charge.

But then things changed. Between the late 60's and early 70's many new faces arrived in Marin County, many with strong opinions about the environment, and those new faces were soon reflected in the makeup of the Marin Municipal Water District Board of Directors. The face of the board changed rapidly from old-fashioned business people to environmentalists. The rather bland subject of water supply, formerly the purview of bureaucrats and civil engineers, became a political issue.

At the same time the Marin County Board of Supervisors began work on the first General Plan for the overall community. In 1970 most of Marin was still zoned for agricultural use. The minimum size of a lot was 7,500 square feet. The new General Plan called for Marin to be divided into three zones; eastern, central and western. The western zone was retained for agriculture, but the central zone was rezoned to A60, allowing a single unit of housing per 60 acres, a ploy to keep out all urban development. Most new development was to be restricted to the eastern region of the county, in the urban corridor around Highway 101.

While a segment of the population didn't like going outside the county for water, whether for personal or political reasons, another segment — farmers, in particular — didn't appreciate the possibility of sharp rises in the cost for water in the future. In 1973 the Water Board passed a moratorium on all new connections to the water system, and in the same year Diet Stroeh was promoted to the position of acting General Manager of the MMWD.

By the 1974 elections the entire MMWD board of directors had resigned and four new members were elected. Two of the new board members wanted to build an intertie to the North Marin District but the two other members were opposed. The fifth board member was open to a political compromise that Diet proposed, agreeing to a pipeline that would allow importation of Sonoma water to Marin but would restrict the overall flow to off-peak periods. This would allow Marin's reservoirs to fill but keep the cost fairly low. It was Diet's first dabble into political maneuvering, a small taste of things to come.

While the county of Marin was thrashing its way through modest growing pains, its sister county of Sonoma was also planning for rapid future growth and increased water usage. That meant planning for new dams and reservoirs, but Sonoma was hung up in its decision-making process because of the endless vacillation from Marin voters. While Marin dithered, the cost of building water storage facilities in Sonoma began to increase. Animosity began to grow in Sonoma toward its southern neighbor. Everyone knew how rich Marin was; why should Sonoma pay the cost of its neighbor's endless foot-dragging?

The MMWD board responded with a clever idea. Why not hold the new General Manager's feet to the fire? The board requested that Diet and his crew come up with a master plan; create a water strategy tied to the Marin County Board of Supervisors' General Plan but one that also included new water conservation strategies, water reuse and reclamation methods, new water sources within Marin, and new efficiencies within the Mount Tamalpais watershed from which Marin derived all its water.

It was a challenge that any engineer would relish. Diet rolled up his sleeves and went to work. He immediately booked rooms at a nice hotel in Marin and took his four top planners there. Once there, he informed them all that nobody would be leaving until such time as a Master Plan was written and finalized. The five men got down to work, plastering the walls of their meeting room with graphs, charts, estimates, plans and drawings. Just four days later a 20-Year Plan was drawn up and presented to the board of directors. The board was blown away with the plan, by its quick appearance and by the thoroughness of its vision. Diet was promoted to General Manager and the 20-Year Plan was implemented.

I don't never have no trouble in regulating my own conduct, but to keep other folks' straight is what bothers me.

~ Josh Billings, humorist

The three buses were nearing San Antonio Creek, north of Mount Burdell near the Sonoma border. The group had already looked at Lower Lagunitas Creek in the San Geronimo Valley, and Soulajule, a valley located between Hicks Mountain and Three Peaks in western Marin. There wasn't anything much in San Antonio Valley in the way of development, just a small creek running among the ranches and hills that could possibly be dammed for a reservoir, and a few farms.

A grumpy crowd of 180 people spilled out of the buses. By now most people were getting a bit hungry. There were no rest rooms or coffee shops or opportunities for refreshment out in rural Marin. Folks were hot and dusty, and some of them were reconsidering why they had decided to come at all.

The huge crowd stood around the country road just above the small creek as Diet explained the possibilities of damming it and the amount of water this region of Marin received on an annual basis and how the water supply could be piped south to meet the main Marin pipeline system. As they stood there in their suits and ties sweltering in the sun, over the hill rode a small group of cowboys, herding cattle from their pasture down to the watering hole.

"Hey, what the hell ya think yer doing?" called out the oldest rancher, a tall man with gray hair, wearing a cowboy hat. He was riding a tall black horse and towered over the group of water board officials and guests. "This ain't no picnic site. This here's private land."

"Good afternoon sir," said Bill Walton, who was along for the ride in his position as a big-time car dealer and political operator. As a rich alpha male who commanded respect during civic meetings, Walton felt he had the authority to speak up for others. "No, you don't understand, we aren't here for any company picnic."

"Then what the hell are ya doin' out here?" demanded the rancher, getting down off his horse and walking toward the group. The other two cowboys, possibly his sons, stayed on their horses, grinning ear to ear as the older folks went at it. "This here is private land. Ya'll got no permission to be out here."

Diet stayed quietly in the background. He'd already made inquiries about this property and he knew the rancher well, a man with a reputation for temper. He let Walton make the introductions.

"Well, sir," said Walton, walking forward with a smile and extending his hand like a used-car salesman, "we are touring the area looking for possible sites to create a new reservoir for the Marin Municipal Water District."

The rancher ignored the hand held out in greeting. He looked from face to face at some of the members of the group, shaking his head as he did so. He held on to the tether from his horse, and took his hat off with his other hand, wiping his brow.

"The hell you are," he said.

"Yes, the Marin Municipal Water District has designated this land as one of three possible locations in the county for a new reservoir," said Walton, "and we're just having a quick look. We won't be long."

"That's right," said the rancher, "you won't be any time at all, 'cause yer leavin' right now."

"There's no need to take that approach," said Walton, the smile on his face slowly eroding. "We are here on official county business and we aren't trespassing."

"You ain't trespassing?" said the rancher. "This here yer land then?"

"Well, no," said Walton, taken aback by the hostility in the rancher's voice. "But it's property that the county could appropriate under eminent domain, should that decision be made. We'll talk to the owner of the property and make a reasonable offer."

"The owner of the property?" said the rancher. "I think yer lookin' at him right now, and ain't nobody ever talked to me about nothin' yet."

"Sorry," said Walton, "I didn't realize."

"Realize what?" said the rancher. "That I'm the owner or that you can't just invite yerself onto private property without permission, or that you can't just steal someone's private property?"

"No," said Walton, "what I meant was that the county would pay appropriate compensation for any property appropriated under public domain."

"Appropriation," said the rancher. "Eminent domain."

"Yes, we have the legal right to obtain whatever property we deem necessary for the public good. Besides, there's nothing out here in this valley. No buildings or houses or anything like that."

"Well," said the rancher, turning and beginning to walk away, "I got a house and it's just over that hill there. That's where I keep my gun. And nobody gonna steal my property unless it's over my dead body."

As soon as the rancher got one foot back in the saddle there was a rush for the buses. Business people, politicians and environmentalists alike jostled each other for seats. Diet sat in his seat just behind the driver, where everybody could hear his voice, but it was Walton's voice that was first raised.

"Gee folks, I'm sorry. I never considered the fact that we might be taking someone's private property," said Walton sheepishly. "It never crossed my mind."

"Have you talked to the person who owns the Soulajule property yet, Diet?" asked Boxer.

"Oh, he'll give us some grief too, but this fella has got a real beef," said Diet. "No matter what site we choose we are going to have some problems."

"Well, Claren, what do you think?" said Boxer. "Soulajule or San Antonio?"

Claren Zumwalt was the environmental coordinator for the MMWD, a man well respected by both the business and environmental communities. So far he had kept quiet on the trip, taking notes and answering questions, but had said nothing.

"It seems the gentleman was a bit angry," said Zumwalt, "and I can see where we might have a legal fight on our hands. The Soulajule site already has a dam built though."

"I think I've seen enough for today," said Boxer. "I'd like to have a look at whatever legal data you have for these three properties, Diet. Plus maps, background material, and preferably some material on this particular gentleman."

Diet said nothing, but smiled. When in doubt, get others in high places to fight your battles for you. And whenever possible, always arrange the results in advance.

12 / The water wars begin

We shall require a substantially new manner of thinking if mankind is to survive.

~ Albert Einstein

Marin County, February 12, 1976

Christmas Day 1975 in Marin County had come and gone, and people marveled over the wonderful weather. The New Year arrived and people had marveled over the blue skies and lovely weather. Dog walkers were out on their paths, joggers were out in the hills, and everyone agreed that the weather couldn't be any better. Weeks went by and everyone agreed that this winter's weather was one of the best in history.

But by early February, things were not so sunny at the MMWD offices . In Diet Stroeh's office, faces were downright cloudy. Board members were calling to see what contingency plans the staff had created in the event that it did not rain that year.

"We have two essential problems. My staff have been keeping an eye on the reservoirs, and I've been going through all rainfall records for over a century," said Diet to a board member on the phone. "The stats show that it doesn't always begin to rain heavily in Marin until January, so we were hopeful. But January now is over, and we're going to have to deal with the fact that there might not be enough rain this winter to fill the reservoirs. We also have to plan if we don't get much rain before the summer, and what we do when water consumption goes up then when it's hot. We may have a real problem."

"What are you going to do about it then?"

"I'll have an answer to you soon," replied Diet.

Diet and his staff sat down and came up with a plan that contained two immediate goals; first, they needed to devise a way to reduce water consumption immediately. Secondly, they had to increase district revenues while decreasing the supply. After much discussion with the board of directors, it was decided to create a whole new rate structure for all water consumers in the county.

The new rate structure created several separate categories of water consumers. There would be different rates for apartments, single-family residential houses, and commercial and industrial users. For a typical single-family home, no penalty would be imposed if the consumption were kept under 90 percent of what that home had used the previous winter. The homeowner would pay a higher rate if the amount exceeded 90 percent, and would pay an additional surcharge if the amount exceeded 125 percent of normal usage.

Diet's strategy was created to deal with the fact that the average home usually exceeded its typical monthly average only in the summer months, often climbing to as much as 150 percent of normal. Owners of new swimming pools, for instance, would be sharply affected by the new rates. This was the opposite of all commodities, where the more of a product you purchased the less you would pay. So MMWD was standing established policy on its head; in their new policy, the more you bought, the more you paid.

Summer and its usual increased usage of water was still far away, so there was no immediate public outcry, but it probably wouldn't take too long before some smart customers brought out their calculators and figured out what was going on.

"Looks like we have bought ourselves some time," said Diet to his staff, "but let's hope there are a couple of good gullywashers in the next month."

On a global average, most freshwater withdrawals — 69 percent — are used for agriculture, while industry accounts for 23 percent and municipal use (drinking water, bathing and cleaning, and watering plants and grass) just 8 percent.

~ Water Facts.com

Berkeley, California, 2006

We are studying some meteorology in this class, not history or geography, but you should know that much of the urban growth of the state of California is owed to artificially created supplies of water, much of it imported over great distances. As arid and semi-arid regions of the state gained access to freshwater supplies, they grew into towns and then big cities, and developers in the process made great fortunes. It can also be predicted that continued population growth and the diminishing supply of available fresh water in California will lead to serious issues in the future, including the escalating price of water.

Although the modern image of California is the Golden State, the world's agricultural breadbasket producing millions of tons of food for export, the truth is much of California is an arid desert. If not for extensive irrigation, much of California would still be the vast desert it was before the construction of all the dams, aqueducts, canals and other marvels of modern civil engineering that have turned the state into an agricultural dynamo.

Take, for example, the vast population growth of the city of Los Angeles, today a polluted metropolitan sprawl that, just over a century ago, was only a small harbor in the middle of nowhere. In 1848, just before gold was discovered in the Sierra Nevada, the population of San Francisco was a mere 800 souls, mostly Ohlone Indians and the Franciscan fathers working to improve their flock's spiritual condition. Five years later it was 50,000 and by 1869, San Francisco was one of the twenty largest cities in the entire country. Meanwhile, a few hundred miles to the south, Los Angeles remained an arid little village with severely restricted access to any fresh water.

In its early days, the only access to water for the tiny village was the Los Angeles River, a small creek that flooded its banks every winter during the rare storms. Most years the Los Angeles basin averages a mere 13 inches of rain, half the annual rainfall amount received by San Francisco. In 1848 Los Angeles had a population of 1,600 people, many of them small farmers eking out a subsistence existence growing dates, artichokes, corn, cabbages and oranges.

Slowly word got out that, with only a little irrigation, you could grow damn near any crop in the L.A. basin and get rich quick. In 1867 the Southern Pacific Railroad decided to run a spur line to Los Angeles, linking the region to the rest of the country by land. While San Francisco was already booming thanks to the Gold Rush, the population of Los Angeles grew slowly, but by 1884 proud Angelinos were displaying their big, fat, homegrown Valencia oranges at the World's Fair in New Orleans.

In 1885 the Atchison, Topeka and Santa Fe Railroad built a competing rail line directly from Kansas City to Los Angeles, precipitating a price war with the Southern Pacific Railroad in which fares to the West Coast dropped to as low as $25. By 1889, tens of thousands of Civil War veterans, farmers from the failing Dust Bowl regions of the Midwest, eager immigrants from overseas, displaced easterners and would-be entrepreneurs poured into the Los Angeles region. In that four-year period alone, hundreds of millions of dollars of real estate was sold in the city. Fortunes were made. The only thing stopping the population surging even higher was the ever-growing shortage of fresh water.

There is a saying in the American West, that "water flows uphill to money." More on that in our next session.

Marin County, February 15, 1976

In an underdeveloped country, don't drink the water; in a developed country, don't breathe the air.

~ Changing Times Magazine

The plan to control growth in Marin County by limiting access to water had been an open secret for many years but the subject finally made its way into the newspapers. Mike Ghiringhelli, later to become mayor of Fairfax, laid it all out in a letter to the editor of one of the local papers.

"In recent years the water district board has been using their position in a political manner to control growth in Marin County. They seemed to want a complete moratorium on all construction," he wrote. "They warned us that our water supplies would not be able to support our ever-growing population if a rain shortage ever occurred. Still, we never obtained any water."

"What if there was a complete moratorium on all building? Would that have prevented the crisis we now seem to be in? Or would it be that, no matter what, a rain shortage such as this would have the present effect?" he asked. "The water district's job is now to announce that we may soon run dry so please don't use water, raise our rates 27 percent and then sit on their duffs and pray for rain. I'd like to see some action about getting outside water into Marin. This would be the only sensible solution to our shortage."

"In all fairness, maybe we can't completely blame the water board, but the attitude here in Marin is, once you have your feet planted then no one else can come in," said Ghiringhelli. "So, then people go ahead and vote down some more water hookups like the last one you did. I'm just going to hope Mother Nature doesn't let us all down."

Alan Littman of Tiburon also shared some of his thoughts on the matter in his own letter to the editor.

"The specter of a water shortage was used to stunt growth in Marin County, thereby greatly increasing the price of housing, increasing homeowners' taxes, pre-empting middle income and young people from residing in Marin," he wrote, "drastically reducing our school population and increasing the problems of our school districts."

"A threat of a water shortage should have been used to provide the necessary capacity to serve the residents of the district," wrote Littman.

"Instead, it was manipulated to create a climate of perpetual rationing in which the water district plans to tell us what plants we shall nurture, how many showers we will take, and to increase our rates."

It seemed the debate, just like the unseasonably warm weather, was beginning to really heat up.

Berkeley, California, 2006

In California, water flows uphill towards money.
~ Anonymous saying in the American West, quoted by Marc Reisner, "Cadillac Desert," 1986

Yes, class, in certain areas of California, water does indeed flow uphill to money. Just as San Francisco went crazy during the Gold Rush, attracting gold miners, sailors, and get-rich-quick desperados, Los Angeles also attracted a motley crew of newcomers looking to get rich. One of them was a poor Irish immigrant named William Mulholland. Born in Dublin, Ireland, in 1855, the son of a humble postal clerk, he moved to California in 1874 and he got a job on a well-drilling crew looking for water. He began his engineering career as a ditch-digger for the city's private water company, clearing weeds out of a canal that ran by his house.

Most people in Los Angeles in 1877 were getting their water from wells, tapping into the accumulated groundwater in the vast Los Angeles basin, an underground aquifer that had taken centuries to accumulate.

The nearest big river was the Colorado, but that river was so far away it wasn't even in the same state. Pumping water to Los Angeles would also have meant pumping it uphill, a physical impossibility at the time, given the technology. But in California, the demand was there; if enough money could be found to build an aqueduct, then water would be imported from somewhere. It was just a matter of where and how.

William Mulholland was an ambitious and ruthless man who became superintendent of the Los Angeles Water Company by 1886. About the same time the city experienced its first extended drought, and most wells began to dry up. The water company went bankrupt and was taken over by the city. The same situation that existed then is starting to happen now in certain small towns in the West; fresh water had to be found somewhere, at any price, or the population would simply drift away. Mulholland and some well-heeled supporters decided the Owens Valley would do nicely, and devised an intricate plan to get control of the valley's real estate, and thereby its water. Although it was 250 miles away in the Sierra Nevada, the Owens River contained enough water to supply a million people. It also had the great attraction of starting its original flow at 4,000 feet elevation. If a long enough pipeline could be built to reach it, the force of gravity would draw the water downhill all the way across the Mojave Desert to the coast.

Mulholland built an aqueduct all the way from the Owens Valley to Los Angeles, a phenomenal feat of engineering that took six years and as many as 6,000 men to build. The aqueduct covered 223 miles, over fifty of them via underground tunnels. When completed in 1913,

the aqueduct increased irrigated acreage in the San Fer-
nando Valley, just north of Los Angeles where most of its
food was grown, from 3,000 acres to 75,000 acres. Thanks
to water, the mad real estate and population boom in the
state of California was on; it hasn't stopped yet.

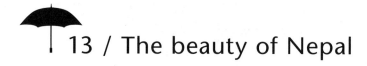

13 / The beauty of Nepal

Our children may save us if they are taught to care properly for the planet; but if not, it may be back to the Ice Age or the caves from where we first emerged. Then we'll have to view the universe above from a cold, dark place. No more jet skis, nuclear weapons, plastic crap, broken pay phones, drugs, cars, waffle irons, or television. Come to think of it, that might not be a bad idea.

~ Jimmy Buffet, Mother Earth News, March-April 1990

Nepal, June 6, 2010

The yarsa, or yak pasture, of Na was basically nothing more than a rock field comprised of giant boulders interspersed with a few bits of grass. It boasted a magnificent outlook across the Rolwaring Valley below. High above the tiny settlement towered the imposing peaks of Chobutse and Kang Nachugo, lining the northern border with Tibet. Yak grazed on the hills, nibbling on whatever tufts of grass they could find. A couple of small stone huts sheltered the yaks during the night and the Magar family from the weather.

Will trudged up the faint trail from Beding, leading the expedition slowly. Moore was right behind. Prayer flags mounted on poles along the trail whipped in the endless wind. Every few hundred yards the party would stop and rest, draining lots of water to combat dehydration, and Will and Walsh would talk about various hikes they had taken around the world.

The weather was changing the face of the planet, both agreed. Glacial melt is a disaster happening all over the world. In the last three decades, Peruvian glaciers have lost almost a quarter of their area. In the next 10 years all the glaciers of Peru, and eventually all the other Andean countries above 15,000 feet, will completely disappear. Not good news for the cities and towns that depend on snowmelt for their drinking water.

A recent report by NASA suggests that a large chunk of a glacier in Peru could break off and fall into a glacial lake anytime. Satellites have detected a crack in the glacier overlooking Lake Palcacocha. The lake could overflow its banks and trigger a devastating flood. The town of Huaraz sits right under the glacier. In 1941 a big chunk of glacial ice actually did fall off, causing an immediate flood that destroyed about a third of the city and killed between 5,000 and 10,000 people.

"Wouldn't it be weird if the same thing happened here?" said Will.

"You know, that's not so funny," replied Walsh. "If a disaster is going to happen here, shouldn't we be going the other direction?"

Will broke out his water bottle, and some dried figs, and passed them around to the group.

"Relax, my man, any flood not going to happen today," replied Will. "These things take time. Scientists are keeping an eye on it. I just want to go see what it looks like up there, for myself. Take some video and some pictures, get a chapter for my book."

Pemaandtheportersshowedupwiththepacksandsatdown.Everyone broke out some snacks and started to nibble. The yarsa lay just above, but they didn't want to scare anyone by walking into the camp unannounced. One of the porters went ahead while the rest of the expedition waited and ate.

As the trekking party sat and relaxed, Sumita Magar, heading back up the path from the Rolwaring River, suddenly saw the group. Sumita, although she had heard of Americans and seen pictures of them, had never met such strange beings before in person. When she spied the expedition party just ahead on the trail, dressed in their strange bright nylon clothing, she stopped and stared.

From where he sat and rested, Will White stared in return. He turned to Walsh, gesturing to the scene laid in front of him, an unending vista of gorgeous mountain peaks and the beautiful young sherpa woman, and smiled.

"Hey, check it out," said Walsh.

"Now that is a beautiful sight indeed," responded Will. "I think I'm going into glacial melt myself."

Nature provides a free lunch, but only if we control our appetites.
~ William Ruckelshaus, Business Week, June 18, 1990

Berkeley, California, 2006

The ramifications of global warming and the effect of higher temperatures on the planet's "frozen freshwater storage system," such as glaciers and polar ice caps, are alarming indeed. In southeast Alaska, for example,

1,987 out of 2,000 glaciers under study are confirmed to be retreating. Another NASA satellite study shows that an area of ancient Arctic ice roughly as large as the Canadian province of Alberta is vanishing every decade as the global climate warms. About 1 million square miles of supposedly permanent Arctic ice has already melted away. The rate of the melt is roughly 9 percent a decade and is speeding up, according to NASA's Goddard Space Flight Center in Maryland.

NASA's findings show that the permanent ice cover in the Arctic is melting at roughly three times the rate scientists had previously estimated. If the melt keeps up at this pace, the permanent ice cover at the top of the earth will be entirely gone before the end of this century. As the dense ice disappears and exposes the ocean for the first time in millennia, the dark blue ocean will pull in greater and greater amounts of solar energy. That will also speed up the rate of the melt. The Arctic Ocean will only partly freeze in the winter and thaw in the summer. Some scientists do not believe this thawing trend is reversible.

A new study of glaciers in a portion of the Antarctic finds that 84 percent of them have retreated over the past 50 years in response to a warmer climate. The work was based on 2,000 aerial photos going back to the 1940s, along with examination of current satellite images. The climate in the southern polar region has warmed by more than 4.5 degrees Fahrenheit (2.5 Celsius) in the last 50 years. When the permafrost melts, gasses long stored in the ice will be released into the atmosphere. This will further increase the rate of global warming.

In the Italian Alps, 10 percent of the glacial ice melted away in the European heat wave of 2003 and experts fear all of it will be gone in 20 years. The alpine glaciers in Switzerland have lost approximately 40 percent of their length at their base since 1850. During the same period their loss in volume is estimated at 50 to 60 percent.

A report from Salford University in Britain shows that the great rivers of Europe that are fed by glaciers in the Alps may run dry in summer seasons if the glaciers evaporate. Major rivers that originate from the Alps include the Rhine, the Rhone, the Po, and the Inn, which feeds the Danube. Mount Kilimanjaro in Tanzania may lose its icecap entirely by 2020, while Glacier National Park in the Rockies could well be looking for a new name by 2030.

If the current rate of global warming continues, most of the earth's 160,000 glaciers will shrink or disappear altogether. Studies show the world's oceans already contain more fresh water than they did 40 years ago. More than 100 million people worldwide live within a mile of a coastline and would be first affected by any rise in the world's oceans.

In dry countries, mountain glaciers can account for as much as 95 percent of the fresh water in river networks, while even in lowland areas of temperate countries such as Germany, around 40 percent of water comes from mountain ice fields. Once the glaciers go, the world will be left with whatever moisture happens to fall out of the sky into lakes and rivers and flows downstream. It will be a much hotter world then, with far less fresh water with which to slake people's thirst.

We have been quick to assume rights to use water but slow to recognize obligations to preserve and protect it... In short, we need a water ethic, a guide to right conduct in the face of complex decisions about natural systems we do not and cannot fully understand.

~ Sandra Postel, "Last Oasis: Facing Water Scarcity"

Will sat in the stone hut of the Magar family, nodding and smiling at Sumita's father while sipping a bowl of chang, the fermented barley beer. It was an extraordinary opportunity for the older man to become extra drunk, because the Americans had already given him a couple of dollars for use of the hut. The old man had killed a chicken and the family pot was boiling with spices for a hot dinner. The fragrant smell drifted around the small hut like exotic perfume.

"You know, boys," said Will, sipping his chang, "Instead of heading straight up to Tsho Rolpa, why don't we just stay here overnight? What's the rush? We've had a tough week. I think we should relax a bit, get more acclimatized to the altitude."

Sumita had changed into her best clothes, and was gaily dressed in traditional Nepalese costume along with a colorful bead necklace and knitted yak wool cap. With her straight white teeth, beautiful smile, shining black hair and slanted Mongolian eyes, she lit up the room. She smiled at Will while filling his cup, then topped up the cups of barley chang for the whole expedition group.

"Me oh my," thought Will. "Who'd a thunk it? Miles from nowhere, in the middle of the Himalayan mountains, and suddenly appears this precious jewel. I have never seen such a pretty girl."

"Well, Will, I have to agree," said Walsh, sipping his own chang and reaching for a second bowl of chicken stew. "We really do need to acclimatize for the climb to 15,000 feet. So we stay here tonight, we climb the glacier in the morning. We'll be back here by tomorrow afternoon. Then we head straight back to Beding."

14 / The price of doing nothing

If you pray for rain long enough, it eventually does fall. If you pray for floodwaters to abate, they eventually do. The same also happens in the absence.

~ Steve Allen, comedian

Marin County, February 18, 1976

The old expression "you're damned if you do and damned if you don't" could have been written expressly about Marin County and the Marin Municipal Water District's ongoing dilemma whether to build more dams to increase water supply or maintain the 1973 moratorium on new connections to control growth. If the board voted to raise rates to conserve water, the public responded to the higher rates — as people always respond to higher prices — by using less. But if the public consumed less water, then the board would realize less revenue. Less revenue meant insufficient funds to pay staff to monitor the new rationing system needed to conserve the water. It was a vicious circle, a Catch 22 of epic proportions.

On February 12 the MMWD board sat down and worked out a new fee schedule for its water customers to go into effect May 1. If it worked, the new schedule would increase revenues to the district while also saving a lot of water. Under the scheme, homeowners would pay more if they used more than 90 percent of what they had used in the past during an average winter month. An additional surcharge would be imposed if homeowners went over 125 percent.

In the summer, consumption normally jumped to 125 percent, from 950 cubic feet to 1990 cubic feet per meter. So, if homeowners kept their water use below 855 cubic feet per month, there would be no penalty. This new rate structure would obviously benefit people who used less. The board also asked the public to adopt "voluntary rationing." Public reaction to these new categories and rationing was muted. Nobody knew what the rates would mean, or who would have to ration what, so there was no reaction.

New York City, June 6, 2010

By the mid-1990s, 80 countries home to 40 percent of world population encountered serious water shortages. Worst affected now are Africa and the Middle East. By 2025 two-thirds of the world's people will be facing water stress. The global demand for water will have grown by over 40 percent by then.

~ Peter Gleick, "The World's Water"

"Look, I want to make one thing clear. We do not use the phrase 'global warming' anymore if we can at all avoid it," said Janet Spalding, at the network news department's weekly planning session. "Is there anybody here who is not aware of what happens every time we use that phrase? All we get is stupid e-mail arguments from viewers about whether it exists or not. From now on, the operative phrase is 'climate change,' and for those who are addicted to using the word 'global,' the operative phrase is 'global climate change.' Do I make myself perfectly clear?"

Jasper Makely was a young up-and-comer in the news department, a hotshot reporter with the meteorology section, he didn't mind getting his nose bloodied or bottom spanked, depending on whom he was contradicting. He put up his hand.

"Uh, does that mean the network's official stand is that global warming does not exist, or does it mean that we have no opinion on it?"

"I seriously doubt that anybody in the media is going to ask your opinion on anything, Jasper," responded Spalding with an icy smile. "However, I will explain things for the hundredth time. It is clear to anyone with an IQ over the drinking age that not only is global warming causing climate change, we are all going to be floating down the proverbial creek without a paddle if we all don't get off our collective fat asses and do something. Network sponsors notwithstanding. I can't speak for the entire network, but I trust that using this new phrase clarifies the news department's position."

"So how come we can't write or say global warming then?" asked Makely.

"Memo to the human resources department," said Spalding, "from now on we make it news department policy not to hire any new staffers with an IQ lower than the President's. To repeat, Jasper, we no longer say 'global warming' simply because we all get sidetracked into useless conversations like this one. We keep covering the topic, daily, but we simply refer to it by a different name. Because getting sidetracked is exactly what the White House, Big Oil and automobile manufacturers want to happen."

"Hey, 'poisoning the planet,' I like that phrase," said Makely. "I'll put that into my news copy tomorrow."

"Jasper," said Spalding, "just be quiet."

We have always had reluctance to see a tract of land which is empty of men as anything but a void. The "waste howling wilderness" of Deuteronomy is typical. The Oxford Dictionary defines wilderness as wild or uncultivated land which is occupied "only" by wild animals. Places not used by us are "wastes." Areas not occupied by us are "desolate." Could the desolation be in the soul of man?

~ John A. Livingston, in Borden Spears, ed., "Wilderness Canada," 1970

Berkeley, California, 2006

Since the construction of the Los Angeles Aqueduct, virtually every river in the state of California has been dammed, and every reservoir that could be built, has been built. There are few, if any, future opportunities to increase the amount of water stored anywhere in the state. What you see is what you get. Unless desalination plants are built along the coast sometime in the future, turning salt water into fresh, there will be no more supplies of fresh water created anywhere in California.

The source of most of California's fresh water lies in the northern part of the state, falling as snow in the Sierra and along the coast as rain. Except for a few small rivers in the north, every river and every drop of water in the state is put to some economic use before it flows back into the ocean. About 80 percent of that water is used for irrigation, turning several interior valleys in the state into agricultural, and economic, powerhouses.

There are over 1,200 major reservoirs scattered throughout the state, and every river except the Stanislaus has been dammed. California has some of the largest reservoirs in the entire country; giant Shasta Lake is an artificial reservoir, as are many other recreational lakes. Most of our rivers flow down from the Sierra Nevada peaks, where the huge snowpack creates spring runoff 10 times greater than that of the Colorado River.

While the enormous Sierra Nevada snowpack creates a huge flow of water into the main rivers and reservoirs, that huge flow is nowhere near enough to satisfy the increasing demand for water in the state. In fact, all of the rivers and reservoirs combined only generate enough to quench 60 percent of the state's demand. The rest of the water comes from underground aquifers, and therein lies a serious problem for the future of the state.

Marin County, February 26, 1976

Water use in the United States alone leaped from 330 million gallons per day in 1980 to 408 million gallons per day in 1990, despite a decade of improvements in water-saving technology.

~ Water Facts.com

Days went by and still there was no rain. Yes, a light sprinkle or two, here and there, but no big gully washers. In total Marin saw 3.23 inches of rain that month, but since it had only rained .31 of an inch in January, 1.49 inches in December and 1.35 inches during November, a lot more rain was needed to get the ground properly soaked and create the runoff needed to fill the reservoirs.

On February 26, the MMWD board of directors met again, and this time faced the obvious. Reservoirs were emptying quickly and drastic measures would be needed or the county's reservoirs might be dry before summer. Implementing new rate structures wasn't enough. Strict water rationing would be needed or else the county would be as dry as dust even before the warm weather arrived.

The board decided that emergency measures had to be imposed immediately, including a 27 percent increase in water rates to make up for any lost revenue expected from a drop in consumption. The ordinance restricted the use of sprinkler systems to water gardens, or using a hose to wash cars or boats. Violators would be warned twice, and then their water would be turned off. There would be a surcharge to turn the water back on.

"We're appealing for cooperation from our customers," said Diet to reporters. "If we get a 25 percent reduction, then stricter rationing methods may not be needed. Stricter rationing might include total prohibition on landscape watering and higher charges for use of extra water above normal consumption. We may need to bring in barges and pump water out of the bottom of Bon Tempe and Phoenix lakes. If we do that, it'll cost up to $800,000. We are heading into a real crisis. Things are going to be tough."

About 6,800 gallons of water is required to grow a day's food for a family of four.

~ Water Facts.com

Until the federal government got into the business of building dams in the 1930s, most of the water used in California for irrigation was from groundwater sources. In the Central Valley, for instance, which at one time was a seabed (now sunken into the ground), in a few short years, between the turn of the century and the 30's, the underground aquifer was almost completely drained by farmers who had turned that region into one of the world's most productive agricultural regions.

When the Central Valley stood on the verge of collapse thanks to the draining of its aquifer, the state's powerful agricultural interests convinced the government to build the California Aqueduct, one of the great engineering feats of the 20th century, a pipeline project so big and complicated it makes the Los Angeles Aqueduct look puny by comparison.

The Central Valley of California was at one time a giant sea that stretched from what is now the Sacramento Delta all the way to the mountains north of Los Angeles. The arid southern two-thirds of the old seabed are known as the San Joaquin Valley, reclaimed land that currently comprises 60 percent of all the arable farmland in the state. At the end of the 19th century, farmers had built small dams and irrigated the more fertile parts of the valley, but the rest of the valley lay fallow. Then came modern machinery based on cheap oil and the farmers started pumping deeper into the aquifer.

By the 1930s, 1.5 million acres of rich farmland were under cultivation in the Central Valley but miles and miles of pipes, from as many as 24,000 wells, had sucked the aquifer down to the bone. In less than half a century the Central Valley water table dropped as much as 300 feet.

The bottom of this ancient seabed is comprises impermeable Corcoran clay, so very little water seeps through it. It rises back up to the surface, waterlogging the land and saturating the crops. During irrigation season the temperature in the valley rises to as high as 115 degrees, causing the water in the ground to evaporate, leaving behind salt. Thanks to this evaporation, thousands of acres of arable land have already gone out of production, covered in layers of salt. The amount of dead and dying acreage is increasing exponentially. It's not only salt that is causing a problem; the process of evaporation leaves behind selenium, a poisonous pollutant. The days of the Central Valley as the world's breadbasket appear to be compromised. Irrigation alone will not keep the industry alive forever.

On the average, each American uses about 160 gallons of water a day at a cost of 27 cents. Bottled water may cost up to 1,000 times more than municipal and may not be as safe.

~ Water Facts.com

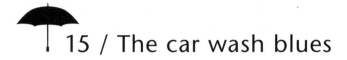

15 / The car wash blues

Water, taken in moderation, never hurt anybody.

~ Mark Twain

Marin County, February 27, 1976

Early on a Saturday morning, a beautiful blue sky was shining and the birds were singing in delight. At his home in the Verissimo Hills in western Novato, Diet was out in the backyard watering his vegetable garden with a can, carefully allocating just the right amount for each plant. It had been a hard week at the MMWD offices, and on weekends Diet always found peace and quiet from the stresses of his job by tending his vegetable garden. Weekdays were for work, but weekends strictly for family business and working in the garden.

The board had decided to impose new rates for water users, in hope of cutting consumption and increasing district revenues. Cutting water consumption by overall volume was one thing; establishing a strict rationing system to conserve what was left of the dwindling supply and getting everyone to buy into the plan was quite another.

"Diet, the phone is for you," Marcia called from the sundeck. Diet and Marcia had met in high school and had married soon after he graduated from university. Diet loved to build houses, and Marcia loved to do the interior design. The vegetable garden was Diet's hobby, though, and he was out there every chance he got.

"Who is it?" he called back.

"I think it's from that reporter at the newspaper," she responded. "Something about the water rationing system that's supposed to go into effect on Monday."

Since the water shortage was now threatening to grow into an official crisis, local reporters had started phoning Diet at the MMWD office for occasional interviews, but this was the first time that any of them had called his home on a weekend.

"Tell him to call back Monday at the office," Diet yelled back. "It can wait."

At the board meeting, the directors had listened to Diet's plan and given their assent, even though everyone knew what the public response was likely to be. There was no choice; staff reported that the county reservoirs were drying up like old prunes. Something drastic had to be done.

Normally the district reservoirs held more than 15 billion gallons of water at this time of year. With the lack of rain, the reservoirs now held less than half that amount. Worse yet, with the warmer weather, plants were starting to sprout and gardens were beginning to bloom and gardeners, like Diet, were out in force watering their roses and lettuce.

"I guess we can put the sprinkler system away," said Marcia, standing on the deck and watching Diet sprinkle his tomato vines by hand. "I don't think we'll be using it again this summer."

To a gardener there is nothing more exasperating than a hose that just isn't long enough.

~ Cecil Roberts, president of the United Mine Workers of America

---

At the MMWD offices, staff and directors had talked long and hard before making a decision that the board then unanimously approved. The voluntary self-rationing measures that the board had requested from the public were not working as well as needed. Starting immediately, emergency measures would be implemented to deal with the water crisis, with the implicit understanding that unless dramatic reductions were accomplished, the county would be completely out of water by the summer.

The emergency measure called for an immediate 25 percent reduction in the overall amount of water used throughout the entire district. It also called for an immediate end to the use of any landscaping irrigation devices, and it imposed a 27 percent increase in water rates to make up for the anticipated loss of income predicted to follow the decrease in usage. Staff and directors alike knew what the public reaction would be.

Without predicting who would be hardest hit, staff knew that the rationing plan could spell serious hardship for community parks, golf courses, home and roadside landscaping, playing fields, nursery businesses, lawns and gardens, or anyone who enjoyed green space and had taken the time and effort to cultivate it.

"This is going to be real tough," Diet said to reporters who called asking for clarification. "We are heading into a real crisis. What we need are a couple of back-to-back storms of about four inches each. If that happens, we hope that we can rebate the increased water charges, but there are no promises."

Diet and his staff went into great detail spelling out exactly what could be watered and what couldn't. For instance, the new emergency measures called for a complete ban on sprinkler systems but allowed the watering of lawns, gardens and shrubbery as long as it was done by hand with a hose. Watering was to be permitted only on alternate days, and only before 10 o'clock in the morning and after 6 p.m. at night. Residents should be alert for any leaks in their water connections, dripping faucets or any other plumbing problems.

The measure banned the use of a hose to wash a car, boat, tennis court, sidewalk or any other hard-surfaced area. The ban did not extend to commercial car washes, which recycled their own water. To wash the family car, the measure suggested a can or bucket be used, as long as the container didn't exceed three gallons.

People were skeptical that you could actually wash a car using a pail. The local newspaper immediately challenged the MMWD board to prove that such a task was actually possible. Board President Pamela Lloyd took up the challenge, bringing her own car down to the MMWD parking lot to meet a crowd of bystanders, reporters and photographers from the local newspapers.

Proving the old theory that the best way to make it rain was to wash your car, the skies grew dark and threatening as Mrs. Lloyd demonstrated exactly how the job was supposed to be done.

"First you fill a two-gallon bucket with soap and water," she explained. "Then you scrub the car with the soapy water, and save the third gallon. When the car is clean, you rinse it with the third gallon."

Mrs. Lloyd followed her own instructions to the letter, and when she was done the car was completely covered in soap bubbles.

"I guess it takes a little bit of practice," she smiled to the cameras. "Maybe the rules of the game should be one gallon for the soap and two gallons for the rinse. I know that people who live in areas where there is no water have always washed their cars this way. It can be done. It has to be done."

Irony of ironies, the skies opened the minute she was finished and her car was immediately rinsed clean of bubbles by the resulting deluge. Unfortunately, the storm lasted only a few minutes, the skies cleared immediately, and the drought resumed.

Nothing so needs reforming as other people's habits.

~ Mark Twain

Marin County, February 28, 1976

It was early in the afternoon and a quite a hot day for early spring. The sun beat down from a cloudless sky. Billy Compton had the Sunbeam Tiger out of the garage and parked in his front driveway with the radio blasting. The local radio station was playing "White Rabbit" by Jefferson Airplane and Billy had turned the volume up loud, trying to wake up some of his house guests who were sleeping pretty darned late from the party the evening before, late even for rockers who seldom got up before noon.

It had been a late night party — very late — celebrating the end of Magic Pillow's latest tour. Magic Pillow was hot, the band's message of peace and love and partying your head off was selling well, and the money was rolling in rather nicely too.

Billy figured the best way to get his day rolling was to wash the car and wake his guests up at the same time, then maybe hit the road for a relaxing drive out to Point Reyes with the hot blond babe who had passed out on the living room sofa the night before from too much wine and dancing and other things.

Billy put the hard top back on the Tiger, rolled up the windows, and began spraying the car with water. He had a new chamois, a box

125

of beer, a bucket of soapy water and the hose connected to the spigot he had finally found, after some dedicated hunting, under the front porch of his house.

There was nothing Billy liked more than washing a cool sports car in the hot sun. Especially when it included drinking cold beer at the same time. This helped cut his hangover from the night before down to a tolerable level, while also getting a fresh buzz going for a new day. He cranked up the tunes on the car radio and started soaping.

"For God's sake, will you turn that stupid bloody thing down," cried Percival Walton, approaching from his own house, once again heading out for a walk with his dog, Roscoe. "You can hear that ruddy noise all the way down the block."

"Hey Percy, how's it hangin' today?" shouted Billy. "Wanna beer? Got some Buds going here."

"No, it's a little early in the day for the consumption of alcohol, I should think," replied Percy, "and will you turn that radio down?"

Billy reached in and adjusted the volume slightly, just enough so he could hear his neighbor's complaints. "What a jerk," he thought. "This guy is such a downer."

"Groovy day, man," he answered. "Just another beautiful sunny day in paradise."

"Can you read?" inquired Percy.

"Of course, man," replied Billy, "every time I get a royalty check I read all the little zeros on the end, just to see how they add up. And I can write too, because I get all these royalties on all the tunes I write, which is like quite a lot these days. Why? Did Keith Richards overdose or something?"

"If you read the local papers," said Percy, pulling out a photocopy of an article, "you might have noticed that a ban on washing automobiles has just been enacted. That includes that silly toy there, if you choose to call it an automobile."

"No way," said Billy, reaching for the paper. "Can't wash the wheels?"

"It might not have occurred to you," huffed Percy, "but there happens to a drought going on, and that means certain restrictions on the inappropriate usage of water. Including wasting water on washing automobiles and sidewalks. There are also major fines for people who do not comply."

"Fines? Wow," said Billy, handing back the newspaper clipping. "Hey man, I haven't been fined all week. We were fined in Santa Barbara for violating the noise laws, but all we got was free headlines the next day, so that's like the cost of doin' business. Ain't nothing free but love, right?"

"If you read the article in question more thoroughly," snapped Percy, "I think you will find that responsible citizens are requested to report infringements of the ordinance banning inappropriate use of water to the appropriate authorities."

"Hey man, if you need to use my phone to alert the authorities, go ahead," said Billy. "I like to be a good neighbor. Call collect, tell her Billy loves her."

"May I point out as well, that in Kentfield the authorities also take a dim view of noise violations," said Percy. "I believe that loud music in the early afternoon qualifies as an infraction of municipal guidelines."

"No kidding," said Billy. "Next time I talk to my attorney I'll be sure to ask him about that. Same time as I talk to him about harassment. I got all these babes chasing me around all the time. And the usual weirdos hassling me, too. You know how it is."

16 / Getting in the swim of things

Be glad that you're greedy; the national economy would collapse if you weren't.

~ Mignon McLaughlin, "The Second Neurotic's Notebook," 1966

Marin County, March 4, 1976

The MMWD boardroom was packed. The main item of discussion was swimming pools, and more than a few folks were hot under the collar.

"To start with, I've got a few facts for you to consider," began Diet. "The average home swimming pool in California takes 20,000 gallons to fill. Whether the pool is being filled for the first time, drained for repairs or cleaning, or refilled for any other reason, that's a heck of a lot of water. Those folks with ample budgets might be able to afford to fill a pool anytime they wanted but if some people in Marin can't take a proper bath in their own tub thanks to rationing – and I've heard from quite a few of them – then they sure as heck aren't too excited about allowing new swimming pools to be filled."

Director Polly Smith was the first board member to speak.

"I think it's psychologically damaging to ask consumers to cut water consumption 20 percent while allowing a few people to enjoy the luxury of filling new pools," she said. "I'm against it."

Director Pamela Lloyd seconded that thought, but was immediately contradicted by a member of the audience.

"The pool building industry here in Marin is a multimillion-dollar-a-year industry," said pool designer Rod Garrett, "and any ban would put them out of business. We've got representatives from the Sunset and Anthony pool construction companies here who'll back me up on that."

"According to my staff, 214 permits for new swimming pools were issued last year in Marin," said Diet. "The proposed ban we are talking about will still allow owners to fill new pools with water trucked in from outside the county. But the amount of water required to fill all these pools is only 14 acre-feet, which is a drop in the bucket of the 8,000 acre-feet that we consider necessary to conserve to see the county through the summer. Nonetheless, it is hard to ask hundreds of thousands of people to conserve water while a few hundred people get the luxury of new swimming pools. I think we ought to study the issue a bit more."

Pool builders had already come up with a few ideas on saving water, suggesting that covers for all new pools be installed to prevent evaporation, banning the draining of all existing pools for maintenance purposes, and requiring that new water conservation devices be installed. In addition, pool builders and service repair companies agreed to launch and pay for an advertising campaign to encourage pool owners to install filtering systems.

"I think in future we can also build smaller and shallower pools to save water," said pool designer Garrett. "For swimmers, a 40-foot pool can be built with a capacity of just under 10,000 gallons. The rest of us might enjoy a 500-gallon hot tub instead, or even a 5,000-gallon fountain."

It looked like the pool builders would carry the argument, but then the protests from the general public started.

"I think that this sort of action is immoral," said Carol Herschleb, "and it sets a very bad example for the community. If I was living next door to someone who was filling a swimming pool, I'd wash my car and water my lawn."

"Wait a moment there," replied director Richard Boylan, "we haven't forbidden the watering of lawns or gardens, only the use of automatic sprinklers. Swimming pools will go long before gardens and food production."

"One minute, I have another thing to add," said pool designer Garrett. "If just 25 percent of the 3,600 pool owners in the county installed filtration tanks, then 42 acre-feet of water could be saved over the summer. That's more than what all the new swimming pools would take. Then we wouldn't have a problem."

"Wait a minute folks," interrupted Diet. "While we are doing our math here, let's get our numbers straight. We've been talking all along about the county saving 25 percent. That's just an average amount measured on a daily basis. If we are talking about the summertime, when it gets a lot hotter, then people start using a lot more water. A heck of a lot more. Right now our figures are based on the county using only 25 million gallons a day. I'm here to tell you that the average summer use in Marin is 42 million gallons a day, not 25 million, so the reality is we have a lot more cutting to do yet."

"The fact is, folks, you can throw that 25 percent reduction figure out the window," he said. "Starting right now, we have to make 40 percent our new conservation target. That means we may soon have to ban all unnecessary water use, including washing your car and any type of irrigation whatsoever. We may also have to hire more staff to patrol the district, and make sure these regulations are strictly observed, if that 40 percent figure is not achieved."

"Swimming pools are only a tiny part of the picture, folks," he said. "They are a luxury. I don't think a lot of people have really caught on to the situation we're in now. We are going to be in big trouble if it doesn't rain soon."

Sixty-six percent of a human being is water. Seventy-five percent of the human brain is water.

~ Water Facts.com

Berkeley, California, 2006

A question has been asked about "global warming." The question is, what's wrong with the planet warming up a few more degrees? Wouldn't that be nice for people who live in Minnesota in the wintertime?

The truth is, an increase of a few degrees will not make for pleasant temperatures around the globe. It will have an extremely negative effect. In the last 10,000 years, the earth's average temperature hasn't varied by more than 1.8 degrees Fahrenheit. At the end of the last Ice Age, temperatures were only about 5 to 9 degrees cooler than today, but even so the northeast United States was covered by more than 3,000 feet of ice. Scientists predict that continued global warming, by a mere 2 degrees over the next century, will mean a rise in sea level of at least 3 feet. That means major flooding during any storms.

It will also mean severe stress on many forests, wetlands, alpine regions, and other natural ecosystems. With warmer weather we will see greater threats to human health, like mosquitoes and other disease-carrying insects and rodents coming north and spreading diseases. We will also be looking at major disruptions of agriculture in some parts of the world. A rise in sea level will affect low-lying areas such as the Mississippi River Delta. Let's not confuse global warming with the phrase "ozone depletion," which is a related environmental issue but actually a separate threat. Global warming refers to the heating of the lower part of the atmosphere, which is the troposphere, because of increasing concentrations of heat-trapping gases. By contrast, ozone depletion refers to the loss of ozone in the upper part of the atmosphere, called the stratosphere.

Ozone depletion is bad news because stratospheric ozone stops incoming ultraviolet radiation from the sun, which can be deadly to plants, animals, and humans. The two problems are related in some ways. For instance, some man-made gases, like chlorofluorocarbons, trap heat and destroy the ozone layer. Currently, these gases are responsible for less than 10 percent of total atmospheric warming, far less than the contribution from the main greenhouse gas, good old carbon dioxide, that invisible substance that emanates from your car's tailpipe.

The ozone layer traps heat, so if the ozone layer gets wiped out, the upper atmosphere cools off, which actually offsets some of the warming of other heat-trapping gases. Sounds good, right? Well, no. The cooling of the upper layers of the atmosphere produce changes in our climate that affect weather patterns in the higher altitudes. Trapping heat in the lower part of the atmosphere allows less heat to escape into space, which leads to cooling of the upper part of the atmosphere. The colder it gets, the greater the destruction of the ozone layer.

Reducing ozone-depleting gases will prevent further expansion of the ozone layer, but eliminating greenhouse gases alone will not solve the global warming problem. However, reducing emissions to limit global warming will also be good for the ozone layer. Have you got that, class?

Nepal, June 7, 2010

A kiss is a lovely trick designed by nature to stop speech when words become superfluous.

~ Ingrid Bergman

Sumita picked up the bowl of chang, finally empty, and went outside her hut, dropping her head to go through the low doorway. As she did, she quickly looked out of the corner of her eye at Will. He lay back, pretending to have his eyes closed, while keeping an eye on her every movement.

"Man, I'm tired," he said. "I've never been up to 13,000 feet before."

"I'm beat too," said Walsh, reaching for the last of the chicken stew, picking up a bone, and gnawing on a leg. "There is also the fact that we have to climb up to 15,000 feet tomorrow, so let's hope that nobody gets seriously affected by altitude sickness. Too much time up at that height will certainly make you tired, if not worse."

"The plan is, we climb up to the lake, take a quick look, and head right back down, right?" said Moore, lying down against his pack and making himself comfortable. "So if anybody gets a reaction to the elevation, we head straight down, no problem?"

"That's the plan, Stan," replied Walsh. "It will take about four hours to get up, less to get down. Will wants some video footage, we're up there maybe two hours, back here mid-afternoon, we head down to Beding to crash."

"Excuse me," said Will, heading for the door, "I need to take a leak."

"So we don't need to bring all the packs way up there?" asked Moore.

"Last I looked, the porters were toting all the gear, Dave," replied Walsh. "I'm not prone to taking risks, but the packs have the medical gear, cameras, food and safety supplies, so the porters can bring them along."

"Will that slow us down?"

"So far, I haven't seen any of us able to keep up with any of the porters," said Walsh, "and we're wearing hiking boots and they've got sneakers. Maybe if we dropped down to sea level the porters would have problems, but at 15,000 feet these guys will leave us in the dust."

Outside the hut, Will walked over to a large nearby boulder, relieved himself, and then stretched. The stars were beginning to appear, and he looked up the dazzling array of bright lights in the purple sky, and at the mighty bulk of the mountain, and was finally happy. Somehow just being in the high mountains, with the endless vistas and giant peaks, was an elixir. Turning, he headed back to the hut when he heard a rustle above his head.

Most Tibetan-style houses in the Himalayas are two-story stone huts, with the first floor reserved for animals and storage. The yarsa of Na was nothing more than a couple of one-story stone huts, with a single two-story structure. On the ground floor of that hut the hikers were resting, and the upper floor — really just an open roof — was used for drying the sticks and small pieces of wood plus the barley that was stored in small bags. Lying down and leaning over the edge of the roof was Sumita, with a big smile on her face.

"Well, hello there, sweet thing," whispered Will. "What the heck are you doing up there, all by yourself?"

Sumita held a finger to her lips, universal sign language for silence, then crooked the finger at Will, indicating he should come closer. He edged closer, holding onto the edge of the roof for balance. Sumita leaned forward and pulled him gently by his hair.

"Kisimu?" she said.

17 / Repercussions to rationing

A leaking faucet can waste up to 100 gallons of water a day.

~ Water Facts.com

Marin County, March 5, 1976

"I think it's time to have a good, hard look at the operations of the Marin Municipal Water District," said a man with a deep voice in the front row. "You've already raised rates 10 percent, so with this new 27 percent surcharge, you're actually raising rates 37 percent."

The public meeting at the Corte Madera Recreation Center had been well publicized. Disgruntled citizens and various taxpayers associations were waiting like hungry lions for Diet Stroeh and the MMWD board of directors. Now that they had a chance to voice their displeasure, people were giving it to Diet as well as they could. Months of frustration came boiling up.

"This surcharge is an excessive amount of money," thundered Coleman Sellers of the United Independent Homeowners of Terra Linda. The overflow crowd jumped to its feet, applauding. People in Marin were mad as heck and weren't going to take it anymore. Rationing to conserve the dwindling supply of water was one thing, but a 27 percent boost in water rates was just too much. Over 200 people crammed into the gymnasium on a Monday night to voice their objections to the surcharges and restrictions. Explanations were wanted and none had been forthcoming.

"So what are you going to do to make sure this short of thing doesn't happen again?" said another loud voice. R.W. Bruce of the Kent Woodlands Property Owners Association was angry, and his remarks were met with a roar of applause from the standing-room-only crowd.

"You should here and now commit yourselves to actively seeking new water resources," said James Reed, standing up. Reed represented the Irate Taxpayers of Marin, the Marin County Taxpayers Association, and the United Taxpayers of Marin. Once again his remark was met with a roar of applause. "Past water boards have been restricting growth by restricting any new sources of water. That's how we got into this crisis in the first place."

"We want guarantees that these rates will be dropped as soon as the drought is over," cried out a lady in the back. More applause.

"I have to tell you that this surcharge is especially hard on the elderly and those on a fixed income," said Sally Ryan, standing and speaking for the Marin County Status of Women Commission. "It places undue penalties on those who have already reduced their water consumption."

When he thought a sufficient number of people had vented their steam, Diet got to his feet.

"We have no choice but to raise rates," he responded, "because water consumption has already been reduced by 25 percent since we imposed the rationing system. A 25 percent reduction in consumption means a corresponding 25 percent loss in district revenue. The water district needs revenue for a wide variety of purposes, including enforcement of the rationing system itself."

"Oh, that's really rich," came a loud voice from the rear. "The more water people save, the more money you charge them. What school of economics did you go to? And what about the rains that fell this past week? Didn't those help raise the water level?"

People were on their feet applauding.

"Yes, indeed sir," replied Diet. "This week's rains have raised the levels of our reservoirs 1 percent, so we are now up to 52 percent of capacity. So far this year we have received 6,000 acre-feet of runoff, which works out to be the driest winter in Marin history. We need a minimum of 10 more inches before the end of the rainy season in April just to get out of our emergency, and that seems unlikely. Even with rationing we are going to be in trouble. Without strict rationing we are going to be in deep, deep trouble, and very soon."

The word "emergency" seemed to have an effect on the crowd and there was a moment of silence. MMWD director Polly Smith took this as her cue to stand up and speak.

"I'd like to point out that district voters have twice defeated bond issues aimed at developing new sources of supply," she said. "We have another bond measure on the November ballot designed to pay for the proposed Soulajule dam, and I suggest that it might be a good idea if voters approve that."

"The rationing plan that we have imposed should be enough to get us through the summer," said Diet, "but we need the extra income for added administration in order to enforce the rationing."

"If we didn't have the added administration, then we wouldn't have the added costs," yelled out a person in the back. "You bureaucrats always want to increase staff. That's about the truth of it."

"We invite everybody to come to our monthly board meeting next Wednesday," said Diet, "and we'll explain the new rates and surcharges in greater detail then."

Marin County, March 6, 1976

About 39,090 gallons of water is needed to make an automobile, tires included.

~ Water Facts.com

There can be no greater insult than comparing any delivery system to the post office. An editorial in the local newspaper on March 5 took exactly that angle, and it was a cruel blow to the nether regions of the MMWD. Readers responded with vigor, and columnists and reporters soon joined the game.

Since being turned into a semi-autonomous business separate from the federal government in 1971, the editorial writer for the local paper pointed out, the U.S Postal Service had managed the rare feat of closing offices, eliminating deliveries in many districts and slowing down the mail while increasing prices.

"Spending more while giving poorer service, it has been forced to increase postage rates," said the editorial. "Higher rates for poorer service have produced a predictable result: People are mailing fewer cards and letters and are sending packages by other means. So the USPS has now begun an advertising campaign to promote use of the mails."

Indeed, the parallels between the MMWD and USPS were obvious. As the newspaper was quick to point out, at the same time that the MMWD had ordered its customers to use less, it was jacking up its own budget about 25 percent. Its budget was, as the newspaper stated, the highest of any Marin public agency. MMWD was spending as if it were increasing water supply and adding new connections, which of course it wasn't.

"If we are to allow our lawns and shrubs to die, our boats to grow rusty and our cars dirty," said the editorial writer, "and to see our quality of life eroded by the water district's restrictions, is it unfair to ask the Water District itself to suffer with us? Or does MMWD intend to continue on the same dead-end road as USPS?"

Letters to the editor took up the war cry and continued the assault.

"Those of us who have been cutting down (on consumption) will have to demonstrate that we are really doing it by cutting another 25 percent more, a neat trick if you can manage it. That would be straight out of "Alice in Wonderland" and "Through the Looking Glass", except those are fictions and funny, and the MMWD's fantasy is a clear and present danger to our pocketbooks."

More letters were written and published.

"As I sit by the window idly watching the rain fall at a 27 percent increase in price, I cannot help but marvel at the American economic system. When in the process of normal events items threaten to become scarce or do not sell with enthusiasm, prices are raised to account for any deficit. Nevertheless we must have faith in our Marin Muni water people. Rest assured that in case of any catastrophe in the water system, they will not sit idly. They will stand on their feet, roll up their sleeves, and make it rain."

Make no mistake, people in Marin were upset at the MMWD. Tension built every passing day as it became clear it was not going to rain in sufficient amounts to eliminate the drought. But the water conservation plan was starting to pay off. Even though March was generally a wet month, in the hot and dry weather people were using about the same amount of water as they normally would.

"Right now district consumers are using about 19 million gallons a day, compared to the usual consumption of between 17 and 20 million gallons a day," said Diet to newspaper reporters. "We expected consumption to go over 20 million gallons in this heat, but people have been extremely cooperative. We've only had to issue warnings to six customers for violating the current rationing system."

Meanwhile, both immediate and long-term forecasts were for continued hot and sunny weather.

Our increasing thirst is a result of growing population, industrial development and the expansion of irrigated farming. In the past 40 years, the area of irrigated land has doubled.

~ The New Internationalist

Public reaction to the rationing system had been mixed since the regulations were first announced. Initially there was no comment, because everyone realized that a crisis was impending and something had to be done. Then people got their bills in the mail with the new 27 percent surcharge and the public mood changed quickly. Money does funny things to some people. Suddenly public interest and the greater good were superseded by private interest. Vague acceptance gave way to personal outrage. Some people wanted to shoot Diet and others just wanted him fired. But private outrage is one thing; public anger is another.

It took a few more days for people who used large amounts of water to figure exactly what the new regulations would really mean. Then the anger really started to percolate. The first to fire a salvo were managers of Marin's hallowed golf and country clubs, when members went to play golf and noticed that the fairways had not been watered and subsequently vented their spleens at staff. Country club managers were more than willing to share their members' concern with the public.

"This ban on watering is going to put us out of business," said Ray Teeters, superintendent of the San Geronimo Golf Club. "We don't have any well water we can use. We will be seeking special dispensation to water at least the tees and greens."

Then the people responsible for irrigating schoolgrounds, city parks, playing fields, boulevards and gardens began to chime in. Mill Valley city officials cried that they were responsible for a 40-acre golf course and 40 acres of city landscaping, and it was all going to die. The Tamalpais Union High School District said that its 57 acres of turf and 20 acres of school landscaping were dying. The San Rafael School District added that its 70 acres of turf was going to dust. The City of San Rafael complained that its 16 acres of public fields would be lost. Marin County officials said that many thousands of acres of state, county and other municipal lawns were at risk.

Pierre W. Joske, Marin County parks and recreation director, was the first to establish a cost to the damage. He noted that a single acre of turf costs about $5,000 just to establish; maintenance costs were another factor. County director of maintenance official Oliver (Skip) Bonner added that it would cost $7,000 per acre to re-establish any turf that died during the hot summer months.

"Even if the playing fields survive, without any watering the ground gets so hard we'll end up with injuries," said Bonner. "Coaches will have to cancel baseball and football programs. Then it will take at least another year to grow the fields back again."

In response to this barrage of public criticism, the best that Diet could manage was a polite response in an interview with the local newspaper.

"I hope everyone realizes that we are in a serious situation. If we don't give up a lawn or whatever it is, we won't have water for anything else," he said. "Storm fronts have been bypassing Marin and Sonoma all spring. We can't depend on any rain. We will start looking immediately at trucking in waste water from our sewage plants to maintain some city lands, but we can't make it rain."

Diet pointed out that West Marin farmers and ranchers were experiencing far more serious problems. They were not plugged into any water district pipelines either, and had been relying on their own wells and ponds to keep their livestock alive. The ponds were already drying up and it wasn't even summer yet.

"I hope the ranchers get together and request the board of supervisors to have the county declared a disaster area by the Governor," he said, "as 29 other counties have already done. We need serious help."

Strangely enough, after their initial show of outrage, only a handful of people bothered to attend the MMWD board of directors meeting a few days later. Responding to the first display of public criticism, the board had already decided to approve a newer and more complex rate structure, ranging from 24 to 29 percent, replacing the one-size-fits-all 27 percent structure formerly planned. The flexible rate structure was designed to help smaller consumers who had already cut back to the bone and couldn't find any more ways to save. The new structure would also hike rates for very large water consumers up to 36 percent.

Directors warned that if the new rate structure and rationing system didn't work, then further increases of up to 50 percent might be imposed during the summer. If that didn't solve the problem, people might have to buy their own water from private sources at even more exorbitant prices.

"People will have to conserve very tightly," said director Bill Filante, "or start making trips to the bank."

The board of directors agreed to start looking at extending the watering ban to include private swimming pools. The board also admitted that it had received a large number of complaints about violations of the rationing system already in place. Under that system, violators would receive only two warnings and then have their water disconnected.

"We've already had about 50 complaints, investigated them and issued five warnings," said Diet. "I think some people are going to have their water cut off."

Most rock journalism is people who can't write interviewing people who can't talk for people who can't read.

~ Frank Zappa

Percival Walton was on the phone to the water district.

"May I inquire with the appropriate person as to where I may report repeated and continued violations of the watering ban?" he asked the receptionist.

"Is this in regard to watering lawns, washing cars or some other violation of the ordinance?" she responded.

"It's in regard to an idiot," replied Percy. "My hippie neighbor washes his car every damned day using a hose, he washes down the sidewalk and driveway, and he washes down his neighbors if they complain. He runs a sprinkler every day on his back lawn, and people run around the lawn under the sprinkler half naked making loud and rude noises. And he plays very loud music."

"I'm afraid I can't help you with the loud music," replied the receptionist. "You are going to have to call the police for that."

"I have called the police regarding this individual," said Percival. "They showed up and asked for his autograph. There were a lot of under-dressed young women on the premises and the police spent more time talking to them than they did dealing with the noise."

"Would you like me to connect you to a staff person who can help you with the watering violations?" she asked.

"Very much so," replied Percy. "Something must be done. I am at my wits' end."

Two-thirds of the water used in an average home is used in the bathroom. Typically 4 to 6 gallons of water are used for every toilet flush.

~ Water Facts.com

Marin County, March 20, 1976

A rainstorm finally hit Marin in late March, dropping 3.5 inches of rain. There was dancing in the streets. The rain immediately alleviated concerns about the need for continued rationing. It seemed that 3.5 inches would put an end to the crisis, but as Diet Stroeh was forced to point out to reporters calling him for comment, the rejoicing was much ado about nothing.

"I know it was a nice little storm," said Diet, "but it was really only a drop in the bucket. We still need a couple of gully washers to solve our shortage. This will do absolutely nothing to alleviate our rationing for the summer."

The 3.5 inches of rain translated into an additional 135 million gallons of water added to the district's reservoirs, but given that the district's capacity was 17 billion gallons, the rain really was insignificant. And since March was near the end of the rainy season, it could hardly be expected to rain in great volume again, although everybody kept their fingers crossed for a downpour.

Since records had been kept in Marin going back to 1889, never had the county undergone two years of extreme drought in direct succession. Drought can be described many ways, but one measurement is "less than 50 percent of the usual precipitation in one year," measured from the beginning of the rainy season. According to MMWD records, the county had experienced several dry periods over several years, including what can be termed the "dust bowl" years of 1912 through 1924, but never back-to-back years of real drought that totally drained the reservoirs.

While the record for total rainfall in Marin was set back in 1889, when a whopping 112.21 inches fell, the average yearly rainfall in Marin is only 50 inches. In 1923 the county received only 19.6 inches of rain, the lowest ever recorded, but it was boosted by a nice downfall of 6.8 inches in January, which caused enough runoff to replenish the reservoirs. That deluge was enough to fulfill the needs of the population of the day, which was much smaller.

In 1912 the county received only 30.02 inches, in 1917 only 20.65 and in 1919 only 23.45 inches, but in between each of those dry years the precipitation returned to normal. There had never been two successive years in Marin's history when the reservoirs were drained to the bone.

In 1975-76, however, the county had received only 22.13 inches of rain. In the winter of 1976-77, the rainfall was only 24.97 inches. During that extended period, the only month where the rainfall exceeded the five inches needed to saturate the ground was October of 1975, when 7.92 inches of rain fell to start the winter season. While that deluge was certainly enough to cause runoff, it never rained heavily again in any one month until November of 1977, when a lush 9.49 inches fell, finally ending the drought. During the 25 months in between, there was never sufficient rain to cause runoff to reservoirs.

By the end of March 1976 the people of Marin had already accepted the inevitable. There would be no big rainstorms coming to bail them out. The long-dreaded killer drought had officially arrived, and another long, hot summer lay directly ahead.

18 / Endless summer

Get your facts first, and then you can distort them as much as you please.

~ Mark Twain

Marin County, March 27, 1976

Blame for a lack of proper foresight was placed squarely on the shoulders of the water district, which had failed to prepare for doomsday. How could they not have known it might not rain? Obviously a drought was going to happen eventually. An editorial in one of the local newspapers pointed that out. Why didn't the water district know this, and why hadn't they predicted it? Why, any idiot could have predicted it!

The newspaper suggested that there was a simple and obvious solution to the crisis. Why not enlarge the size of the reservoirs in the water district, and thereby save more water for such a possible crisis?

"A revered former official of the Marin Municipal Water District has suggested this approach to the board, privately," said the editorial writer, "but so far there has been no sign that contemporary officialdom has paid any attention."

The general public soon took up the hue and cry. Yes, why not enlarge the reservoirs? Why, there's a simple solution to our crisis! Why didn't somebody think of this before? No need for any pipelines to Sonoma or emergency rationing! Letters were written in local papers, venting the fury of those whose rosebushes and lawns were dying.

In his own defense, Diet offered his own opinion of the situation.

"In reference to Mr. Jerald R. Cochran's letter regarding the deepening of Nicasio Reservoir to increase water supply, the district has taken this into consideration, along with the raising of the dam itself," wrote Diet. "Either possibility will not affect the rain that falls in the Nicasio watershed. The dam was designed and built so that we may store the total amount of water the entire watershed could ever yield. Enlarging the reservoir would not increase the amount of water available during a dry period."

In short, if it doesn't rain, there is no water to store, no matter what size dam you build. Diet's comments summed up the situation rather well, and put a temporary end to public speculation about simplistic remedies.

Meanwhile, it was announced that police and firemen would join MMWD staff during the summer months to help catch violators of the water rationing ordinances. They said violations of the rationing ordinance would be reported immediately to the water district for quick action. Fire chiefs, in a joint meeting on March 11, also noted their concern about the amount of water that would be available over the hot and dry summer months for firefighting.

Diet thanked the fire and police officials for their offer, and assured the public that these new watchdogs would only be watching for violators during their normal patrols, and wouldn't be sneaking around when they weren't supposed to. He also announced that water consumption was still 9 percent over the rationing goal.

Marin County, December, 1976

Few things are harder to put up with than a good example.

~ Mark Twain

By the end of May, the MMWD board decided to end their patrols looking for violators of the strict No Watering policy. Some 35 employees had been out searching neighborhoods very diligently, looking for scofflaws and water bandits, and had turned up virtually nothing.

"It just wasn't worth the cost," admitted Diet. "On Wednesday, which was the hottest day of the year so far, the patrols only spotted half a dozen violations. I think it's great that we don't need the patrols anymore. I expected a lot more violations, but I'm really glad there aren't many."

Since the ordinance was enacted, a total of 111 warnings had been issued. Most were for minimal offenses, like watering in the middle of the day. Enforcement or not, warned Diet, the county still wasn't meeting its rationing goals. The average daily use hovered around 28 million gallons, some 3 million gallons above the stated goal. Unless district customers cut their use by at least 40 percent over the summer, the reservoirs would be empty by fall. That awful news prompted yet more angry letters from homeowners in the district.

"I couldn't help feeling bitter and amused the other night when I read that our local water district has decided to dismiss a number of temporary investigators they had hired to look for violations during our current water crisis," wrote J.W. Johnson of Ross. "I couldn't help wondering where they had been looking. If they would like to accompany me some night on my evening stroll I think they would find enough violations in the form of automatic sprinklers to keep them busy."

May, June and July came and went and not a drop of rain fell. In August the skies opened and it rained a meager total of 1.73 inches, and September followed with a grand total of 1.33 inches, but both drizzles were immediately soaked up by bone-dry ground. Lawns and gardens continued to die, and people looked constantly to the sky for relief. But at the same time, people were also looking closely at their water meters and adjusting their daily consumption habits, and finally water conservation started to really take hold.

On September 16, Diet announced that there was some good news; thanks to the public finally buying in to conservation warnings, MMWD reservoirs still held 5.5 billion gallons of water in its six reservoirs, enough to last the rest of the calendar year. Or until the annual winter rains, hopefully, commenced again.

"Usually we'd have about 10 billion gallons left by now, out of our total capacity of 17 billion," he said to the press. "Rationing and water conservation techniques have lowered daily summer consumption to 24 million gallons a day compared to our daily summer average of 40 million gallons. If we didn't ration severely we'd only have 2.9 million gallons by now, and we'd be pumping the bottom of the lakes at a multi million-dollar cost. Without these savings, we'd be completely out of water."

There was even better news.

"According to the U.S. Weather Bureau, we'll have heavy rainfall in the next 30 days," he said. "Given our usual rainfall, reservoirs should be back up to 80 percent by February, so rationing and surcharges will come off when we hit that figure. If there are tremendous amounts of rain before then, the board may look at the situation earlier."

Even better, construction of the intertie pipeline between MMWD and the North Marin Water District was completed over the summer, and MMWD was able to import 6000 acre-feet of water from Sonoma through North Marin, using it to provide water for the MMWD's northern areas such as Lucas Valley.

William Wilson, North Marin's operations manager, said that his district would soon turn to the Russian River, because the ongoing drought had lowered the water in Stafford Lake, its traditional supply. Wilson said that another dry year would severely reduce the amount of water available from the Russian River, and result in strict rationing in the North Marin Water District too.

"But it will have to be a very dry year," said Wilson, "because the Russian River is a very large river and has a lot of water in it." Winter forecasts were for heavy rain, so the point seemed moot. The worst was over, and people settled back and waited for the winter rains to commence.

A lawn is nature under totalitarian rule.

~ Michael Pollan, "Second Nature," 1991

The U.S. Weather Bureau was partly right. It did rain, but nowhere near the massive amounts it had been predicting. In October a mere .79 inches of rain fell, just enough drizzle to get people's hopes up. But October is often a dry month in Marin, and the real rainy season seldom starts before November.

But by mid-November the predicted storms had not materialized, even though some clouds finally appeared in the sky. The total rainfall for the month turned out to be a paltry 2.35 inches, falling in dribs and drabs here and there, once again not enough to produce runoff. The parched earth eagerly soaked up the water, and in a few minutes it was as if no rain had fallen at all.

By November 15, the MMWD board of directors was at wits' end. After much discussion, the board decided it was time for some serious action, and voted to turn to the option of last resort, which was cloud seeding. The board approved spending $16,000 on a scheme to wring some moisture out of the thin clouds that dangled in the sky but adamantly refused to drop any water on the parched citizens of Marin, heading for points north and south instead.

The seeding was termed "experimental only," and was to be limited in scope so that it did not require state-imposed environmental review procedures. The plan called for the installation of two or three silver iodide generators along Bolinas Ridge. Each generator was to be fired by butane gas. Silver oxide was to be injected into each burner's flame, converting the chemical into microscopic crystals, to be carried upward on the burner's warm exhaust flow. When the crystals reached the passing clouds, each one became the nucleus of a raindrop. Or so the theory went. The effectiveness of cloud seeding depended on several factors, including wind patterns.

"The effect this year might be minimal," replied Diet to questions from reporters. "We just want to see what happens."

District Engineer Bernie Heare said the experiment could result in as much as three inches of rain to the county's watersheds, and rain might fall on nearby communities such as Petaluma and Santa Rosa too. However, other communities farther away, such as Sacramento, might be adversely affected if Sacramento's usual winter rain fell on Marin instead. Cloud seeding was, admittedly, an inexact science. Left unsaid was the fact that nobody in Marin cared what might happen to Sacramento, because nobody in the capital seemed to care what had already happened to Marin.

Adding to the confusion, Diet reminded all and sundry that there were other angles to cloud seeding to be considered. Such as flooding. What would happen if the cloud seeding efforts were too successful, and the heavens opened?

"My staff is still researching whether the district must buy additional insurance against possible lawsuits resulting from the cloud seeding," said Diet. "Officials at the Santa Clara Water District have used this seeding technology before and their insurance premiums have not increased."

So in one fell swoop Marinites had gone from worrying about the lack of rain to worrying what would happen if too much rain fell. Not that all their worrying amounted to much; the clouds were seeded and nothing happened.

In December the clouds finally opened a bit, and a total of 4.18 inches of rain hit the ground, spread out over the course of the month, almost enough to cause runoff. But the ground was so dry it soaked the rain up like a sponge. The reservoirs stayed at the same low levels, but the public's fears were partially allayed. Rain had fallen. Rainy season, it appeared, was just around the corner. It was just a matter of time.

19 / The crisis commences

It's tough to make predictions, especially about the future.

~ Yogi Berra

Marin County, December 14, 1976

Diet Stroeh sat in his office at the MMWD headquarters in Corte Madera, looking out the window at the sky. Clouds turned the winter sky to gray, but it still didn't rain. Sipping his morning coffee, he leafed through the daily newspaper, looking to see what cheerful reports the paper might be carrying that day. As he did, a big black cloud settled down over his features. Although it had finally began to rain — not enough to fill any reservoirs, but certainly enough to give people hope that the drought might be over — the news in the newspaper regarding the drought was not good.

Diet picked up the phone and called his secretary, Marge, his regular sounding board. "Have you seen today's paper? Grab a seat. I want to read something to you."

An editorial in a local newspaper clearly indicated that not everyone was happy about the direction things were going. Conservation and rationing meant belt-tightening and sacrifice, and even after 12 months of following a rationing program many people still felt that somebody — people others than themselves — was to blame for the lack of water in Marin. Many still wanted to find a more traditional response to the problem of supply and demand; that is, instead of restricting their demand, they wanted more supply. A lot more supply.

Lots of people were convinced that MMWD didn't have a clue what it was doing. That argument was exemplified by the editorial in the morning paper. Headlined MMWD's Inconsistent Foresight, the editorial writer tore a strip off Diet's hide, and questioned his engineering credentials too.

"Holy cow," said Diet, holding up the newspaper to Marge, and pointing to the editorial. "Listen to this crap, will you?"

" 'If the directors and staff of MMWD would devote as much time and effort to finding water as they do dreaming up ways to restrict its use, there might be enough of the stuff to go around," claimed the editorial writer. "The MMWD board had foresight in preparing for the worst, but unfortunately they have no foresight at all when it came to finding new sources of water. Sensible citizens,' " quoted Diet, with smoke coming out his ears, " 'come up with ideas now and then. Many of us are aware that there are vast amounts of underground water in Marin. Why, the hills are full of it. Old San Rafael is dotted with filled-up wells. Why, sump pumps have to be used in the basements of some downtown businesses. A relatively shallow well will strike water almost any place.' "

Diet paused for a moment, breathed deep, regained his composure, and continued.

" 'Does MMWD explore this? "No, its directors are more interested in restricting water use than in finding water. It would be nice if those that run the district would make the job for which they were elected their first order of business.' "

Diet paused for a moment, sat back, and thought.

"Wow," said Diet, "the board of directors is going to love this."

"What's all this, about the hills are full of it?" asked Marge. Aside from being a beautiful young lady, she was Diet's right hand gal and a bright person to boot. "What are they full of?"

"I know who is full of it, and I know what they are full of," said Diet. "Take a seat and take this letter. I have a few things I need to say to clarify the issue."

Private wells were being dug in backyards, and sometimes in front yards too. The reality of the situation was diametrically different from the fanciful picture painted by the newspaper. While some lucky people did indeed strike water, the majority of people in Marin who paid contractors a lot of money to dig wells received no discernable result. There was, in fact, little underground water to find. It seemed everybody in Marin had a clever idea to find water. Dowsing, the ancient art of finding water with a bent stick, made a comeback. Everybody and their dog were out in their backyard, bent over like covens of old witches, dowsing for water.

In fact, over 500 wells had already been privately drilled in Marin by desperate homeowners during the past six months, and nearly all had come up dry. There is no vast hidden aquifer underneath Marin County. Some private wells were sunk down over 600 feet deep before the property owners despaired, gave up and accepted the obvious. The lucky homeowner who struck any source of water was the rare homeowner indeed.

But that didn't stop certain people from boxing Diet's ears in the press. Somebody had to take the blame and anger, and why not the man who instituted rationing? Blame was just something that came with the territory. Diet sighed and took another deep breath, looking out the window at the sunny skies.

"For God's sake, when the heck is it ever going to rain again"? he wondered out loud.

"As you always say, when it's good and ready," said Marge, sitting down with her pen to take the letter, "and not a minute before."

Denial ain't just a river in Egypt.

~ Mark Twain

Berkeley, California, 2006

How will global warming affect soils, class? Well, warmer global temperatures are expected to cause an intensification of the hydrologic cycle, which means we can expect more evaporation over both land and water. The higher evaporation rates will lead to greater drying of soils and vegetation, especially during the summer. We can also expect major changes in the distribution and timing of rainfall. The combination of a decrease in summer rainfall and increased evaporation could mean more severe and longer-lasting droughts in some areas. Increasing drought frequency will affect our ecosystems, coastal systems, and fresh water.

We can expect drier summers at northern high latitudes. Less winter precipitation falling as snow and warmer temperatures will mean earlier drying of soils in the spring. An increase in the ratio of rain to snow means accelerated spring snowmelt. A shorter snow season means rapid, earlier, and greater spring runoff, followed by a reduced summer flow. In other words, we can expect very heavy flooding in the spring, not so good for people living behind levees.

The environmental consequences of the summer 1999 drought in the eastern United States give us an example of what may come. Without fresh water to rinse out rivers and streams, salt water encroached farther up rivers in many areas of the mid-Atlantic coast. The high salt content threatened water supplies in some cities and prevented farmers in some areas from irrigating their crops. It also led to low oxygen conditions in certain bays, causing fish kills.

Drought also means wildfires. During 1997-98, a strong El Niño caused extremely dry conditions and large forest fires in many areas of the world, including Indonesia, eastern Russia, Brazil, Central America, and Florida. Droughts have been relatively frequent since the late 1970s in some areas where drought usually accompanies El Niño events. Global warming may produce a quasi-permanent El Niño-like condition in the Pacific basin, interrupted by more extreme cold La Niñā events. If the frequency of El Niños increases, the frequency and severity of droughts and forest fires may also increase.

Marin County, January 19, 1977

In theory there is no difference between theory and practice. In practice there is.

~ Yogi Berra

Christmas came and Christmas went, and Santa was not generous in his gifts to the parched citizens of Marin County. By mid-January of 1977 people started to whisper some really awful questions. What if it doesn't rain soon? Can we actually survive another year without rain? No way! Hey, what if it never rains again? For the first time, instead of "drought," certain people in high places were quietly uttering the word "disaster" behind closed doors.

Diet called an urgent public meeting at the Marin County Civic Center for January 19. It was time to discuss the worst case scenario with his customers: what to do if it didn't rain at all that winter, again?

As befits upscale Marin County, the Civic Center is an astounding work of art, created by world-famous architect Frank Lloyd Wright. Complete with pale blue circular roofs and a golden spire jutting into the sky, the Civic Center looks like a giant spaceship touched down from outer space, nestled across several adjacent hills. Loyal Wright fans from all over the world came here just to look at it.

On the evening of January 19, there were no Frank Lloyd Wright fans at the Civic center. There were certainly no J. Dietrich Stroeh fans either. Rather, the room was packed with angry taxpayers wanting to know what was going to happen to their extremely expensive properties if somebody didn't come up with a scheme to find or import some water, immediately if not sooner.

People were packed into the room like sardines and the spillover crowd was jammed into hallways, spectators in the back craning their necks for a view. A loud and angry buzz filled the air. Anxious taxpayers wanted to know just what the heck the water district, specifically General Manager J. Dietrich Stroeh, was going to do about the impending disaster. He's the one that shoved rationing down our throats! Did that work? Hell no! Why, it's been nine months since you could wash your car without getting an earful from your neighbor! Where is the progress? Where's the good news?

The entire MMWD board of directors was in attendance, sitting on a dais at the front of the room, behind a raised podium at which Diet was supposed to talk. Being politicians, the board cleverly said nothing. If anybody was going to go down with the ship, it wasn't going to be them.

In front of the angry crowd Diet stood all alone, armed with a hastily written speech typed on several sheets of flimsy yellow typewriter paper. On those pages lay his future as an engineer and as general manager of the water district. In fact, so did the future of Marin County, because if people didn't get access to a lot of water soon, the entire county would be more than a disaster zone; it would be a dead zone.

Diet got up in front of the crowd, shuffled his papers, and cleared his throat. "Hello folks," he said. "Glad you could all make it."

The rumble in the hall died down to a whisper, then all was silence. You could hear a pin drop. All eyes were on the podium. It was make or break time for Marin County. Was the richest county in America going to turn into a dustbowl and blow away in the wind? Diet cleared his throat again, and began to speak.

20 / The turning point

I've had a wonderful evening, but this wasn't it.

~ Groucho Marx

Marin County, January 19, 1977

"Can you folks hear me in back?"

Diet was dressed for the event, as he always dressed for any business occasion, in a snappy suit, this one a beige number with matching vest and colorful tie, aviator glasses and classy dress shoes. On this occasion, however, his tie was loosened and his voice was tight. He knew the importance of the evening's agenda, what it meant to his career and what it meant to the citizens of the county he'd always called home. Lawns, gardens, Open Space lands, lakes, reservoirs, creeks, school yards, playgrounds, golf courses; every green space and living thing in the county was turning to dust. This wasn't just a drought that he was addressing; it was the future of billions of dollars worth of very expensive real estate, and the fate of 170,000 very thirsty — and angry — customers.

"I know through the telephone calls that my staff and I have received that many of you are very upset and concerned, and quite frankly

I'm fired up about the water situation myself," he began. "I've been meeting with state officials, and local officials — I'm talking about San Francisco now, and East Bay MUD, and Sonoma County — for the last month, and they are starting to get quite concerned for themselves too. If you have been reading the daily newspapers, you can see they are also starting to talk about rationing in their own districts, even though they are tapped into the state water supply."

A low murmur when through the crowd; the mention of San Francisco and other districts becoming worried about their own sources of water was certainly news. Maybe even welcome news; misery loves company.

"We could talk all night about how this situation happened, but the fact is we are now in a crisis situation, and the question is what the hell are we going to do about it?" said Diet. The word "crisis" denotes some urgency, and at this point many in the crowd stopped muttering and paid strict attention. The dirty word had finally been spoken; a government official had broken the silence and admitted a disaster was in the offing. It was now official. OK, now what?

"I spent an hour today with San Francisco officials. All of a sudden these guys are very concerned. You know and I know they have been laughing at us here in Marin — at least Herb Caen, the columnist at the Chronicle, has been having a good laugh at our expense — but now they find themselves in the same boat," he said. "We were all talking today about the snowpack in the Sierra. That's where San Francisco gets its water. It hasn't been raining down here, so it hasn't been snowing up there. So, no snow, no water."

"The East Bay is the same. They are going to a rationing system immediately. So far, everybody has been talking about sticking their straw into the Russian River up in Sonoma. That's been their ace in the hole," he continued. "But guess what? The water in the river isn't there anymore. The supply has dropped from 450 feet per second, which is a factor of flow, way down to 50 feet. Statewide and regionally, the weather is turning into a disaster any way you look at it. We in Marin aren't going to get any water from the Russian River."

Diet paused to clear his throat. The room was as quiet as the grave. Marin's ace in the hole, the Russian River, was just a joker.

"You might want to boot me out of here tomorrow, but after tonight you might have a better understanding of the situation and what we are going to have to do about it," said Diet, turning and pointing to a chart hanging on the wall behind him. "The present situation is that we have only 4 billion gallons of water left in our lakes. Total. The lakes can hold 17 billion. Normally at this time of winter we are at between 12 and 14 billion. And the lakes are not refilling. So you see where we're at."

There wasn't a single hand in the air. People sat rapt, looking at the charts. The lines showed a sharp downward curve, heading toward oblivion.

"Yes, I know, we had some rain back in the beginning of January, but the fact is that it takes about five inches of rain before the ground in Marin gets saturated. Only then do we get runoff into the reservoirs. Anything else is just a tease," said Diet, pointing at the figures. "This is the situation we have faced for nearly two years now. The harsh reality is that I have no idea if this drought is going to go on for a third year, or a fourth, or even forever. It's frightening. This whole situation is unreal."

Again the crowd started to buzz. First the "crisis" word, then "disaster" and now "unreal," a leftover from the hippie vernacular of the 60's; this wasn't the kind of talk they came to hear. Where are the soothing words of comfort, news that fresh, clean drinking water will be shipped in by barge or tanker and everyone's problems will be solved and we can go golfing again?

"I see some of you smiling when I use the word 'unreal.' Well, you shouldn't. It really is unreal," he said. "This drought breaks all records. I'm not lying to you. There has never been anything like this in our history in Marin. I've checked all the data going back over 100 years. Just to get back to a normal situation we are going to need about 36 to 48 inches of constant rain, and as soon as possible, and I just don't see that happening."

The audience started to buzz again. Four feet of rain? No, that wasn't likely to happen, but what about trucking in water from somewhere?

"Hang on. Yes, sir, I see you there in the back of the room with your hand up, but I'm sorry, I'm not taking any questions right now," he said. "I know what you are going to say. Everybody has said it to me already. January and February are our wettest months and we usually get most of our annual rainfall then. And we still have March and April to go yet. Now, if you asked me last year if I thought we would go all winter without rain, I would have said: 'Never happen.' If you had said to me that we would go another year without rain, I would have laughed at you. It has never happened before. But it's happening now. We can't afford to assume it's suddenly going to rain in the next month or so. We have to act now. Immediately."

There was rumbling in the audience, but it died down to a whisper as he raised his hand. Diet had their full attention now.

"In fact, one member of the water board asked me just that exact question last month, about the chances of a drought like last year ever happening to Marin again. And I said to him: 'There is about a 1 percent chance of it not raining this year.' So you can fire me right now if you want, because obviously I was wrong. Way wrong."

A woman in the front row gave out a nervous titter. There was a low hum as people murmured to their neighbors. If the board fires Diet, who the heck is going to be in charge? Does anybody else know what is really going on anyway? And what the heck is happening with our weather?

Everything is funny as long as it is happening to somebody else.

~ Will Rogers

"I usually don't believe much in weather predictions, but I am starting to become a believer when they say that it won't rain," said Diet. "The predictions from the U.S. Weather Bureau are that the next 30 days will be dry as well. Yes, bone dry. Some folks say we usually have a big storm in February. I don't know if we will, they don't know, you don't know, nobody knows. What my board of directors has suggested we do is plan for a worst-case scenario, because that's what it looks like is going to happen. So we have to plan for the possibility that it will not rain again this year."

The silence in the room was now audible. A chair squeaked and everybody turned to look at the offender. Diet reached under the table and pulled out a second set of charts, hand drawn in marker pens on a big piece of poster board. On it was a series of squiggles in green and black.

"The green line that sweeps upward and off the chart is our normal flow into the reservoirs. We normally get 58,000 acre-feet of runoff a year into them. An acre-foot is just that, an acre of water that's a foot deep. For those that like plain numbers, that's 326,000 gallons," he said. "The red line on the chart is the winter of 1975-76. That's last year. The orange line way down there at the bottom is what we have received as of this entire year, which is a lousy 2,500 acre-feet."

"Last year we had only 7,000 acre-feet, so we couple that with what's left in storage and we come up with a new rationing plan which I am going to explain right now. What that means is, we are all going to have to cut our current meager water consumption by 57 percent more, starting immediately. That's on top of what we have already cut. That refers to every man, woman and child in the entire county."

The silence was broken by gasps and moans. Rationing was already causing enormous grief and discomfort. Cut it by another 57 percent? How? That's impossible.

"How the hell are we going to do that?" he said. "I know, we've already cut everything back to the bone. But here's how. We are going to send out census cards to every single house in the county, and find out exactly how many people live in each house, and assign an exact amount of water consumption to each and every house. People living in each house can decide what they want to do with their allotment. We will do this immediately, and we will implement this emergency allotment program starting the first of February, which you can see is less than two weeks away."

Utter silence in the building. You could hear a pin drop. Diet paused for a moment to clear his throat again, then laid down a bomb." People who do not meet their exact water allotment, right down to the last gallon, will have their water service cut off. Entirely."

This startling announcement brought a huge gasp and shouts from the crowd. What? In less than two weeks there will be no water? Not months or years down the line, but right away? No water will run from the tap if you exceed your limit? Nothing at all? It's inconceivable! Nobody can live without water.

"The only way you will get your water back is through the installation of a flow restrictor that will be installed on your meter," he continued, waving the crowd to quiet. "Also, water rates will go up again, starting immediately. Basically, we are talking doubling the price. Right now."

With this announcement the entire crowd stood up and started yelling. First we were talking water rationing, now we are talking real money! Question period or not, P. Worthington Walsh of Ross was on his feet in a flash, arm in the air, feet on his chair, and mouth already moving. Citizens of the extremely wealthy town of Ross such as Walsh were not used to such impertinence from the hired help. His rose garden was already dying, the back lawn had turned to dust, the swimming pool had gone green, and now this!

"Why don't you cut back on the damned personnel budget if you need more money?" shouted Walsh, in a curt, clipped tone reminiscent of the army general he once had been. "Cut back on staff. Why, you can barely drive down Sir Francis Drake Boulevard without seeing a water district truck along the way. That's how you solve problems, son. It's the old-fashioned way. Tighten the belt. During the war we all cut our budgets and we got by with whatever resources we had."

"Thank you for that suggestion, sir," said Diet with a smile. "We have already received that specific suggestion, and thousands more just like it. We're already cut to the bone and will continue to cut. But not our staff. In fact, what we are going to have to do is actually increase our water district staff, again, and do it immediately."

The crowd started to boo, and loudly. More staff? Again? Insane!

"We have had a tremendous number of calls to staff for our help," shouted Diet, motioning for the crowd to quiet, "and things are going to get a lot worse. Let's get this straight. What we have now is a complete environmental disaster in the making. The board of directors has already directed staff to start moving on obtaining supplemental equipment and new personnel. Cutting back on staff is just not an option."

People were now on their feet and yelling. Double the rates? Fire the bastard!

"Why don't you get off your asses and drill some wells?" yelled a leather-lunged taxpayer from the back.

"Quiet please, folks. Quiet. I have more news. Yes, tomorrow we will be looking at drilling 75 wells throughout the district," Diet continued in a loud voice, speaking over the buzz. "But bear in mind that the last well we drilled yielded only seven gallons per minute. That's only enough for one family residence. We are talking about needing anywhere from 1,000 to 2,000 gallons per minute. Drilling wells won't work for everyone."

"Why don't you just seed the clouds? That's a lot cheaper," a red-faced lady from the front row yelled out in an angry voice.

"There has been a lot of talk about weather modification, or cloud seeding as you call it," responded Diet. "We have already tried that. The water district rejected it again for a fairly simple reason; if you don't have any clouds, then you have nothing to seed. There aren't any clouds. But I appreciate all the ideas people are bringing forth."

"When are you going to bring in water tankers, then?" asked P. Worthington Walsh, back on his feet.

"We have been looking into the idea of trucking or barging water in from elsewhere," Diet continued. "I just found out at 5 p.m. that we can pick up potable water from Stockton, down in the delta, using 4 million-gallon ships. This could be dropped off at the old sugar refinery near San Quentin and piped into our water system through the 12-inch pipe we have there."

The crowd began to quiet down. See, what's the problem? Why all the fuss? You simply bring in water from elsewhere and put it into a pipe. Simple fix, let's get on with it, quit the damned complaining.

"The problem with that particular solution is that it costs about $7 per 1,000 gallons, and right now the water you are using costs only 80 cents," said Diet. "You do the math."

There was quiet while people did the math.

"We are looking at desalination plants, but they would take years to build. Who knows if they would work or what the cost? But that's not a solution for today. There are some springs on the south side of Mount Tam but they would never serve the entire population," continued Diet. "The fact is we are looking at anything and everything to find water, but the short answer is that we need some water right now, not next year, not five years from now. An awful lot of water. Right now."

Not only is there no God, but try finding a plumber on Sunday.

~ Woody Allen

At this moment James Reed seized the opportunity to leap to his feet and shout out his opinion. Representing the Irate Taxpayers of Marin, the Marin County Taxpayers Association, and the United Taxpayers of Marin, Reed was living proof that not all residents of Marin were left-wing hippies, and that a staunch conservative viewpoint was well represented in the county.

"This crisis has been created by the water district itself, because you have failed in the past to secure new sources of water for the county," said Reid. "Last year you imposed a 27 percent surcharge on water bills. Now you want to raise the rates again? You should have known that this crisis was going to occur."

At this statement, much of the audience stood and cheered. Diet merely smiled and continued his speech when the noise abated.

"As I mentioned earlier, this morning I talked with the general manager of the San Francisco Water District and it looks like they will also be going to rationing. So will the entire East Bay," he said. "But what is happening, I think, with the agencies around the Bay Area and across the state and even with the water agencies across all the western states, is what I call the 'lifeboat syndrome.' Which is an opinion held by those communities that still have water, like southern California, which might be described as: 'I'm OK, Jack, I've got mine, so why the hell should I care about you?'"

More angry shouts from the crowd. The enmity between northern and southern California had been a fact of life for so long no one remembered when it started. This time, however, it was personal. That's our northern water you have down there in Los Angeles!

"You might ask, 'Why does all the water from the north of the state go down to Southern California?' They have been asked to cut back a bit on their usage in the L.A. Metropolitan region, and come off the Colorado River to the tune of about 250,000-acre feet so those of us in the northern part of the state can use it," said Diet. "The people I have talked to down there have indicated quite bluntly they are not going to do so. They are not going to start any sort of rationing whatsoever, or even talk about any kind of conservation programs. What they have said to me, quite bluntly, is, 'We planned ahead for our problems, you plan for yours.' That's nice, but what will happen is that the entire Central Valley agricultural district will get wiped out, along with us here in the Bay Area."

People were on their feet again. More angry shouts and yelling. Some folks were getting thirsty just from shouting.

"I've been told that the entire snowpack in the Sierra Nevada will be gone in 2 to 3 days," said Diet in a matter-of-fact tone, and the crowd quieted. "I have just written a letter — and my board of directors has a copy — to the governor, requesting an emergency session of the state's water agencies."

"Nobody in the rest of the state cares about us here in Marin. They figure we are rich and can just buy our way out of the problem. The fact is, we can't. Nobody can," he said. "But if I can get San Francisco and then the East Bay agencies on board, maybe I can get the ball rolling and then the Central Valley will come on board. On our own, we are in the same bind as any other small community. Nobody cares. But if I can convince higher authorities that this is a state disaster in the making, maybe we can get some action. We have to do something immediately."

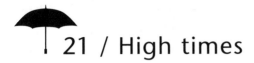

21 / High times

If we knew what we are doing, it wouldn't be called research, would it?

~ Albert Einstein

∏epal, June 7, 2010

Will scrambled over the loose, rough scree of the moraine wall that acted as a dam and kept the waters from Tsho Rolpa Lake from bursting their banks and hurtling down to the valley below. It had been a hard three-hour climb up the rocky Rolwaring Valley, following the thin path of the river that flowed from the lake, but Will was eager to finally arrive at a destination that he'd been researching for so long. He sat down on the rocks of the moraine wall and opened his water bottle and savored the sight, panting with exertion.

"Well, dudes, this is it," yelled out Will, as members of the expedition slowly arrived over the edge of the moraine wall one by one. "Ain't it worth the effort, Bob?"

"Let me catch my breath for a moment and I'll tell ya," gasped expedition leader Walsh, flopping down next to Will. "I'm glad we're here, but I'll be happier when we can turn back and head the other direction."

"Not so fast, my man," answered Will, "we've got some research to do yet."

"What research?" said Walsh. "I thought you said you just wanted to take a look at the lake, and take some video. Well, here it is. Have a look and shoot some video, and let's go, because we're scheduled to be back at Beding tonight, and I don't want to be up here if it starts to rain."

The surface of Tsho Rolpa was a milky blue, a mix of water, silt, sediments, broken rock and snow. Even at an altitude of 15,000 feet the lake didn't freeze, thanks to regular movement of its waters as it flowed through the moraine wall.

A small research station and sluice gate stood atop the moraine and let the water drain, part of an experiment by the Nepalese government to control the expansion of the lake. Major funding had come from the Netherlands. The Dutch, master dam builders, had been involved for over a decade with the Nepalese government in efforts to mitigate the dangers of glacial lake outburst floods at several Nepalese glaciers.

On this day the research station stood empty. A sluice gate installed in the dam allowed a controlled release of water. Cables had been installed to stabilize a large number of boulders jammed into the notch below the dam. It was a makeshift operation, but it worked well enough to temporarily stabilize the lake.

Tsho Rolpa Lake lies at the foot of the Trakarding Glacier, which itself is in slow but constant motion, movement that sends down an occasional barrage of stone avalanches to the lake below. The glacier crept along slowly, down from the mountain above, to the edge of the lake. From time to time large chunks of ice broke off from the glacier and fell into the lake, each drop accompanied by a loud boom as it hit the water. Ripples from each hit spread across the lake in an expanding pattern.

"So, are we going to meet some engineers here, and get data on the water flow, or what's the scene, Will?" asked Moore. "I thought you wanted to do some research?"

"No, I knew that there wouldn't be anybody up here right now," replied Will, sipping on his water bottle and watching while the last of the expedition porters arrived. "They have some automatic measuring devices to keep track of the flow, and that data gets sent down to Kathmandu electronically. You remember those sirens I showed you as we climbed up the valley, and those wires that looked like old-fashioned TV aerials? That's part of the early warning system, should the lake suddenly expand and blow its banks."

"And what, exactly, would cause this lake to blow its banks?" asked Walsh, looking down at the waters flowing through the sluice gate. "It's being drained by this sluiceway."

"Don't worry, it would take some cataclysmic event, like the glacier falling into the lake," said Will, opening up his pack and pulling out a piece of yak meat. "Relax, we're safe here. Let's have something to eat before we head over to the glacier. Want some dried yak?"

The saddest aspect of life right now is that science gathers knowledge faster than society gathers wisdom.

~ Isaac Asimov, "Book of Science and Nature Quotations," 1988

Berkeley, California, 2006

Tsho Rolpa Lake has expanded considerably in the last decade, thanks to warmer temperatures in the Himalyas. It is now 2.6 kilometers long, half a kilometer wide, and 132 meters deep. It is the largest glacial lake in Nepal and it is holding millions of tons of water in its tenuous grasp.

Typically, class, the instability of such glacial lakes is resolved by a "glacial lake outburst flood," or GLOF. Once the banks of the dam are over-topped, even slightly, the entire moraine wall tends to give way quite rapidly. Millions of tons of water are spilled in minutes. It's an awesome sight, one where you don't want to be standing underneath in order to watch the show.

The occurrence of GLOF hazards all over the world is becoming more frequent, probably due to increased global warming. Glacial lakes can be destabilized by a variety of factors, which can occur individually or in spontaneous combinations, which is where the real danger lies.

Often the weight of a slowly growing glacial lake eventually puts enough pressure on the moraine wall to collapse it. Heavy precipitation, or meltwater from within the glacier, can also put sudden pressure on the wall. Earthquakes, rockslides, or avalanches may also shake the moraine, or cause high waves that impact the loose moraine. The inner ice core of a moraine dam itself may also be undermined by warming, or by increased seepage as lake waters rise. So there are a number of bad things that can happen, sometimes all at once.

Then we have what is known as the GLOF "cascade process." A GLOF high in the mountains delivers an initial surge to an artificial dam, causing that dam to also give way, and then the next, and so on, like a game of dominoes. The key element of any GLOF is the instantaneous release of enormous volumes of water and rock, producing sudden peak flows that are many times greater that the seasonal peaks associated with annual monsoon rains.

The cascade effect is even more pronounced when a GLOF flow is piggybacked on top of a seasonal monsoon deluge. Eyewitnesses have described roaring walls of water up to 60 feet high thundering down mountain canyons. GLOFs can cause major damage along valleys up to hundreds of miles away. There is little doubt, for instance, that a sudden breach of Tsho Rolpa would wipe out most of the villages and towns downstream for a hundred miles.

On August 4, 1985, for instance, the glacial lake Dig Tsho below Langmoche Glacier in the Khumbu region of Nepal suddenly blew and sent a 45-foot-high surge of water and debris down the Bhote Koshi and Dudh Koshi rivers for nearly a hundred miles. An estimated one million gallons of water was instantly released, creating an initial peak discharge of 6,000 feet per second. That spectacular natural event destroyed all the bridges for 40 miles downstream.

In 1981, the Sun Koshi River in China, with a peak discharge estimated at 10,000 feet per second, destroyed a large section of the China-Nepal highway and impacted 30 miles of valleys in Nepal. A 1977 GLOF near Ama Dablam in Khumbu destroyed all the downstream bridges for 30 miles.

In 1998, the British Columbia Hydro Authority from Canada and American company Meteor Communications installed an early warning system in Rolwaling Valley. Several water level sensors were installed along the river channel immediately downstream from Tsho Rolpa to detect the onset of a blow.

Within two minutes of a GLOF exploding, the discharge would be detected, relayed, and received by 19 warning stations downstream. Each station, powered by a 12-volt battery charged by a solar panel, would trigger an air horn backed up by an electronic siren. The alarm is supposed to give people within earshot a few minutes to escape. Otherwise, everyone will be killed and the valleys below will be immediately destroyed. It would be like putting some ants in a washing machine and flicking the switch. Of course, with steep mountains on both sides of the valley, aside from the problem of how you are supposed to escape, there is always the paramount question of where you are supposed to escape to. When faced with a GLOF blowing its lid, the old expression "run like hell" suddenly takes on a new meaning.

We've arranged a civilization in which most crucial elements profoundly depend on science and technology. We have also arranged things so that almost no one understands science and technology. This is a prescription for disaster. We might get away with it for a while, but sooner or later this combustible mixture of ignorance and power is going to blow up in our faces.

~ Carl Sagan

Nepal, June 7, 2010

While big black clouds billowed up from the plains far below and loomed behind Kang Nachugo, a few miles away on the Trekarding Glacier the sun was still shining with incredible intensity. What had been a freezing environment in the early morning was a hell of white-hot heat by noon.

Will had smeared zinc ointment all over his face as protection from the burning rays. At 15,000 feet, with the reflection off the snow and glacier beating on him, it was an outdoor bake oven.

Will had stripped down to his T-shirt and was sweating profusely. Climbing up from the moraine dam toward the glacier, he led the expedition team carefully, Walsh right behind. The glacier was melting rapidly, leaving gaping ice bridges over crevasses the team had to cross, and the going was very slow.

"Say, Will, you know what?" said Walsh, casually, following right behind. "These ice bridges could give way as they melt in the heat, you know."

"If we all got together and jumped up and down on a bridge, maybe the overall weight would make a dent in the ice," answered Will, stepping slowly and testing each step before he committed his weight. "Every bridge we've crossed must be at least 20 feet thick. If it were five or 10 feet thick, I'd pick another route. Relax, and enjoy the view. Not many people in the world have ever seen a glacial lake perched in a mountain bowl at 15,000 feet. Take some pics, dude. And keep your eye open for a good camping spot just above the glacier."

"Campsite? What the hell are you talking about? We're retreating down to Beding to camp tonight."

"No, I want to go way up on top, look down on the lake, and get a wider picture of the lake, the dam, the spillway, the river, everything."

"That's crazy, Will. Have you heard about high mountain glacier lassitude? Like, how it starts to affect the human mind at around 15,000 feet? I think you're coming down with a dose."

"Hey man, I'm not in rapture. I'm not losing my mind, I feel great," replied Will. "I've been waiting for years to make this trek. Now that we're way up here, I'm not going to stop halfway."

"Look, I'm the trek leader, and we agreed that we would camp at Beding tonight. I don't think it's safe up here. There are falling rocks, and this ice is not stable," said Walsh. "It's melting. And we have some nasty clouds down there that look like they'll be arriving up here very soon."

"Yeah, I know, but if I had told you before we were coming up past the glacier to camp, you would have said 'no.' But I'm paying the bills, and I still owe you half the agreed fee, which I will happily pay you with a nice bonus when we get back to Kathmandu. But for now, we're going up."

Behind them, and below in the distance, giant black cumulonimbus clouds boiled and churned as the monsoon worked its way up from the Gangetic plains.

It wasn't the Exxon Valdez captain's driving that caused the Alaskan oil spill. It was yours.

~ Greenpeace advertisement, New York Times, February 25, 1990

Berkeley, California, 2006

Satellite coverage is ideally suited for monitoring changes in the earth's landscape, including glacial advances and retreats. A satellite provides scientists with critical information used for surface mapping and monitoring of dynamic conditions and changes over time. Aside from looking at glaciers, they can do good things like monitor active volcanoes and thermal pollution and coral reef degradation. They can map surface temperatures of soils and geology, and measure surface heat balance.

For instance, an earth-monitoring instrument aboard a NASA satellite has recently observed a potential glacial disaster-in-the-making in Peru. High up in the snow-capped Cordillera Blanca lies a glacier that feeds Lake Palcacocha. This lake is located high above the town of Huaraz. A big crack has been observed in the glacier. If a big enough chunk breaks off and falls into the lake, the ensuing flood would overflow the banks and could hurtle down to the Rio Santa Valley below. It would arrive, and flood the entire city of Huaraz and destroy its population of 60,000 people, in less than 15 minutes.

Peruvians call glacial flood-bursts, or GLOFs as we know them, by the Spanish title of "aluviones." Since 1702, aluviones caused by glaciological conditions have repeatedly caused death and destruction in the Rio Santa Valley. In 1941 an aluvione destroyed approximately one-third of Huaraz, killing as many as 7,000 people. Since then, the Peruvian government has emphasized control of the water level in Lake Palcacocha and other lakes in the region that pose similar threats.

Nepal, June 7, 2010

Dave Moore didn't like yak meat. He wasn't a big fan of freeze-dried meals, either. He disliked trekking across an unstable glacier even more, but mostly he kept his thoughts to himself. Worst of all, he had a splitting headache caused by the extreme altitude and heavy exercise involved with climbing in wet snow in the heat.

Sneaking behind a giant boulder to relieve himself, he had sent an update to the White House about what was going on, but he wondered what good it was going to do for the President to know that his one and only, crazy son was taking life-threatening risks again, when there was nothing that really could be done about it. Getting the President pissed off was never a wise career move. Then again, saying nothing to him was not much of an option either.

Theoretically a helicopter could be sent from Kathmandu for a rescue, but there were several problems associated with that. Although he was not an expert on the subject, Moore thought that 15,000 feet was probably too high for any helicopter to safely fly. Also, it would have to arrive before the monsoon did, an event that looked like it would happen any day. Helicopters don't fly well in torrential monsoons or blinding whiteouts. If the chopper showed up, where would it land? And how would you force Will to get on it? At gunpoint?

Moore was following Walsh and looking for an excuse to bump past Walsh and get closer to Will, all the while keeping a close eye on the nearby crevasses they were crossing. If Will fell in a crevasse, Moore felt he might as well jump right in after him, which would be preferable to explaining to the President of the United States how his one and only son had died not five feet away from his protection.

"Hey, Will," he yelled up the line to White, 10 feet ahead, "look over there."

At the 16,000-foot level, a few hundred yards above and to the expedition's right, an avalanche sent rocks and snow tumbling down the slopes of the mountain and into the lake far below.

"This is like Russian roulette, crossing this glacier," said Moore to Walsh, just ahead in line. "This definitely is not safe. I'm totally beat, too. Why don't you tell Will to forget about this research crap and just turn around? We can camp down by the dam."

Looking down, he could see that the crevasse they were passing over was filled with a murky green ice water. Anybody falling into the crevasse would drown in its icy grip within a few seconds.

"He's not listening to me," answered Moore glumly. "I told him we need to turn around."

"Hey, dudes, calm down. In two minutes we'll be off the glacier and safe on stable ground," yelled back Will, stepping carefully across the ice bridge. "Two more minutes, so don't lose it."

Meanwhile, behind the Americans, the sherpa porters spat into the snow, complaining about the threat of falling boulders, muttering endless chants of "om mani padme hum" to appease the demons of the Himalayas. This senseless trek was angering the gods of the mountains. These rich Americans had no business being here. Best to turn around, they thought, but none of them said anything. Moore had just told them who Will was. The son of the President of the United States wasn't someone you argued with. And they had not been paid, either.

Only two things are infinite, the universe and human stupidity, and I'm not sure about the former.

~ Albert Einstein

Berkeley, California, 2006

It's not just the glaciers of the world that are melting, class. Ice is melting everywhere at a steadily increasing rate. Rising global temperatures are lengthening melting seasons, thawing frozen ground, and thinning ice caps. These changes are raising sea level faster than was earlier projected by scientists, and threatening both human and wildlife populations. Arctic communities face more violent and less predictable weather, rising sea levels, and diminishing access to food sources. Polar bears will soon face a severely reduced food source. If the melting continues, the bears may become extinct by the end of the century. Seals, walruses, and seabirds will also lose key feeding and breeding grounds along the ice edge.

Shipping through the Arctic will increase as ice melts and new shipping routes become available. The length of the navigation season along the northern sea route is projected to increase to about 120 days by 2100, up from the current 30 days. If ships use the Northwest Passage, oil spills and fisheries depletion can be expected.

An estimated 15 percent of the Arctic tundra has already melted, an area roughly three times the size of California. By the end of this century, the southern permafrost boundary is projected to shift northward by several hundred kilometers, changing regional vegetation patterns.

The Greenland ice sheet is the largest land ice mass in the Northern Hemisphere. It holds enough fresh water to raise the earth's sea level by 24 feet were the entire sheet ever to melt, which could happen if the global temperature rises by 3 degrees Celsius. Satellite data show Greenland's ice has been melting at higher and higher elevations every year since 1979. Global sea level has risen almost 20 centimeters in the past century. According to the Intergovernmental Panel on Climate Change, sea levels are guaranteed to rise by at least three feet by 2100.

Washington, D.C., June 8, 2010

In Washington, D.C., Alvin Brunanksi, press secretary for the president, took the phone.

"Well, it's been quite a while. How are things with you and the network?"

"Excellent, sir," answered network news anchor Janet Spalding. "I'm sorry to hear that the President won't be participating in our special program on climate change today. Is there any way we can get you to change his mind?"

"Actually, I think we'll have something to say very shortly on that subject," responded Brunanski smoothly, "but today may be a bit premature. I'll be sure to have my people call you in a few days, as soon as we know a little more. But, no, today just doesn't work for us."

"The word making the rounds is that the White House is finally willing to reopen talks with the European Community and other signatories to the original Kyoto treaty," said Spalding, not missing a beat. "Have you got a comment on that we can use on this evening's news?"

"I most certainly do, Janet," replied Brunanski, with a laugh. "It's this: Rumors are just like excuses. Everybody has one, and they all serve the same purpose. Best to wait for hard facts, don't you think?"

Congressman John Burton, 1970's
Photo courtesy of John Burton

Supervisor Barbara Boxer, 1970's
Photo courtesy of Barbara Boxer

Sally Stanford, Mayor of Sausalito, 1970's
Photo courtesy of Steve Bogel

Congressman John Burton and Supervisor Gary Giacomini
Photo courtesy of Gary Giacomini

MMWD General Manager Diet
Stroeh and MMWD Chairman
of the Board Bill Filante
Courtesy of MMWD photo archive

Richmond Bridge pipeline
Courtesy of MMWD photo archive

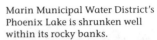

Marin Municipal Water District's Phoenix Lake is shrunken well within its rocky banks.

Bon Tempe Reservoir was one of the last district lakes to be emptied.

Dry bed of Nicasio Reservoir
Courtesy of MMWD photo archive

Lake Nicasio: nearly dry

Three-gallon car wash MMWD Director Pam Lloyd 1976
Courtesy MMWD photo archive

Diet Stroeh standing in the middle of a dry Nicasio Reservoir

Stroeh is Named New Marin Manager

J. Dietrich Stroeh has been appointed the new general manager of the Marin Municipal Water District.

Stroeh, 37, named acting general manager in November following the retirement of William R. Seeger, was among five finalists out of 150 applicants for the post.

Two of the final candidates were from Southern California, one was from the East Bay and one from Minnesota.

"We realized that we had just as much talent right here in Marin County," said board president Jack R. Felson, commenting on Stroeh's appointment.

Stroeh, a resident of Novato, for 30 years, first joined the water district as a junior engineer in June 1960. Since then, he has worked as assistant, associate, senior and principal engineer. He was named manager of the engineering division in 1971.

Stroeh is a graduate of San Rafael High School and the College of Marin, and received his civil engineering degree from the University of Nevada.

Stroeh is named new General Manager for the Marin Municipal Water District Courtesy of MMWD photo archive

WATER FOR MARIN—J. Dietrich Stroeh, manager of the Marin Municipal Water District, stands atop pipe carrying water to parched Marin County across the Richmond-San Rafael bridge. Six-mile line, finished in 47 working days, was turned on Tuesday.
AP Wirephoto

MMWD General Manager Diet Stroeh with state water official at pipeline dedication, June 7, 1977

Tsho Rolpa Glacial Lake

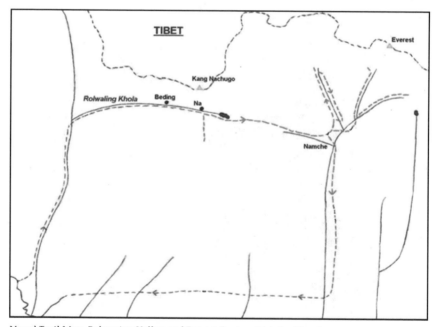

Nepal Trail Map, Rolwaring Valley and Everest Region, Map by Alan Ingram

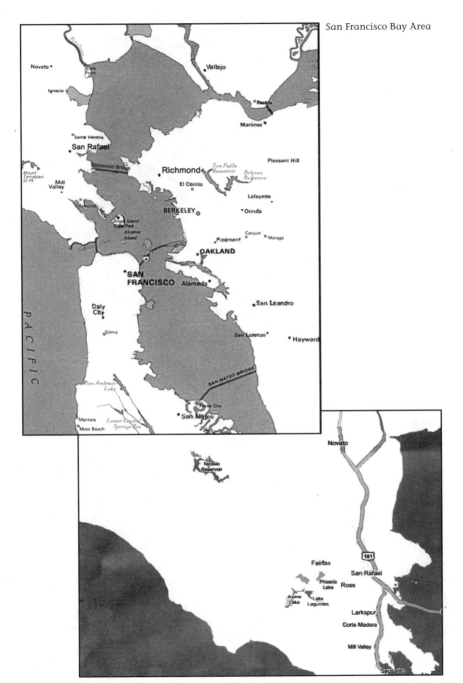

San Francisco Bay Area

Marin County

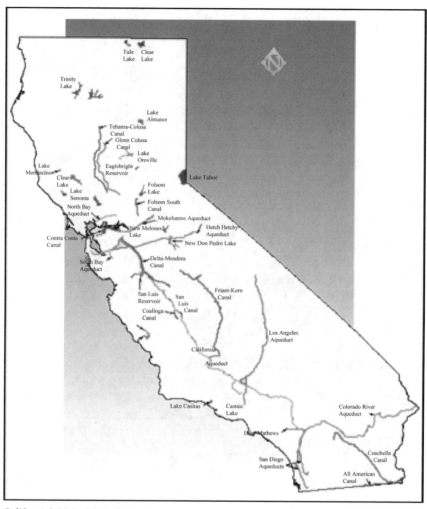

California's Major Water Projects

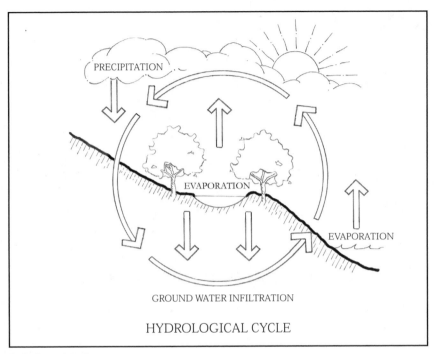

Hydrological Cycle

22 / The 11 a.m. news

I don't know the key to success, but the key to failure is trying to please everybody.

~ Bill Cosby

Marin County, January 25, 1977

For such a small county, Marin had somehow managed to become nationally famous. Perhaps this was because of the hippies, many of whom moved from Haight Ashbury and other San Francisco neighborhoods into Marin starting in the late 60's, bringing along with them famous rock bands like Jefferson Airplane and The Grateful Dead. Along with the artists came fans, followers, and other artists. But in 1977 Marin managed to become extremely famous for its bucolic lifestyle, thanks to a Marin writer named Cyra McFadden, who started writing a satirical column in local newsweekly The Pacific Sun, a series she called "The Serial." Her column soon evolved into a best-selling book, and was eventually made into a movie. In The Serial, McFadden satarized Marin County culture brilliantly.

"Welcome to 1970s affluent Marin County, California; the cutting edge," wrote McFadden. "These beautiful people are all headed for A

Fully Actualized Life, which is a heavy trip since they want EVERYTHING material AND a highly spiritual life."

Almost 30 years later, proving that some things hadn't changed in Marin, journalist David Brooks revisited the topic of lifestyle in his best-selling "Bobos in Paradise," labeling people who want a spiritual life, along with lots of material possessions, as the "bohemian bourgeois," or Bobos for short. Whatever the label, the Marin lifestyle was simultaneously envied, mocked and derided by media pundits and social commentators alike, many of whom seemed to secretly want to live in magical Marin while publicly poking fun at the people lucky enough to live there.

No one mocked Marin more than famed San Francisco newspaper columnist and man-about-town Herb Caen, who, by the mid-70's, had become a cultural icon in the Bay Area. Caen regularly had a good laugh about Marin and its drought, mocking Marinites who "went visiting relatives in the East Bay just so they could enjoy a good hot shower."

Caen was not the only columnist or media figure enjoying a good laugh at Marin's expense. One by one, reporters and weathermen began to cover the ongoing soap opera of the "rich little county that couldn't." Marinites couldn't wash their BMWs, couldn't soak in their hot tubs, and couldn't save their expensive real estate from turning into dust. It became a ritual on the six o'clock TV news for every weatherman to check in with Marin County, to see if it had rained yet.

Of course, all of California and the western United States was also suffering from the same ongoing drought but Marin, in its snobbishness, had cut itself off from the state water system, relying on its own rains to fill its reservoirs, so it was fair game for media to poke fun at the county. Marin was isolated, a victim of its own selfish behavior, and, besides, wasn't Marin the hot tub capital of the world?

At the MMWD offices in Corte Madera the phone started to ring incessantly with media calls, not only from San Francisco, but also from media outlets across America. Had it rained yet, Diet? When was it going to rain? Bets were placed on what date it would rain. In fact, there were so many media calls that Diet was forced to make a decision. Either he could answer them all, or none. There was also a third choice. He could hold a daily media conference and deal with the nonsense all at once.

And so were born the infamous "11 a.m. media scrums" in front of the MMWD offices, wherein Diet labored to keep a waiting world informed of brave little Marin County's efforts to find some water, any water, somewhere, and somehow transport that water to its citizens, so that people could water their lawns and gardens before all of Marin County turned into a modern version of the Great Oklahoma Dust Bowl. And maybe even take a hot bath in the bargain.

You got to be careful if you don't know where you're going, because you might not get there.

~ Yogi Berra

"So, Diet, is it going to rain today?"

Charley Hunter had gained a reputation as something of a wit in the Bay Area TV news market. It was Charley Hunter's job to come up with a fresh one-liner every morning, simultaneously inquiring about the weather while mocking Marin County for an amused Bay Area audience that couldn't get enough of the soap opera. Hunter alternated between car wash jokes, hot tub metaphors and questions about cloud seeding, all the while maintaining a rubber-faced grin.

It was Diet's job to be the straight man, enduring the humiliation of being the general manager of a water district that didn't have enough water left with which to brush your teeth while facing the alarming prospect of soon not having any at all, and the repercussions that come along with an endless drought, such as very high property values going right down the dumper. Diet's answers were unfailingly polite, as he brought an eager

TV audience up to speed with the day's doings in the land of drought.

"The forecast for today, and tomorrow, is sunshine," said Diet, squinting into a bright sun that belonged in the middle of an Australian summer rather than in the middle of a northern California winter. "The weather is lovely, and perfect for hitting the beach."

"So it's not going to rain?" inquired Joel Bartlett, a handsome young reporter who went on to a 30-year career as a TV weatherman in San Francisco. "OK, what's your water-saving tip for today?"

"Hang on, what's the latest news on acquiring any water, Diet?" interrupted Bob Hayes, a local AM radio reporter whose sad assignment was trying to get something newsworthy out of the daily conferences. "Any luck arranging tankers to bring water down from Canada?"

"Why, I'm glad you asked that," replied Diet, reaching into his pocket for a piece of paper on which he had written some notes. "Of course, we are looking into every place we can to buy some water, including Canada. I'm pleased to say we are close to a deal regarding leasing some water tankers and bringing water in from the north, if we decide to go that way. We are also looking at importing water by barge from Stockton, and people have been very kind in sending us their suggestions as to various other ways we can find some water. I'm sure we'll have a decision soon."

"You've been saying that for several days, Diet," said Hunter. "Sounds like you haven't solved the issue yet. What about towing some icebergs in from Antarctica?"

If stupidity got us into this mess, then why can't it get us out?

~ Will Rogers

Letters had indeed been rolling into the MMWD offices from many sources. Barge water down from Canada. Dig a ditch around the base of Mount Tam and collect storm water (however, it would have to rain for this solution to be practical.) Lay down plastic sheets under eucalyptus trees in the Tennessee Valley and collect overnight evaporation. Build a giant wind tunnel on the Golden Gate Bridge and collect the fog. Everybody thought you could collect the fog and turn it into water, somehow. One constituent wrote a long letter to the MMWD offices, explaining that there was a drought because there were too many dogs and cats in the county.

"The suggestion has been made that we bring some water down from Washington state," said Diet to the camera crews as they jockeyed for the best angles. "We have contracted for the tanker trucks and already begun to study how we clean them. They will all have to be disinfected. Then there is the problem of where we will unload the tankers, and how people will get to them, and how 170,000 people will get the water home once they pick it up in their cars from a central depot. I'm afraid that particular situation is very Third World, except for the fact that the actual cost of that water looks more like room service at the Ritz Carlton."

"What about the icebergs, Diet?" asked Hunter, always ready to slip in an absurd comment. "Are you really studying the possibility of bringing icebergs up from Antarctica?"

"Actually, yes. We have somebody looking into it, but the numbers don't look very encouraging financially," responded Diet. "The currents will allow us to do it, towing them northward along the Chilean coast, and they won't melt entirely before they get here, but where do you store the icebergs once they are here and how do you magically turn ice into water? Those are a few of the problems we're looking at."

The TV crews all pushed forward at this remark, directors signaling frantically to their crews to zero in on Diet's face as he laid out the scenario.

"So you're serious about the icebergs, then?" said Hunter.

"I have said on many occasions that we will look into every possibility when it comes to bringing water to Marin County. We are facing a disaster. If we have to dig a ditch all the way to Oregon, we will."

"Tell us more about the penguins, Diet," said Hunter.

"The idea is that we could tow the icebergs into Tomales Bay, because the currents won't allow us to bring them into San Francisco Bay, and we could create a small port there and drive bulldozers up on to the icebergs," he continued. "We could mine the ice with bulldozers, and grind the ice up on the spot, and slurry it up a new pipeline to patch into the Marin Municipal pipeline system."

Reporters were frantically taking notes, as Diet spoke. Ports! Slurry! Bulldozers! Pipeline! Amazing stuff.

"Of course, we'd have to do an Environmental Impact Report first, especially if the penguins jump off and wander all over the coast. Imagine penguins walking down the main street in Tiburon. There'd be panic, and we'd need the Humane Society on board with us, so to speak. So, yes, there are lots of things you'd have to consider."

"Penguins?" said Hunter. "How about killer whales? Any whales in the picture?"

"Give it a rest, Charley," said Diet. "I'll see all you good folks here again tomorrow. Same time, same place."

My choice early in life was either to be a piano player in a whorehouse or a politician. And to tell the truth, there's hardly any difference.

~ Harry S. Truman

The idea of towing icebergs to California was a serious suggestion, and it spawned many other serious suggestions along the same lines. Perhaps the most ingenious ways to solve the drought crisis came from the active and agile mind of Congressman John Burton, who served as a state and federal elected official in several capacities in San Francisco, Marin and

Sonoma counties for several terms. Of all the eccentric, dynamic or just plain crazy people to ever live or work in Marin, Congressman John Burton may be placed right at the top of the list. His flamboyant and outspoken style suited Marin perfectly, and the drought was just the kind of crisis that Burton loved.

John Burton spent 40 years in public service. He began his career as a deputy attorney general before his election to the State Assembly in 1964. He was elected to Congress in 1974, before returning to private life in 1983. In 1988, he returned to the State Assembly, and he moved on to the State Senate in 1996.

In total, Burton served in the State Assembly for 16 years, and in Congress for eight years, before stepping down from public office after publicly admitting that he had developed a drug problem. After treatment Burton returned to the California Senate, where he remained as its president until the end of his term.

Friends and foes described Burton — and he had many of both — in a wide variety of ways, none of them bland. In reference to his often coarse language, one critic described him as "a walking expletive with no deletion." One former legislator defended his "big, volcanic, temper tantrums" as "almost always for real things." Suffice to say that Burton would probably never have been elected anywhere else in the United States, but in Marin County he fit right in.

In an impassioned speech before Congress, Burton defended his home turf, lambasting the media for its treatment of Marin County, in particular a TV special broadcast by NBC that managed to leave a lasting impression on the nation about Marin's distinct personality.

"Mr. Speaker, on the evening of July 20, the residents of an entire California county, Marin County, were portrayed by NBC in a TV special titled 'I Want It All Now' as a self-indulgent conglomeration of eccentrics, hedonists, narcissists, and irresponsible adults," thundered Burton. "The sting of this unfair portrayal is still being felt in the county and has most certainly left an ugly scar on the nation's image of Marin County. The program was one of the most irresponsible pieces of journalism I have ever seen. It has grossly deceived a national audience about the people and lifestyle in Marin County, and has brought television journalism to a new low."

Burton went on for chapter and verse, but his point was well made, even if his oratory did nothing to change the country's perception of Marin as a spoiled and self-indulgent community, an image that persists to this day. But if Marin is perceived as a crazy place full of wacky people, what is there to make of Burton's own actions in regard to the drought?

Ninety percent of politicians give the other 10 percent a bad name.

~ Henry Kissinger

"Diet," said Charley Hunter, bright-eyed and bushy-tailed the next morning at the 11 a.m. media scrum, "what do you think of Congressman Burton's latest idea for dealing with the drought that he announced this morning?"

"No doubt Congressman Burton has some excellent ideas for dealing with the drought," replied Diet, keeping a straight face while adjusting his tie. "We've discussed a few of them. Now, we all know that while we here in the West have suffered a deep drought, folks in the East have been getting a lot of snow. Congressman Burton and I discussed his idea of filling boxcars with snow and shipping it out here."

Reporters started frantically taking notes again. This was news. Boxcars filled with snow? Wow, what a great idea! Why not?

"Unfortunately, I pointed out to the congressman that, because of the time frame required to ship the snow all the way out West, and the heat we are experiencing out here, it would likely melt. The congressman and I also discussed his idea of commandeering a squadron of C-124 transport planes, and filling them with snow, so they could get here faster."

"Wow, how is that plan proceeding?" asked an eager reporter in the back, pencil in hand and taking down quotes.

"Well, I pointed out to the congressman that as soon as snow starts melting, the water will start sloshing back and forth. Imagine flying a C-124 over the Sierra with several tons of water sloshing back and forth. You get the idea."

"Did you hear the congressman this morning on the radio?" asked a newspaper reporter from the national media contingent. "He has a new plan, nothing to do with planes or trains."

"Actually, I have not," answered Diet, looking directly at the reporter as he did so. "What, exactly, has the congressman proposed today?"

"The congressman has proposed that he get President Carter to bring the 6th Fleet to San Francisco Bay," explained Hunter. "We aren't at war and the fleet isn't doing anything special. Then they'll berth in San Pablo Bay, and the fleet will use their nuclear-powered desal plants to create water for the county. Sling a pipe over the side of the ship, run it to shore, and there's instant fresh water, problem over."

"What," said Diet, "the 6th Fleet? That's pretty interesting, but I think there might be a problem with that idea too."

"What is that, Diet?" asked Hunter.

"Well, to start with, those gigantic ships draw about 20 feet of water, and San Pablo Bay up here is only two feet deep at low tide. It's a stupid idea."

That night, over dinner, Diet got a phone call from Burton.

"Why did you say on TV that I was stupid?" demanded Burton. "I'm trying everything I can to help you out, even calling the President, and this is the thanks I get?"

"I didn't say you were stupid, John."

"The press has been calling me, telling me that's what you said."

"No, I said it was a stupid idea, and it is. Imagine the 6th Fleet, beached, sitting high and dry in San Pablo Bay. What would that look like on national TV? Thanks for suggesting the trains and planes and the 6th Fleet, but what we are going to need is a plan that actually works."

23 / Sitting on the dock of the bay

The best way to get a bad law repealed is to enforce it strictly.

~ Abraham Lincoln

Marin County, January 27, 1977

"You bureaucrats are all bastards," came a loud voice from the back of the crowd, a rough, cigarettes-and-whiskey voice. "You're always trying to screw the little guy."

"That news will come as a shock to my parents, Sally," yelled back Diet, standing on a soapbox to make himself heard. What he wanted to say was: 'That would be the first time you haven't charged to screw people,' but you don't say that to people in public. And certainly you don't say it to the mayor, especially if the mayor is Sassy Sally Stanford.

Diet's public relations policy of meeting with water consumers, whether singly or in groups, was really paying off. In ones and twos, then in a steady trickle and then with a rush and a roar, consumers came in to MMWD offices, holding aloft their water bills like they were death notices, aghast at what had transpired within their household budget when they weren't paying any attention.

While most Marinites were well aware of the drought by now — hell, it was in all the newspapers and the talk around the water cooler was all about brushing your teeth in a jar and dabbing your pits with a wet sponge — and while most of them were actively participating in the campaign to cut their water usage if for no other reason than to stop their household budgets from going down the drain, there were still the occasional profligates who somehow thought that Diet's stringent rules and regulations didn't apply to them, and they hadn't paid much attention until the bill arrived in the mail. Then they headed down to the MMWD in a foul mood, looking for blood.

Not all Marinites were rich, of course, and it's likely that a lot of the ones who were rich got that way by paying strict attention to the bottom line, but rich and poor alike shared the same attitude when it came to money. They did not like spending it on simple household basics like the water bill (a nice chardonnay was another story) and, like all good Americans, whether Republican or Democrat, they hated paying taxes to any level of government.

Water had been so cheap and clean and easily available forever in Marin — all you had to do was turn on the tap and let it flow — that nobody had paid much attention to the price. But consumers who were used to paying $50 a bill every two months, and hadn't bothered to stop watering the rosebushes and hosing down the sidewalk, were now paying $500 per bill and by gosh, somebody was going to answer for it.

That somebody was J. Dietrich Stroeh.

Diet usually met the angry ratepayers in the MMWD boardroom. Patiently he would explain to each person, couple or group, whether they were owners of laundromats or apartment renters, that notices had been mailed to everyone in the county concerning the rationing system. Warnings had been publicly issued about the new costs for those who ignored their strict household allotments. Shocked at the rise in costs, consumers would go home muttering something about "using paper plates from now on," while planning to go to Mom's place over in the East Bay just to use her bathtub.

The association of restaurant owners, however, was just too large a group to fit into the MMWD boardroom. So many people showed up ready for a confrontation with Diet, they would have spilled out into the corridors and down the hallway and out into the lobby. Nobody was more steamed at the new water rates than the restaurant owners. Well, the nurseries and golf courses and hospitals and long-term care homes weren't too happy either, but restaurants really use a lot of water. Not only is there a lot of cooking and cleaning, but for some strange reason their customers also seemed to be using the bathrooms a lot more, too, just the last month or so.

The restaurant owners of Marin were hit hard when the full rationing system took effect, so when the word got out there was going to be a meeting to protest the new water rates, over 100 managers and staff arrived at the MMWD offices to voice their displeasure. Although he had better things to do than argue with irate restaurateurs, Diet met them head on. In the MMWD back parking lot, that is.

Clothes make the man. Naked people have little or no influence on society.

~ Mark Twain

"I'd like to thank you all for coming down here today," said Diet smoothly, standing on top of a small wooden orange crate that one of his staff had pulled out of storage so he could see over the heads of the crowd. As always, Diet was immaculately dressed for the occasion in his signature three-piece suit, aviator glasses, new tie and polished shoes. He believed the best way to maintain authority was to dress and act the part. Clients could show up in jeans and flip-flops, but they wouldn't ever catch him without a dapper suit. Clothes, as the saying goes, make the man.

There were managers, owners, and wait staff from Tiburon, Mill Valley, Sausalito, Corte Madera, Larkspur, San Rafael, Novato, and all over the county. Heck, Diet could even see the owner of the saloon from way out in Point Reyes Station, a tall guy with flaming red mutton chop whiskers who always wore a cowboy hat, standing at the back of the crowd with his arms akimbo like a human scarecrow, a big sheet of white paper that looked suspiciously like a water bill clamped between his teeth, glaring.

"What are you sons of bitches trying to do, put us all out of business?" came the whiskey voice from the back again. "I ain't gonna pay this friggin' bill."

"Thank you for coming down here today, Sally," said Diet, raising his voice to be heard above the hubbub. "I'll be glad to show you how we can all chip in and save a lot of water during this current crisis."

"Crisis? What crisis? The only crisis is these goddam outrageous rates that yer charging," replied Stanford. "The second crisis is gonna be when I sue yer skinny ass."

"You tell him, Sally," yelled Bill Masters, owner of a seafood restaurant in San Rafael, waving his own bill in the air. "This is the price we have to pay for these damned bureaucrats not planning ahead for the simplest thing like a water shortage. All they ever do is pass the buck on to the taxpayer."

"Shortage, what shortage?" thought Diet to himself, although he said nothing out loud. There is no shortage. This is a disaster." But what he said to the crowd was somewhat different.

"OK folks, here's what we are going to do. Each and every one of us in Marin is going to have to dig deep and find ways to save water, and that includes all restaurant owners," he said, clearing his voice and speaking up to make sure he could be heard by everyone, even Sally Stanford at the back. "But I understand that commercial enterprises are not the same as residential households, so we are going to create a separate system for you. And we're also asking you to help us to come up with new ways to save water."

"I'm using paper plates down at the Coffee Mill," said Jim Schwartz. "That way we don't use any water at all."

"I stopped giving customers a glass of water unless they ask for it," chipped in Mabel, who was only a waitress at the Coffee Mill but who had showed up at the meeting because customers were giving her a hard time and she wanted to give somebody else a hard time, and who better than the jerk who started the water rationing program in the first place?

"Those are good ideas," replied Diet, raising his voice again to be heard. "Anybody else got any good ideas on how to save water?"

"We stopped watering our flowers," yelled a voice over to the side. And so it went, from angry voices yelling at Diet to energized consumers eager to challenge each other about how many gallons they could save. In a few minutes, the crowd started to get together in small groups to swap ideas. Using his newly found PR strategy of asking for public input, Diet had turned the crowd from an antagonistic lynch mob to an energized group of lawful citizens."

Soon the crowd began to disperse and Diet got down from his box and made his way to the back door of the MMWD offices. And who should be standing there but Sally Stanford herself and D. Walter Peppers, attorney at law and famous instigator of lawsuits against public bodies?

"I'd like a word with you," said Peppers, even more resplendent than Diet in his three-piece suit, fedora and ivory cane, looking like some desperado from a Wild West show. "In your office if you don't mind. Now."

"We got something to discuss," said Sally Stanford, "and I don't think it's something you want to broadcast to a crowd, buster."

Live in such a way that you would not be ashamed to sell your parrot to the town gossip.

~ Will Rogers

To understand Marin, first you need to understand the town of Sausalito. Sausalito is a slice of Marin in miniature, a beautiful and progressive community where creative and freethinking people, such as artists and writers, come to work, congregate and discuss the issues of the day. And to understand Sausalito in the 70's, you need to understand Sally Stanford and how the heck she ended up as mayor of Sausalito.

According to historical archives, Sassy Sally Stanford was the most famous hooker and madam in San Francisco's notoriously bawdy history, and in a town that is world-renowned for bawdy behavior and wild living, that's quite an accomplishment.

Sally Stanford was born in San Bernardino County on May 5, 1903. Sally's life on the wrong side of the law began at 16, when she eloped to Denver with a man who boasted he was the grandson of a former governor of Colorado. Sally helped him cash some checks he happened to have stolen. She was sent to the Oregon State Prison at Salem for two years for obtaining goods under false pretenses.

Sally came to San Francisco in 1924 and entered the sex trade as a hooker and went on to become a madam. Sassy Sally (the name came from a popular song of the time, "I Wonder What's Become of Sally?") finally took the last name Stanford because she liked the Stanford University football team and thought the moniker gave her some class. Stanford was arrested so many times she got fed up and decided to become, in her own words, "a square."

Sally moved to Sausalito in 1948 and bought the famous Valhalla Restaurant, a showplace dining establishment located on the waterfront with a great view of San Francisco. She fought city planners with a vengeance, and tussled with authorities on many occasions. Eventually she decided to run for office in order to rectify the situation and get the upper hand. She won a seat on Sausalito's City Council in 1972, and in 1976 was re-elected with the majority that made her mayor. She was 72. Only in a place like Marin County could a wild woman like Sally Stanford become the mayor.

Never let your sense of morals prevent you from doing what's right.

~ Isaac Asimov

Diet's desk at the MMWD offices was a cluttered mess. The walls were decorated with slogans promoting water conservation. Pamphlets were stacked upon tables, waiting for mailing to water consumers, outlining various methods in which consumers could keep within their household allotment. But keeping within bounds was not something with which Sally Stanford was familiar.

"First of all," said her lawyer, Peppers, opening an envelope and holding up a sheet of paper, "there is no way that my client is ever going to pay this outrageous bill."

Sally sat on the other side of the desk from Diet, dabbing her eyes demurely with a hankie and pretending to cry. Even at the advanced age of 72, she was not above acting a role; her lawyer was really only there for window dressing. There was a serious principle involved. It was called money, something very near and dear to Sally's heart. Normally she would have torn Diet's head off using language that would make a stevedore blush, but today was all about money, so Sally sat there sobbing.

Even at this late point in her life Sally took every opportunity to present an imposing image, with her thick head of dark black hair —

although going gray, almost white in parts — swept up high on her head in a bouffant. She affected deep red lipstick and heavy rouge, plucked eyebrows and large earrings. The only thing missing from the picture was her longtime friend and confidante, her green Amazon parrot Loretta, usually found perched on her left shoulder and whispering sweet nothings into her ear. As mayor of Sausalito, Sally could do any damned thing she wanted, and she usually damned well did.

If women didn't exist, all the money in the world would have no meaning.

~ Aristotle Onassis

"Who do you think you are, presenting my client a bill for $2,500 for water?" demanded Peppers in his opening salvo. "Are you piping Perrier straight into the water system these days or simply trying to balance the district budget on the backs of hard-working taxpayers? It's outright extortion, that's what it is. Do you think that money runs like water? There is no possible way that my client can afford to pay this amount."

"If you can afford to pay Walter Peppers to represent you," thought Diet, "you can certainly afford to pay your water bill." But, as usual, what he said out loud was something different.

"Haven't you seen the literature my department has been sending out to water customers?" he asked, looking directly at Sally and ignoring Peppers. "Are you not aware there is a severe water shortage?"

"I don't normally drink . . . water," Sally replied in her whiskey-and-cigarettes voice, taking the hankie away from her eyes for a brief moment. "I prefer something . . . stronger."

"Everybody has to do their part in saving water or else soon we won't have any water left," replied Diet, reaching for a pamphlet and handing it to Sally, who ignored it , indicating that Peppers should take it. "If you go over a certain set amount, then extra charges start to kick in. I know for a restaurant that maybe difficult to achieve, but we all have to try. But I tell you what; I'll make you a deal."

At the mention of a deal — language she understood — Sally put her hankie away and sat up straight. Talking money was her kind of language.

"OK, whaddya got?

"Well, let's start by my asking you what your average water bill comes to."

Strangely enough, for a person who didn't drink water and had no idea that there was a water shortage, Sally had a fairly accurate idea of what her water bill actually was.

"OK, it's $250, give or take."

"Here's what I am going to do then," said Diet, reaching forward and taking the bill from Peppers' hand. "I'll make you a deal. I am going to put this bill away in my desk here, and if you reach your allotment and stick to it, then if we ever get through this drought I will tear your check up. In the meantime, if you just write me a check for the $250, which is what you normally pay, we'll call it a deal for now. How's that?"

Sally looked amazed. "You would actually do that?"

On a good Friday night at the Valhalla, Sally might make that amount of money just from the bar alone, but two and a half large was still two and a half large, and she had never talked to a bureaucrat before who didn't treat her like an adversary, and she started to cry again.

"Would you really do that for me?"

"Yes, ma'am, I will," said Diet, taking the bill and putting it in a drawer, and pulling out a pen. "If you could just sign a check for me now, we have a deal."

Sally smiled. It's not often you can strike a reasonable deal with a bureaucrat.

"See you in a few months," she said.

All truth passes through three stages. First, it is ridiculed. Second, it is violently opposed. Third, it is accepted as being self-evident.

~ Arthur Schopenhauer

24 / The Sacramento blues

It is amazing what can be accomplished when nobody cares about who gets the credit.

~ Robert Yates

Sacramento, February 5, 1977

By now, what had been happening in Marin County was daily news all over the state, and the word was getting around that pretty soon it might not only be Marin, but a lot of other counties in California where water was starting to get pretty low. Just to the north of the Bay Area, the Russian River was so low that Sonoma County wouldn't share its water with anyone. The City of San Francisco and the East Bay towns were also going to institute rationing, even though they were hooked up to the state water system.

The Director of Water Resources in the State of California was Ron Robie. Robie was an old friend of Diet Stroeh, and Diet had called Robie on several occasions about the possibility of getting water from the state system somehow, somewhere, and shipping it to Marin County. Until now, there had been no response, but things were starting to change.

Ron Robie, sensing a statewide disaster in the making, finally responded to Diet's repeated messages, and called an emergency meeting of all affected water districts to the state capitol in Sacramento. All the big hitters showed up, including officials from the federal Bureau of Reclamation, the State of California, the San Francisco Water Agency, the East Bay Municipal Utilities District, and the inland valleys. At the end of the table was a guy from little old Marin Municipal Water District named Diet Stroeh.

It was agreed that the goal of the plan was to find a way to get water to every district. Marin was to get emergency water from the delta system, somehow and somewhere, and ship it somehow, probably by tanker trucks to a dock in the East Bay, and then ship it again by barge to a dock near San Quentin. From there, the idea was to tap in to the MMWD somehow, and get the water to its 170,000 customers. But nobody knew where exactly in the delta to get the water from, or how. There was no legal arrangement for sharing water in the state of California. Either you had your own supply, or you didn't.

Given that the situation in Marin was desperate, there was some urgency to the talks, but the reality was that other, much more powerful constituencies could also be affected negatively, and soon. For instance, Kern County, in the heart of the great agricultural breadbasket of the San Joaquin Valley, looked like it might be running short of water soon. The origin of the water that ended up in the San Joaquin Valley was the Shasta Reservoir in the north of the state, which was fed by snowmelt from the Sierra. Shasta's reservoir was getting very low, and powerful agricultural interests in the San Joaquin were starting to get quite concerned.

The meeting began early in the morning. The key to getting any movement on deadlocked talks was to convince the Los Angeles Metropolitan Water District to release some water from the total amount of acre-feet they had contracted to purchase, water that emanated from Northern California. Technically and legally speaking, the water belonged to Los Angeles, but physically speaking it was stored in Northern California, then flowed south to the Sacramento Delta from Mount Shasta, and from there via an aqueduct to the south and eventually to Los Angeles. To arrange any sort of deal, all the water districts in attendance had to agree to share that water to some degree, because water is not a static substance; it is a fluid, almost always in motion, passing through various constituencies. Who could say who owned what, where and when?

Kern County needed the largest block of water. The City of San Francisco looked like they might need a large block too, and little Marin County stood down there at the end of the line with its humble request for 10,000 acre-feet. On their own, Marin County voters had no political power to influence gigantic L.A. Met, but Diet knew that there was strength in numbers, and the key was to get the balance on your side.

When it appeared by early afternoon that all of the water authorities might actually end up on the same page and strike some sort of deal, suddenly officials from the federal Bureau of Reclamation announced that they could sign no official document without official agreement from Congress. The federal government controlled a lot of water in the delta, and it was essential that the right parties in Washington actively participate in any agreement. At this point, sensing that everything was going to fall apart, Diet lost his cool and announced he was leaving.

It was a desperation move. Diet knew that any agreement required approval from every player in the room, not just a majority. Threatening to leave was the only card he could play, but the Bureau of Reclamation officials refused to budge. They had no authority with which to sign any legal agreement, they said. The truth of the matter was, neither did Diet. His threat to pull the plug on the meetings by walking out was just a bluff.

To stop his meeting from falling apart, Robie got on the line and phoned Governor Jerry Brown. Brown got on the line and read the riot act to the federal officials. "Sign something or other" was the ultimatum and never mind the details. Politics would be taken care of later. It was an all-or-nothing situation, and Brown had a lot of political pressure to deal with from many sources also threatened by drought. Politics being politics, all the parties in the room agreed to sign a vague "memorandum of understanding" stating that they would agree to share water, a political compromise that carried less weight than the paper on which it was written.

Nonetheless, Diet's strategy had carried the day. He had some sort of legal agreement to get his hands on some water, somewhere, and if nobody knew any details such as how and who and why, those could all be worked out. The fact that Diet's own board of directors knew nothing whatsoever about the memorandum, nor had they agreed to any MOU, was only a minor detail. They had to agree to an agreement, any agreement that might get them water; what choice did they have?

Nobody at the meeting knew where the agreed-upon water was coming from, and where it was going, or how to get it there, or any other significant details. But they had a deal to cooperate, somehow. That's all that really mattered. One way or the other, Diet was going to get some of that state water and bring it home to Marin. Just like at every other stage in the ongoing drought saga, he had no authority, no money, no budget and no specifics. Details would be worked out later. But it was a start.

Self-sacrifice enables us to sacrifice other people without blushing.
~ George Bernard Shaw

Marin County, February 5, 1977

At the Stroeh residence in the Verissimo Hills, Diet collapsed with a sigh into his big easy chair in the living room, his favorite one with the view of a grove of old oak trees just outside. It had been a long, hard day, and the drive back from Sacramento was stressful as well, fighting rush-hour traffic on the way back. The Richmond-San Rafael Bridge had been an especially tough slog, and as he drove across the bridge looking at the bay, Diet wondered just where barges would load and unload.

"How'd it go?" asked Marcia, bring Diet a nice, cold drink. "Any luck?"

"I think so, but it's too early to say yet what's going to happen, so I'm not going to celebrate," he answered tiredly. "I managed to get some sort of agreement from all the general managers to share some water, so that's a victory of sorts. But how we go from there remains to be seen. How are the kids?"

"I put them to bed a few minutes ago," she said. "I have to tell you something you should know. You've been out at meetings every night, so you haven't heard them, but we've been getting phone calls here."

"From who? The media again? Tell them to call me during the day at the office."

"No, not this time. Well, yes, we had a call from a newspaper in New York, but they apologized when they discovered what time it was out here. No, we've had a few calls from people here in Marin. Disgruntled customers, I think you can call them. I tell them this is a private residence, and to call you at work, but some of them have been rude."

"Well, just tell them to call me at the office, or hang up on them if they are rude," said Diet, standing up and stretching. "I apologize that my work bothers you and the kids here at home. There's nothing I can do about it."

"It's not just here at home," said Marcia. "It's at school too. Christina said some of the kids have called her names. Their parents have been saying nasty stuff about you. How you are the person responsible for this crisis."

"Oh, that's just great. First they get me at the office, now the family here at home," moaned Diet. "Next they'll be stopping me at Safeway, in the vegetable section, threatening me with rutabagas."

Average amount of water (in liters) needed to produce a kilo of food: Potatoes 1,000; Wheat 1,450; Rice 3,450; Chicken 4,600; Beef 42,500.

~ Water Facts.com

Getting an agreement to move some water out of the California delta into the Bay Area might have become doable when general managers of certain key water districts at the Sacramento meeting realized that there was really no way to physically accomplish the task. Agreeing to something that's impossible is easy. Doing the impossible requires a little more time and effort. Saying "yes" just buys time to say "no."

The California water supply system of reservoirs, aqueducts, canals, rivers and pipelines criss-crosses the entire state like a giant jigsaw. Engineers had been at work building it for over a century, turning what had been essentially a desert green through monumental effort. Basically, most of the water in the state came from over there and was needed here. Except for the northern part of the state, very few communities used water that wasn't transported for many miles through pipes or canals of some sort.

Overall, the state of California averages a meager 22.7 inches per year of rainfall. That meager average would be less if it weren't for the Northern California coastline, which receives two-thirds of all the rainfall in the state. But that water doesn't drain into rivers that can be tapped into by cities in the south. Most water used in Southern California comes from the Sierra, where it drains into dozens of small rivers that drain into the Sacramento and San Joaquin rivers.

California has 82 rivers, the longest of which is the Sacramento at 400 miles. The Sacramento drains 22 million acre-feet per year, compared to 16 million acre-feet for the Colorado River. The full runoff of streams in California is estimated at 71 million acre-feet per year. The Sacramento-San Joaquin Delta alone encompasses approximately 738,000 acres with over 700 miles of waterways.

While this appears to be a monumental amount of water to move around, the population of California in 1977 was 16 million people (today it is 36 million, and projections are that the population will reach 48 million by 2020) and in 1977 those 16 million people needed every drop. On average, one person's personal and industrial needs in California are 250 gallons per day. Actually, counting all the water they consume, every person in modern America requires 1,300 gallons of water per day to produce all the food, fiber and energy they consume. Demand has always fueled supply, but by 1977 the supply was barely enough to go around.

The East Bay gets its water piped in from the delta and the Sacramento River through Contra Costa County. San Francisco gets its water from the Hetch Hetchy reservoir high in the Sierra Nevada in Yosemite National Park, where it runs via pipeline to the East Bay hills and then underground to San Francisco. The East Bay actually has two different pipelines into which Marin could possibly tap; its own and San Francisco's. The funny thing is these two pipeline systems don't meet. Each system is separate and unique. So agreeing to tap into that patchwork of pipes to somehow bring water to Marin was easily said, but virtually impossible to do.

There was also the small question of how Marin was going to pay for tapping into the supply and getting it to Marin, which nobody wanted to discuss right away, possibly because they didn't think it was possible to do it. But a meeting was scheduled anyway, to see if it could be done.

A 4-year-old child could understand this report. Run out and find me a 4-year-old child. I can't make heads or tails out of it.

~ Groucho Marx

The meeting of Bay Area water district general managers and their technical staff took place in the water district offices in Hayward. The general managers of the Contra Costa Water Agency, Alameda District Agency, East Bay Municipal, San Francisco Water Authority and the MMWD all sat down together, pulled together maps and drawings of their separate systems, and made a depressing discovery. There wasn't any way to get the water to Marin. There was no connection that even came close.

"Let's start over here, in the east," said Bob Billings, the general manager of the Contra Costa Water Agency, pointing to a giant map on the wall. "The piping system starts right at our principal water source, the Mokelumne River Basin over in the Sierra Nevada range. Water is stored at the Comanche Reservoir and the Pardee Reservoir, then the Mokelumne Aqueduct starts at Pardee and runs the water to Stockton, then through Contra Costa County over to Antioch and Pittsburgh, where it takes a dip southward to Walnut Creek. Then the pipeline veers left past Lafayette and Orinda, and fills up our reservoirs at San Pablo, El Sobrante and San Leandro. From there the East Bay MUD water supply system runs through a network of reservoirs, aqueducts, treatment plants, and distribution facilities that extend all through the East Bay area."

"South of us," he continued, "you've got the Zone 7 Water Agency, the Tri Valley's water wholesaler. If you receive your water from the California Water Service Company, or the City of Livermore, the City of Pleasanton, or the Dublin San Ramon Services District, then your water comes from Zone 7."

"Whoa," said Diet, holding up his hand and pointing to the map. "Wait a minute. There's got to be an easier way to look at all this data, or we'll be here all week. Here we are, the MMWD way over in the west across San Francisco Bay, right here in Marin County. We have two ways to get water there, either via barge across San Pablo Bay, or via the Richmond-San Rafael Bridge, where we might get lucky and get permission to run a pipeline. So the question becomes, how do we run water from way over here in Hayward, north to a point near the Richmond shoreline?"

"I have an idea," said a voice in the back of the room. It was Bill Jenkins, a junior engineer from the Alameda Water Authority. "Nobody seems to have mentioned anything about money yet, so I don't know what kind of pipeline we can build, but if you look closely right here" — everybody looked closely at a map of the East Bay piping system — "these two pipelines are only about 20 feet apart. You have the East Bay MUD system right here, and the San Francisco pipeline running by it right here. They almost touch."

Everybody in the room crowded close to the map to take a look.

"If the MMWD had the money," said Jennings, "all you have to do is construct some sort of connection between the two pipelines. San Francisco treats the water first, then you switch it over to East Bay MUD system, and then you run it north to Richmond using our pipes, near the Richmond Bridge where the EMUD line stops, and then you build a pipeline over the bridge to Marin, and that oughta do it."

There was complete silence in the room for a full 30 seconds while everyone looked at the map.

"Twenty feet?" said Diet. "Build a connector 20 feet?"

"Well, yes," said Jenkins. "You'll have to get the two agencies to sign off on it, but we have those gentlemen right here in the room, I believe. The East Bay MUD system runs all the way north to Point Richmond. If you take a look at the map, that's right next to the Richmond Bridge, where you already mentioned you could run a pipeline across to Marin. You'd have to build a new pump station there at the east end of the bridge, of course, and a pump station over in Marin, but that would be easy."

"Pay for a 20-foot connection? Of course we'll pay for a connector," said Diet. "Not a problem, we'll pay for it."

"You'll have to get permission to run a pipeline across the Richmond bridge too, of course," said Billings. "You'll have to deal with the folks over at CalTrans, and get their permission, and good luck doing that."

"I'll deal with CalTrans later," said Diet. "Let me look at that map again. It's a miracle."

It takes two gallons to brush your teeth, 2 to 7 gallons to flush a toilet, and 25 to 50 gallons to take a shower.

~ Kid's Water Facts.com

---

25 / Governor Moonbeam Comes to Town

People prefer to follow those who help them, not those who intimidate them.

~ C. Gene Wilkes

Marin County, February 11, 1977

California has always had a history of electing people to the Governor's office who probably couldn't get elected as dogcatcher elsewhere, or else politicians so progressive that even California voters couldn't keep up with their wild ideas. Ronald Reagan and Arnold Schwarzenegger, both movie actors nearing the end of their careers, were elected to high office in California thanks to their colorful personalities, access to vast sums of money, and an ability to paint a positive picture of a better tomorrow. But of all the politicians ever elected as governor in the biggest and most influential state in the union, nobody was ever more colorful than Jerry "Moonbeam" Brown, who came to Marin at the height of the drought to see what all the fuss was about.

Jerry Brown was a born politican. His father, Edmund G. (Pat) Brown, had been Governor of California for two terms prior to losing the 1966 election to Reagan. The younger Brown also had politics in his blood from an early age, and in 1974 he became Governor of Californa, succeeding Reagan. Brown served two eventful terms, and later became mayor of Oakland.

During his governorship, Brown pushed the limits of what could be accomplished politically, especially with environmental issues. In 1978, Chicago Tribune columnist Mike Royko invented the nickname "Moonbeam" in connection with Brown's proposal that the state purchase its own satellite to provide emergency communications. The "Moonbeam" nickname stuck, and soon became associated with Brown's "way out " politics, radical even in those radical times. Many of Brown's ideas are now considered progressive and some have become simply conventional. Almost 20 years later, Royko would admit that Brown, despite the silly Moonbeam moniker he had tagged him with, was just as serious as any other politician.

But back in 1977, a visit from Jerry Brown to your town was somewhat like the arrival of a pop star. In fact, Brown dated pop star Linda Ronstadt for a while, adding to his celebrity. The drought was on everybody's lips, but it was Jerry Brown that was in everybody's head, when the governor came to Marin's Civic Center to ask about the drought.

Being in politics is like being a football coach; you have to be smart enough to understand the game, and dumb enough to think it's important.

~ Eugene McCarthy

"Well, what did Brown say about the drought?" asked Marcia over dinner that night. "Is he going to impose mandatory water rationing on the entire state or not?"

"He didn't say whether he supports mandatory rationing," responded Diet, reaching for the potatoes. "He knows it would be political suicide to force it on people. He didn't say much at all, he just asked everyone a lot of questions. He asked me if I thought mandatory rationing was the way to go, and I said yes. He asked the President of the San Francisco Board of Supervisors, who said he didn't think it was necessary at this time, and that drew a lot of boos. A couple of state representatives said they would present legislation on Monday that will require all state water officials to draw up emergency plans, describing how they are going to cut water consumption in their own districts by 25 percent. Oh yeah, and the general managers of all the water districts signed that Memo of Understanding we agreed on in Sacramento."

Under the MOU, Marin County would receive between 6 and 10 million gallons of water per day, starting May 1. The bulk of the diverted water would go to farmers in Kern County in the inland desert, and the rest to the Bay Area. Oh yes, Marin and Kern County each would have to pay the L.A. Met Water Authority $50 per acre-foot for the water they received.

Marin water users, meanwhile, were continuing to use less and less water every day. The current rationing allotment was 12 million gallons a day countywide, but daily use had actually dropped down to an unbelievably low 9.4 million gallons.

"If we keep at these current daily use levels, we might be able to make it about another 300 days, right through summer and to next winter," said Diet, "even without any new supplies. And if it doesn't rain by next winter, at least we'll have some water, either via barges or coming through this pipeline we have to build."

"Any news on that?" said Marcia.

"I've sent my staff to chase down CalTrans officials, find out who

216

we need to talk to. They are the ones who control the Richmond-San Rafael Bridge. I'm on a winning streak, so maybe they'll says yes and let us use the bridge to carry a pipeline. Otherwise we'll have to use barges."

"By the way, have you talked to your board of directors yet about all these deals you've made, and what it's going to cost the consumer?"

"No, I haven't, because I haven't tallied up the costs yet. My only interest right now is getting the water somehow. We'll figure out how to pay for everything later on."

"Has it occurred to you that your career at the water district is over if any of these deals fall through?" asked Marcia.

"There's really been no time to call a board meeting yet and vote on any of these issues," said Diet. "I'm flying by the seat of my pants. But to answer your question, yes, I know my ass is grass if I don't pull this all off."

"Did you install those new telephone lines down at the office yet?"

"Yes, we added six new trunk lines and six new receptionists. We're getting a thousand calls a day right now, and people are still picking up the low-flow showerheads, and the rationing plan is really working."

"Well, that's some good news, at least," said Marcia, gathering up the dishes and heading for the kitchen. "That makes two days in a row with some good news."

"Yeah," mumbled Diet to himself as soon as she was out of the room, "and this afternoon we ran out of low-flow showerheads."

There is more stupidity than hydrogen in the universe, and it has a longer shelf life.

~ Frank Zappa

Billy Compton wound the Tiger down into second gear, braked sharply, and tore through the curve while heading uphill for Point Reyes Station. It was one of his favorite driving routes. He had started heading north from Kentfield along Sir Francis Drake Boulevard, always congested until you got past Fairfax and into the San Geronimo Valley where the suburbs ended and you finally got into open road.

From San Geronimo he headed uphill, steeply, heading for Nicasio, the motor of the Tiger purring. He blew by the little village center in a puff of smoke, his engine responding to his downshifting with a contented rumble, then north to the Nicasio Reservoir, which he noticed was virtually dry, and then he was at the four-way intersection, choosing a hard left toward Point Reyes. At the bridge over the creek he swung a hard right, shifting madly into a lower gear for the climb uphill.

There was something about racing around the hills of western Marin that cleared Billy's head of all the cobwebs, blew away his blues, and, more importantly, killed his daily hangovers. There were virtually no cops out here in the west county, and very little traffic. Out here he could forget about all his woes, the fact that his manager wanted the band to record another album even though he didn't have enough songs written, and another tour looming, and royalties and back taxes.

"Greedy, everybody's greedy," thought Billy, gearing down and slowing up as he approached the little town of Point Reyes Station, pulling in at the pumps to get gas. "Why doesn't everybody relax and just take it easy?"

Listing his hassles in his head, Billy's mind turned to his neighbor Percy. "Now there's an uptight head case if I ever saw one," thought Billy, letting the attendant fill the tank with high-octane gas while he rolled up an illegal cigarette, his own high octane. "That geezer really needs to mellow out, or get himself some earplugs, whatever works."

Percy, at the same moment, was finding his own way to mellow out. As soon as the sound of the Tiger's tailpipes descended down the Kentfield hills, Percy ducked into his garage, unwinding his garden hose.

He quietly pushed the hose through the hole that he had made in the hedge separating his house from Billy's. Slipping through the hole himself, he quickly went over to the water tap that emerged from the back of Billy's house and screwed his hose into the tap.

Percy turned the hose on very low, then scampered back through the hole in the hedge to his own house. Quickly, he ran the hose over to his cherished rosebushes, geraniums and fuchsia bushes. Satisfied that the water was flowing smoothly, he tiptoed back to Billy's house, where he turned the volume of the hose up a little higher. Then he walked down to the edge of Billy's driveway, hiding behind the hedge as he did so, and took up a forward position near the sidewalk, hunkering down to listen.

"I don't know what makes more noise, that stupid music he plays, or that silly automobile he drives," thought Percy to himself, "but at least with that damned auto I can hear him coming a mile away."

Not everything that can be counted counts, and not everything that counts can be counted.

~ Albert Einstein

Pouring himself a stiff drink, Diet retreated to his home office. There, he closed the door and reached into his briefcase, pulling out a folded newsletter from the California Water Resources Association. He turned to the page marked Editorial and began to read. As he read, he sipped on his scotch and began to grind his teeth.

The headline for the article said everything it needed to say: "Marin Water Rationing – The Fruit of No-growth Planned Water Scarcity." Diet scanned the article quickly, and swore while reading.

"Failure of the Marin Municipal Water District to build facilities to tap and store nearby Russian River water," read the article, "is the true reason for its drastic order February 1, 1977 instituting water rationing. Yet, in a recent radio interview a member of the Marin water district board falsely blamed Southern California for the Marin County water crisis."

"Los Angeles — which has an advanced water conservation program — was accused of failing to conserve water. Southern California's per-capita consumption is one of the lowest in the state. It is unfortunate when one area of California blames another for its own lack of planning and action to meet an inevitable problem."

"A few years ago, when a previous board of the Marin Water District sought voter approval for building an aqueduct to the Russian River, population control groups obtained a court injunction preventing the agency from informing the public of the facts. A misinformed public then rejected the aqueduct proposal. Then the population control people gained control of the Water District board and lost the manager who had been advocating the Russian River aqueduct."

"This new board promised a 'do-nothing' policy, except to urge conservation by water users and press for reclamation of wastewater. Now the Marin County public is paying the price of so-called population control via planned scarcity. Each citizen may only use 47 gallons of water per day — about one-quarter of normal usage — water prices are being doubled, and use in excess of the limit results in water disconnection, with a $35 fee for reconnection. All this should serve as a warning to the entire State that water is too vital to be used as a population control tool."

"Well," thought Diet, "this really ought to help speed things along. Wait until the board gets a hold of this . . ."

26 / Planning the pipeline

Optimism is the madness of maintaining that everything is right when it is wrong.

~ Voltaire

Marin County, February 12, 1977

The MMWD offices were bustling. Six new receptionists had been hired to handle the endless barrage of phone calls, either from angry water customers whose bills had gone through the roof, or from customers who wanted to get low-flow showerheads, or from media people trying to interview Diet, or from Marin organizations that wanted to meet with Diet and express their concerns about future water supply.

Diet was in his office, talking to senior staff, explaining that Chevron was pleased to donate some 5,000 oil barrels that water board customers could use for storage of water if and when Diet ever found any water, and all that staff had to do today was figure out how to clean 5,000 dirty barrels that had been used to store oil, when Marge walked in.

"There's a phone call you really have to take."

"Who is it from, the President? Am I going to be given the Medal of Honor, or just get arrested?"

"It's Dick on the phone. He says he has some information for you. You're going to like it."

Dick Rogers was one of Diet's senior staff. Senior staff had been allocated to find water tankers to ship down water from Oregon or Canada, or to lease barges that could get water across the bay from any port that was selected. Rogers had also been assigned the dirtiest job of all, to dog CalTrans officials until he found the right person with the authority to discuss the use of the Richmond-San Rafael Bridge for a pipeline.

"Dick, tell me something good. Did the Canadians offer to give us free water when their hockey rinks melt in the spring? Have you tracked down the people we need to talk to about shipping by tanker?"

"Better than that. I have not only found the person we need to talk to at CalTrans, he has talked to his bosses, and we already have an answer."

"OK, lay it on me. What did he say?"

"He said 'yes.'"

"He said 'yes' to what?" asked Diet.

"He said yes, that we could get their official permission to use the bridge to lay the pipe," replied Rogers. "How do you like them apples?"

"Yes!" yelled Diet into the receiver. "This is it! You've done it!"

"Hang on to your hat, Diet. It gets better."

"How can it get any better?

"Well, there's more," said Rogers. "It's about the price."

"Let me guess," said Diet. "He wants a million bucks, upfront, in unmarked bills. But how did you get him to respond so quickly?"

"It was simple, really. All I did was tell him about our drought situation, and he said he already knew all about it," said Rogers. "It's been in all the papers, and they thought we would call eventually. He said a pipeline was the only obvious solution, and they already had a board meeting."

"This is it! This is the key! All we have to do is get water from the delta through the East Bay over to Point Richmond somehow, and now we can run it across the bridge!" shouted Diet into the phone. "I love you! How can it get any better?"

"Have we given any thought as to what it might cost, Diet?"

"Of course, he wants my first-born child. He can have her too, she's too expensive to put through school. I told you not to worry about the money, we'll deal with all that later. We don't have any money, so what's the difference?"

"Since I had him on the phone," said Rogers, "I thought I'd push my luck."

Diet paused and took a breath, thinking about the fact that he had put the topic of money so far on the back burner it was almost invisible, and now it was going to blow up in his face. Then he exhaled.

"OK, Dick, let me have it."

"CalTrans is going to let us use an entire lane of the bridge for as long as we need. As . . . long . . . as . . . we . . . need," said Rogers, drawing each word out slowly. "Plus, get this. We don't have to hang a pipeline over the edge of the bridge, or do anything crazy. And they are going to lease a lane to us for the grand total of a buck a year."

"Dick," roared Diet, "I love you and I love CalTrans. Give me the name of the guy who agreed to the deal, and we'll send him a crate of wine."

"Always pleased to be of help," said Rogers.

Hanging up the phone, Diet turned to his staff.

"OK, guys, roll up your sleeves, we have work to do. By May 1, L.A. Met is going to let us have some water. By June 1, we need to have a pipeline constructed, ready to rock and roll across the Richmond Bridge. Let's get to it. Send me my engineering guys."

"Oh yeah, one thing," he said. "Nobody talks about costs, whether it's the pipeline or whatever. Especially with the media."

Human history becomes more and more a race between education and catastrophe.

~ H. G. Wells

Berkeley, California, 2006

Today, class, we are going to talk about the future demand for water in the state of California. You may remember that, back in the late 80's and early 90's, there were a couple of minor droughts in the state. I say "minor" in that the state suffered several dry years in a row, and rainfall was below average, and there were serious problems associated with that. For instance, exceptionally dry weather usually brings increased fire danger.

But for a real drought, we have to go all the way back to 1976-77, when there were two years back-to-back where rainfall was insufficient to fill our reservoirs here in Northern California. Those of you who have been studying their history will remember those dates as a real crisis, especially in Marin County, where they almost ran out of water entirely.

Since 1977 the state of California's population has doubled, so we need to look ahead to the future and start to calculate how much water we will need if there is another drought like 1977. If you will turn to the reports that I have passed around to all of you, let's look at the one by the Public Policy Institute of California, that looks at what the public demand for water will be by the year

224

2030. Now, you will note that the PPIC is a non-partisan, non-profit institute, so they are not anti-business, or an environmental activist group. They have compiled this report so that the public will be informed about our future needs for water, which, according to this report, may be considerable.

According to the PPIC report, by 2030 we will have approximately 14 million more people living in California than we have today, or approximately 50 million people. Judging by other estimates, that is a conservative figure. Some estimates have placed the figure at 48 million as early as 2020, but who is to say?

At the current rate of consumption of 232 gallons per person per day — that's a figure that includes personal and industrial use, by the way, not just how much water is needed for your morning shower — that constitutes approximately a 40 percent increase in total water usage in the state of California.

Those who have been paying attention to what is happening in the world, including the fact that glaciers are melting in the Sierra, will have concluded that a 40 percent increase in water usage by the public is not possible, for many reasons. One of which is that we cannot increase the water supply in California by 40 percent. We'll get back to the issue of water supply in just a moment, but first let's take a look at where that expected increase in water demand is predicted to occur.

In America today you can murder land for private profit. You can leave the corpse for all to see, and nobody calls the cops.

~ Paul Brooks, "The Pursuit of Wilderness," 1971

According to this report, much of this water will be going for landscaping in the hot, dry inland valleys that will see the bulk of population growth. Before we jump immediately to the question of landscaping, first let's ask ourselves why people would want to live in the desert.

There are several answers for that, one of which is cost. Anyone who has attempted to rent or buy property here along the coast of California, or anywhere near a big city, knows all about the cost of housing. It's another simple example of the old law of supply and demand. Many people want to live in California, and those with the ability to pay can afford the asking price of a million dollars for a simple home. We have seen how much the cost of housing has risen in the Bay Area during the last decade. You have to be rich to live here. Either that, or you are willing to pay everything you have just for housing.

According to this PPIC report, the largest areas of growth will be outside of Sacramento, in the San Joaquin Valley, around San Bernardino, and in Riverside Countys east of Los Angeles. Leaving aside the San Joaquin Valley for a moment, you will see that the other three areas all have one thing in common: they are situated just outside of big cities that are predicted to get even bigger. So, yes, these are suburbs we are talking about, and just imagine the commute to your job in those areas. Can anyone say, "Thank goodness for air conditioning"?

The San Joaquin Valley is a bit different from the other areas, because right now all we have there are small cities like Fresno, Modesto and Bakersfield. These cities are predicted to grow for different reasons than Los Angeles. For instance, a lot of people who retire in California will sell their homes, move from the coast and settle in senior communities in the foothills of the Sierra, a trend that has already begun. Also, lower-income people have to live somewhere too, and the higher cost of living is already pushing many people out of the Bay Area and the L.A. region to the foothills.

Now, back to the matter of landscaping that I mentioned earlier. California is not the Third World. People are not going to leave the outside of their homes as dust patches. It's simply human nature to improve the quality of your personal real estate. To date, much of the landscaping style in California has come from the aesthetic sense of folks who have moved here from elsewhere, and much of their taste is East Coast in nature. So we have all these wide green lawns, and big gardens, both requiring a lot of water.

In the future, especially in the hot inland desert valleys, you are not going to see people landscape their homes with lots of trees and plants that require a lot of water. It will just be too expensive. Same for coastal cities. Probably many of the people who own homes along the coast, or any area that is already built up, will eventually switch to landscaping that is drought-friendly.

In 2001, this PPIC report found that a state law requiring developers to prove in advance that they have lined up enough water for new residents is working well. But the report also found that one-sixth of all large municipal water utilities in existing communities have failed to submit water plans that show the same encouraging result. A lot of communities have not yet written adequate supply-and-demand projections.

In the past decade, California has made great strides in cutting the indoor usage of water. We have mandated low-flow toilets and showers with stringent plumbing codes and water-efficient appliances. It's the usage outside of the house where we are having problems. Half of all the water used in homes built in inland valleys today goes for landscaping and irrigation, as compared to only one-third on the coast. This is a trend that has to stop.

California is already looking to places such as Las Vegas for answers, where they heavily promote the use of native plants and restrict the use of water. There are no big green front lawns in Las Vegas. You can't simply stand on your porch and water your sidewalk there; you'd get arrested. Golf courses, parks and roadway medians are also using nothing but recycled water, a trend that is also catching on in California.

You can get out your calculators and figure out how much water we Californians need to save in the future. This PPIC reports says that, with new conservation methods, we should be able to meet the demands that a population of 50 million people will bring. Of course, that's making the assumption that our current supply is going to stay the same. I think that's a big error. Who knows how much water we are going to lose as the glaciers melt, snow falls as rain, and the planet warms up?

If you are going through hell, keep going.

~ Sir Winston Churchill

Marin County, February 13, 1977

Medieval philosophers who imagined what hell must look like almost always described it as a place of fire. The human subconscious fears fire, because fire burns and causes great pain. In medieval times, outlaws were sometimes burned at the stake. Everyone fears fire and the damage it can do. Fires often accompany drought, and when they start, there is often no water to put them out.

Fire authorities took great pains during the drought of 1977 to make sure that fire did not get a foothold in the tinder-dry woods. Elaborate measures were taken to ensure that fires would not get started accidentally in the rolling hills and open spaces that characterizes so much of the county. But human nature and hard work only go so far. Fate has a hand in our future too.

"We were just plain lucky. It could have been a disaster," said Marin County Fire Chief Richard Pedroli, whose department increased fire prevention, beefed up fire patrols, and asked cooperation from citizens and the media.

Pedroli's department found that, on average, 45-50 tons of accumulated burnable material per acre was scattered around the Mount Tam watershed. His team made contingency plans for a holocaust. An elaborate mutual aid program was set up among all Marin County fire departments. Accelerated fire prevention programs were installed. Everything that could be done, was done. Expanded patrols of watershed lands were launched. Clearing of overgrown fire trails became a priority.

On high fire danger days, parts of the Mount Tam watershed were closed to the public. The entire Bolinas-Stinson Beach road was closed for two years. Three water tanker planes were stationed nearby at Santa Rosa.

Everyone in fire prevention crossed their fingers and toes and prayed for the best. The public didn't know it, but had a blaze started in the vast woodlands that cover much of rural Marin, there would have been little anyone could do to stop it. While the drought threatened to destroy lawns, gardens, plants and trees, wildfire had the potential to destroy everything.

27 / The pipeline commences

I find that the harder I work, the more luck I seem to have.

~ Thomas Jefferson

Marin County, February 13, 1977

"Well gentlemen, what we have here is a classic good news/bad news situation. The good news is that we have the go-ahead to build a pipeline across the Richmond-San Rafael Bridge. The bad news is that we don't have any money with which to do it."

Diet was in a very fine mood as he invited his top engineers into his office. Suddenly, all the clouds of confusion that had been plaguing him for almost two years had been blown away, and all that remained was a simple engineering problem. How to build a pipeline across a bridge, with no budget and also in record time? The fact that nobody on his staff had any idea how to do it was not important. Engineers are engineers, he thought. They are born to solve problems, and the harder the problem, the better, so they are gonna love this one.

"So that's the bad news?" asked Ron Theisen, one of Diet's top guys, young enough to love a challenge but experienced enough to know

231

what was possible and what wasn't. "We don't have any money to build it with? How's our credit at the bank?"

"Don't you worry about the money," replied Diet. "That's my problem. I'll get it somewhere. Go ahead and spend whatever you need. Money is not the problem. That's not the bad news."

"OK, I'll bite," said Theisen. "If we don't have any budget whatsoever to work with, what's the real problem?"

"Well, the bad part is that we have to construct the pipeline by June 1, which is when we will be able to get water into the pipe from East Bay MUD. We have to be as ready as our partners in our planning."

"Wait a minute," said Theisen, "June 1? That's only three months from now. We can't design, build and complete an entire six-mile pipeline in three months. Can't be done. We don't even know where to start."

"Not true at all, chief," replied Diet. "It's three and a half months from now. Plenty of time if we don't waste it talking all day."

"Let's get serious here for a minute," said Ralph Gertz, who was already a civil engineer when Diet was still in college, and was used to doing things in a logical fashion. "We are talking six and a half miles of piping, plus two pump stations? We don't have any money, we don't know the first thing about where we are going to get the piping, and we have to build two pump houses without owning any land on either side of the bridge, and we have to do it in 14 weeks?"

"Don't worry about the pump houses, that's my concern," said Diet, "all you have to do is design and build the pipeline."

"OK, that's simple, forget the pump houses. So let's knock a few days off the timeline right there," said Gertz, puffing on his pipe. "Then we can probably get the job done by Christmas, which is about nine months from now. Since it cannot possibly not rain three years in a row, we'll get the pipeline up and running just when it does start to rain."

"Sorry guys, we need the pipeline right now, not then. And please don't tell me it won't rain three years in a row," said Diet. "Three months ago I told the board that there was about a 1 percent chance of it not raining again this year, and look where we are now. So here's the deal. We need the pipeline up and running before summer. We are going to lose a lot of livestock, expensive real estate and property values if we go all summer trying to get by on emergency rations, which are getting tighter everyday. Plus we might lose this deal. There are lots of people unhappy with the deal. We can't sit here and say it can't be done. Got to be done now, or else."

"Or else what, Diet?" said Gertz. "What's the 'or else'? Or else it doesn't get done in three months?"

"No, Ralph me boy, that's not it," said Diet, standing up and opening the door. "Or else I will find myself some people who will do it. That's the 'or else' we are talking about."

Diet held the door open. There was complete silence in the room. Each man was lost in his own train of thought, mentally canceling weekends and holidays and calculating exactly what would need to be done.

"Can we hire more personnel?" asked Theisen. "As many as we need?"

"I already told you, hang the cost," said Diet, looking Theisen right in the eye. "Money is not the issue here. Go get yourself a marching band. I'll get the money, somehow, somewhere. What matters is that we have finally found a source of water. All we have to do now is get the damned water here to Marin. Immediately. Enough said. So, gentlemen, where do we stand?"

It was so quiet you could hear the clock on the wall ticking. Diet held the door open, looking at each man one by one. Finally Theisen put up his hand.

"Can I ask a simple question?"

"Fire away, Ron," said Diet, keeping his hand on the door.

"How the heck do you expect us to get started, what with the door wide open letting in flies?"

"Atta boy, Ron," said Diet, closing the door, rolling up his sleeves and sitting down at his desk. "OK, let's get started."

The Safe Drinking Water Act of 1974 represents the first time that public drinking water supplies were protected on a federal level in the United States. Amendments were made to the SDWA in 1986 and 1996.

~ Water Facts.com

Berkeley, California, 2006

There has been a lot of discussion among some of the students as to whether or not there is such a thing as global warming. We all read the newspapers, and we all know that there is uncertainty among some scientists and members of the government as to the real nature of the phenomenon, as to whether it is man-made or not.

Let me say, first of all, that we are not discussing the totality of global warming in this class. Our emphasis is only on water, and to what extent the global fresh water situation is being affected by climate change. To that end, I must say that it is a proven fact that the planet is warming up, and it is most certainly proven that the cause for the rise in the temperature has been an accumulation of greenhouse gases in the atmosphere, chiefly carbon dioxide.

For instance, data from the Mauna Loa Observatory in Hawaii, regarded as one of the most accurate on the planet for measuring changes to the upper atmosphere, shows that levels of carbon dioxide have reached historic highs. According to lab director Pieter Tans, the latest measurements are the highest ever recorded, but, more worrisome, they also follow an upward trend. Since 1958, when measurements were first taken, there has been an increase in carbon levels every year. While the rate increase slowed a bit during the past year, Tans warns us that the overall growth rate during the past decade has been accelerating twice as fast as during the 1960s.

Kill my boss? Do I dare live out the American dream?

~ Homer Simpson

Marin County, February 15, 1977

Diet was on the phone with a parts manufacturer in the East Bay.

"We already have a buyer for that pipe," said Doug Marsden, of Peninsula Piping. "There will be a premium to be paid if we cancel or postpone the contract."

"I don't care what the cost is," said Diet. "Tell the other water district to stuff it. No, wait; just say the Marin water district faces an emergency. We need the piping more than they do, and we can't afford to wait."

"I'll have to check and call you back."

"What's that? No, I don't want you to call me back," said Diet. "I need an answer right now. Cancel that, the only answer I'll accept is 'yes,' and I need the piping right away."

"How much piping are we talking here?"

"Enough for six miles," said Diet. "Of course I'll be happy to pay a premium."

Although CalTrans had given the MMWD permission to use the bridge, the agency had a few stipulations. First, the pipeline would have to be installed on the outer lane of the upper deck. Second, it had to be supported on wooden cradles. CalTrans had a fear of earthquakes, and of the pipeline somehow twisting or moving with temperature fluctuations, so they refused to allow the pipeline to be laid directly on the bridge deck itself. The bridge itself also moved in the wind and with traffic. The cradles would have to be designed to suit the job, and they would have to be custom made somewhere, because they didn't exist.

There was also the question of which company would build the pipeline itself. That problem was a little easier to solve, because many companies in the Bay Area would jump at such a lucrative job. Of course, the main problem was that the MMWD did not have the money to pay for the pipeline, or for the construction, but as long as nobody asked the $64,000 question, Diet was not going to volunteer that small tidbit of information.

Ron Theisen knocked on Diet's door and entered.

"Great news. We found a company down in Texas that will drop what they are doing and manufacture the pipe couplings. For a premium, of course. But they say shipping it here is a problem. If it goes by ship, we are looking at the Panama Canal route, and that will take a few months."

"Forget it. Tell them to airfreight the couplings in. We want them in three weeks."

"Air freight? Six miles worth of couplings? Are you kidding? Do you have any idea what that would cost?"

"No idea whatsoever, and I don't want to know either. At least, not today. Tell them to make the couplings and air freight them here and give me an exact date when we can expect delivery. When you know all the details, then tell me what it will cost. I don't want to know today. I have a bigger problem."

"I'm not sure I want to know what that is."

"We are going to need a pump house on the east side of the bridge.

West side, no problem. I can twist a few arms here in Marin to get the land. But I haven't been able to find any property for sale near the bridge in Richmond. All I need is a patch about 20 feet by 30 feet, but there's no such real estate available. I've got an oil company that will sell me five acres of worthless abandoned parking lot, but I do know that five acres of waterfront is one thing we can't afford. "

Meetings are indispensable when you don't want to do anything.

~ John Kenneth Galbraith

In between meetings with various members of various water boards, and meetings with his staff, and the obligatory morning meetings with the media, Diet faced daily face-to-face meetings with groups, companies and individuals who were in an uproar over their skyrocketing water bills. Especially angry were large consumers of water, such as hospitals, which found it very difficult to cut back and which — unlike restaurants, car washes and laundromats — were not in a position to increase charges to their patients. The sick and elderly must be cared for, drought or not.

MMWD staff contacted each and every large consumer of water in the entire district, starting a survey of water consumption while advising clients of various ways that even more water could be saved. In return, the hospitals and retirement homes reported back to MMWD staff exactly how much water they were currently saving, and what methods they were employing to cut back even further.

For example, the Redwoods, a retirement home in Mill Valley, advised MMWD staff of their in-house water conservation program.

"We have 150 independent living apartments, 150 residential care apartments, and a 58-bed skilled nursing facility," wrote administrator Mr. Jean Naquin. "For 1976, our daily rate of consumption was 32,238 gallons in the spring. As of our last billing we have reduced our consumption down to 19,500 gallons per day. We have stopped completely any watering of grass and trees. We have taken measures in our kitchen and nursing facilities to conserve water. We are considering cutting back use of the dishwashers, and reducing frequency of baths for patients, but we must ascertain the health risk first. I don't think we can cut back any further without compromising the health and safety of our residents."

At Nazareth House, a long-term care facility in San Rafael, Mother John explained that they, too, were doing their part.

"In summer our average daily usage is 15,265 gallons per day. Our current usage is down to 8,200 gallons per day," she wrote. "We no longer serve water with a meal. We are using paper plates for meals, but the expense is prohibitive. We have had individual talks with all residents about water conservation and we speak about it at Mass. Last summer we drilled a well, but found that the water is not potable. The patients are receiving fewer baths, and we are changing the bedding less frequently. As for your inquiry as to how much more we will be able to cut back, I find that I am unable to answer that question."

New York City, June 8, 2010

Janet Spalding studied the report her assistant producer had handed her first thing that morning. She turned to her head producer and tossed the report on the table.

"I'm not convinced we can get the ratings we need unless we have the President make an announcement about replacing Kyoto," she said. "All the polls say the environment has dropped off the radar recently, what with the economy going down the dumper. For the ratings I want, we're going to need more than what we've got so far."

"Every indication from the White House is that some sort of major announcement will be forthcoming shortly, but it won't be today," said

Tom Jenkins, her senior producer. "But everything else is falling into place nicely. Every single one of our correspondents has some sort of breaking news lined up, and we can't sit on the entire bundle for much longer, or else we are going to get scooped. Heck, we already got scooped on that Maldive Islands evacuation plan story. It's not every day that an entire country just packs up and moves."

"We gave that story away, if I remember correctly," said Spalding. "It was going to leak like a broken faucet anyway. That freelancer we used was available to the highest bidder, so we tossed it to Global for free and now they owe us big time. We don't have anybody in Southeast Asia who is any good, and that freelancer wasn't going to sit on the story for much longer, and we may need Global for the special."

"Speaking of, we need to go over all the correspondents again before the end of the week," said Jenkins. "Some of the data has changed, plus our guy in Bangladesh is making noises like he's drowning. The monsoon there has flooded him out of his hotel and now he wants to report from India instead."

"If he gets on a plane, he might as well fly home and pick up his paycheck along with his pink slip," said Spalding. "I want pictures of him doing the dog paddle. If the whole country is going to float out to sea, I want him on a raft shooting images. Tell him that directly, yourself."

"You got it."

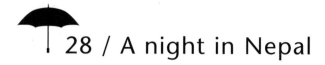

28 / A night in Nepal

Before you criticize someone, walk a mile in their shoes. That way, you'll be a mile from them, and you'll have their shoes.

~ Jack Handey, humorist

Nepal, June 7, 2010

The sun went behind the mountain with surprising suddenness. The moment it disappeared, the temperature dropped like a stone. Immediately the trekking party, which had stripped down to T-shirts and pants in the blazing afternoon heat, started putting on layers. The sherpas broke out the tents and put them up in a matter of minutes. The landscape faded from bright white to pink, with long black shadows flinging themselves off the mountain like slingshots.

"Put yourself in my shoes," said Will to Bob Walsh, who was in a sullen mood, brought on by a high-altitude headache and Will's stubborn insistence on camping high above the lake. He wasn't happy at all with Will's stupid grandstanding at a crucial moment in the trek. He hadn't planned on the party staying at the lake anyway; at 15,000 feet it was way too high an elevation, and he had planned for the party to descend to

240

Beding at 12,000 feet. "If I told you I wanted to come all the way up here, you would have said no."

"Of course I would have said no," replied Walsh, fumbling with a Power Bar. "I don't lead expeditions into danger, and you wouldn't have booked my company if it had a reputation for doing stupid or dangerous things."

"Hey, look at the fabulous light," replied Will, breaking out his video camera. "Sunset over the Himalayas, a dark green lake below, black clouds down over the plains, crystal white mountains. Have you ever seen a prettier sight?"

Walsh said nothing. He was too angry to argue, and too preoccupied with getting everyone fed before the light disappeared. They were running low on packaged food, and would likely have to subsist on yak meat and barley meal for the next few days. The sherpas were trying to cook on their Primus stove. They prepared freeze-dried dinners for their clients, then supped on some *chaura*, specially treated rice, along with *tsampa*, the Tibetan form of coarse barley flour stirred to a lukewarm porridge. They topped off their meal with *pika tscha*, the ill-reputed Tibetan buttered tea made of Chinese tea, salt, and soda mixed with rancid yak butter.

Will pulled out a small bottle of orange brandy and tipped a few drops into everyone's tea, a special treat at the highlight of the trip.

"I want to apologize to you guys for making you come up here," said Will. "First thing in the morning I'll get video coverage of the lake, the dam, the sluice gate and the whole scene from up here, then we can leave immediately. We'll be back down to Na by noon."

Dave Moore said nothing. He also had a headache, and was in a foul mood too. It was way too high up here for him to sleep, and just the thought of avalanches was sure to keep him awake all night.

Usually, terrible things that are done with the excuse that progress requires them are not really progress at all, but just terrible things.

~ Russell Baker, political commentator

Berkeley, California, 2006

California is rich in many ways, class, but despite what you think, being rich in water isn't really one of them. If you look at the map a little more closely, you'll find that the supply of water is separated from the demand in both space and time. Over three-quarters of California's water supply comes in the winter and spring months, in the form of rain and snow, but the greatest demand for it is in the summer and fall. Also, three-quarters of the supply falls north and east of Sacramento, while most demand occurs well south and west of the state capital.

In the future, demand for water in California will be made much more difficult than it already is, because climate change will increase the spring runoff and reduce the late summer runoff. According to the Union of Concerned Scientists, the latest climate projections suggest that the temperature will increase substantially in the coming century. The exact rate of increase will have much to do with the amount and timing of further emissions of fossil fuels into the atmosphere. Heat-trapping gases will certainly raise the temperature, but we don't know yet what amounts of greenhouse gas pollution will be permitted in the future.

The lower end of some estimates indicates that planetary temperatures will rise about 4 to 6 degrees within a century. The higher-end estimates range from 7 to 10 degrees. Summer temperatures are expected to rise more substantially than previously estimated. Winter precipitation is estimated to either rise slightly, or drop up to 30 percent. Previous estimates had predicted that there would be huge increases in precipitation thanks to global warming, but the latest projections show a different picture.

Rising winter and spring temperatures will have profound impact on the Sierra Nevada snowpack. Warmer winter rainstorms and earlier spring snowmelt will change the timing of mountain water runoff. Water managers will have to choose between capturing winter runoff for summer use, or maintaining reservoir space for spring flood control. Lesser stream flow in summer months will disrupt California's water supply system.

Lesser stream flows in spring or summer will also require costly changes to California's intricate infrastructure of aqueducts and reservoirs. Transporting water from the Sierra, or from the Colorado River, to Southern California may be far more costly with different water flows. Great changes will be needed in the hodgepodge of institutions that currently administer California's water supply and delivery system.

Projections for California's future temperatures show two different scenarios, depending if and when environmental protection action is taken to reduce or eliminate greenhouse gas emissions. The most optimistic projection envisions a rapid transformation to clean energy technologies, a transition that would allow greenhouse gases to peak by mid-century and start to decline below current levels by 2100. The pessimistic projection sees continued and intensive reliance on fossil fuels, allowing heat-trapping emissions to continue to grow throughout the century. Heat-trapping gasses remain in the atmosphere for many decades. The climate of the next century is dependent on the actions that are taken during the next decade.

Average winter temperatures in California are projected to rise 2.4 degrees Fahrenheit by mid-century under both projections. By the turn of the next century winter temperatures will rise by 4 degrees under the best-case scenario and between 5.5 and 7 degrees in the worst case. The degree of temperature increase will vary greatly from region to region within the state. Generally, inland areas — already the hottest parts of the state — will get hotter than the statewide average, with the coastal areas also seeing higher temperatures but not as hot as inland regions.

Using these forecasts, winter precipitation, which now accounts for most of California's annual total, should decrease between 15 and 30 percent. If the more optimistic temperature levels are realized, then California may experience winter precipitation increases of about 5 percent. Earlier projections, using older data, had predicted a doubling or even tripling of California's winter precipitation, an optimistic scenario not likely to be realized as long as fossil fuels are burned as an energy source.

∏epal, June 7, 2010

Where does the white go when the snow melts?

~ Anonymous

As soon as the sun went behind the mountains, the temperature dropped below freezing and the expedition members snuggled into their sleeping bags inside their tents. Perched on a small ledge of gravel at the top of the glacier, the tents were jammed close together to take advantage of the only flat space they had been able to find. Each member of the trek was left alone with his thoughts. Would some rocks come tumbling down overnight and strike someone asleep in the tents? Would they get safely down in the morning? Would it rain or snow?

"Seems like the monsoon is way early this year, don't you think?" said Walsh, lying in his bag, unable to sleep.

"Yeah," replied Will, from the sleeping bag into which he was curled up like a ball, "but it doesn't always arrive on schedule. In fact some years it doesn't arrive at all. Way up here, at this height, who knows what will happen. Maybe it'll snow."

"We've got several more days of hiking after this," said Walsh. "We are going to get wet."

"Ah, we got wet before," said Will.

"Yes, we got wet earlier," replied Walsh, "but we were down low and those were spring showers. Getting stuck in the monsoon at this elevation isn't something I planned on. We should be down at Beding right now, heading east first thing in the morning. I don't want to be stuck up at 15,000 feet if heavy rain starts to fall."

"Maybe it will snow at this elevation."

"It's too warm for snow," replied Walsh, "a lot hotter than I remember it ever being in the spring. The freezing level up here can rise as high as 16,500 feet, but if we drop down to 8,000 feet it will rain like hell when the monsoon starts. The rivers will rise so high we can't cross. We have some bridge crossings to do, and I don't want to get stuck trying to cross a Himalayan bridge in the middle of a downpour."

Some 97 percent of liquid freshwater is stored underground in aquifers. Up to 2 billion people, a third of the world's population, rely on it. Aquifers are most severely depleted in parts of India, China, the U.S., North Africa and the Middle East. It can take centuries for aquifers to recharge, so the world is currently running a groundwater overdraft of 200 billion cubic meters a year. Pollution is a major problem; there are over 10 million different synthetic chemicals in use today.

~ UNEP, Global Environment Outlook 3

Berkeley, California, 2006

Continuing with our study of the Himalayan region, class, it's important to remember that climate varies with altitude. At about 6,000 feet, the average summer temperature is a nice and balmy 75 degrees. When you get up to 13,000 feet, it is rarely above freezing except in the daytime in summer. Down in the valleys, summer temperatures can soar up to 95 degrees. In the eastern Himalayas especially, rainfall can be quite heavy and floods are common.

Depending on elevation, temperature and precipitation can change very quickly. Within the space of a few minutes the sunshine can disappear and there can be monsoons, floods, high winds, snowstorms and rain. Heavy rainstorms are possible during July and August.

The Indian Meteorological Service divides the year into four seasons. The relatively dry, cool winters run from December through February. The dry, hot summer starts as early as March and runs through May. The southwest monsoon arrives sometime in June and continues through September when the predominating southwest maritime winds bring rains to most of the country.

Theories vary about the origins of monsoons. Over the centuries, observers have attributed monsoons to thermal changes in the Asian landmass. More recently, meteorologists have added other factors, like the barrier of the Himalayas and the sun's northward tilt, which shifts the jet stream north. Hot air over southern Asia during April and May creates low-pressure zones that suck in cool, wet winds from the Indian Ocean. These circumstances set off a rush of moisture-rich air from the southern seas all over southern Asia.

The pre-monsoon season of April and May is a transition period, often with many cloud-free days, but temperatures are on the rise. By mid-May, the freezing level can rise as high as 16,500 feet at times. This period coincides with significant snowmelt, which causes rivers and streams to rise substantially. Warmer temperatures increase the risk of avalanches.

On some peaks, precipitation has been observed five times greater on the mountain peaks than in the valley itself, usually falling during the day when strong upslope and valley winds occur. In the valley, rain may fall only between late afternoon and midnight, depending on the winds.

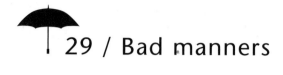

29 / Bad manners

One of the symptoms of an approaching nervous breakdown is the belief that one's work is terribly important.

~ Bertrand Russell

Marin County, February 16, 1977

The phone rang at the Stroeh home. It was suppertime, not a time when the family wanted to be interrupted by phone calls.

"Kids, if that's one of your friends, please tell them to call back later," said Marcia, putting plates on the table. "Suppertime is family time, not phone time."

Christina picked up the phone. At 14, she was the oldest of the three girls, and the most responsible.

"Hello, this is Christina."

"Is Dietrich Stroeh there?" said a strong male voice.

"No, he's at a meeting."

"He's always in a meeting," said the caller. "I called him at his office about a dozen times and he's always in a meeting. Saying you are in a meeting is just an excuse when you don't want to talk to people."

"Maybe you'd better talk to my mom," said Christina, handing the phone over while making faces to her sisters.

"Is this Mrs. Stroeh?" asked the caller.

"Yes, it is. Who is this? It's dinner time, and we don't talk on the phone during dinner in this family."

"I knew someone would be home if I called at this hour. I want to talk to Dietrich Stroeh," said the caller in an angry tone. "You can never get through to him at his office. Now I see you can't even get through to him at home."

"That's because he isn't here. He's out at an urgent meeting. Who is this? If you are a member of the media, you can simply show up at the water district offices at 11 in the morning and he will answer your questions then."

"No, I'm not in the media," responded the man on the other end. "And if I go down to the water district I just may punch him in the nose. Do you know what this so-called water allotment is doing to my business?"

"Of course, I don't," replied Marcia, now angry herself. "You're not the only person in Marin who is suffering because there is no water. Everybody is."

"Yeah, but there is only one person who can do something about it," said the caller, "and he doesn't even have the guts to answer the phone. If he spends all his time hiding, how can he get anything done? Tell him to barge some water into Marin soon, before we all go broke."

"I suggest that you tell him that yourself," yelled Marcia, "and please don't call here again."

With that she slammed down the phone and turned to the girls.

"That's why we don't answer the phone at dinner time," she said.

"Mom, where is Dad?" asked Jody, the second-oldest daughter.

"He's in a meeting," said Marcia, angrily. "He is always in a meeting."

If everything seems under control, you're just not going fast enough.

~ Mario Andretti

Diet was at a meeting. In fact, he was explaining his latest water conservation actions to his board of directors, and updating them on the latest meetings he'd had with major consumers of water, including laundromat owners and the directors of various county hospitals. Even by sharpening their pencils to a fine point, it was becoming apparent to Diet that you can't get blood from a stone, and that everybody was doing the very best they could to save water.

"Since our last board meeting, I met with representatives of the commercial laundry owners to see how our latest rules were affecting them," he said. "Human nature being what it is, since we ordered the last rationing cuts more and more people have been taking their laundry out to the laundromats so they can save on their home water bill. My conservation committee would like to ask the board to consider postponing the installation of the flow restrictors in the event that a laundromat exceeds their allotment for the first two billing periods."

In January, MMWD directives had been issued to all households and commercial water users across the county. All businesses were handed a flat 57 percent cut across the board. Households were allotted water according to a sliding scale, according to the number of residents in the house, ranging from 49 gallons per day for a single resident to 32 gallons per person per day for a household of seven or more people. MMWD was billing its customers on a two-month cycle. Those who didn't cut their usage down to their allotment were automatically cut off.

"I have here some more correspondence received from various operators of convalescent hospitals and long-term care facilities. I have to say that it's obvious that everybody is doing their part," said Diet, pulling out a huge stack of letters. "For instance, Walter Hekimian of the Terra Linda Convalescent Hospital reports that they have cut their usage from 11,400 gallons a day down to 9,400. From what I have been reading, I think that some in-house restrictions have actually been too severe, and too close to the danger point of risking contamination and infection problems."

"Over at Marin Convalescent Hospital, they have installed buckets in all showers, and the captured water is being used on plants. Kaiser Hospital tells us that whirlpool baths have been replaced by hot packs, the air conditioners have been turned down, and the water fountains have been turned off."

"I have to say that I think our staff and inspectors have been very vigilant with all commercial operators. My information is that abuses by homeowners to date have been very rare. In fact, I think we can safely say there are about 170,000 volunteer meter readers in the county right now, and about 170,000 water police too. The people of Marin County are doing a fantastic job in conserving water."

Your grandchildren will likely find it incredible — or even sinful — that you burned up a gallon of gasoline to fetch a pack of cigarettes!

~ Dr. Paul MacCready, Jr., aeronautical engineer

Berkeley, California, 2006

Sometimes, class, when we are discussing the effects of climate change on our planet, we tend to overlook the most vulnerable people in our society, the elderly. While

251

it is possible for younger people to move their place of residence, or deal with the various effects like heat, droughts or floods, the elderly have no such mobility or ability to deal with climate change. Think of it this way. You may be young now, but the grim scenario that we are painting in this geography course, of a future where it is going to be much hotter, is the future in which you kids are going to live. You kids will be the elderly people affected by this climate change. How does that strike you?

A recent scientific study — conducted by 19 scientists from several universities and research institutions, including Stanford University, the University of California and the Scripps Institution of Oceanography — finds that by the end of the century, rising temperatures could lead to a huge increase in heat-related deaths. Since people are living longer and longer these days, just imagine this scenario. You kids will be about 90 years old when this happens.

One study, from the National Academy of Sciences, gives the most detailed projection yet of changes in California as temperatures increase. If the use of fossil fuel continues upward at its present rate — which is something we don't want to even think about, but is quite possible — the study determined that summertime high temperatures in California could increase by 15 degrees in some inland cities.

Have you ever been out to Death Valley? In the summer? These temperature increases will put the climate of certain inland cities like Fresno, Stockton, Modesto and Bakersfield, on par with that of Death Valley now. The study also sees a reduction of somewhere between 73 and 90 percent in the snowpack in the Sierra Nevada.

So guess what happens to water supplies for the San Francisco Bay Area and the Central Valley? If we see significant increases in the use of renewable energy, like wind and solar power, the study says that fossil fuel emissions could push average high temperatures up by only 4 to 6 degrees. Even so, Yosemite Valley will then be as hot as Sacramento is today.

In cities like Los Angeles, the number of days of extreme heat could increase by four to eight times. Heat-related deaths in Los Angeles, which averaged 165 annually during the 1990s, could grow as much as seven times.

Higher temperatures could also have devastating consequences for wine grapes, which could ripen more quickly and be of poorer quality. So, troubles ahead in Napa and Sonoma valleys. Cows will produce less milk. In fact, agriculture as a whole will be greatly affected by rising temperatures, and agriculture is sure to be allocated far less water than it receives now. But never mind the farmers for now. Just think what the world will be like when you kids get old.

By 2025, two-thirds of the world's people will be facing water stress. The global demand for water will have grown by over 4 percent by then.

~ NJAWWA.com

---

30 / Looking to desal

The American people are very generous people and will forgive almost any weakness, with the possible exception of stupidity.

~ Will Rogers

Marin County, February 26, 1977

It was just after 4a.m. when the phone rang. Diet turned on the light above the bed and struggled to find his glasses.

"Who is it?"

"Mr. Stroeh? This is Reggie Miller here at KCBS. How are you this morning?"

"Reggie, do you have any idea what time it is?"

"Sure, it's quarter after four."

"I'm glad that they have clocks down at KCBS. And phones. It's too bad they don't have any common sense," said Diet. "What the hell are you doing, calling me at this time?"

"I've been trying to get a response from you for two days, Mr. Stroeh," responded Miller. "You're a hard man to get hold of."

"How about this, Reggie? When I get hold of you, I'm going to throttle you."

"Hey, you don't have to be that way, Mr. Stroeh."

"Let me repeat it again, Reggie. It's four in the morning. I was up working until midnight last night. I was asleep when you called. What way do you want me to be?"

"Well, now that I have you, how about a quote on the San Quentin situation? I was down there interviewing the warden and he said the prisoners were going to save enough water to get Marin through the whole summer."

"Do they still have the death penalty down there at San Quentin, Reggie?"

"Well, I guess so."

"Good, because I will call the warden and recommend you for the position," said Diet, slamming down the phone. He turned to Marcia, who had woken during the exchange.

"What kind of idiot phones people at four o'clock in the morning?"

"The same kind of idiots that phone here at six, seven, eight and nine o'clock," she responded, reaching for the light switch. "Only they don't happen to work for radio stations, nor are they usually that polite."

Irrigation of the land with seawater desalinated by fusion power is ancient. It's called "rain."

~ Michael McClary, author

Berkeley, California, 2006

Just north of San Quentin in Marin County, along the shore you'll find the Marin Rod and Gun Club, the Marin County Wastewater Treatment Plant, and — these days — a small test desalination plant on which the staff of the MMWD is conducting tests to see if it's possible to turn San Pablo Bay (which is mostly salt water) into a source of drinking water.

The $1.2 million pilot plant is studying various ways of treating, filtering and desalting the waters of San Pablo Bay. Depending on what is learned, and the political climate, a full-scale plant could provide Marin with 5 million to 10 million gallons of drinking water a day, enough to serve about 15,000 homes a year.

If the desal plant is built, the county would still require conservation in periods of drought. The district now pipes Russian River water to 184,510 customers in Southern and central Marin, but the only available pipeline has reached capacity. The district built a pilot desalination plant in 1990 and operated it for four months, but desalination was deemed to be too expensive at that time. Studies would also determine whether the desalination process eliminates pharmaceuticals, mercury and pesticides.

Estimates are that it would cost as much as $100 million to build a full desalination plant in Marin, and construct a new network of pipelines. MMWD officials won't commit at this date as to the source of power for the plant, other than to say they will buy it from PG&E. The desalination plant, if built, would be 100 percent publicly owned and operated.

I gather that several other desalination plants are proposed for California. Although the Marin County desal plant would be publicly owned and operated, at least six of these other proposed facilities would be privately owned, or operated under joint private-public ownership. Making water a profitable commodity will inevitably lead to changes in conservation efforts in California. As the cost of desalinizing continues to decline and the possibility of profit rises, municipal supplies of water run the risk of being taken over by private companies. Water reclamation and water quality could be compromised by the profit motive. It would also remove our largest constraint to endless population growth in the state, which is a limited supply of fresh water. New and endless sources of fresh water could result in more population growth and the need for more infrastructure.

There is no such thing as an infinite resource. Currently we have a consumerist lifestyle in California that seems to require all of us endlessly consuming more and more of everything. Even in Marin — hey, especially in Marin — you can see that happening. We have larger cars, larger homes and — especially this — we have much larger people. In our technologically fixated society, we think technology can fix anything. Just like the creation of hybrid and hydrogen cars, desalination will allow us to keep consuming without ever conserving.

Altogether, the proposed desalination plants along the shores of the Pacific would provide water for approximately 170,000 households. As technological advances make desal increasingly cost-effective and as the cost of importing fresh water from faraway sources to cities increases, there will be a bigger and bigger push for more desal plants.

The prospect of limitless supplies of water from an untapped resource comes just at a time when California is finally noticing its water limitations. According to the Pacific Institute in Oakland, despite the state's endless growth, California could meet its future water needs, up to 11 million more Californians, simply through conservation.

The use of solar energy has not been opened up because the oil industry does not own the sun.

~ Ralph Nader, quoted in Linda Botts, ed., "Loose Talk," 1980

Desalination is common in other parts of the world, particularly the Middle East, where Israel and Saudi Arabia have both built desal plants to provide much of their drinking water. Worldwide, more than 15,000 plants are operating. The reason that desalination has never taken hold here in the USA is because, until lately, plentiful freshwater supplies and high costs kept it from being competitive.

Today, however, population growth in coastal areas is straining traditional water sources in California, Texas, Florida and other regions. Technological advances have nudged the cost of desalinated water closer to that of traditional freshwater sources such as lakes, rivers and aquifers. Aquifers are our natural underground water storage systems that serve millions of people. In some regions, desalination can squeeze more out of depleted aquifers by treating groundwater that's naturally brackish.

Pressure for fresh supplies of drinking water will intensify mostly in coastal areas, where 53 percent of U.S. residents live on just 17 percent of the land. A study by the National Oceanic and Atmospheric Administration estimates that 27 million more people will live on American coastlines by 2015.

Some California officials say desalination plants will take pressure off expensive imported supplies, such as water from the Colorado River. Critics, however, point out that three-quarters of the state's water is currently used by agriculture. Crops such as cotton, alfalfa and rice are low-value crops, water-intensive and heavily subsidized. Eliminating these crops from subsidies could create a potentially large new source of water, removing the need to build desal plants which are, by the way, often powered by polluting fossil fuels. More on that in another class.

Marin County, February 28, 1977

At the morning press conference in front of the MMWD offices, media reps were having a field day with Diet. They knew something was up, but they couldn't pin him down.

"You're looking a little more chipper today, Diet," said a reporter from the local newspaper. "What's up, did an iceberg beach itself on the Marin Headlands?"

"There has been some progress made in negotiations to find and import water into Marin County," answered Diet. "As for the penguins, we have worked out a deal with the Marin Humane Society to have the birds kept at the animal shelter until such time as we can afford to ship them back, along with all the journalists who are apparently fond of free rides."

"Aside from the penguins, Diet," said Joel Bartlett of KPIX, "what does the United States Weather Service have to say about the 30-day forecast and the chance of rain in March?"

"I say my prayers, but the only reliable way of knowing what is happening with the weather is to tune in to you, Joel."

"Well, there's a chance of rain in the next few weeks, as far as I understand," said Joel, "but there was a good chance of rain in January and February too, and look where we are now."

"Where we are, gentlemen, is up a creek without a paddle if we don't find ourselves some water soon, so if you don't mind I'll just cut short this chat and go look for some."

"Why not simply make it rain, Diet?" said a voice from the back.

"If I was able to make fantasies come true," said Diet over his shoulder, heading back into the building, "I'd be working for the media."

31 / The desal solution

I refuse to have a battle of wits with an unarmed person.

~ Bumper sticker

Marin County, February 28, 1977

It was late in the evening. Marcia was out visiting a sick friend and Diet was at one of his many meetings, so Christina was babysitting her two sisters. At 14, she was old enough to make dinner and make her sisters go to bed, although this time they were not cooperating and Christina was starting to lose her cool.

"If Mom comes home and sees that you are not in bed she is going to get mad at you," she said, standing in the doorway of the living room where her two sisters were watching TV. "She's also going to get mad at me if I don't make you get into bed. So turn that TV off."

"In a minute," said Jody. "The program is almost over."

"Not in a minute," snapped Christina, "you've been saying that for 20 minutes."

The phone suddenly rang in the kitchen and Christina went to pick it up.

"Hello, is Dietrich Stroeh there?"

"No, he's not, can I take a message?"

"Yeah, you can take a message all right. You tell him that if he doesn't get that pipeline connected soon, I'm going to come over to his house with a pipe myself and connect with his head."

"I beg your pardon?" said Christina. "What did you say?"

"You heard me, kid. Give your head a shake. This is a warning. If he doesn't get off his ass and get his job done, there are going to be some serious consequences. That stupid board of directors doesn't want any new water, does it? So that we never build any new houses? This bullshit has been going on for too long. A lot of people are pissed off, and we're tired of your father making jokes on TV every day."

"Are you threatening my dad? I'm going to call the police," said Christina, her voice shaking. "How dare you threaten him? Do you know how hard he's working?"

"Yeah, consider this a threat. I know where you live. You got a nice big house, and your father makes a lot of money, and he's on TV every day making jokes," said the caller, his voice rising too. "They should fire him and get rid of that board too, and find some people who know what they're doing."

"So you think it's going to help, phoning here and threatening his kids? You're a really brave guy, aren't you? My father would punch you in the nose if he caught you talking to his kids like this. I'm going to tell him what you said. Give me your name and he'll call you back."

"Ha, you must think I'm really stupid. Like I'm going to give you my name and phone number," yelled the caller. "What I'm going to do is come over to your house sometime. Maybe it's time to light a fire under your dad. Let him know that other people are really suffering while he plays this game of going on TV every day, pretending that he is doing something while nothing ever happens."

"I know who you are," said Christina.

There was a long pause on the other end.

"What?"

"I recognize your voice. I know who you are. I'm going to tell my dad that you called and what you said. Boy, is he going to be mad."

There was a long pause on the other end, and then the line went dead.

"Stupid jerk," said Christina, hanging up the phone.

"Who was that?" said Jody, wandering into the kitchen.

"Somebody who stayed up too late," she replied. "Like you."

I bought some powdered water, but I don't know what to add to it.

~ Steven Wright, comedian

Berkeley, California, 2006

For those of you who have been asking, — no, desalination of saltwater is not a new idea. Ancient mariners used a simple system of desalination centuries ago, what we would call solar distillation. You simply let the sun heat salt water, and what evaporates is condensed on a cooler surface, leaving behind the salt. The idea goes all the way back to Aristotle in the 4th century B.C.

In modern times, the first desal plant was built back in 1862 in Key West, Florida, when Fort Zachary Taylor used a simple form of distillation for its water source. Florida has always had a problem with water, especially its groundwater, which is brackish. Tampa Bay launched a desal plant just a few years ago, with a lot of problems ensuing from the brackish water from where the plant is located.

Instead of using sun to heat water, more recently desal plants started to use artificial heat sources to distill water. You need a lot of energy to do this, so distilled water can end up being expensive. They use distillation aboard large ships these days, and in the Middle East — Saudi Arabia and Kuwait, for instance — because those places have their own oil. The farther away you get from your energy source, the more expensive desal becomes.

Modern desalination plants employ a process known as reverse osmosis. Salt water is forced through a type of membrane, removing most of the salt molecules. Currently it takes about 2,000 gallons of salt water to make 1,000 gallons of fresh water, or a 2–1 ratio. It's expensive, but not as expensive as it used to be because new technology has improved the whole process.

Industry sources tell us that, in the past 20 years or so, the cost of producing membranes has dropped by 86 percent and their productivity has increased by 94 percent. The time it takes to pump water through the membrane has dropped about 50 percent as well, so suddenly the costs of desal are starting to look pretty good, especially as the cost of fresh water acquired from the usual sources, like lakes and reservoirs, continues to rise.

There are about 15,000 desal plants around the world now, producing about 8.5 billion gallons of fresh water daily, with reverse osmosis technology being used in most new plants. One problem with reverse osmosis is that the membranes need fairly clear salt water in order to function well. In Tampa, they found that turbid water can contain organic material that gunks up the works. Desal means you've also got a lot of brine to get rid of, which can be a problem depending on the location of the desal plant.

The third major problem with desal lies in the amount, and source, of the energy that is needed. Many big desal plants are located right next to a power plant, which helps the economics of it all. If there are no transmission lines to be built, there is a discount. Price is important, of course. You can't just suddenly triple the cost of a commodity like water without the voters or consumers being all upset.

Marin County, February 28, 1977

Marcia hung up the phone in anger.

"It never ends," she yelled at Diet. "Media calls, crank calls, always during dinner, every night and now we are getting them late at night. We ought to disconnect the phone."

"I'm sorry, I wish I was here every night so I could deal with them myself," said Diet, lying down on the couch with a wet cloth on his forehead. "Just tell everyone to call me at the office."

"Everybody says they can't get through when they phone the office."

"Who was it this time?"

"Some woman complaining about the fact that her garden has turned to dust and her water bill has gone through the roof, and it's all the fault of the board of directors who refused to allow any new connections as a way to stop any new growth in the county and now even old-timers like her are getting hurt. The same old silly story as always."

"Who else?"

"The local calls are always customers complaining about their water bills and when are we going to get any new water? And the local media asks about politics. The national media always asks about the weather, but the local reporters are always asking about the board of directors dragging their feet, and stuff like that. As if I can comment about it."

"I'm really sorry that you have to take these calls. Maybe you should just hang up on them."

"I tried that. They call back, more angry. But I can't ignore the phone. Half the time it's for the kids, or me."

"I'm pretty frustrated too. My neck is stuck out as far as I can stick it. As a matter of fact, my neck is as sore as hell. Can you do me a favor and rub it?

"I sat down and wrote a letter to the board today."

"What? What did you say in it?"

"Don't worry, I didn't send it. Here, you read it while I rub your neck."

Dear Board of Directors:

After several sleepless nights and tears shed, I feel compelled to write you. I am writing this on my own, as I, too, am unable to leave things unsaid or unresolved. For several years, Dietrich has spent considerable time and emotional energy in smoothing ruffled feathers, cooling down the press, trying to get some unity on the board, keeping over 200 employees together and functioning, and — last but not least — trying to keep water flowing.

He has taken his job very seriously and has contained his frustration repeatedly. There are lots of people wanting to be listened to, no matter what the time of day or night, and each with his own idea of what should or should not be done. He has attended meetings, and more meetings, where nothing was decided. He has kept his cool the entire time.

I realize it's not my place to comment, but when all of you are finished with him, the children and I are the ones who pick up the pieces. We watch him grow old before his time. I realize he could do what the last manager did, and quit, but he has invested 17 years of real concern for the water district and the community and he is truly dedicated to his job. He is a "team player" and I hope the teamwork can be re-established. I just think the responsibility shouldn't be on his head alone.

Sincerely, Marcia

"Whew," said Diet, handing the letter back to Marcia. "Are you going to send it?"

"I don't know, what do you think? Will it make the situation worse?"

"Well, let's see. I have the media on my back, about 170,000 angry customers, you and the kids are mad at me too because I am never home and people are calling here with threats, and now we have the board of directors angry. How about I phone up your mother and insult her so we can add her to the list?"

"When is all this going to end?" said Marcia, quietly.

"Finally," quipped Diet, getting to his feet, "a question I can answer. That's easy. When it rains."

"OK, then, smart guy," retorted Marcia, "if you are so smart, why don't you make it rain then?"

"Geez," said Diet, flopping down in the couch, "here we go again."

For every complex problem, there is a solution that is simple, neat, and wrong.

~ H. L. Mencken

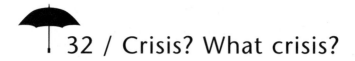

32 / Crisis? What crisis?

Beauty fades . . . dumb is forever.

~ Judge Judy

Marin County, March 2, 1977

Billy Compton turned to Suzie Sweet, lead singer for the band Screaming Meemies.

"Don't bogart that, if you please."

It was a swinging party. Everybody was there. There were record executives, musicians, groupies and assorted hangers-on. Music blasted off the back porch and bounced off the walls of the garage, over to the gigantic hot tub and to the swimming pool where most of the party was gathered. Billy and Suzie were sitting on the edge of the pool, dangling their feet in the water.

"Great party, man," said Suzie, passing over the smoke. "Great record, too. Like your recent one, I mean. You can dance to it."

"You can dance to all of them, if you can dance," replied Billy, regarding Suzie's taste in swimming attire with great appreciation. "Wanna get in the pool?"

"I don't want to get my hair wet."

Suzie's hair looked like a giant Medusa's wig, piled high in deep curls on top of her head. It was her second-best attribute.

"Say, how come you keep the water level in the pool so low?"

Billy looked down into the pool, which was filled with only about two feet of water. The pool was filled to the top when he bought the house, and he wasn't sure exactly how deep it was then, but it certainly was a heck of a lot deeper then than it was now.

"It's evaporation, that's what happens," said Billy. "It's been hot all winter long. Normally ya don't go into swimming pools in Marin in March. It's just been hot for weeks, so I thought I'd throw a party. I guess that's how the water disappeared. It just, like, you know, evaporated."

"If you jumped in, the water's so low you might smack your head," said Suzie.

"I've done enough things to my head already," said Billy. "We certainly don't want that to happen."

Suddenly there was a lot of shouting. Billy looked up to see what it was. His neighbor Percy was standing in the middle of Billy's driveway, waving his arms, and yelling. Billy let his swimwear appraisal go for a moment, and sauntered over to where Percy was standing, arguing with Bobo, bass player for the Meemies.

"Say, are you deaf?" asked Percy, as soon as Billy approached.

"Gettin' there, for sure," answered Billy. "My doctor says I ought to wear earplugs, but I told him it's enough trouble remembering just to bring condoms to the concerts."

"Listen, will you turn down that bloody volume?" demanded Percy. "You can hear it down in Mill Valley, for Chrissake."

"What's shaking down in Mill Valley?" asked Billy. "I haven't been there since we played Sweetwater."

"I'm afraid I'm going to have to tell you, I've notified the police of a noise infraction."

"Don't be afraid, man," said Billy. "Fear is the basis for most neuroses. Did you know that?"

When we try to pick out anything by itself, we find it hitched to everything else in the universe.

~ John Muir

Berkeley, California, 2006

Desalination plants have been built in some cities in America where the economics make sense. The rising price of fresh water and the dropping of the price of desalinated water have played the largest role, but part of the story has to do with the rising cost of energy.

The major sources of energy in the United States currently are hydroelectricity, natural gas, coal, nuclear and gasoline. Small amounts of electricity are generated by solar, wind and geo-thermal power, but you can't run an energy-hungry operation like a desal plant with solar or wind power.

In California, nuclear power is basically a non-starter these days. Having a good part of your state sitting on top of a gigantic earthquake fault line will do that. Nobody wants a nuclear plant to be involved when massive tectonic plates start shifting around deep in the earth. Although nuclear power certainly has its supporters, especially among those who visualize the enormous profits at stake, and those who are critical of the possibilities of alternative energy sources like solar, to date there have been no city councils along the California coastline raising their arms in the air and calling for nuclear facilities to be built in their backyards.

So, in California, that leaves two major sources of energy to power desal plants, either hydroelectric power or natural gas. Proponents of natural gas tend to point out that there are few, if any, unexplored possibilities to create new sources of hydroelectricity in California. Any major dams that can be built have long since been built. The amount of energy generated by hydroelectric power is finite.

A few years ago, when certain energy firms were caught manipulating the energy market by closing down power plants for "maintenance," Californians discovered just how close we are to maxing out the energy grid. So, to build and power major new desal plants in California will require new sources of energy.

Proponents of natural gas point out that it is a clean, dependable source of energy. In fact, during the 2001 energy crisis, then-Governor Gray Davis signed legislation allowing many new natural gas plants to be built in the Bay Area, built by private sources and without any taxpayer dollars involved. While it costs hundreds of millions of dollars to build a new natural gas plant, profits were such that private companies were keen to do so, as profits would quickly accrue to pay off the debts. Then the price of natural gas went up, of course, throwing a lot of those plans into limbo.

There is also the important consideration that natural gas emits carbon dioxide, and guess what, class? Carbon dioxide is the leading cause of global warming on the planet.

Marin County, March 2, 1977

"Who is this head case?" demanded Suzie. "What's his problem?"

"Good afternoon, madam," replied Percy. "Pleased to make your acquaintance. Most unfortunate to meet under such trying circumstances. Lovely bit of swimsuit there."

"How come you talk so funny? Are you, like, English or something?"

"Yes, that is correct, madam. I'm definitely a something. Actually what I am, is a neighbor, an aggrieved neighbor, one with a complaint about the noise volume. I wonder if you would be so kind as to take your stereo system and deposit it in the bottom of the pool where it obviously belongs."

"Actually, we're running a little low in the pool, Perce," said Billy. "Water level's a little lower than usual."

"Hey," said Suzie, standing next to the hedge leading to Percy's backyard, "are you like a florist or something? This place looks like a jungle back here. I've never seen so many flowers."

"Just a hobby, madam," replied Percy smoothly. "Would you care for me to show you around my garden, or are you over-dressed for such strenuous exertion?"

Berkeley, California, 2006

You can trace the roots of the present energy crisis all the way back to the OPEC oil crisis of 1973. In the wake of historically high oil prices, everyone panicked and we in the U.S. urgently went looking for new sources of oil. Prices stabilized, but when the Asian financial crisis of the late 90's sent oil prices crashing down to $10 a barrel, research and development of new sources of oil basically stopped. Thanks in part to cheap oil, our economy boomed again, once again outstripping the shrinking supply of oil. World markets reacted as markets always will to short supply situations, and the price of oil shot up again. By summer of 2001 the price of crude oil topped out at $30 a barrel and refined gasoline was nearly $2 a gallon at the pump.

Then came the technological revolution, and the economy went crazy, and the high price of fossil fuels didn't cool the American economy. Both newly elected President George Bush and then-Governor Davis agreed on a simple solution to the need for more power in California to meet the needs of the digital economy. "Let's get some more gas going while the going is good, and hang the fallout. We won't be around to deal with the consequences anyway."

In five years since energy deregulation, California's economy had grown 32 percent and demand for electricity had grown 24 percent, or 6,000 megawatts. Experts disagreed wildly on the exact amount of power that new technology took from the grid — it depends greatly on exactly what you include in the technology sector — but 8 percent new demand seemed to be a conservative figure. One thing everyone now agrees on: energy consumption shows no sign of declining, either in California or anywhere else.

California gets about 24 percent of its power from hydroelectric plants, both within the state and through purchases from the Southwest and the Northwest. In the Columbia River Basin, home to 30 Bonneville Power Administration dams, snow levels were down 50 percent during the so called "energy crisis." Data gathered by the French TOPEX/Poseidon satellite shows the entire Pacific Ocean continues to be dominated by a distinctive pattern of cool and warm waters that repel El Niños, which typically soak California with winter snows. Long-term dependence on snowfall does not constitute a wise energy policy.

Ongoing denials from gas and oil companies notwithstanding, the atmospheric level of carbon dioxide is, or soon will be, higher than it has been for the past 420,000 years. And the world's number one polluter? Not smokestack-belching China; it's still the good old gas-guzzling U.S.A.

Although proponents expound its virtues in comparison with diesel and other fossil fuels, when burned to create electricity, natural gas emits large quantities of nitrous oxide and carbon dioxide. The main component of natural gas is methane, along with traces of butane, propane, ethane and water vapor. Despite the addition of very expensive "scrubbers" on the latest natural gas power plants, these gases still contribute to the greenhouse effect, especially given the huge amounts of gas all these new plants cumulatively burn.

My country is the world, and my religion is to do good.

~ Thomas Paine

Marin County, March 2, 1977

Officer Dalton was a bit perplexed.

"Who was the person that called to register a noise complaint?"

"Well, it sure wasn't me," replied Billy, who had turned down the stereo's volume to talk to Percy and had forgotten to turn it back up. "Might have been my neighbor Percy over here. He likes to make phone calls."

Officer Dalton ambled over to the next yard, where he found Percy talking to a woman who was wearing three hankies, one of which was on her head and the other two conveniently placed where they would do the most good. Percy was showing her his roses.

"Lovely day for the middle of winter, officer," said Percy, amiably. "Nice day for a party."

"Did you call in a noise complaint?" asked Officer Dalton, taking his eye off Suzie for a moment to look at the roses she was studying. "And haven't I been here before?"

"I haven't been keeping track of the number of noise complaints," answered Percy, "but I'm in a good mood today. Since the noise no longer seems to be an issue, I, for one, am willing to forget about the problem for now."

"He's like a florist or something," said Suzie to Officer Dalton. "These sure are beautiful roses."

"Why don't you pick a few for yourself," responded Percy quickly, "and Officer, here are a few for your lovely wife, if you will."

33 / A matter of the heart

You're not a real manager unless you've been sacked.

~ Malcolm Allison, English soccer coach

Marin County, March 2, 1977

Highway 80 runs straight as an arrow from Sacramento to the Bay Area, first across a flat plain, past Davis to Vacaville, then up a slight rise and down into Vallejo, where you turn west and follow Highway 37 along the northern shores of San Pablo Bay to Marin County. It's a 77-mile, 90-minute blast along a six-lane freeway, usually through heavy traffic comprising commuters between the capital and San Francisco, with a heavy mixture of long-distance semi-trailers clogging up the slow lanes thrown in for variety. Many people make the commute on a regular basis — business people, government workers, commuters who have jobs in the Bay Area but can't afford to live there — but Diet Stroeh only went to the state capital for business.

Today's business had been simple. Find some money to pay for the water he'd already found but couldn't afford. The financial commitments were starting to mount up. He had a deal with the Los Angeles Metropolitan

Water Authority for enough water to last Marin County the entire summer, but he had no commitment from his board or anyone else to raise water rates, again, or any other local source of money to pay for the water. He had ordered coupling for six miles of piping from Texas, deliverable via airfreight, without mentioning his lack of signing authority. He had agreed to pay for connection of pipelines in the East Bay, and he also needed to put out a contract to actually build the pipeline. He had no money to pay for any of this, and he'd had no real authority to make these decisions but, flying by the seat of his pants, there was really no time to hold a board meeting, and he had the nagging feeling that if he did, then things would become far more complex.

So far, the board had been quite supportive of all his decisions, but were laying low in the background, as befits all good politicians, watching which way the wind blew. If Diet pulled off his coup — finding water for Marin, thereby stopping the county from drifting away like dust in the wind — he would get the credit and glory. If he got caught short somewhere along the line, as in being unable to build the pipeline or find the money to pay for it, it would be his own neck on the line. He could kiss his career goodbye, and he knew it.

Today's trip to Sacramento, for instance, had been a failure. His overtures to state politicians had produced no action, and certainly no commitments of any financial support. Reading between the lines, the message was that Marin was a very rich county, and if it refused to join the state water supply system, then it was damn well on its own and could pay for its own pipeline. Lining up a deal with L.A. Met had been the state's main contribution to easing Marin's drought crisis; now Diet was on his own and he knew it.

It was somewhere around Davis that the tension and the overwork and the long hours and the endless meetings and the frustration and the anxiety rose up from his subconscious, where they had lain like dank weeds for weeks, silently growing in the dark places of his mind, and burst forth into his consciousness. Mentally, he started a checklist of things yet to do and meetings yet to call, and underneath the 18-hour days was the silent horror that he had committed himself to a course of action wherein a certain amount of luck would be necessary to come out on the positive side of the ledger, and counting on luck is not usually a component of any engineer's thought process.

Toting up his worries, Diet began to sweat. It was a warm day, but not warm enough to raise a sweat. He wound down the window an inch and got a blast of air. Finding he still couldn't breathe, he wound the window back up but he still couldn't get a full breath. He loosened his collar, putting his tie in his pocket, but by now his attention wasn't on the road but on his chest.

"I can't believe it," he said out loud, to no one, "I can't breathe."

On the right, a sign indicated an exit to the outskirts of Vacaville. Struggling hard to maintain his composure, Diet pulled over to the exit and drove slowly along the off-ramp to the first place he could safely stop. Parking the car on the side of the road, he opened the door and staggered out. Leaning against the side of the car, he wondered if he was having a heart attack. His chest was so tight he couldn't get a breath, and he felt quite light-headed.

"My God," he thought. "Am I going to bite the dust right here, in the dirt on an off-ramp to Vacaville? That's not the way I planned to check out."

Behind him the traffic roared and growled on I-80. A dirty haze filtered up from the freeway and the air reeked of gasoline. The sky was a pale robin's egg blue, with a smattering of clouds drifting in from the Pacific, light gray in tone but getting darker to the west.

"I wonder if it's going to rain?" he thought, as he blacked out.

Guidelines for bureaucrats: When in doubt, ponder. When in trouble, delegate. When in doubt, mumble.

~ James H. Boren, author and political commentator

Berkeley, California, 2006

I think that Marin County has some of the finest drinking water of any small-sized community in America. At least, what comes out of my taps in Marin tastes great. Pure Marin County rainwater could be bottled and sold in stores, and there would likely be a lineup to buy it.

People in Marin, take our gorgeous scenery and relaxed lifestyle for granted, assuming that our wonderful drinking water is a given right. Marin's water doesn't emanate from some nasty, brackish groundwater, with snakes and alligators defecating in it. Marin's water isn't shipped through dirty pipes from some industrially polluted river and treated with enough chemicals to make your teeth shine in the dark. Marin doesn't get its water from some lake full of algae, soapsuds and coffee grinds. Marin's drinking supply is pure, sweet, God-given rainwater.

However, should we in Marin decide, as so many other communities have already done, to add desalinated water to our water supply in order to soften the effect of any future droughts, another picture would emerge. Some people in the bottled water trade have described desalinated water as "dead water." It is perfectly clean; in fact, all salt, dirt, minerals and other organisms have been scrubbed right out of it during the reverse osmosis process, and then water officials have to decide what minerals to put back in again. No, the problem lies elsewhere.

While modern technology, such as reverse osmosis, does a great job of removing known contaminants from the water supply, modern technology is also guilty of creating a whole bevy of new compounds — known to scientists as "emergent contaminants" — that are rapidly entering the water supply. While defying quick analysis, two emergent contaminants have already come to the attention of researchers and been tagged with handy initials.

Pharmaceuticals and "personal care products" have collectively been named PPCPs by researchers looking into the side-effects that these products may or may not have on our bodies, if and when they contaminate the water supply. PPCPs consist of dozens of recently invented chemical compounds, ranging from prescription medications to soaps, fragrances and sunscreens. As biology teaches us, what is consumed by, or applied to, the human body is eventually excreted, along with any chemical residue that has not been metabolized by the body. Unlike many known pollutants, PPCPs are not regulated by governments and their side-effects on the body, when recycled through the water supply and consumed, are not known yet. However, early research is showing some alarming results.

Modern sewage treatment is, by and large, very effective in removing known contaminants from any effluent discharged back into the water supply system.

The efficiency of that treatment depends on a wide variety of factors. One factor pertaining to emerging contaminants is the sheer volume and complexity of PPCPs entering the aquatic environment, although currently PPCPs are present in such small levels that they can be difficult to identify. But as public usage of PPCPs increases, they may present a potentially serious health risk to the general public.

PPCPs were only identified very recently, when a 2002 U.S. Geological Survey of 139 streams found minute, although detectable, amounts of PPCPs that hadn't been found before. The compounds most frequently found were steroids and non-prescription drugs. Also found in varying quantities were antibiotics, prescription medicines, detergents, fire retardants, pesticides and hormones. Researchers and activists have since called for action into further sampling of the nation's water supply as related to PPCPs.

"Pharmaceuticals are potentially ubiquitous pollutants because they could be found in any environment inhabited by man," reports an article in the 2003 Bulletin of the World Health Association, "although currently there is little evidence they are present in sufficient quantity to cause significant harm."

Among the chief offenders are estrogen, both natural and synthetic, and anti-depressants, which can cause a wide variety of behavior changes in fish and shellfish, including the same "calming" effect they were designed for, in use by in humans. Synthetically "calmed" fish do not survive in a predatory environment.

Ninety-eight percent of the adults in this country are decent, hardworking, honest Americans. It's the other lousy two percent that get all the publicity. But then, we elected them.

~ Lily Tomlin

Synthetically calmed, Diet lay on the sofa in his living room, pondering the strange variables in life and sipping his drink. As far as he saw it, he had two options. On the one hand, he needed to get the pipeline built, find money for the pipeline and for the water that he had purchased without a source of money pay for it. And to build it, plus keep his board of directors happy, and pay some attention to his family. Oh yes, keep the media happy too, and keep 170,000 customers happy while simultaneously jacking up their water rates while cutting their supply. Oh, and figure out the politics of dealing with six different water districts, all of which had different goals and objectives that differed from his, and couldn't really care a fig if Marin County withered away.

On the other hand, if he didn't find some way to offload some of his problems, he wouldn't have any problems to worry about, because he would likely suffer a heart attack and die. While he was pondering these variables, Marcia came home and found him lying there.

"My goodness, what happened to you? You look as white as a sheet! Did you see a ghost?"

"I've had a tough day," he explained. "Plus, I don't think I am well." He explained his trip to the state capital, and his failure to locate any funding, his stress and his subsequent anxiety attack.

"You had better see a doctor right away."

"I did go to the hospital, and the doctor said it was extreme anxiety, but not a heart attack. What I need to do is see a psychiatrist," he moaned. "I really need to have my head examined. What was I thinking when I said that finding some water was all that was important, and I'd find the money later? Now I don't even know where to look for any funding. I'm an engineer, not a politician."

"Well, then, there's your answer," said Marcia. "It's time to call a politician and get them to go find the money. That's their job."

"I don't even want to raise the subject of money with my board. They'd just say that I was the one who put the cart in front of the horse. It's my problem, and I have to fix it myself."

"No, when I said politicians I didn't mean your board of directors," she said. "They might have gotten elected but that doesn't make them professional politicians. No, you've got to go for the top."

"I should just pick up the phone and call the President?"

"I doubt Carter knows or cares where Marin is," she said. "No, I meant who is at the top, locally? How about John Burton?"

"John Burton? How about getting me another drink? I need less stress in my life, not more."

The society that scorns excellence in plumbing as a humble activity and tolerates shoddiness in philosophy because it is an exalted activity will have neither good plumbing nor good philosophy; neither its pipes nor its theories will hold water.

~ John W. Gardner, activist for youth

Berkeley, California, 2006

We were talking about desal plants and emerging contaminants in our water supply.

PPCPs are hydrophilic, or "water-loving," and can survive easily in an aquatic environment. For instance, hormones, especially growth hormones that escape from cattle feedlots, can be a significant issue, particularly here in California where feedlots in the inland desert can possibly leak hormones into the water supply. It's just a short hop, skip and jump from the desert to the delta, and from the delta into the bay, and into your glass of drinking water.

Synthetic and natural hormones interfere with the signal pathways in the brains of fish. They are suspected of some nasty things, including the feminization of male fish and abnormal reproduction in alligators. Male fish in some areas are growing ovaries and in some cases are trying to lay eggs. This isn't a good thing. Besides hormones, which also include birth control pills, traces of aspirin, acetaminophens, and epilepsy, high blood pressure and high cholesterol medicines can exist in treated wastewater. Preliminary studies also indicate that low levels of anti-depressants such as Prozac and Zoloft may cause metamorphosis in frogs, affecting their mortality.

While pharmaceuticals are a serious issue, other PPCPs, such as personal care products, could evolve into even more of a problem because they greatly exceed medications in their widespread use. For instance, some researchers say that the widespread use of antiseptic additions to soaps causes inadvertent destruction of beneficial microorganisms. Antibiotics can affect algae development and disrupt the food web. Scientists have identified over 60 compounds derived from detergents, cosmetics and hous hold cleaners that can interfere with the vital processes of the body and cause hormonal imbalances.

PPCPs are entering the environment in small amounts, but those amounts will increase quickly as the population in California grows. Medications that are applied to the skin, from the nicotine patch to various lotions, wash off and go down the drain too.

Most unused drugs clogging up the medicine chest are routinely dumped down the toilet eventually. In fact, the dumping of drugs into wastewater results in much higher amounts entering the waste stream than from simple human excretion. Very few pharmacies accept unused drug prescriptions, or take back unwanted drugs, or recycle any drugs. All unused drugs eventually go into our water supply.

The cumulative affect of PPCPs upon human beings is not yet known, which, for many scientists, means that action is needed to limit the influx of chemicals into the water supply. On the other hand, the lack of any definitive data on the issue means that, to date, virtually nothing is being done to stop PPCPs from entering the nation's water supply. Something to think about, class.

34 / Building the pipeline

Setting an example is not the main means of influencing others; it is the only means.

~ Albert Einstein

Marin County, March 5, 1977

At the MMWD offices, Diet met with his engineering staff in the boardroom. He rolled up his sleeves, put his notes on the table, and closed the door.

"Well gentlemen, where do we stand?"

"The first thing is, I've met with CalTrans, and they are adamant about a couple of items," responded Ron Theisen. "Firstly, as you know, they don't want the pipeline sitting right on the bridge deck. It has to be hung off the ground somehow, whatever way we decide to do it. The pipeline will be exposed to the elements, unlike every other pipeline we've built, which were all underground. When the pipeline is empty, no problem, but when it's full, it will have much greater mass, so it'll be very heavy. CalTrans does't want any leaks, so we have to design everything with an eye toward maximum flexibility, and allow the pipeline to move when it needs to."

"Let's get on it," responded Diet. "What else have you learned?"

"I also met with the Bay Area Toll Authority, which is an agency underneath CalTrans and which actually runs the bridge. We'll need to deal with them directly in any matters regarding the bridge itself, like closing one lane and how that will affect rush-hour traffic. Normally we'd have four to six months of design time for a project this size, but we are going to have to design and order everything in the next couple of weeks, so I have set up a schedule whereby we meet with the toll authority on an 'as-needed' basis."

"Good," said Diet, "already we are rockin' and rollin.' So what else?"

"Evidently, above-ground pipelines need to be designed to allow for a lot of flexibility," said Theisen, "which is why, when you see any above-ground piping, it has all these loops and twists and turns built into it somewhere. The piping never goes in a straight line for too long. But here we have a bridge that is straight as an arrow for almost four miles, and the lane we are allowed to use is only 10 feet wide, so we are going to have a real challenge to find a way to build curves, twists or loops into the pipeline design."

"Not a problem. I'm sure you gentlemen will find a way to do that. Clever bunch. Every good engineer loves a challenge. Next?"

"On either side of the bridge we'll need to build pump stations, and link to the underground water systems in the East Bay and Marin," said Theisen, looking at his notes. "We can't start any design process until we know exactly where the piping will run and where the pump houses will be."

"I'm working on that already. I'm going to talk to Chevron soon about using some of their property. Next?"

"We have broken the overall schedule down into three parts. First, the design stage, which is where we are now," said Theisen. "It's hard to design the overall plan when we only know the middle section, which is the bridge. But we are started on the bridge design already. Second, the buying and ordering of parts, most of which are contingent on the design phase, but we've already ordered the expansion couplings. Third, there's the actual building phase. We'll need to put out a bid package for that as soon as possible."

"OK, so we move on the bid package right away, we move heaven and earth to find the piping itself, we continue with the design, and we meet again in two days," said Diet, standing up and gathering his notes. "We'll see you all here on Thursday morning, at 9 a.m. sharp. Go kick ass."

I have not failed. I've just found 10,000 ways that won't work.

~ Thomas Alva Edison

Berkeley, California, 2006

Well class, if fossil fuels such as oil, gas, coal, and natural gas are not sources of sustainable energy, and nuclear power has serious drawbacks like earthquakes and cost and storage issues, and alternative energy won't work for any number of reasons — wind and solar power can't offset the loss of oil, and their production process requires fossil fuels in the manufacturing process — well, we really have our shorts in a knot, don't we?

Either we are going to find a way to safely store spent nuclear fuel, and suddenly find some new sources of uranium, or we can forget about nuclear power happening here in California. Hydrogen may be an acceptable way to generate power for some uses, but I doubt it's going to be a way to run our cars in the near future.

In short, we really have our work cut out for us if we are going to find a way to replace fossil fuels with a reasonable alternative soon. And we'd better find it quick, because the planet is going to be so hot in a century that we'll all need to have air conditioning, and there goes the energy grid, because no appliance is as energy consumptive as an air conditioner.

Luckily there are people looking into hydrogen for uses other than running cars, and other research into what we need to call "clean fuel," or else the planet will turn into a bake oven. So it's encouraging to hear that an international consortium has been formed to take a serious look at creating nuclear fusion.

Let's not confuse fusion with old-fashioned nuclear fission, which is another kettle of wax entirely. Fusion, which doesn't exist yet in a commercial function, entails the process of atoms combining at extraordinarily high temperatures. The challenge is to control the energy in a self-sustaining reaction in which heat released by fusion can be used to generate electricity.

Old-fashioned nuclear fission is generated by uranium, which is proving hard to find. Fusion uses deuterium instead, also known as heavy oxygen, which can be obtained from water. Existing nuclear reactors involve the splitting of large atoms, a process that leaves behind highly radioactive waste that remains deadly for thousands of years. Using fusion instead, waste stays radioactive for a short period of time.

This fusion project is a $13 billion project that will be jointly run by France and Japan, backed by an international consortium of financiers. The reactor will be located near Marseilles in southern France. Construction of the 500-megawatt reactor is expected to take 10 years, with most research taking place in Japan. A demonstration power plant should be online by 2030, and a commercial plant by mid-century. The long-term potential is for a virtually limitless, environmentally acceptable and economically competitive source of new energy. We hope.

Before we all wet ourselves with joy and excitement, let us remind ourselves that, as of today, fusion remains a complete unknown. We have discussed before that expecting technology to save our planet and change our lives for the better has been a bit of a fool's game up to date, but who knows? Maybe this time we'll get it right. Certainly we cannot continue to pollute our planet any longer in the fashion of the last 50 years.

Marin County, March 7, 1977

It is horrifying that we have to fight our own government to save the environment.

~ Ansel Adams

"I understand you've located a source for the pipes we need for the pipeline, right here in the Bay Area?"

Diet and senior staff were once again huddled in his office at MMWD headquarters, touching base on construction of the pipeline. Maps and charts were hastily pinned to the walls. Boxes of reports and files were piled against one wall. Atop a bookcase, a clock counted down the hours to deadline day.

"Yep, got some good news, Diet," replied Theisen, "we've located a supplier right here in the Bay Area who'll get us what we need in very short order. So when we need the pipe, it'll be ready."

"Terrific! There's one less problem to worry about. Now, what else ya got?"

"We're going to need a pair of massive concrete structures to be erected at either end of the Richmond Bridge to hold the pipeline up in the air, and we'll need to know as soon as possible where the pump houses are going to go," replied Theisen. "I've also got some good news from Chevron. They have their own plant just off the end of the bridge in Richmond, all those pipes you can see when you approach the bridge, and they have given us permission to have our pipeline cross their property if need be. So there are two hurdles down already."

"OK," said Diet, "I'm going to need to talk to Chevron anyway, see if I can get permission to use some of their property for a pump house. I'll get on to them just as soon as I get back from Washington"

"Going for a quick vacation, Diet?" quipped Theisen, who had canceled his own holidays to work on the pipeline.

"Ha, I wish. No, I go hat in hand to the nation's capital to see if I can find some money. We don't have a dime to pay for anything yet. I've struck out here in California. Maybe the feds will give us the time of day."

New York City, June 8, 2010

"I want to cut that section about organic gardening from the end of the show," said Spalding. "What's it running, a full 45 seconds?"

"It got bumped last night too," said Kathy Creedy, an old-timer whose career with the network went all the way back to the turn of the century. "And it's 42 seconds."

"OK, we're going to bump it again to tomorrow, and if something hot comes up tomorrow, we'll bump it into the middle of next week too," said Spalding. "I want that report about the bankruptcy and unincorporation, or whaevert the legal phrase is, of that suburb outside of Las Vegas that's been disconnected from the water supply."

"It's not really in Las Vegas, and it's a really depressing subject," said Creedy, fighting for her work to stay on-air. "We always like to keep a kicker at the end of the broadcast, to counteract all the awful news we scare people to death with. That's your own rule, Janet."

"Yes, so in that case we'll move the story about the adoption agency to the end, because it gives off a nice glow. We'll move the Vegas story up in the mix, right after the Amtrak derailing."

"May I ask why the Vegas story is causing such a flutter?" asked Creedy. "I haven't seen the footage or read the script."

"It's a 'first of many,' story, so there will be lots more where that came from," said George Mitchell, who had produced the piece. "You are going to see towns all over Arizona, Nevada, New Mexico — anywhere there's no more water to be had — throw in the towel and shut the light. They're turning into ghost towns. You ain't seen nothin' yet."

"More importantly," interrupted Spalding, "I want a series of stories that lead us right into our network special on climate change that we're working on, and I want those stories to be all ours. We'll get back to the 'green gardening' stuff after the special. In the meantime, think brown."

Washington, DC, June 8, 2010

"I got a letter from Will in the mail today," said Claire White to her husband.

"A letter?" said the President. "Do you mean an email? Will must be in Namche Bazaar by now. They'd have an Internet connection there.

He's a few days early, I think."

"No, an actual letter," she said, holding it up for her husband to read. "Slug mail. He knows I love to collect the stamps."

"What did he address it to? First Lady, the White House, the Excited States of America, like last time?"

"Sweetheart, you know he uses those special envelopes we gave him. The computer scans the code, the letter gets pulled out of the mail, and gets sent directly here."

"Oh yes, I remember now," said Will White Senior, scanning the letter quickly. "It says here that everything is going fine. Stamped Kathmandu. Must have sat in the airport there a few days. Still, it got here in a week though."

"You know and I know that if things were not going fine with Will that he would call on the phone."

"Yes, except where he is, there are no phones."

"Is Dave keeping a close eye on him? He has a satellite phone."

"Of course, dear," he said, handing back the letter. "You know I wouldn't let our boy get into any danger. We have a team and a helicopter standing by, and our consul has a direct line to the Nepalese ambassador. If he breaks an ankle or even breaks wind, Dave will let us know."

"I like that boy Dave. He's a good boy. Played for Army, didn't he?"

35 / Water and oil

There are no passengers on Spaceship Earth. We are all crew.

~ Marshall McLuhan, 1964

Marin County, March 7, 1977

By now the hunt for fresh water in Marin County had taken on many new facets. Some people were under the impression that a gigantic aquifer, or underground water table, was lurking somewhere under the county, and that all water officials had to do was tap into it by drilling wells and Marin's water problems would be solved. Over 600 private wells were dug throughout the county, and a few lucky property owners actually tapped into some small pockets of water, especially those in the Ross Valley where a modest aquifer did exist. But, by and large, wells everywhere were coming up dry. MMWD staff dug some wells too, just in case they got lucky, but they either came up dry or yielded only a modest flow, sufficient for one household at best.

The ancient art of dowsing, or water witching, suddenly made a big comeback. You could see people all over the county walking around with forked sticks, bent over like hunchbacks, looking to strike liquid gold, but few found any water. Suggestions were made to build a giant ditch all around Mount Tam and catch any water that ran off the steep slopes, but it was pointed out that you needed some rain in the first place in order to catch any runoff. Like cloud seeding, you needed a basic resource from which to start.

Some of those with the financial means to do so quietly imported water by truck, especially in the wealthier communities of Ross and Kentfield, but the general public did not have the money to do so.

While water officials and the general public did whatever they could to find some water, people in the county's growing "alternative community" came up with some ideas of their own. A plan was hatched to hold a giant "rain dance" on top of Mount Tam, and see whether the karmic energy of thousands of people chanting and dancing would help.

The day of the planned rain dance dawned cloudy, which put some of the crowd in a bad mood until people realized that for rain you need some clouds. Rock bands played, people danced, the crowd chanted, drummers drummed, the clouds gathered, and — miracle of miracles — it actually began to rain! The hippies went home ecstatic that the Great Marin Drought had finally ended, thanks to their entreaties to the great rain god in the sky. Perhaps the copious amounts of smoke emanating from the festival helped seed the clouds.

Unfortunately, the deluge quickly tapered off to a shower, and the next morning things were back to normal. Or abnormal, depending on your point of view. At any rate, the modest rainfall on the day of the rain dance constituted the only moisture for the entire month, and the drought quietly resumed its deadly creep the next morning.

A people that values its privileges above its principles soon loses both.

~ President Dwight D. Eisenhower, Inaugural Address

Berkeley, California, 2006

Well, class, the theme of our discussion today is "water is the new oil." To project what will happen in a world of scarce and expensive water, let's look at what is happening right now with fossil fuels such as oil. Since water has also become a commodity in growing demand, we can project that the same thing that is already happening with fossil fuels will happen with fresh water, sooner or later. Probably sooner.

In short, the days of cheap oil are over. Those of you fortunate enough to own a car, if you gassed up on the way to class this morning, may have noticed that gas prices aren't dropping. Gas has been so cheap for so long, at least in comparison to what it costs in other countries that apply taxes to it, we have expected prices to stay low forever. For years we in America have been stuck in a sort of Jiminy Cricket kind of thinking: that is, anything we wished for hard enough would eventually come true. We wished we could consume anything we wanted as long as we wanted. And we have, but with oil, those days will soon be over.

We are about to go through the same process with fresh water as we have with oil, the difference being — as our ancestors proved, living without plastic — that you can survive without oil, but you certainly can't live for long without water.

As James Howard Kunstler explains in his book "The Long Emergency" — which, by the way, I recommend you read — the short but spectacular age of cheap oil brought us many of the comforts and luxuries to which we have become so accustomed. It may not be public knowledge, but much of what we eat, wear, watch, play with or consume is either made partly of oil or oil by-products. Many of our creature comforts — everything from central heating to air conditioning, pharmaceuticals to food — are also related to oil in some manner. Most importantly, it is vital to understand that fossil fuels are the world's chief source of energy, and that without access to cheap energy the world is going to change, very dramatically and very soon. Fresh water will be part of that equation.

Kunstler explains that the most important aspect of this energy crisis — and we need to understand this — is that it is going to be permanent. When fossil fuel runs out, it won't come back. It will be gone forever, and the alternatives are few. We seem to think that technology can supply all our answers, but in fact the reverse may be closer to truth. Since we have burned so much fossil fuel in the last 50 years, and polluted the planet to the point where it's quickly warming up, our looming energy problems will coincide directly with the climate change we've already created. One crisis will exacerbate the other.

Remember the law of supply and demand: the less there is of any commodity, the more that commodity will cost. Demand for oil from China, with its manufacturing sector going nuts, and from India, where the middle class is now bigger than in the United States, has shot up exponentially. The United States passed its own oil production peak way back in 1970, and since then our production has dropped steadily while our consumption continues to grow. We now have to import about two-thirds of our oil, and, if we continue to consume oil like

Arab sheiks on a consumer binge, the situation will soon get much worse. There is no replacement for oil. There never will be. New supplies of oil will only continue to get more difficult and expensive to extract.

To aggravate energy matters, American natural gas production is also declining. Because of the oil crisis of the 1970s, nuclear plant disasters and acid rain, we decided to make natural gas our national energy solution. Half the homes in America are heated with natural gas. Any natural gas imported from overseas would have to be shipped in pressurized tanker ships to special terminals, and there are only four such ports in America. Prices of natural gas have only one way to go: up, way up.

Alternative energies are not going to keep us in the luxury to which we have become accustomed. Solar and wind systems require substantial amounts of energy to manufacture and without the support of a fossil-fuel economy, they aren't affordable. Some people have been musing about hydrogen, but we are not going to replace gas-guzzlers with vehicles run on fuel cells in the near future, if ever. For one thing, the current generation of fuel cells is largely designed to run on hydrogen obtained from burning natural gas. Also, the nature of hydrogen — it's really explosive — presents expensive obstacles in storage, transport and use. Anyone remember the Hindenburg?

Big agriculture is talking about replacing oil in part with ethanol, but their plans are predicated on using oil and natural gas to produce the fertilizer and weed-killers to grow the biomass crops that would be converted into ethanol or bio-diesel fuels. This is an obvious net energy loser. And proposals to distill trash and eco-waste into synthetic oil depend on maintaining the huge waste stream produced by a cheap oil and gas economy in the first place.

Coal is a huge contributor to greenhouse gases and presents many health and toxicity issues. Nuclear power has huge problems associated with storage and disposal of waste. Uranium as a fuel is also a resource in finite supply. In short, there is no easy answer to our looming energy crisis.

As I just said, in 2004 China became the world's second-greatest consumer of oil, surpassing Japan and following us. China's surging industrial growth has made it increasingly dependent on the same oil imports we are counting on. If China wanted to, with its gigantic military machine, it could easily walk into some former Soviet republics in central Asia, such as Kazakhstan, which has untapped supplies of oil. Is America prepared to contest an Asian land war with the Chinese army? Perhaps more importantly, can the U.S. military permanently occupy regions of the Middle East without bankrupting our economy?

The world's energy crisis is a time bomb waiting to explode, but it is nothing compared to what will happen when countries start to run out of water. After all, diminishing supplies of oil merely mean a diminished quality of life. Diminishing access to fresh water supplies means death. And the more fossil fuels we burn, the more we raise the planet's temperature, oblivious to the fact that we are melting away the ice that provides us with so much water.

Marin County, March 8, 1977

Joel Bartlett was working the afternoon shift as a meteorologist for San Francisco's KPIX TV, but, living in Marin, it was part of his job description to cover any "weather-related community events" in that county, and what weather event could be more important than the Great Marin Drought? So at 11a.m. every day, Bartlett turned his nifty little Volkswagen Sirocco onto Highway 101 and zipped up to Corte Madera, where he joined the daily media scrum at MMWD headquarters, looking for new information.

"Hey, Joel, when's it going to rain?" asked a radio reporter from the East Bay, waiting for Diet to make his morning appearance. "You're the expert."

One of the drawbacks of being a weatherman was that other reporters, and the public, would always ask you what the weather was going to be that day. Sometimes it's a joke, other times people are serious. Talking about the weather is only human nature, but in the midst of an endless drought the questions were becoming tedious.

"It's going to rain when there is sufficient moisture in the sky to form clouds," responded Joel, cheerful as always. "When those clouds become saturated, the weight of each drop will become such that the law of gravity shall prevail, nature will run its course, the drops will fall, and it will rain. Unless it doesn't."

After weeks of questioning, there were basically only two themes that remained at the scrums; water conservation or importation? The media was, quite frankly, tired of hearing about conservation techniques. They had heard every variation on the subject, from pouring leftover bathwater onto the shrubs, to brushing your teeth in a cup of tea rather than letting the tap run. Bartlett himself had demonstrated water conservation techniques on TV so many times he could have filled the Pacific Ocean.

Since conservation lectures were wearing on viewers' nerves, importation of water had become the theme of the scrums. Since the memorandum of understanding between Marin County and East Bay MUD and the State had become a matter of public record, the line of questioning had devolved into queries about the pipeline. When was construction going to start? When would it be completed? When would water flow through the line? How much was all this going to cost? How long would the water run? Most importantly, of course, was the age-old question of when it was going to rain.

"Say, Joel," remarked Fred Thompson, a radio reporter from San Francisco, "We're taking bets. A buck is the minimum and you get to pick your own date. You in?"

"I'm afraid that my professional capacity as a weatherman prevents me from making that wager," responded Joel, "but where did you say the pot is at now?"

For 200 years we've been conquering Nature. Now we're beating it to death.

~ Tom McMillan, quoted in Francesca Lyman, "The Greenhouse Trap," 1990

Berkeley, California, 2006

Last class we were discussing the work of James Howard Kunstler and his book, "The Long Emergency." Kunstler's theory is that we have entered an age of slow decline because we have based so much of our society on the plentiful supply of cheap fuels, and that the escalating price of a diminishing supply will have serious repercussions for our future.

Kunstler explains that, as a society, we made a set of un-fortunate choices somewhere during the 20th century, thanks to our infatuation with the automobile and the cheap prices we paid to fuel them. Perhaps the worst choice was to let our towns and cities rot away. We re-placed them with suburbia built on top of a lot of the best farmland in America. We made housing subdivisions, highway strip malls, and regional shopping centers the backbone of our economy, and we happily jump into the car to go between home, our places of work and our shop-ping centers. When we are forced by price and scarcity of fuel to stop our endless driving and mindless shopping, and the endless manufacture, transportation, promotion and consumption of consumer items, the bottom will fall out of our consumer-based economy.

Soaring energy prices are bound to rearrange our lives and make our lifestyle intensely local. We will need to downscale virtually everything we do, from the way we work and the way we trade the products of our work, to the kind of anonymous communities we currently live in, to where and how we grow our food. When it's $7 for a gallon of gas — right now it's $9 a gallon in downtown London, England — we won't be commuting 50 miles to the office or 25 miles to the nearest big-box store for some snacks; we'll be working at home or working and shopping much closer to home. Anything organized on a grandiose scale, whether it is a government or a corporate entity, will wither away as cheap energy evolves into very expensive energy.

Our mega-mall society will not survive long when energy prices double. WalMart and Costco stores won't be such bargains anymore. Transporting goods 12,000 miles from where they were manufactured, perhaps in a forced labor camp in China to Des Moines, Iowa, will no longer be inexpensive. Given the coming conflicts over energy supplies, supply lines could easily be interrupted by military contests over oil. The nations that have been supplying us with ultra-cheap manufactured goods will have internal conflicts of their own to resolve. Like, how cheap will these products be when the nations from which we import will also be struggling with their own energy famine?

The days of enormous, ego-inflating, gas-guzzling vehicles will be gone. With expensive gasoline in short supply, and tax revenue disappearing, our roads will surely suffer. The interstate highway system does not tolerate partial failure. The interstates are either in excellent condition, or they quickly fall apart. The commercial aviation industry, already on its knees financially, is likely to dwindle to a few carriers and prices will certainly rise. The sheer cost of maintaining gigantic airports won't justify the operation of reduced travel.

Big Ag, as they call it here in California, could be in deep trouble. Corporate food production will no longer be cheap as industrial agriculture suffers from a scarcity of cheap oil. The costs involved in importation of fossil fuels will mean that we will have to grow more of our food much closer to home, and not on the mega scale of today. Food production will be more labor-intensive than it has been for decades. Stoop labor will make a comeback.

Of the 1,200 species listed as threatened or endangered in America, 50 percent depend on rivers and streams.

~ Water Facts.com

Those regions of the country that have prospered thanks to cheap oil will be in trouble. For instance, the southwest will suffer when cheap energy becomes expensive energy. Hot-weather states like Arizona and Nevada, currently experiencing population booms, will be short of water as well as cheap energy. Imagine Phoenix without cheap air conditioning. Never mind that, imagine much of America without air conditioning.

If moving commodities great distances will increase their cost, as cheap energy is replaced with expensive energy, what will happen with cheap water?

Taking Southern California and in particular the mega-sprawl we call Los Angeles as one example, it has been importing ultra-cheap water for decades from Northern California and Arizona. As demand for that water increases, so will the price. Already we have a situation where Northern California rivers, and their fish populations, are withering away as water is diverted to urban centers in the south. How long before fishers, recreational interests, environmentalists and northern urban communities retaliate in the courts?

In the Sun Belt states, golf courses and retirement communities are popping up like mushrooms, totally dependent on cheap water and air conditioning for their existence, as are booming cities like Phoenix, Tucson, and

Las Vegas. What will happen to these communities as the cost of water — and the hydropower that creates the energy upon which all modern conveniences are based — greatly increases in price?

Water, like oil, is a commodity that we cannot do without. Whereas with oil we will merely suffer and adapt, without access to water — especially clean, fresh and cheap water — our societies will change in ways that, at present, we can only contemplate. Water indeed is the new oil, and we are rushing blindly into a future where both commodities will be in much shorter supply. Perhaps it's time we stopped and planned ahead for this eventuality.

Just as with oil, where we will have to redesign our communities and our lives to reflect the realities of price and supply, we will be forced to eliminate the inefficiencies of water supply and control that we currently tolerate. Thousands of water districts cannot compete against each other, not with growing populations and diminishing supplies; the costs would be astronomical. Necessity will force America into a different system of water supply, and water control. After all, oil may be viewed as a luxury, but you simply cannot live without water.

36 / Mr. Stroeh goes to Washington

My grandfather once told me that there are two kinds of people: those who work and those who take the credit. He told me to try to be in the first group; there was less competition there.

~ Indira Gandhi

Marin County, March 9, 1977

"I have come up with an idea."

"Good, that's better than coming down with a cold," said Marcia, putting the dirty dishes in the dishwasher. "Would you mind passing the plates and sharing that idea with me?"

"You may remember that when Jimmy Carter was stumping for votes out here . . ."

"How could I forget?" she said. "I still wake up nights thinking about it, my heart pumping."

"OK, I get your point, but when Carter was out here scrounging up money and votes in California, he stayed at Arnold Baptiste's house here in Novato."

306

"That's exciting. We are talking the same Arnold Baptiste who is President of the Marin County Board of Supervisors?" she asked. "Pass me the cutlery."

"One and the same. The reason Carter stayed there is because he and Arnold are old friends. Carter is a Democrat, and the Democrats need California in the next election, right? So I asked Gary Giacomini, who, as you know, is vice-chair of the Board of Supervisors, to set up a meeting with Arnold, and to ask Arnold to set up a brief meeting with Carter in Washington. Or Carter's people, most likely. Gary called me back today to say it's all set up. Maybe I can scrounge some money there."

"Really? Now, that's a good idea. So when are you going to Washington?"

"Three days. I'll represent the water district, and Gary will go, and Bill Filante as the president of our board, and John Burton from the House of Representatives, and Burton has persuaded Senator Cranston to come. So we are all set. Maybe we can squeeze some money out of Washington, because we sure aren't going to get it from Sacramento."

"What's your pitch? Why would the White House care about little old Marin County?" she asked, hanging up her apron. "I doubt they've ever heard of us in Washington."

"It's the same scheme I used in Sacramento. On our own, we're sunk, but if we tie it in to a larger issue, then maybe we'll get a fair hearing," said Diet. "If I tell them it's not just Marin running out of water, but the East Bay and the entire Bay Area and key parts of California, well . . . They need California votes, don't they?

"Good luck," said Marcia, "you're going to need it. Probably not a good idea to come back if you don't get the money. Call collect from Albania."

Berkeley, California, 2006

America is a country that doesn't know where it is going but is determined to set a speed record getting there.

~ Laurence J. Peter, educator and author of "The Peter Principle"

Experts in the field of energy predict that California will need 1,000 new megawatts per year to keep up with a growing population. As you should know, one megawatt provides energy for 100,000 homes, and government sources are predicting that another 14 million people will be living in California as early as 2020, so we need lots more energy.

A few years ago, Governor Arnold Schwarzenegger was approached by lobbyists to commit California to import electricity from Wyoming, Nevada and Utah, via a new 1,300-mile transmission line. The energy from the so-called Frontier Line would come from more than two-dozen new power plants to be built in those states, all fired by coal. California committed $2.5 million for research and planning, while private interests would provide start-up capital.

Officials in the energy field have been quick to point out that all these new power plants will use new technology that reduces toxic emissions to near zero, by turning coal into gas. That process adds about 25 percent to the overall cost. However, politicians like Wyoming Governor Dave Freudenthal said that gasification technology is too expensive, and Wyoming won't do it.

California's air quality is already considered poor by federal standards, but right now Wyoming, Nevada and Utah have relatively clean skies. They also have an abundant supply of coal. But, new technology that removes pollutants from emissions or not, coal-fired power plants emit twice as much carbon dioxide into the air as do natural gas plants. These new power plants would also emit mercury, which settles into lakes, reservoirs and rivers and causes great damage to aquatic life.

There is some good news, though. The power companies proposing these new power plants won't begin construction until they have signed contracts with California state utilities. The California Public Utilities Commission has already enacted a law requiring more renewable power and restricting carbon-based power supplies.

Speaking of renewable energy, in response to the coal-fired strategy, New Mexico Governor Bill Richardson proposed his state create a new agency to issue bonds that would pay to link new wind power projects in New Mexico with California. And activists point out that there are still other alternatives to explore instead of coal, like geothermal power, which exists in great abundance under the Salton Sea in southeast California. So we have two ways we can go.

Washington, March 12 , 1977

To shorten winter, borrow some money due in spring.

~ W.J. Vogel, scientist

It was a large, walnut-paneled conference room with long wooden tables facing each other in the middle. Security was tight just to enter the "Little White House," as it is known in Washington political circles. Through the windows, you could see the real White House right next door.

Of the 20 people present, the Marin contingent was placed at an end table, signifying their low standing on the political totem pole. Congressman John Burton sat at the head of their table, along with members of Senator Cranston's staff. Other Marin officials sat next to Burton, and at the far end of the table sat Diet Stroeh, a small frog in a very big pond on his very first visit to The Hill, and a nervous frog at that. President Carter was absent, attending to more important issues, but he'd sent some top advisors to the meeting in his place.

After greetings were exchanged, people talked about the weather, as people will do when maneuvering for an opening to more significant issues. My goodness, wasn't it cold in the East? Worst winter in living memory. More snow than you could ever handle. Nice and dry out West, though. Too dry, that's the problem. Could be a real problem there. Yes, very dry. After small talk was dispensed with, the meeting suddenly got very serious.

"Mr. Burton, we understand that your constituency comprises several affluent cities and towns in the San Francisco Bay Area," said Richard Carswell, a senior advisor to the President. "From all the media coverage that we've seen, it appears that Marin County may in fact be one of the wealthiest counties in the entire nation. Could you kindly explain then, why one of the richest places in the country would come to Washington looking for handouts? If you are short of water, why can't you simply have some water trucked in? Do you think that Marin County is so special that the federal government should simply subsidize it? What kind of funding are we talking about?"

"Well, sir, I have here with me several elected officials from the county of Marin and the water district and I am sure that they could explain the specific details a lot better than I can," responded Burton smoothly. "I'm just the go-between, as it were. Mr. Giacomini is the vice-chair of the Marin County Board of Supervisors. Perhaps he has a better understanding of the issues involved."

Gary Giacomini scrambled to his feet, hastily straightening his tie, grabbing a handful of papers as he rose.

"Thank you, Representative Burton," he said. "Marin County indeed does have some significant problems pertaining to water, or the lack of it, as you may have seen on the TV news or in the press. We are badly in need of fresh water, and we have arranged to build an emergency pipeline across a local bridge in order to get that water from the East Bay Municipal Utilities District folks, who are tied in to the state water supply. However, Marin is a small county and we are not in the position to fund the entire cost of building the pipeline and buying the water, all by ourselves."

"What, exactly, are the costs involved of building this pipeline?" inquired Carswell. "What are we being asked to assist with?"

"Well, as vice-chair of the Board of Supervisors, I have prepared notes as to the costs to the county of the actual drought, but I am not privy to the pipeline costs. The person to ask about all the details is the general manager of the Marin water district," said Giacomini, turning to look at Diet. "Luckily, he happens to be sitting right here. He has all the facts and figures. Mr. Stroeh can explain everything and what we need to do about it."

There was silence in the room. Outside an open window a bird chirped. You could even hear the traffic as it roared along distant Pennsylvania Avenue. Carswell cleared his throat.

"Well, Mr. Stroeh?"

Diet sat there dumbfounded. With no political authority, he had asked to attend the meeting as an observer. He was merely along for the ride. He had brought some figures and statistics, but he had no arguments prepared, no written speech, not even any speaking notes; everything was in his head. He'd expected Burton or Cranston to carry the ball, while he stood on the sidelines as an interested bystander. Suddenly the spotlight was turned on him, and like a deer in the headlights, he was stunned.

"Uh, yes, thank you Gary," stuttered Diet as he rose to his feet. "Thank you Mr. Carswell and all the gentlemen here today who have taken time out of their busy schedules to come down here today and help us with this urgent issue. As Mr. Burton previously stated, we have a drought happening in Marin, a drought like we have never seen before. In over 100 years of record keeping, there has never been a situation like this."

"If I understand correctly from my briefing notes," said Carswell, "Marin County is not tied in to the state water system. You have chosen to go it alone in the past when it comes to storing water. Now, when you need some help, for some reason you come to Washington looking for handouts. Why not go to Sacramento?"

"Yes sir. Yes, of course. Actually, uh, we've been to Sacramento already. They believe that their contribution was to smooth the way for a deal that allowed us to get access to some state water, which we have done through a deal with L.A. Met. So, theoretically we have access to some water, but the problem is that we have no way to get the water to Marin County. The East Bay area of San Francisco is tied in to the state water supply, and East Bay officials have agreed to let us use their pipelines to move the state water from the delta area to their pipelines. But we have no way to move the water from the East Bay pipelines over to Marin County. So we've started building a pipeline over the bridge, but we need some help to pay for the pipeline."

"You've already started work on this pipeline?"

"Yes, sir, we have. Time is very tight. It hasn't rained for over two years in Marin, and we have a long, hot summer coming up. We have 170,000 customers who stand to lose their properties, livestock, and businesses if we don't get some water soon. We felt we had to move on this."

"So you are building a major project, but you have no way of paying for it?"

"Yes sir," said Diet. "You could say that. Along with the water, we're also running out of time."

"I still don't understand why you don't just raise taxes, or assess yourselves, or whatever needs to be done," said Carswell. "I've heard already that Marin is one of the richest counties in the country. Surely you can afford to pay for your own construction projects?"

"Well, actually it's not that simple," said Diet. "Marin is not the only place where people are hurting. The entire Bay Area is now going to water rationing; San Francisco and the East Bay are about to be in trouble too. Democratic constituencies, all of them, I should mention. It hasn't rained in two years in the entire region."

"Yes, I've heard about that," said Carswell, sitting up straighter. "Go on."

"Actually, the entire state of California is suffering from a severe drought, or soon will be because the rainy season is now over and we are heading into summer again with no sign of rain at all," explained Diet. "Actually, it's not just California. The drought is beginning to creep up into Oregon and Washington state, and I hear that they are having some problems in Denver, and all over Colorado too. In total, we are talking about 24 western states going dry, mostly Democratic constituencies, by the way. They may not be in the same tight spot that we already are in Marin, but that doesn't mean they won't be in some serious trouble soon."

Carswell turned to his left and began speaking to an aide, who quickly left the room. Federal officials behind Carswell started to whisper to each other. Soon their entire table was in a buzz. Carswell turned back and faced the Marin delegation.

"You are saying that two dozen western states are facing an emergency drought situation?" inquired Carswell, writing notes in a black leather binder. "An entire region of the country that could be legally referred to, if and when it comes to public discussion, that could be referred to as a federal disaster area?"

"Uh, sure, yes, you could use those terms," said Diet, turning to look at Giacomini and Burton, who were both staring at him with tight smiles. "It's definitely going to be an emergency situation all over the West, soon. Yes. Very soon, and it's already a certified disaster area in Marin County. We certainly don't have enough water to get ourselves through the summer, and the rest of the Bay Area is going to rationing, and Kern County is in serious shape, too."

Carswell turned to another Carter official sitting behind him, and the two began to whisper. Turning back to Diet, he looked at the piece of paper he had in his hand.

"I don't believe you've answered my questions as to total cost considerations yet."

The total figure that Diet had in mind was $6 million, to cover all the costs of buying water and building the pipeline. Maybe they could squeeze by with $5 million, but that was just for Marin. He quickly multiplied that number in his head to account for all of the state of California, plus 23 other western states, and then added a few zeros to round out the numbers.

"Uh, about $650 million would be more than sufficient for all 24 states, I guess," he said, swallowing.

A loud buzz went all around the room, as if someone had started a race car inside a small garage. Carswell reached for an empty water jug and began to bang it on the table, like a judge in a disrupted courtroom. Giacomini and Burton both continued to stare at Diet like he had lost it.

"Order, please, gentlemen," Carswell said loudly. "Could we have some quiet please?"

"You've gone and blown it now," whispered Giacomini. "Where the heck did you get such a stupid number? Are you crazy?"

"It just popped out of my head," whispered Diet. "It was a nice round number. Maybe I should have just stuck with the $6 million for Marin."

"Sorry," said Carswell, loudly, motioning to the whole room for quiet. "Sorry, Mr. Stroeh, that's impossible. There's no way that we can authorize that figure. The best we could ever do would be half that, maybe $350 million, maximum."

"Done," said Diet without any hesitation, looking over at Burton and Giacomini and nodding. "It's a done deal, problem solved, thank you very much. We're very grateful. I'm sure that Represetative Burton will say the same."

"Representative Burton, there's an environmental bill going through the House and Senate tomorrow morning," said Carswell. "Do you think you could write a rider to that bill, stick this on the end of the bill as an earmark? Get it through a House vote?"

"If you give me the legal wording tonight," responded Burton, "I'll attach it to the bill in the morning, and I assure you I will find the votes to make it happen."

"Mr. Jamieson of Senator Cranston's contingent," said Carswell, "when it comes through the Senate in the afternoon, will the Senator support it and does he have the votes to get it through?"

"No problem," said Jamieson. "You can count on the senator. The votes will be there."

"OK, gentlemen, I'll talk to the President later today," said Carswell, rising, "and I'll phone you on Monday. Thank you for making the trip all the way out here. Somebody will be giving you a call soon."

"Thank you," said Burton, rising from the table to shake hands all around. The Marin contingent made its way to the door. Once in the hallway, Burton turned to Diet and winked.

"Welcome to Washington, Diet."

37 / Full alert

Nepal, June 7, 2010

Honest criticism is hard to take, particularly from a relative, a friend, an acquaintance, or a stranger.

~ Franklin P. Jones, businessman

Will lay in his sleeping bag, trying to sleep. His breaths were short and shallow and his head hurt. At 15,000 feet, he was coming down with another aspect of mountain sickness. Around midnight, by the glow of his watch dial, he felt the need to answer to nature, but getting out of his warm bag into the sub-freezing air was too much to endure, and he crawled back into the bag again.

"This was a mistake. We really shouldn't be up here," he thought. "I shouldn't have forced this down everyone's throats. But I just gotta get some footage to take back, show people what the whole scene looks like. I just hope we don't get nailed by a rock."

The walls of the tent shook with icy blasts, and the wind sounded like a lost soul crying in the wilderness. All night, dozing only fitfully, he dreamed dark dreams, with visions of falling into a crevasse and drowning, and woke up several times with a start. By dawn, he was exhausted from the altitude and lack of sleep. Sticking his feet into frozen boots in the morning didn't help his mood either.

"Just think, we could have left our boots by the fire in that hut down in Na, instead of freezing our butts off way up here for no good reason," said Dave Moore, trying to sip some lukewarm tea the sherpas had brewed out of melted snow, while nibbling some stale biscuits. "The scenery was nicer down there, too, if you know what I mean."

"Yeah, she's gorgeous, alright," replied Will. "How old do you think she is? 19?"

"They age rapidly up here in the high mountains. All that sun, bad food, cold," said Moore. "She looks older than she really is. But yeah, I guess she's no more than 18 or 19. Too young for you, old man."

At 6 o'clock in the morning, the stars still like diamonds in the black skies above, the giant shadow of the great mountain blocking half the heavens. As the light slowly grew, the tracks of rock falls heard during the night became clearly visible. As the group packed up and started to leave, a sherpa guide started to chant quietly in an off-key voice, his daily prayers just a whisper on the wind.

"I wish that guy wouldn't do that," said Moore. "All this praying gives me the creeps."

"How so?" said Will, slinging his video camera around his neck on a strap.

"All this praying, it makes me feel like someone has just died. Or else somebody is going to die," said Moore. "We have no business being up here. There were rock falls all last night. We could have been killed in our sleep."

"Not me," said Will, bringing his video camera up to his eyes, as the first warm rays of the sun burst over the edge of the mighty mountain. "I never slept, so I had nothing to worry about."

"Well, get your damned video footage and let's get the hell out of here," snapped Walsh, groggy and ill-tempered. "Before the sun warms up and we get nailed by some avalanche."

As the sun rose over the mountain, a golden glow arose with it. Will panned his camera over the whole landscape, shooting the trekking party as they slowly stepped down to the glacier on their way back to the lake. His lens lingered over the lake itself, and on the little hut next to the dam where a researcher would stay while monitoring the lake, and he panned over the moraine dam in which a drainage chute had been inserted. Moore sat down in the snow behind Will, watching.

"Say Dave, how come you're hangin' around way up here if you think it's so unsafe," he said, while he panned again across the barren landscape. "You should be heading down with the others."

"Just watching your back, Will," said Moore. "Somebody's got to do it."

"Just like what you've been doing all along, right? Hey, I'm not stupid," said Will. "Every trip I go on, my dad sends some jerk like you along to watch out for me. You guys come from, like, a robot factory or someplace. Does the Secret Service send everybody to the same barber shop?"

"I don't know what you're talking about Will," said Moore. "The girls like it."

"OK," said Will, shutting down the video camera and putting it back in its sack. "Watch my back if you like. Just don't get between me and the pepperoni pizza when we get back to Kathmandu. And stay away from the sherpa girl when we get down the hill, too."

"I don't know what you're talking about again, Will," said Moore, getting up and starting to walk. "This altitude is getting on everybody's nerves. Let's just cool it, right?"

On the way down, both men stopped frequently for rests. Moore went slowly, stepping aside to let Will cross any snow bridges across the crevasses, never more than a step behind. Each time Will stopped and stared at Moore, but neither man said anything. By noon the expedition was back at the lake, safe. Will lined the whole party up in front of the moraine dam, and had a group photo taken by one of the porters.

Instead of sun filling the sky as it had the day before, dark clouds came climbing up from the Rolwaring Valley so the hiking party didn't linger, quickly moving over the dam and descending to the river valley below. A few hours of downhill hiking would get them back to Na.

Drops of rain began to fall, and soon it was raining heavily. Every once in a while a member of the party would glance over his shoulder, checking to make sure the dam was holding. Downhill was warmth, a dry hut with food and cooking fire and pot, and a pretty girl who might cook a hot lunch. The rain started to come down even harder. Will began to sing again. No one picked up the refrain, and the porters picked up the pace, making double time down the rocky track.

Stopping to tie his boots, Dave Moore reached into his daypack and pulled out his satellite phone. Flicking it on, he waited for the dial tone while watching the party disappear down the trail below him. After a moment the signal light came on and he dialed a number in Washington.

"Boys, we have a problem," he said. "Pass the message on to Big Daddy. I think it's time to put that chopper on direct standby. It's starting to rain, and we may be in deep doo doo soon. I'll call back soon, but get the motor running just in case. Looks like by tonight the rivers up here will be running wild. I don't think we can make it to Namche Bazaar. We're gonna need a rescue."

The struggle to save the global environment is in one way much more difficult than the struggle to vanquish Hitler, for this time the war is with ourselves. We are the enemy, just as we have only ourselves as allies.

~ Al Gore

Berkeley, California, 2006

It's time to talk about something called "equilibrium warming," class. Those who have been reading their textbooks will know what that means; for those of you who have been lazy, I'll explain how it all works.

We are living in what some scientists call the "Anthropocene Age." For those who have never heard the term, it was coined by Dutch chemist and Nobel Prize winner Paul Crutzen a few years ago. Historians call the age in which we live the Holocene, dating it back to the last Ice Age. Crutzen argues we should call this new age the Anthropocene instead, because mankind has become so dominant over the planet that we are capable of altering the planet on a vast geological scale.

It was Crutzen who suggested that the starting date of this new age should be the 1700s, because that's when James Watt perfected the steam engine and let loose the gods of war. War against the planet, that is. The steam engine begat the Industrial Age, and the Industrial Age begat carbon dioxide poisoning, and the world has never been the same.

Back before the steam engine started puffing little clouds of coal dust into the air we breathe, carbon dioxide levels around the planet stood still at a fairly healthy 280 parts per million. This was the same amount of carbon that Jesus breathed. It was the same amount when the druids built Stonehenge 2,000 years before Jesus, and 2,000 years before Stonehenge, when the first cities of mud huts were built.

When Watt flipped the switch on the first steam engine, the first batch of coal dust was launched into the air. Carbon dioxide levels rose slowly at first, taking over 150 years to reach 315 parts per million. Then, all warmed up, carbon dioxide got on a nice little run. By the mid 1970s, carbon stood at 330 ppm, and by the mid 1990s, it was 360 ppm. Just in the past decade, carbon in the atmosphere has grown at a startling rate.

For every increase in carbon levels, the earth experiences a related rise in temperature, which is what we call "equilibrium warming." At the current rate we are going, we'll be at 500 ppm by mid-century, which is almost double what it was when Watt invented his infernal combustion engine. The last time the air was that dirty was during the Eocene Age, about 50 million years ago. In those days, sea levels were 300 feet higher than today and reptiles swam in inland seas.

Carbon dioxide is a "persistent gas," which means it hangs around a very long time. Hard stuff to get rid of. Once carbon gets in the air, it takes about a century to disappear. So the recent carbonization of the air is practically irreversible. It will take a lot longer to clean the planet than it did to make it dirty.

The future of the planet has long been known to scientists, but politicians and the general public seem to be in either a state of ignorance or a state of denial. Probably both. It seems nobody wants to talk about carbon or do anything about it. But coral reefs are rapidly disappearing, and polar ice caps are melting, and glaciers are disappearing, and soon much of our fresh water will be polluted.

The average American is responsible for emitting about 12,000 pounds of carbon into the air per year. That's right, six tons per person! The United States is by far the biggest polluter on the planet, thanks mostly to the gigantic cars we drive. We also hold most of the cards when it comes to closing down the game. If we want carbon dioxide levels to stabilize, and to keep the global temperature from rising to the boiling point, it's time for us to get off the pot and do something.

Everybody looks to America to take the lead on this issue, but then we point to the factories in China and India and say we aren't the only ones polluting the planet. Which is true. And what about those people cutting down all the rain forests in Brazil, and the clear cutting of trees in Southeast Asia? But it seems stupid to be looking to farmers in the Amazon to take command of this planetary crisis. It's gotta be us. Or, to be more precise, it's up to you kids to do something, because that's your future that's going up in smoke, and your parents don't seem to care.

Marin County, March 22, 1977

Work is of two kinds; first, altering the position of matter; second, telling other people to do so. The first is unpleasant and ill paid; the second is pleasant and highly paid.

~ Bertrand Russell

Ron Theisen had out his slide rule and was doing some computations. Engineers did not have computers in 1977, except for clumsy designs in which you had to insert software disks to make them start, sort of like old-fashioned wind-up gramophones. Slide rules by Texas Instruments were the high-tech tools of the day in the MMWD offices.

Theisen was working on a design problem that seemed insurmountable. It became apparent that the pipeline for the bridge would have to run a mile eastward to get to where a pump station would be built, and in the course of that mile the pipeline would have to run above the piping at the Chevron refinery. His job was to figure out how to match piping systems, and to design the MMWD piping to run above and over the Chevron piping, all without knowing where the pump house would eventually be built.

On the west end of the bridge in Marin, the pipeline would go underground at the Rod and Gun Club, somewhere, and stay underground until it arrived at the Canal District in San Rafael, where it would go under the canal. Another pump station would have to be built somewhere on the other side of the canal in the Loch Lomond neighborhood.

Heading south from the Rod and Gun Club another pipeline would connect to Ross Valley, somewhere. Another pump station would have to be built at Greenbrae, on the banks of Corte Madera Creek. In the same fashion that Diet had been forced to operate from the beginning, it was all cart-before-the-horse planning. Just as Diet had pushed the green light button before knowing where he would get any money, piping designs would be started before engineers knew where they were going.

The phone rang in Theisen's office.

"Hello?"

"Hang onto to your hat, Ronnie boy! Have I got news for you!"

"OK, Diet, you've seen a national weather forecast and you guarantee it's going to rain by the end of the week?"

"Better than that, chief," said Diet. "Even better than that. It's never going to rain again, but we will be made in the shade

323

anyway. Yes, you betcha, we've got the money, Ronnie, we've got the money."

"Who did you have to kill?" said Theisen. "Or did you rob a bank?"

"Well, I haven't actually got the money in my pocket, but I have a promise from the feds in Washington and the money will be coming soon."

"You got a promise from a politician?" asked Theisen. "Why, that's just like money in the bank, isn't it? Did you shake hands on the deal? And did you remember to count your fingers afterward?"

"Be a cynic, but I'll be home tomorrow and give you all the details."

"OK," said Theisen, "and by the way, congratulations."

Berkeley, California, 2006

Class, we've been talking all semester about climate change and its effects on our water supply for the future. Fresh, clean drinking water, that is. We know that 99 percent of the water in the world is salt and no good for drinking, and the one percent that is left is in the process of either melting or getting polluted.

But it's not just human beings that are going to be affected by climate change. Higher water temperatures are threatening the world's fish by stunting their growth and reducing their food stocks. According to the World Wildlife Fund, climate change is causing the world's rivers, lakes and oceans to heat up, and many species of fish are being affected. Those of us who eat fish ought to be concerned about this.

Some species, like salmon, catfish and sturgeon, cannot spawn if winter water temperatures rise too high. Freshwater fish may not be able to breathe because less oxygen dissolves in warmer water. Fish populations are also moving to cooler waters, which causes problems for other fish that rely on them as a food source.

For an example of that, 120,000 seabirds starved to death in the Gulf of Alaska back in 1993 because their normal prey had moved from the surface down into cooler waters, and the seabirds were not able to dive deep enough. The same type of die-off is happening on many bodies of water around the world today.

Aside from the fact that fish are dying in large numbers from pollution, over-fishing and now climate change, there is the more serious economic realization that fisheries worldwide generate more than $130 billion a year, employ at least 200 million people, and feed literally billions of people who have no other source of protein.

So it's not just people on dry land that are going to be affected by warming waters. The entire food chain, including all the animals that live on fish — seals, polar bears, whales, whatever — are all going to be affected too. Global warming is a crisis that affects land and sea alike.

38 / Show me the money

Luck is the residue of design.

~ Branch Rickey, owner of the Brooklyn Dodgers

Marin County, March 19, 1977

"Hello Mr. Stroeh?"

"Yes, this is Dietrich Stroeh. How may I help you?"

"My name is Richard Badger and I'm with the Federal Disaster Relief Office and I'm calling you from Denver. How are you today?"

"Fine, and even better now that you have called."

"I'll be in Oakland in a week or so and I thought perhaps we ought to meet. I understand that you know all the details concerning the disbursement of $350 million in funding for the western drought disaster aid."

"Say what?"

"Weren't you in Washington recently with Representative Burton about getting funding for drought relief in 24 western states?"

"Absolutely," said Diet, "I'm the guy. But I can't say I know all about western disaster relief. I'm just the general manager of the Marin Water District."

"Well, I was given your name as the point person to call," said Badger, "and I was told by Representative Burton that you knew all about the drought and the funding mechanisms for disaster relief for the western states."

"Uh, right, yes, of course," said Diet, "but as for disbursements of grants and loans and that sort of thing, I thought that was your department."

"Yes, we have the money but I'm not sure how we are going to handle the disbursement of the funds. This is the first drought that our department has had to handle and I'm afraid there's no magic formula for disbursement. We are just going to have to work it out."

"With me?" said Diet.

"You're the person who I was told to call," said Badger. "Representative Burton said you have all the figures and information we needed to know."

"I tell you what," said Diet, "why don't we get together in Berkeley as planned and we can go from there. How's your schedule look for this week? I'm kinda busy but I'm sure I can push things aside and get over there."

Water is a good servant, but it is a cruel master.

~ John Bullein, writer, 1562

Berkeley, California, 2006

Those who have been doing their homework know that accurate rainfall statistics have been kept in California since 1849, since the Gold Rush. People arrived here in California from all over the country, and from Europe and Asia, and that's where our California history really begins. No, you don't have to remind me, there have been inhabitants of California for about 12,000 years. One theory holds that the people we now call Native Americans, or Indians, arrived in North America across a land bridge from Siberia after the last Ice Age, which ended about 10,000 years ago, give or take a millennium. There are other theories now evolving as to origin of Native Americans, but one thing is sure: when Christopher Columbus arrived on these shores from Europe in 1492, he thought he'd sailed around the world and arrived in India.

There is something of a problem when it comes to record keeping that only started in the 1850s. Since we like to count in cycles of 10, we tend to measure time in terms of decades and centuries. Usually a century, at least in our current thinking, is plenty of time by which we can measure historical events such as weather. If you look back over the last 100 years or so, we can see episodes of drought and wet years, and using those measurements we think we can get a sense of what to expect in the future.

For instance, and I've mentioned this instance several times, we had a real drought in California in 1976 and 1977. We've had several dry periods in California over the last century and a half, but 1976 and 1977 were

328

special in that they ran back to back and very little rain fell at all for 25 months. Between 1987 and 1992 there was also a period of five years when it didn't rain much either, and there have been several similar brief periods of "minor droughts," but never have we had an actual disaster situation because our reservoirs and aqueducts have allowed us to store water, and move it around where it is needed.

But as we are about to find out, in the cosmic scope of things, a century is actually just the blink of an eye. You need to go back much further than a few hundred years to get an idea of what constitutes typical, average or normal weather here in California. As it turns out, measuring weather starting just in 1849 could be a big mistake. The period of 1850 to 1880, which was when European settlers first arrived and started keeping track of the weather here in California, includes some of the wettest years in the last several millennia. In other words, what we have come to consider as typical California weather patterns might not be so typical after all, but actually a rare exception to the norm.

How do we know this? Were the natives keeping track for the last few millennia, measuring rainfall in their hats and scratching notes on tree bark? No, the reason we know this is because of recent research into California's rainfall history, research going back over a thousand years.

According to that research, evidence from an increasing number of lakes, rivers and marshes in western North America — and southern South America too, if you want to look elsewhere for confirmation — shows that the period we call the Middle Ages brought extreme droughts to California that persisted in excess of two centuries.

As we have discussed before, our reservoirs in California might be able to hold enough water to last from three to as many as five years, but a drought of 20 years — never mind 200 years — would certainly spell the end of what we know as modern California. For those planning for the future, whether housing or water management, this might be a topic worth looking into. As in, when did these droughts happen? Perhaps more importantly, why did they happen? Far more importantly, we might ask ourselves, just what are the chances of a nightmare of that magnitude ever happening again?

Whether you think that you can, or that you can't, you are usually right.

~ Henry Ford

Marin County, March 28, 1977

Diet pulled his old Buick into the parking lot just off Telegraph Avenue in downtown Berkeley and wondered what he had gotten himself into. He had no figures about western U.S. droughts, or any knowledge of what the other 23 western states affected by the drought needed in the way of funding to overcome their drought conditions. In fact, all he had in his briefcase was a bunch of papers indicating what it was going to cost the Marin Municipal Water District to buy water from L.A. Met, what it was going to cost to build a connector between two separate water systems in the East Bay, and what is was likely to cost to build a pipeline across the Richmond-San Rafael Bridge. He knew as much about the situation in Colorado, Nevada, New Mexico and Arizona as he did about Canada. But he knew that Richard Badger had a bag full of money to hand out, and he was going to get his district a slice of the pie.

The street address he had been given didn't seem to be right. Diet was expecting a hotel, but the address seemed to indicate a nondescript office building. He entered and took the elevator to the 12th floor. When the doors opened, the entire floor was empty, revealing a space much larger than the conference room in the "Little White House" in Washington. There wasn't a stick of furniture to be seen.

"Hello?"

"Over here, Mr. Stroeh."

In the middle of the room behind a pillar, Diet noticed a table and two chairs. Sitting at one chair was a young gentleman wearing a dark business suit, with papers spread out on the table in front of him. A patch of fluorescent lighting shone above the table; otherwise the entire floor of the building was dark.

"Mr. Badger?"

"Pleased to meet you, Mr. Stroeh. Pardon the unusual facilities. I tried to book a hotel conference room but there was nothing available on short notice."

"Fine with me," said Diet. "We could meet in the bar if you want. Anything that's convenient for you."

"Actually, the federal government leases this space in this building, but I didn't know it was empty. As long as we have some light to see by, that's all we need. Please sit down. Now, I'm quite curious, can you tell me what this funding is for, exactly?"

"Sure, I can tell you what the money is needed for in Marin County, because I'm the general manager of the water district there, and we have experienced a severe drought now for almost two years," said Diet.

"I'm afraid that, as far as the rest of the western states go, you are going to have to deal with those folks one on one. All I have is information about my own district."

"I'm sorry, I was led to believe that you were speaking on behalf of a larger group," frowned Mr. Badger. "I believe my notes said that Representative Burton called an emergency session on behalf of 24 western states who were in crucial situations regarding the drought."

"No doubt Representative Burton will be happy to explain that process to you when you speak with him next," answered Diet smoothly, "but all I am authorized to discuss is the state of affairs in Marin County."

Actually, until such time as he had a real deal, Diet had no authority to speak on behalf of anyone, because — once again — it would be his board of directors who made the call in regard to borrowing or spending any money. But if he didn't come up with a promise of money from the feds in the first place, or from any other source, he knew what the board might elect to do, and it wasn't a vote he wanted to have happen.

"Ah, yes, I haven't had the pleasure of visiting Marin County," said Badger, "but I have certainly heard all about Marin on the national news. You live in a beautiful county, I hear, Mr. Stroeh."

"Thank you, yes, it's very nice. Very dry, right now, though. Dry as a bone."

"I believe I saw a national TV show explaining how Marin was among the richest counties in the entire country," said Badger. "Why are you coming to the federal government for assistance? I don't understand why you can't simply purchase water in bulk from someplace and have it delivered."

Here we go again, thought Diet. Does it ever end?

"Actually, sir, it's not quite that simple."

So Diet went through the whole preamble, explanation, summary and wrap-up all over again, explaining to the disaster relief man that Marin was not connected to the state water supply, that everything had been tried, from towing icebergs to anchoring the 6th Fleet in San Pablo Bay, that nothing had worked out, and that you couldn't expect 170,000 people to line up for water from a truck; even if you could, the cost of buying and transporting that water would bankrupt even the rich folks from Marin.

"That's quite a good story about the penguins," smiled Mr. Badger, "and the 6th Fleet stuck in the mud in San Pablo Bay conjures up some humorous images, but let's get down to brass tacks. How much money do you need to borrow?"

"Borrow?" said Diet.

"The federal government is not a bank, Mr. Stroeh. Plus, there is the added factor that Marin has gained a national reputation as the hot tub and chardonnay capital of the western world. How would it look if I went back to Washington and reported that I had just given Marin County $20 million dollars?"

"No need for any such problem to occur," answered Diet smoothly, "because we don't need any $20 million. The grand total is likely to be closer to $6 million and of course we would be most appreciative of a grant. No doubt the voters of the county would remember the favor at election time."

"Normally what we do is grant 20 percent and then loan the other 80 percent," answered Badger, "depending on the circumstances and ability to repay."

"I hoped that you could make it something like a 50-50 deal."

"Marin is far too affluent a constituency for me to make any such arrangement," said Badger. "They'd take my desk away in Washington."

"How does 60/40 sound?" said Diet, crossing his fingers under the table.

"I think the best we can do a 70/30 split, loan to grant, with 3 percent interest."

"Three percent?" thought Diet. "For three percent I'll go down to the parking lot and wash and wax your car."

"You drive a hard bargain, sir," he said, "but the county is in difficult circumstances right now and beggars can't afford to be choosers. If you can guarantee the money can get to us by June 1, we have a deal."

"I'm sorry, I can't guarantee anything of the sort," responded Badger, shuffling through his papers. "A vote may have to be taken in Congress."

"I have every confidence in your ability to accomplish the task," said Diet, fingers again crossed under the table. "It's just that we have already started the construction phase of the pipeline, and our completion date is June 1, and it would be nice at the opening ceremonies to announce that the project is actually funded."

"Yes," said Badger, "I can imagine it would look rather bad if you completed the project and then had to tell the voters there was no way to pay for it."

"Three percent interest, you say?"

"Best we can do."

"Excellent rates, much appreciated," said Diet.

The two men shook on the deal, arranged for theoretical transfers of payments should the loan be approved, and agreed to meet again soon. Diet got into the elevator and floated all the way to the ground.

"I did it. I did it," he thought. "I can't believe it, but we actually have a promise for the money. I wonder what they are going to do with the other $344 million?"

The activist is not the man who says the river is dirty. The activist is the man who cleans up the river.

~ Ross Perot

Berkeley, California, 2006

Recent research clearly shows that California has experienced two "mega-droughts," one lasting around 900-1100 A.D., which, if you have your slide rules handy, works out to be 200 years. The second mega-drought lasted from 1209 to 1350.

Any drought of any extended length we might undergo poses serious problems for all of California, especially Southern California, and in particular the Los Angeles metropolitan region, which gets nearly all of its water from other sources. The crisis in the Middle Ages affected not only California, of course, but many other parts of the world as well. The climate changes that occurred were part of a global weather pattern that brought warmer weather to Europe, but also helped contribute to a "mass collapse of hydraulic civilization," as some have termed it, in other regions of the world.

How do we know all these things? Ah, that's a most interesting question. Thanks to the latest breakthroughs in technology, we have found ways to measure the precipitation of various regions of the world by carbon dating tree rings in specific locations. In our next lesson we will discuss specific regions that were affected by this prolonged drought in the Middle Ages, what the effect was, and how this data is so pertinent to the future of our planet, and specifically California.

39 / Severe and persistent drought

Nothing is impossible for the person who doesn't have to do it.

~ Bumper sticker

Marin County, April 30, 1977

It wasn't until late April that construction finally started on the pipeline over the Richmond-San Rafael Bridge. MGM Construction, a Bay Area company, got the contract. The first phase was the Richmond end of the bridge, which was the most complicated work. Two crews worked full time, 10 to 12 hours a day, taking up two lanes of the bridge as they installed the wooden cradles and laid piping on top of the cradles. Initial concerns were that rush-hour traffic would cause horrendous backup but, surprisingly, the traffic was light and no backups occurred.

MMWD sent a full-time inspector to keep a sharp eye on things, but as the days and weeks proceeded, the project rolled out as smooth as silk. The inspector reported back two or three times a day to Ron Theisen at the MMWD headquarters, but no real problems occurred. While the construction of the pipeline was under way, MMWD staff worked furiously at designing the pump stations at either end of the bridge, and to make connections to the already existing piping systems in Marin and the East Bay. Theisen visited the construction sites about once a week, but no problems arose that couldn't be fixed on the spot.

Meanwhile, back at MMWD headquarters, Diet Stroeh kept a sharp eye on the clock and on what was left of the water supply in Nicasio Reservoir, which was getting very close to rock bottom. A bridge, submerged long ago when the valley was flooded, appeared out of the murk, its crumbling roadbed emerging into the sun for the first time in many decades. All the fish in the reservoir had long since died, and the cracked lakebed was scattered with carcasses on which the crows heartily dined.

Pipeline or no pipeline, everybody in Marin kept a weather eye on the sky, praying for some spring rain. There were some cloudy days, and even a few light showers, but the heavens persistently refused to open. Day after day rolled by with meteorologists forecasting no rain for Marin County. There was some rain to the north in Sonoma, and some sprinkles farther down in the South Bay, but it seemed that Mount Tam created some sort of barrier in the sky that forced the clouds away from magical Marin County.

In April of 1977, usually a wet month for the county, only .51 of an inch of rain fell in Marin. May was not much better, racking up a feeble 1.96 inches spread over several brief showers. By now, everybody in Marin knew that you needed a whopping good gullywasher to get the pipes flowing. But by now, it seemed, everyone had come to the same conclusion; it wasn't going to rain that year and the speculation had been reduced to guessing if, not when, it might rain the following year. June records show a pitiful 0.02 inches of rain fell in Marin, not enough to put a shine on your car, and by then the final chances of any rain for the season were completely over. Pipeline coming or not, it was time to really tighten the belt for another long, hot summer.

The impossible had finally happened. When asked what the chances were that it could go two full wet seasons without any rain in Marin County, Diet Stroeh had told his board it was virtually impossible. Now the only possible thing left to find out was if it would ever rain again.

The Rio Grande is the only river I ever saw that needed irrigation.

~ Will Rogers

Berkeley, California, 2006

As we were discussing in the last lecture, research on the history of drought here in the Golden State shows that we have experienced "severe and persistent drought" in the Americas during the Middle Ages. Since we have only 150 years of rainfall data by which to ascertain what is the normal or typical precipitation here in California, it is my own assumption that we may be relying on completely misleading data as we plan ahead for possible future growth in the state. In particular, we may have the wrong impression of what the future holds for us in terms of precipitation as the world's climate starts to change.

Recent research shows that natives once lived on the lake floor of what we now know as Owens Dry Lake, a body of water that evaporated after an aqueduct was constructed to bring water to Los Angeles from the Sierra. Before the aqueduct was built, Owens Lake was the southern terminus of the Owens River, which drains the eastern watershed of the Sierra. Exploring the lake floor, researchers found proof that the 112-square-mile lake was greatly reduced somewhere back in the early medieval period, and had become a desert playa on which natives were living. This seemingly innocuous data has ominous implications for the future water supply of Los Angeles.

Through the study of ancient tree stumps that were exposed when water levels in Mono Lake in the Sierra dropped over 50 feet between 1940-1982, as rivers feeding it were diverted to provide water to Los Angeles, research shows that trees once grew on what is now the floor of Mono Lake. Carbon dating of the rooted stumps of ancient cottonwoods and Jeffrey pines shows that Mono Lake was greatly reduced by drought during the Middle Ages. Then the trees drowned when water levels began to rise again. By carbon dating the outermost tree layers and counting the tree rings, researchers were able to construct a precise chronology of the medieval droughts.

Other scientists have shown, through the drilling of core samples of mud from underneath San Francisco Bay, that sedimentation levels in the bay abruptly fell while salinity rose during the same period, showing a drastic decline in freshwater flow into the bay and an increase in salt water. Other researchers in the American Midwest have found evidence that during the same period the great sand hills lost their plant cover and began to grow, turning parts of eastern Colorado and western Nebraska into an American Sahara. Lake levels in the upper basin of the Colorado River — the origin of water that currently flows to Los Angeles — also fell sharply.

Remains of bodies recently found in ancient Chumash burial grounds in what is now known as Ventura County in the Los Angeles region show a radical increase in the number of violent deaths from wounds during the same period, possibly an indication of fierce tribal fights over water rights. We also have evidence of the disappearance of the sophisticated Anasazi society in the American Southwest during the same period, and the dramatic decline of the Mayan society in Central America, and the collapse of the Tiwankaku civilization in the Andes.

The prestigious journal Nature has published new scientific evidence, based on core samples of lakebed sediments, showing that the collapse of the Mayan civilization occurred somewhere between 880 and 1000 AD, the same period as the California mega-drought. Other civilizations that are now known to have fallen during the same timeframe include Angkor Wat in Cambodia and the Tula in Mexico.

Does the fact that the world is currently getting hotter mean that the world is going to get drier in the near future, and that a repeat of the medieval droughts is likely? Not necessarily, say a lot of scientists. It all depends on shifting weather patterns, and no one knows yet precisely which way the patterns will evolve. But one thing we do know: aside from rainfall that is stored in lakes and rivers, much of the world's fresh water is frozen in glaciers and snowfields, and the glaciers are rapidly melting as the global temperature rises, as it most certainly is.

You cannot motivate the best people with money. Money is just a way to keep score. The best people in any field are motivated by passion.

~ Eric S. Raymond, author

Marin County, May 2, 1977

At a private session of the MMWD board of directors, Diet Stroeh presented the costs of the ongoing drought to his directors, along with news that the federal loan — theoretically approved — would come at a nice interest rate of only 3 percent, said amount to be added to the current debt load if and when the federal monies ever arrived.

"It's impossible yet to put a dollar figure on the costs that will be required by the county's taxpayers to rebuild all the private lawns and gardens that are being destroyed, or the public playgrounds and sports fields that are turning to dust," he said. "We aren't counting all the golf courses whose fairways have died, because those are private expenses to be borne by private interests."

"I'm not counting all the boulevards and public spaces that have turned brown, because those are municipal costs. I'm not counting the public or private school yards that turned to clay, because those costs must be tallied by the school boards themselves. I don't have any idea of the costs to the farmers whose fields and pastures are disappearing, or whose livestock have died. Fortunately, these items are not my concern, and we won't have to pay the costs incurred."

"However, the costs to the MMWD itself have been considerable to date, and they are indeed our concern. So far, the damage to our budget is $1.5 million for the pipeline and pump stations. Add in other expenditures, such as MGM Construction's bill for building the pipeline, and the total construction costs are $3,591,930. Throw in the purchasing of 10,000-acre feet of water from L.A. Met, and our total debt is approaching $5 million."

"The actual cost of the pipe for the pipeline itself is $1.8 million. That includes 800, 41-foot sections of 24-inch pipe installed on top of wooden stands, on the right lane of the upper deck. The pipeline capacity is 9 million gallons per day, which is the average amount used by customers so far during the drought."

"We are going to have to assess a special fee, on top of everything else we have charged our customers to date, to every meter in our district. My suggestion is that we hold off on any such announcement for a while," he said. "First of all, let's wait until the pipeline is complete and the water is flowing. Secondly, let's wait until the loan from Washington has arrived. Then we'll have a better idea of the exact costs we are going to have to pass on to our customers."

The board unanimously agreed and the motion was passed.

Don't blow it — good planets are hard to find.

~ Quoted in Time Magazine

Berkeley, California, 2006

Yesterday, class, we were talking about evidence that there was a centuries-long drought during the Middle Ages. You will recall that scientists carbon dated tree stumps that reemerged when lake levels dropped during a drought in the 1990s. Anaerobic conditions in the waterlogged stumps prevented their decay. For instance, areas studied include Tenaya Lake in Yosemite National Park, the West Walker River, and Osgood Swamp near Lake Tahoe. At the West Walker River site north of Mono Lake, diversion of rivers and irrigation of nearby agricultural lands had deprived the lake of water, lowering it 170 feet from its natural height and revealing tree stumps. Carbon dating of the stumps shows that the trees died around 900 A.D. The extreme depth at which the stumps were found clearly indicates that earlier droughts in ancient California were more severe and prolonged than previously estimated.

The four California sites are all vulnerable to variations in winter precipitation from Pacific storms traveling on mid-latitude westerly winds. Droughts in this region of the world are attributed to a poleward contraction of the northern circumpolar vortex. The same phenomenon probably occurred in the Middle Ages, involving a simultaneous contraction or change in the wave patterns of the polar vortices in both the northern and southern hemispheres. Evidence of severe drought is also found in lakes in Patagonia, South America, where stumps of ancient beech trees put the approximate dates of tree death around 1100 A.D.

California is extremely vulnerable to even a slight drying of the climate. If medieval warming made the jet stream turn north of California, there are many scientists who wonder if the current trend toward global warming will create a similar effect in California in the future. Those who have become accustomed to a steady supply of snowmelt runoff from the Sierra may be badly misunderstanding California's long-term climate tendencies.

Research has shown us that one of the wettest periods in California's history ended just before the turn of the 20th century, and that California may be on a slippery downhill slope, headed back to its more usual arid state. As that climate change occurs, we will need our dependable sources of frozen snow and ice to supply us during our driest months. Now, class, we may have a serious problem on our hands.

The planet's glaciers are rapidly melting as global temperatures rise. Many of California's glaciers have shrunk. These days the Sierra contains approximately 498 ice features, including perennial ice patches and mountain glaciers. The largest glaciers are Palisades, Dana, Lyell, Kneiss, Maclure, Mendel, Darwin, and Goddard, all of which have retreated between 30 and 70 percent over the past 100 years. Photos taken by early explorers a century ago show a much larger snowpack on all those glaciers.

Recent results from climate modelers do not bode well for the state's snowpack. The latest forecast, published in the Proceedings of the National Academy of Sciences, predicts the state may lose up to 90 percent of its snowpack by the end of this century, if the precipitation that we normally receive falls in the form of rain rather than snow. If that unfortunate situation occurs, then we will receive a much higher volume of runoff all at once, and earlier in the year. If that occurs, then we not only have the dangers of heavy flooding — something that should alarm anyone planning to build or live in the valley floors near Sacramento — but we will have less water later in the summer and fall seasons, when we really need it. The state of California, so dependent on its system of reservoirs and aqueducts, may have to drastically change its methods of water management. Class, we have a problem.

40 / Stress, the silent killer

Obstacles are those frightful things you see when you take your eyes off your goal.

~ Henry Ford

Marin County, May 5, 1977

"You answer it, please."

"I believe we made a deal. We would alternate answering the phone," said Marcia. "I answered it last, so it's your turn."

"When it rang last time it was a wrong number, so that doesn't count."

"For goodness sake, will you get up and answer the phone before we all go crazy?"

Diet sighed, pushed his plate away, and got up wearily from the table. He wasn't really hungry anyway, but since he so seldom got to eat with the family at dinnertime, he didn't want to get up. The phone never stopped ringing, and ignoring the calls just made the callers phone back again.

"Hello?"

"That you, Stroeh?" A deep, masculine voice was on the other end of the phone, along with heavy breathing. He didn't recognize the voice.

"Yes, Dietrich Stroeh here. Who is it? How can I help you?"

"This is Al Rizzuto calling. We've met before. At the Civic Center. I'm the guy who asked you when you were going to stop dicking around and get some damned water into this county before we all go bankrupt. Rizzuto Construction. You remember the name?"

"I'm sorry, Mr. Rizzuto, I don't remember the name. There were a lot of people at the Civic Center meetings. Rizzuto Brothers Construction rings a bell though. You were building those units in Terra Linda, I believe? A condo development?"

"That's right, supposedly a condo development. If you drive by the hospital you can see it, half finished, the foundations in and a lot of wood framing standing around, doing nothing. Been like that for six months, you can't miss it."

"How can I help you, Mr. Rizzuto?"

"You wanna know why the condos are sitting there like that, foundations in and not much happening?"

"I can't say that I have been spending a lot of time thinking about it, Mr. Rizzuto. The fact is I have had a lot on my plate, including a leg of chicken going cold, and also a lot on my mind lately. I'm sure you know all about the drought."

"Know about the drought? I could write a book. I been to all the meetings, I wrote you a letter and I been trying to talk to you for months. You're a hard guy to get a hold of."

"I'm in the middle of dinner right now, Mr. Rizzuto. I think I mentioned the chicken. There is a piece of pie involved too. Can you call me back at my office, during office hours?"

"Really? I called you there a bunch of times, your secretary said she'd pass the message on. Fat lot of good it does calling you there."

"I'm afraid I get an awful lot of mail and phone calls at the office, Mr. Rizzuto. I try to answer them all, but sometimes it can take a while."

"Yeah? Well, here's another thing you ought to be afraid of. I got a lot of my own money sunk into them condos, and I can't afford to sit around for years while you guys twiddle your thumbs. The bank is after my ass for payment, and I'm going to be after the ass of a few of your board members soon if we don't get some damned water into this county. I put good money into some campaigns the last election, and I ain't gonna do that again. The board is gonna hear about this, and then you are going to hear about it from them."

"I already hear from my board frequently, Mr. Rizzuto. On a regular basis. I hear different things from many of them. Was there someone in particular I should expect a call from?"

"Look, let's cut to the chase here. When is that damn pipeline going to be finished, so I can call the bank and keep my own house? I been waiting all winter for you guys to run some water into town, and I can't afford to wait all summer too."

"If you read the papers, Mr. Rizzuto, you will have noticed that the pipeline is proceeding smoothly, and the announced date for completion of the project is June 1. You can take that to the bank."

"June 1? OK, I can live with that. It runs past that date, the bank is going to pull my loan. They pull my loan, I pull someone's chain. I pull that chain, it's your neck on the line."

A drowning man is not troubled by rain.

~ Proverb, Persian

347

Berkeley, California, 2006

Those of you who think that it's a trifle warm in the room today may be right. According to a new scientific study just released, the warming of the world in the last century is greater, and more widespread, than at any time in the past 1,200 years.

In the current issue of Science, researchers Tim Osborn and Keith Briffa of the University of East Anglia in Great Britain, the leading British climate research center, present analysis of tree rings, fossil shells, ice cores and actual temperature measurements from 14 locations around the world, showing that the current warming trend is the most extensive global weather change since the days of the Vikings.

Researchers were able to reconstruct the Northern Hemisphere's climate as far back as the ninth century. Currently the increase is about one degree above normal and two degrees warmer than the last century. However, the last decade has seen the sharpest increases, with all 10 of the warmest years on record occurring since the mid-1990s.

A report from the Goddard Institute for Space Studies puts eight of the past 10 years at the top of the charts for warm weather around the world. That report claims that 2005 was the warmest year in recorded history, while the National Oceanic and Atmospheric Administration and the United Kingdom Meteorological Office rate 2005 as the second-hottest year in history, after 1998.

All three studies agreed that 2005 was the warmest year in recorded history for the Northern Hemisphere. Temperatures in that hemisphere were 1.3 degrees hotter than normal. The high temperatures are a special cause for concern because 1998's temperatures were assisted by an El Niño event, which typically helps drive up temperatures. Overall, the Earth has warmed up 1.4 degrees this century, with most of that rise happening in the past 30 years.

Marin, May 5, 1977

Marcia was putting the dishes away, and handing them to Diet for drying. The kids were in the next room, playing Monopoly.

"I hate it when these people call here all the time. Especially at mealtime. Why don't we just take the phone off the hook from now until June 1?"

"That would be nice," said Diet, reaching to put the plates up on the shelf, "but the guy has a point. It's impossible to get through to me at work. I told my secretary to hold all my calls, I just don't have time to talk to people anymore. I have meetings scheduled all day long. Half of the people at meetings chew my ass out too. Today it was a couple of golf course superintendents, telling me they were going to lose their fairways this summer if we don't get some water. I told them to instruct their customers to stop taking divots."

"Well, thank goodness June 1 is coming soon. How is work on the pipeline coming along?"

"Things are coming along great. We're going to set a world record, pull off a three-year job in six weeks. I keep waiting to hear that we've ordered defective steel or a catastrophe like that, but so far, so good. The pipeline isn't the real problem."

"Don't tell me there is something else," said Marcia, pulling the stopper on the sink and letting the water go down the drain. "Nobody threatening to quit, I hope?"

"No, worse than that," said Diet, watching the water go down the drain. "I haven't heard a word back from Washington as to when we are going to get our money. Nobody is returning my calls. I know how this Rizzuto guy feels."

"Don't worry, you'll get it. Relax and put your energy into other things."

"I can't relax. There are too many other things to worry about. But one thing is for sure. Come June 1, when we have the big ribbon-cutting and all the bigwigs will be there, I sure don't want to be cutting any ribbons while admitting the fact that we don't have any money to pay for the project. If we don't get that money by June 1, my career is going straight down the drain, just like that dishwater."

The bare earth, plantless, waterless, is an immense puzzle. In the forests or beside rivers everything speaks to humans. The desert does not speak. I could not comprehend its tongue; its silence.

~ Pablo Neruda

Berkeley, California, 2006

Purdue University has been busy. The staff there has been so kind as to create the most comprehensive climate model ever to predict the long range future weather of the United States. Their study predicts more extreme temperatures throughout the country, and more extreme precipitation along the Gulf Coast, in the Pacific Northwest and east of the Mississippi.

Run on a cluster of supercomputers, the Purdue study includes many factors not previously included in earlier reports, such as the effects of snow reflecting solar energy back into space, high mountain ranges blocking weather fronts, ocean currents, cloud formations, vegetation cover, greenhouse gases, and hundreds of other data sources. The climate changes the Purdue study predicts are large enough, class, to substantially disrupt our nation's economy and infrastructure.

The Purdue team required a period of five months to run the data on a cluster of mega-computers at the Rosen Center for Advanced Computing on Purdue's campus. With an improvement over previous computer models, several key observations about the change in climate over the next century were observed. The team checked their model's performance by analyzing the period from 1961 to 1985. The study isn't perfect, but Purdue reports they would need a computer cluster at least 100 times as powerful as their current model to improve their accuracy.

The results are alarming. The desert Southwest will experience more heat waves and the heat waves will be of greater intensity. The heat waves will coincide with less summer precipitation. Periods of extreme heat will increase in frequency by as much as 500 percent. Water is already at a premium in the Southwest, and over the next century even less water will be available for the region while the population is predicted to increase rapidly. This is not a good combination.

The Purdue report says that the Gulf Coast will be hotter and will receive its precipitation in greater volume over shorter time periods. The study projects more dry spells interrupted by heavier rainfall. Flooding will be a serious concern.

In the Northeast, summers will be longer and hotter, and heat waves will last longer. In fact, the entire continental United States will experience an overall warming trend. Winter temperatures will rise, and the duration of winter will shrink. In summary, the Purdue model shows in accurate detail that climate change is going to be even more dramatic than previously predicted in any other study.

41 / Making the prime time news

Humanity is acquiring all the right technology for all the wrong reasons.

~ R. Buckminster Fuller

New York City, June 8, 2010

"So, how many feeds can we handle at the same time?"

In the network studios in downtown Manhattan, Janet Spalding was putting together the last touches of her network news special on global climate change. Tomorrow the show would broadcast. The network had put considerable effort into researching, producing and promoting the show, which would air live from a dozen points around the globe, where reporters were stationed at "flash points" where climate change was occurring in dramatic fashion.

"On a split screen, we are going to run four faces at a time, and at the bottom of the screen we'll have the ticker running with the other four names, each with a tiny one-inch icon showing a stop time version of their face," said Trisha McNab, her executive producer. "We'll stay with the first group of four, interviewing in sequence from top left, clockwise, and when we jump from that group to the second group, all the second group of faces will appear together on the split screen simultaneously, while the first group fades to the bottom, where they become small icons in the right-hand corner."

"You introduce the second group by name," she continued. "They nod but don't talk when introduced, then we cut to the first reporter and that face fills the screen. The other three faces we shrink down to two inches, on the left side of the screen while the ticker tape runs at the bottom."

"OK, sounds good," said Spalding, "but we've got cut-ins from the Washington politicians to handle as well."

"When we jump from the reporters to the politicians, we cut the reporters' feeds from the screen entirely," said McNab. "We can't have a dozen feeds and faces running all at once, we'll drive the viewers crazy."

Across the continental United States, the network had positioned six reporters at various locations where climate change was already happening. After extensive discussions, the news department had decided on Oklahoma City as an example of the Midwest, where local water departments were severely restricting access to the Great Oglalla Aquifer. They would cut to Pahrumph, Nevada, representing the Southwest, where several small towns had been abandoned as supplies of water from the Colorado River were cut off.

The network had a reporter in Shreveport, Louisiana, as a Gulf Coast example; the entire coastline was under threat of rising sea levels. They'd jump to Key West, Florida, to show the future of that region as seas rose. Philadelphia, Pennsylvania, was representing the Northeast, at risk for great storms. Stockton, California, would show the future of the Inland Valley if the levee system in the delta were to break during a spring flood.

Overseas, the network had a reporter in the high Andes Mountains of South America, where shrinking glaciers and low water supplies threatened the future of several cities. At great expense, the network had stationed a reporter aboard a cruise ship just off Antarctica, where great chunks of ice were breaking off the land mass. In the Netherlands, a reporter was ready to interview senior politicians about the future of that nation's extensive system of dikes, seriously threatened by rising sea levels.

In the Pacific Ocean, the network had stationed a reporter in the low-lying nation of Kiribati, where the entire population of 75,000 people was threatened with evacuation as the seas rise. In Sydney, Australia, the network had a reporter on the scene to discuss the future of that country, as its record droughts continue.

In Asia, a reporter was stationed in Bangladesh, a sea-level country where the summer monsoon was threatening over 150 million people with deadly flooding. Another reporter was stationed in the Maldive Islands, where the 2004 tsunami had swept over the island like a wave, a dire warning that the entire country could be under sea level in the future.

"What are the last-minute chances of getting anybody at the White House to make an appearance?" asked Spalding. "Can you put the squeeze on the Secretary of State? I've given up on the President saying anything."

"I wouldn't hold my breath getting anyone to talk," replied McNab. "We are zero for a hundred asking that bunch to talk. I'd expect a reply out of Thomas Jefferson before anyone at the White House utters a squeak. The President has them all in lockdown mode. But I'll keep the pressure on and see if anyone breaks."

Aquifers are most severely depleted in parts of India, China, the United States, North Africa and the Middle East. It can take centuries for aquifers to recharge, so the world is currently running a groundwater overdraft of 200 billion cubic meters a year.

~ Water Facts.com

Berkeley, California, 2006

In what are certain to be water wars between various major players in California in the near future, the Central Valley irrigation districts are quietly signing federal contracts that assure their farms ample water for the next 25 to 50 years. In the western San Joaquin Valley, farmers are currently producing water-dependent crops like cotton, melons, tomatoes and almonds worth about $1 billion a year, all sustained with water from California's northern rivers. Those kinds of profits speak loudly to the federal administration.

The water used in the Central Valley is being diverted from the Sacramento and San Joaquin rivers, the Trinity River in the far north, and the Sacramento Delta, where fisheries have declined drastically. A lot of this diverted water is going to something called the Westlands Water District, located southeast of Fresno. At 600,000 acres, this is the nation's largest irrigation district. There are about 2,500 farmers in Westlands, and they are currently receiving about 1.15 million acre-feet of water annually at a special discount rate. They are also successfully renewing their long-term contracts at prices far below those paid by any cities.

Westlands buys its water from the federally administered Central Valley Project, which also supplies water to a third of California's cropland and about 50 cities, including Sacramento and San Jose. Westlands contracts with the Bureau of Reclamation, the federal agency that overseas the whole Central Valley Project.

The discount rates will run for 25 years, with an option for another 25-year renewal.

Traditionally Big Agriculture has always received a special discount for water. For instance, the Marin Municipal Water District pays a hefty $500 an acre-foot for water from the Russian River, while Westlands pays as little as $31 an acre-foot for its federal water. The excuse has always been that the farmers are growing food, which is good for the nation.

There are a lot of critics, mainly environmentalists, who say that Westlands is going to receive much more water than they have in the past under their new contract. In the past, Westlands usually received only a portion of its annual quota, which was based on the availability of delta water; that is, whatever was available after water quality standards for San Francisco Bay and the delta were met. Critics also say much of this Inland Valley acreage should be taken out of production because the irrigation produces toxic water runoff, some of which may drain into state waterways.

The decision of federal agencies to allocate more water to corporate agriculture is a disturbing trend that should cause alarm to water district managers in urban areas who depend on northern rivers for their cities' drinking water supply. This federal decision reverses the tradition of allocating available water equally among farmers, urban areas and projects designed to help the environment. For instance, the 1992 federal Central Valley Project Improvement Act led to some environmental restoration in the Central Valley, the delta and San Francisco Bay.

The creation of CalFed, an agency that brings together state and federal agencies, also allowed more fresh water into the delta and Bay Area. About 800,000 acre-feet of water flowed into the delta, but under the Bush administration in 2003, CalFed created something called the Napa Agreement, which has ended up moving the balance of power to Westlands.

Corporate agriculture is causing more problems to the state than merely locking up discount sources of cheap water that urban areas will soon wish they could access for their own drinking supply. Drain water in the western San Joaquin Valley has been contaminated with selenium for decades. When lands in this desert area are irrigated, salt, boron and selenium present in the soil dissolve, and then rise to the surface. Crops can grow in the presence of selenium, but not in boron or salt. So the soils must be flushed to remove the poison. The drain water has to go somewhere, and in the middle of the desert there is no place for it to go. Selenium is highly toxic to fish and wildlife. Some of the 600,000 acres of the Westlands Water District are so waterlogged that 40,000 acres have already been removed from production.

The best solution might be to take at least 300,000 acres of polluted farmland out of production, permanently, but Big Ag in California is too powerful politically to allow that to happen right now. In the long run, however long that may be, the huge agricultural breadbasket we call the valley may not be commercially or environmentally viable.

Marin County, June 2, 1977

I never said most of the things I said.

~ Yogi Berra

The delivery truck pulled up at Billy's house with a squeal of brakes. The driver leaned out the window and yelled to Billy, who was lounging on the front porch with a cool bottle of Bud.

"Hey, where ya want these barrels to go?"

"You see that driveway there?" asked Billy, indicating Percy's house next door. "Drive up to the back and stack them against the side of the house."

Heading into his own house, Billy came back out with a bag that he tucked under his arm and ambled over to Percy's house, where the truck was parked at the back of the driveway. The driver was stacking the barrels against the wall, filling up the driveway. Since Percy did not own a car, being in a state of temporary cash depletion, there was no reason not to block the garage doors. Work in the accounting business being slow these days, Percy was currently out on one of his frequent walks, a fact that Billy had earlier ascertained with his binoculars from the living room window. Billy stood thoughtfully by, slowly sipping on his beer, counting as the driver unloaded the barrels, watching the street carefully for signs of Percy's return.

"Ya know, this has gotta be the biggest load a talc I ever delivered. Watcha gonna do with all this stuff?" asked the driver, wiping his brow in the summer heat. "Open up a chain of beauty parlors or what?"

"Thanks, man," said Billy, slipping a $20 bill into the driver's shirt pocket as the deliveryman climbed back into the cab. "I appreciate you taking all the bags apart at the store and pouring them into these barrels."

As the delivery van pulled away, Billy darted over to the barrels and quickly slapped labels on the side of each one. In the distance he could hear Roscoe barking. Percy took frequent walks, but he was seldom gone long. Darting back to his own front porch, Billy sat out on the front steps where he couldn't be missed by passersby, put up his feet on the railing, and waited.

"I see that you are hard at work, as usual," said Percy, red-faced and puffing from his hike up the hill, "putting together great thoughts for the edification of adolescent girls, I assume?"

"Yep, got some good lyrics for my next song percolating," responded Billy. "Do you know any words that rhyme with dork? Hey, want a Bud?"

"What the bloody hell is all this?" exploded Percy, ignoring the offer of free beer as he suddenly noted the barrels stacked in his driveway. "Are you using my property as a convenient location to store your excess bloody beer barrels? Where the hell did all those things come from?"

"Just had them delivered, Perce," said Billy, sauntering along behind as Percy strutted over to his own driveway like a bantam rooster checking on his flock. "A present for you, for putting up with all my parties. Kind of a way of saying thanks."

"A present?" responded Percy, stooping down to peer at the labels on the barrels. "What the hell do I need with a lifetime supply of beer? Get this bloody rubbish out of here before I call the police. You're just using my property as a place to keep your excess booze."

"Ain't beer in the barrels, Perce," said Billy, bending over to point at the label. "It's powdered water."

"Powdered water?" exclaimed Percy. "My word, I've never heard of such a thing."

"Latest thing on the market, just out," said Billy, kicking one of the barrels for emphasis. "Kinda expensive, but money's not an issue here. More of a principle of the thing."

"What principle?" asked Percy, trying to pry the lid off one of the barrels.

"Well, you know that old saying about 'neither a borrower or a lender be'?"

"I am familiar with the adage," said Percy, tugging uselessly on the lid, "but I had not established you in my mind as someone familiar with literary or biblical references, especially those of philosophical import."

"Seems to me that you got a good lawn and garden going here, Perce," said Billy, taking a sip on his beer while giving a nod toward Percy's back yard, which was a riot of green and colorful flowers and foliage, "and with this drought and all, might be hard this summer keeping it goin'. I thought maybe I'd lend a hand, on account of all the noise problems and all, from my parties. My own pool is gettin' kinda low these days, all this heat causin' evaporation, so I can't help you with any real water. So I thought I'd get you the second-best thing."

"Your pool is getting low?" inquired Percy, avoiding looking Billy in the eye. "I hadn't noticed. Mine was empty for quite a while, until lately. Rather expensive to repair, even more expensive to fill these days, what with the price of water going through the roof."

"Yeah, well try this stuff instead," said Billy, nodding at the barrels over his shoulder while walking away. "Shovel it on deep on all your plants, spread it around the whole yard. Lots there, should last you all summer."

"Um, yes, well, thank you," mumbled Percy in a low voice, watching Billy walk away while tugging on the lid of the barrel. "Very sporting of you. Powdered water, indeed. Never heard of such a thing."

42 / Down on the levee

The universe is not required to be in perfect harmony with human ambition.

~ Carl Sagan

Nepal, June 8, 2010

Sumita sat at the fire, a pot of barley meal and dried yak meat simmering in a large pot. As soon as she had seen the hiking party returning down the valley, she had washed and changed into her best clothes. Dipping into the meager store of food on the roof, she quickly started a hot luncheon meal. Her father carried a pot of chang out into the front yard, welcoming the hiking party with a wooden bowl of the milky liquid. It was a modest party, but a party nonetheless. Mountain climbed, mission accomplished, welcome the conquering heroes.

"What ya think, Will?" whispered Bob Walsh, nudging Will with his foot as he sipped from the bowl of chang. "That the best thing you've seen in a month of Sundays, or what?"

Will, sipping from his own mug of chang, didn't answer. Nodding, he didn't take his eyes off Sumita as she scooped spoonfuls of the barley meal into bowls and passed them around. Smiling, she handed a brimming bowl to Will, her eyes downcast as she did so. Reaching for it, Will casually brushed her hand, causing Sumita to twitch, spilling a small amount on his hand.

"Mmm," said Will, smiling, taking his hand and licking the broth from his fingers with his tongue. "Very tasty. Finger-lickin' good. I always prefer my barley mush with a little rancid yak butter."

Sumita, although not understanding a word, blushed. Will licked his fingers slowly, trying to catch her eye. Her cheeks glowing red under her darkly tanned skin, she kept her eyes down, pouring more barley mush into another bowl, and passing it to Walsh.

"You know, Will, I think you are making that girl embarrassed with your poor table manners," said Walsh, sipping from his bowl. "Perhaps you ought to restrain yourself a moment, until you've had the opportunity of proposing marriage to the sweet thing. Bring her back to Kathmandu, have a royal wedding, maybe slaughter a few goats for the occasion."

"I could go for a little goat right now," said Dave Moore, "or even a big goat. Time to celebrate. Went to see the glacial lake, and nothing fell on our heads. But we gotta go now, before we get stuck here."

"Easy with that chang," said Walsh, pointing his finger at the porters. "We aren't staying here today. Enough goofing around. Time to get the heck out of here before this rain makes the river impassable."

"Ah, we've got plenty of time to make it back down before dark," said Will. "It's only a few miles, and downhill. Let's wait for the rain to stop. We made it up the mountain, I got my video footage, and nobody got hurt. And, by the way, gentlemen, my apologies for my risking people's lives on our little detour. The footage of Tsho Rolpa Lake is going to get me on the speaking circuit for sure. I thank you for indulging me in this little adventure. Relax, what's the rush? The scenery down here is even better than the scenery up there."

"Well, you finish the mush by yourself then," said Walsh, getting up and dusting himself off, "because the rest of the group is now heading to Beding. We'll see you there tonight, and if you don't show up we'll be leaving for Namche Bazaar first thing in the morning."

The porters got up to go. Moore looked at Will, and Will looked at Moore, and Moore looked at Sumita, who ducked her head and made herself busy picking up the bowls. Moore looked at Will one more time, shook his head, and headed for the door. Then he stopped and turned.

"We'll see you in a couple of hours, right?"

"Not a problem, bro. I'll be there," said Will. "Maybe Sumita here will walk down with me. Looks like the monsoon is here, and it's probably time to leave here anyway."

Berkeley, California, 2006

We've been talking a lot about future drought, and what climate change will do to the state of California, and how that change will affect our future drinking water supply. Next we are going to discuss another possible natural disaster, one that might happen as early as tomorrow.

First of all, let's sum up. The state's reservoirs can only hold water for a couple of years, and if it doesn't rain during that time frame we are in big trouble. Let's suppose that pesky Pacific high pressure zone stays lodged up in the North Pacific, as it has in the past, and we don't get our usual amount of rain. What do we do then? Tow icebergs from the Antarctic?

We've gone over how warmer air temperatures in the past few decades have reduced the size of the Sierra Nevada glaciers, which currently supply us with a nice, steady flow of runoff during those hot summer and early fall months when we need it most. We've discussed how much the air temperature has risen in certain parts of the planet recently, as in Alaska, where glaciers are retreating at an alarming rate. We have theorized what will happen to glaciers and our snowpack over the next century if warmer air temperatures produce rain instead of snow.

Now, instead of talking about future events, let's talk about what could happen tomorrow. Something that would rob the state of its drinking water immediately. What we urgently need to discuss in California is the delta and the levee system built up around it to store and direct much of our fresh water supply. What will happen to the delta if there should be a big earthquake, which all of our scientists say is bound to happen? It's not a question of if, but when. And we are way overdue for the "big one."

How many of you have seen coverage of the series of hurricanes that have hit Florida and the Gulf Coast states the last few years? Meteorologists have warned for years that warmer air and water temperatures would increase the severity of hurricanes originating in the mid-Atlantic and traveling through the Caribbean or Gulf of Mexico. Scientists have said that these new storms would be more frequent and more severe than in the past, and they were certainly right. But when a big one hit a major city located at sea level — in fact, the ground under New Orleans has subsided over the years and is now under sea level — the levees designed to protect the city broke, and the resulting flood caused more damage than did the hurricane itself.

When the hurricane hit and the levees broke, the government assured us that emergency forces were in place to secure the damage. What everyone immediately discovered is that the forces of nature are much stronger than we thought. You can't stop a hurricane, and you can't corral a flood and make it do what you want. Water, as we have discussed, is 9,000 times heavier than air. Air, whipped into a hurricane, can cause catastrophic damage, but it doesn't even begin to compare to the damage that water can do when it gets loose.

There is also, for our purposes in this class, the more important aspect that all this water that is stored in the delta is fresh drinking water, and if it is let loose then there goes most of the water for the people of California to drink. Whoosh, in a flash it's all gone, and it's not replaceable. Think about that for a while.

Over 50 percent of the population of developing countries is exposed to polluted sources of water. If current trends continue, by 2025 two-thirds of the world's population will be living with serious water shortages or almost no water at all.

~ Water Facts.com

New York City, June 8, 2010

Janet Spalding swore under her breath. On the phone with an undersecretary for the chief of staff at the White House, she had been put on hold again, a sure sign that key people at the White House were getting fed up with her incessant phone calls. Today was the latest in a long line of calls her staff had placed to the President, the Secretary of State, the Vice president and a host of other senior government officials. Since she had not received an official refusal from anybody she had invited to appear on her live television special, that meant there was still hope that one of them might possibly relent. The politics of the day were as variable as the weather.

"Hello, Ms. Spalding?"

"Yes, surprisingly I'm still here."

"I've been unable to reach the Secretary directly, but his chief of staff has just notified me that it may be possible for him to spare five minutes for you during the broadcast, but right now he is unable to confirm his participation."

"When, exactly, do you expect that he will confirm his schedule for tomorrow?"

"The Secretary is in a meeting with the President right now, and when he returns to his office I will ask his chief of staff again. I will get back to you this afternoon for sure."

"Tell the Secretary that the amount of time left in the program for anyone from the administration is now down to two minutes. All I'd like him to do is comment on climate change issues pertaining to Asia, South America and Europe, and no comment will be required about what is happening here in the United States."

"That's fine, Ms. Spalding. Would it be possible for you to fax or email the script for the program in advance, so that the Secretary can familiarize himself with the issues?"

"I'm afraid that is against network policy. I'm sure the Secretary has heard the phrase 'climate change' before. Tell him it's something like global warming, only he has our guarantee that we won't be using that particular phrase in the program, given that it seems to make some people in the government so nervous."

Every day, 6,000 people, mostly children under the age of 5, die from diarrhoeal diseases.

~ Water Facts.com

Berkeley, California, 2006

We were theorizing what will happen to California's drinking water when a big earthquake hits in or near the delta. According to Lester Snow, who happens to be the director of the California Department of Water Resources and should know a thing or two about it, we stand to lose the drinking water supply for two-thirds of the state for an entire year. A major earthquake in the Northern California anywhere near the Bay Area itself would likely be an unmitigated disaster, but if you add the possibility of losing two-thirds of your water for the entire state for a year, well, that goes beyond the definition of a disaster. It would be a national emergency. New Orleans was described as the greatest national disaster in American history, but what we all saw in New Orleans would be a drop in the bucket compared to an earthquake that broke the delta levees.

According to Mr. Snow, a "moderate" earthquake of 6.5 on the Richter scale could collapse 30 levees, flood 16 delta islands, and damage 200 miles of additional levees. It would also damage or destroy at least 3,000 houses and 85,000 acres of farmland.

If there were a major earthquake and extensive breaks in the levee system, salt water would rush into the system, mixing with the fresh water, rendering much of the water supply worthless for drinking purposes. It would also cause an immediate shutdown of the pumps that send water south to the San Joaquin Valley and to all of Southern California, including the metropolitan Los Angeles area. That's about 15 million thirsty people right there. Can you imagine 15 million people without water for a year?

Any major earthquake could also damage the pipeline that leads from Hetch Hetchy to San Francisco, so you could say that most of the Bay Area's population of 6 million people would also be without any water supply for an undetermined length of time. Any earthquake above 6.5, which earthquake experts tell us is quite possible, would almost guarantee a complete breakdown of the Northern California water supply, if it hit in the wrong place. It's possible for the Northern California area to be hit with a quake of 7.0 on the Richter scale, or 7.9, or even an 8.0. It happened in Alaska a few years ago. This is something we should all be concerned about.

Widespread levee breaks, without an earthquake, also could imperil the water supply for 22 million Californians. A report by the Department of Water Resources says that levees in the delta are deteriorating and that new housing on flood plains is putting many more people at flood risk. Money to maintain levees, however, has declined sharply in state budgets during the past few years.

Much of the delta was cheaply filled in a century ago for farming. Ground level behind the levees has been sinking ever since, in some areas to 25 feet below sea level since their construction. Houses in a new residential area north of Sacramento could be inundated with up to 20 feet of water if the wrong levee breaks. It's not hard to imagine; levees settle over the years and can become unstable. Rodents can open up passageways for water to seep through. If a log rots over the years — and lots of logs were shoved into old levees during their construction — an air space can be created that catches water and compromises a levee.

The state looks after 1,600 miles of levees that protect at least a half-million people, including more than 600 miles of levees built on unstable peat soils. Few levees anywhere in the nation are built to more than a 100-year standard. In the Netherlands, levees along the Rhine River are built to a 1,250-year standard. As I've already said, trusting records that go back only a hundred years is pure foolishness. If the state of California experiences a heavy spring flood, exacerbated by early snowfalls followed by heavy rains, melting glaciers and early runoff, we could easily experience a "thousand year" flood. Say goodnight to your water supply then.

Marin County, June 3, 1977

If all the world's water were fit into a gallon jug, the fresh water available for us to use would equal only about one tablespoon.

~ National Rivers System

The Marin Municipal Water District offices were very busy, which was business as usual. The phones were ringing, as always, with people calling and complaining about their water bills. Diet's secretary buzzed him from the front lobby.

"Diet, you have a visitor."

"Who is it, the Pope? I'm very busy right now."

"Almost the same thing. It's Mayor Stanford from Sausalito and she says she wants to see you right away. Or else."

Stanford waltzed into the room, again accompanied by her lawyer, D. Walter Peppers. This time, instead of crying, she was smiling broadly. Peppers hung back behind her, his hat in his hand, looking sheepish.

"Can I help you, Mayor Stanford?" said Diet.

"I believe you are holding on to something of mine, buster," said Sally, helping herself to a seat, and indicating that Peppers should do the same.

"I'm sorry, ma'am," said Diet. "I'm very busy right now. The county is running out of water and we have a ton of people who are angry about their water bills. I'm not sure I understand what you're talking about."

"It's in the drawer," she said.

"I'm sorry? What drawer? What has that got to do with anything?" said Diet.

"That drawer," said Sally, pointing to Diet's desk. "Open the bottom drawer."

Slowly, looking at Sally quizzically, Diet opened the drawer to see what she was pointing at. There was the usual assortment of papers, stapler, pens, and miscellaneous office supplies found in most desks. "What is it, ma'am?"

"I believe you have a bill in there for $2,500," she said with a big smile. "I believe you said if we ever got through this stinkin' drought you would give it back to me. Cancel it. Building a pipeline means that the drought is over. It opens next week, right?"

"Why yes," said Diet, a smile breaking through on his own face. "Yes, I did say that. I had totally forgotten. I believe that we agreed that if you stayed within your allotment for the duration of the drought, I promised to tear up the bill."

With that, Sally held out her hand for the bill. "Give over," she said.

"Wait just a minute," said Diet. "How do I know that you have actually stayed within your allotment?

Sally turned to Peppers and held out her hand. "Show the man, Loverboy," she said.

With a flourish, Peppers reached into his briefcase and pulled out a sheaf of papers, each numbered and held together with a paper clip. He handed the entire pile to Diet.

"I believe, sir, that if you examine the monthly water usage you will note that not only has my client stayed within the allowed monthly usage, or allotment as you so crudely put it during our initial discussions," said Peppers, "but I think you will find that my client has actually stayed well below the so-called allotment for her classification of business. Which is, as you know, a water-intensive operation."

Diet went through the invoices one by one, studying each one carefully. Indeed, just as Peppers said, the monthly bill for the Valhalla restaurant was not only well below the allotment, in each successive month the amount of usage had actually dropped.

"That's really impressive," said Diet, looking up from the invoices and smiling at Sally. "I'm a man of my word, and I'll be glad to tear up your bill."

Reaching into the desk, he pulled out the bill that Sally had received six months before. Holding it up theatrically, he carefully tore it in half, then quarters, and dropped the pieces of paper into his trash can.

"Done," he said, and sat back in his chair.

"Just one thing," he said, as Sally and Peppers rose from their chairs and made their way to the door of his office. "A question: I'd like to know how you did it. That's really impressive savings. What did you do, switch to paper plates? The Valhalla is a fancy operation. Did people complain?"

Indeed, the Valhalla was a swank and imposing restaurant, with a large sundeck right on Richardson Bay, the famous cityscape of San Francisco looming far in the distance through the famous fog that often drapes the bay. Valets took your coat and parked your car. It was a place where customers expected to see not only a glass of water on the table, but perhaps a bowl of roses too.

"Yes, paper plates," said Peppers with a forced smile.

"Nah," said Sally, with a smile and a wink. "Don't believe a word the chump says. I closed the men's."

"Sorry?" said Diet. "What did you do?"

"I closed the men's. The toilet. I closed it since I saw ya last," said Sally. "Put a sign on it saying 'under repair.' Left it that way for six months."

"What?" said Diet, amazed. "But what did your customers do?"

"I made the guys piss off the end of the deck," she said. "Some of them complained, but I set them straight. I'm the stinkin' Mayor, and I can do whatever I want."

We have the Bill of Rights. What we need is a Bill of Responsibilities.

~ Bill Maher, TV talk show host

Berkeley, California, 2006

In 1997, more than 50 California levees collapsed during rainstorms, killing eight people, forcing the evacuation of 100,000 people and destroying 24,000 homes. Levees have failed more than 140 times in the past century. Many were hastily constructed a century ago, when farmers simply pushed back dirt to protect crops. Over the years, they were lengthened and built higher, but the internal structure of many is not solid. A levee break in Stockton during dry, sunny weather in June 2004 flooded 12,000 acres of farmland and caused $150 million in damage. The cause is unknown because rushing water washed away the evidence.

This Jones Tract failure in June 2004 created a lake more than 50 percent larger than Contra Costa County's Los Vaqueros Reservoir. Crews worked 25 days 'round the clock to fill the 500-foot breach with 200,000 tons of rock, and it took about six months to pump out the water. University of California Professor Jeffrey Mount predicts that there is a 2-in-3 chance that a major storm or earthquake will cause widespread delta levee collapse in the future.

Senator Dianne Feinstein called the New Orleans levee failure a wake-up call for California. She sponsored CalFed legislation that authorized $90 million to repair the most vulnerable delta levees. Since then, the corps has identified 200 repairs in 12 levee systems that need work. Approximately $1.3 billion is needed to complete the job, and according to a 2000 state analysis of delta seismic risk, it may not be possible to make the levees earthquake proof. Assemblyman John Laird of Santa Cruz tried to set up a framework for reporting on the condition of the levees, and a reliable source of funds to repair them, but his bill, AB 1665, failed to come to a vote.

Most of this data we've talked about today pertains to earthquakes. We haven't even talked about the possibility of major floods collapsing the levees. The gradual elevation of sea level, linked to global warming, simply compounds the risk. Scientists predict California coastal waters may rise as much as a foot over the next 50 years, and possibly even three feet over the next 100 years. You know, maybe it's time we all moved to higher ground.

43 / My cup runneth over

Everywhere water is a thing of beauty gleaming in the dewdrop, singing in the summer rain.

~ John Ballantine Gough, American temperance orator

Nepal, June 8, 2010

The trekking party and the porters reluctantly stepped outside the yak shelter in Na into a heavy rain. Sumita followed, picked up the water jug and pointed toward the river, indicating that she wanted to go down and get more water. Will stepped aside and indicated with a bow that she should go first.

"We'll see you guys in a couple of minutes," said Will, taking the water jug from Sumita and putting it under his arm. "Be right back."

"Hey, man, it's starting to pour," said Moore. "We got to leave."

"Go ahead, man," said Will, heading down the steep path toward the river. "I won't be five minutes."

"Let them go, two young lovers," said Walsh, watching the pair quickly disappear downhill. He picked up his daypack, hoisted it to his back, and went over to help the porters load their heavy packs. "Let's get back to Beding, and then back to the trek. This stupid detour has gone on long enough."

"We can't just leave Will behind," said Moore, scrunching his neck in the ever-increasing downpour. "Let's go get him."

"How you going to force him to come?" said Moore. "You got a gun? Look, he wants to be alone with the girl for a minute, understand? He's in love."

"It isn't right to leave him behind," retorted Moore. "What if he doesn't show up in Beding?"

"Look, we'll be in Beding in an hour or so, dry out, and wait for Will. If he doesn't show, I'll round up a posse, come back and hog tie him. I am like, totally fed up with all these stupid delays and detours."

"It's still not right to leave him," said Moore, refusing to budge.

"What are you, his mother? Or do you have the hots for the girl yourself?" said Walsh, beginning to walk down the trail.

"Hey, man, you need a punch in the head or what?" yelled back Moore, not moving.

"Hey, man, you can stay here too if you want," yelled Walsh over his shoulder. "You can both stay here forever if you want, but the trek is now getting back on track."

Moore ran down the trail and caught Walsh by the arm.

"What if Will doesn't show?"

"He'll show, alright. He might be dazzled but he's not brain dead. Look," said Walsh, holding up two daypacks. "I got his pack right here. He doesn't have any food, no sleeping bag, no rain gear, nothing. He'll show up in Beding alright. That guy can't go an hour without eating and in about two minutes he's going to be completely soaked."

Walsh took Moore by the arm and started walking down the trail, dragging Moore along with him. Moore kept turning his head back to look for Will.

"We'll get wet the next few days, but we'll be OK," said Walsh. "It's not getting soaked that worries me, it's the rivers rising. A couple of hours of this stuff, the rivers will be five feet deeper."

"The river will be five feet deeper? How about that damned lake we just left? How much deeper will it be then?" said Moore. "It was just about over its banks when we were there. Yesterday afternoon, that glacier was melting, it was so hot. How about five feet of rain falling on it? What then?"

"The same thing as last year, and the year before that, I suppose," shrugged Walsh, keeping a brisk pace and one hand on Moore's jacket. "The monsoon shows up every year, like clockwork. It rains one heck of a lot. Will said that lake always drains, and it's never overflowed yet."

"What does he know? What if a really big chunk of that glacier breaks off and slides into the lake?" asked Moore, shrugging off Walsh's hand, turning again and looking back. "What happens if you add a lot of rain and a huge chunk of ice at the same time? Have you given any thought to that?"

"I have, and that's one reason why we need to get out of here immediately. The only way to get Will to leave that girl behind is to put some pressure on. We leave him behind now, he'll get soaked. That'll set his head straight," said Walsh, walking even faster. "We gotta get out of here, now. Look at what's coming our way"

With that, both of them looked up at the sky. The clouds were black, boiling up from the valley far below, and it was raining like hell. The porters were already far ahead, heavy packs notwithstanding. A strong wind swept up the valley from the south, the sky rumbled and growled, and thunder crackled from somewhere in the distance.

Moore slowed down, then stopped.

"I gotta take a leak," he said.

"Hell man, I don't care what you or Will gotta do," said Walsh, as he kept walking. "Just get it done and get down to Beding quick. We gotta get out of this place now."

Stopping behind a huge boulder to relieve himself, Moore reached into his pack, pulled out his satellite phone and turned it on. "Mayday, Mayday. Washington, this is Walker One," he said. "Time for disaster relief. Talk to me, boys, we now have a problem. Talk to me right now. Time to get that chopper airborne. We have a problem."

In Jakarta, Indonesia, the poor pay water vendors 60 times the price of water from a standard connection; in Karachi, Pakistan, 83 times; and in Port-au-Prince, Haiti, and Nouakchott, Mauritania, 100 times.

~ Water Facts.com

Berkeley, California, 2006

Class, you may remember just a few years ago when the Jones levee collapsed near Stockton. That was no 100-year flood, or earthquake. The levee just gave way. It was old, like the rest of the delta levees. To refresh your memories, let me remind you that this single levee collapse cost about $100 million to clean up. We may never have a final accounting of the cost of the Louisiana flood caused by Hurricane Katrina, but the New Orleans levees that gave way were built to withstand a 250-year flood, while California's delta levees have only been built to a 100-year standard, if that.

The California Department of Water Resources tells us that a major flood of the lower Sacramento River, which is guaranteed to happen, would cause at least $14 billion in damage. It would flood about 130,00 acres under an average of five feet of water, and damage or destroy 93,000 homes, 3,400 businesses and over 500 industrial sites. In other words, it would make the Louisiana catastrophe look like a bad rainstorm.

Going back to the subject of earthquakes for a minute, the department of water resources says that a 6.5 earthquake near the western delta would breach at least 30 levees, weaken or undermine an additional 200 miles of levees, and pull 300 billion gallons of salt water into the delta. It would close the pumps that send water to Southern California for a year. On top of all that, it would generate up to $40 billion in economic damage for the next five years.

L.A. Met currently contracts for 2 million of the 4 million acre-feet of water that moves through the delta every year. L.A. Met has 18 million customers. It's not just the Los Angeles metropolitan area that depends on water from the delta. Everything south of Hayward relies on it. That includes Silicon Valley and all of the San Joaquin Valley, where the dairy farmers and big agricultural interests contribute most of the $30 billion a year the state earns from agriculture.

Every once in a while, people in high places talk about building a canal around the entire delta, just in case the levees fail, which of course the levees are going to do at some time. But every time the idea is raised, somebody else screams bloody murder, like what happened back in 1982 when Proposition 9 was put on the ballot. The idea of a canal was defeated 62 percent to 37 percent. In the Bay Area the "no" votes totaled 95 percent.

You see, if a canal of some sort were actually constructed, there are lots of people who think that Southern California would no longer care what happens to the
delta, which may be true. The delta's indigenous fish population is already at an all-time low, and many people
suspect that too much water is already heading south. But
any way you look at it, if the levees fail, the entire state
will be in an emergency situation the likes of which will
make Hurricane Katrina look like a tempest in a teapot.

---

*One gallon of gasoline can contaminate approximately 750,000
gallons of water.*

~ Water Facts.com

Washington D.C., June 8, 2010

---

*The recommended basic water requirement per person per day is
50 litres. But people can get by with about 30 litres. Say five
litres for drinking and cooking and another 25 to maintain
hygiene. The reality for millions comes nowhere near. The
average U.S. citizen uses 500 litres per day, while the British
average is 200.*

~ The New Internationalist

"Mr. President, sir, I hate to interrupt, but there is an emergency call that I think you should take."

"Oh, really, who is it? The President of Iran saying he has a nuclear bomb in a suitcase?"

"No, sir, it's the gentleman from the Secret Service whom you said should be put through any time he calls," said the presidential aide. "He's on line two."

President William White was in bed, reading reports about the disastrous agricultural situation in the American Midwest, where long-term projections were for yet more drought. He quickly punched line two.

"Rich, what you got?"

"Sir, our agent in Nepal has gone to Code Red. He believes the situation is deteriorating rapidly and that a chopper should be deployed immediately."

"Call our consul in Kathmandu and get the bird in the air. I want hourly updates, no matter what time of day. Get the medical team ready at the hospital, and call Moore back immediately. Tell him to call me here personally the first chance he gets. I want to know exactly what's happening on the ground. Now, what else do you know?"

Marin County, June 7, 1977

Engineering is a great profession. There is the satisfaction of watching a figment of the imagination emerge through the aid of science to a plan on paper. Then it moves to realization in stone or metal or energy. Then it brings homes to men or women. Then it elevates the standard of living and adds to the comforts of life. This is the engineer's high purpose.

~ Herbert Hoover

"Hey, Diet, how ya doing?"

"Top notch, chief," said Diet to one of the local newspaper reporters. "Nice day."

It was a warm and sunny day, hardly unusual because it had been warm and sunny nearly every day for 25 months in a row, but in many ways it was a very special day. Today was Pipeline Day. Parking his car on the temporary lot just east of the Richmond Bridge, Diet checked his tie in the car's rear-view mirror. As always, he was nattily dressed for the occasion. Today was a big day, but he was relaxed. The job had been accomplished, on time and under budget. Today was just for the formalities.

Tests run on May 25 had indicated that the pipeline was functioning perfectly. His staff had run 750,000 gallons through the pipeline across the Richmond Bridge to the pump house near the Rod and Gun Club in Marin. At first the water was a bit brown and murky, but that was expected given that the pipes hadn't been washed and connections to the East Bay water supply had never been tested. Within a matter of minutes the muddy quality had disappeared and the water ran clear as a mountain stream.

More importantly, to his immense relief, he had quietly received official notification from Washington a few days before that the loan to pay for the pipeline had been approved. When the ribbon cutting was held, he could hold up his head with satisfaction that the job was done, and done right. Nobody needed to know the details, about how close a shave it had been. He'd keep that information to himself.

Strangely enough, there were no TV cameras for the ribbon cutting, and only a smattering of newspaper and radio reporters in attendance. The fun had finally gone out of the media game of cat and mouse a few weeks earlier, when it became apparent that the pipeline was bang on time and straight on schedule. Only disasters make front-page news; successes get buried on the back pages. There was still no sign of rain, but the citizens of Marin County were finally going to get their long-anticipated supply of water, and there was no fun in mocking that.

Official dignitaries were few and far between. Governor Jerry Brown was in Sacramento, attending to affairs of state. Water Resources Board Director Ron Robie sent a representative. Marin and local officials turned out in numbers, because certainly Marin voters cared whether or not the water came on line, but state and national officials kept a low profile. After all, the drought was still going on, and people all over the western U.S. were suffering, and there was nothing to celebrate in that.

Diet kept his speech short. Parking lots at the end of bridges are not exotic locations, and nobody wanted to hang around and admire the view.

There are about 60,000 community water suppliers in America.

~ Water Facts.com

"It's been a long struggle to find a way to get water to Marin County, and I hope we all learn a good lesson from what has happened," he said. "It's imperative that all water districts find a way to cooperate in the future, because at any time any one of us could find themselves stuck in the same position."

"Marin is unique in that we are not connected to the state water system, but other districts could find themselves in a bind of their own, whether they are connected to the state system or not," he continued. "Water is obviously essential to everyone, and we cannot simply say 'too bad' if any one district has problems. People cannot survive without water, and there will come a time when this same sort of thing happens to some other district. The lesson is that we all have to pull together to create a system where people work together, not work against each other."

"I'd like to thank all the managers of all the water districts in California that worked together to make today a reality, and the state and national officials who participated in this complicated solution. It took everybody working together to make it happen, and that should be a lesson to folks in the future when the next big drought hits."

The podium at which he spoke was simply a box balanced on a big stool, with a handful of microphones dangling from the top of the box. There was no large water wheel to turn, no actual connection to the pipeline running along the edge of the parking lot a few yards away. He simply touched a button that sent a signal to the pump house a few hundred yards away. In the pump house a MMWD engineer turned the actual wheel. There was no sound, no fireworks, no sign that the water was moving through the pipe, but by looking at the instrument panel the engineer could see the dials flickering. He leaned out the pump house door, waved and gave the thumbs up.

"Ladies and gentlemen," said Diet. "The system is now on line. We have water! I officially declare the Marin pipeline open."

Nepal, June 8, 2010

What is the appropriate behavior for a man or a woman in the midst of this world, where each person is clinging to his piece of debris? What's the proper salutation between people as they pass each other in this flood?

~ Buddha

Will took the pail from Sumita. Smiling, he pointed to the riverbank where she should sit. He drew the pail of water and sat down next to her. Both of them stared at the river rushing by. What was there to say? In a minute he would have to get up and walk away, to his giant world of politics and the global environment. She would return to the hut, and her tiny world of goats and yaks, and all would be as before.

"The only words I know in Nepali are: 'Can I get a bottle of beer?'" said Will, staring ahead at the river. "I bet you don't even speak that dialect. I bet you don't understand a word I am saying. But I'd sure like to see you in a fancy dress at the annual ball at the White House. Boy, that would put a buzz up the butt of all the bureaucrats in Washington."

Sumita said nothing. She had never even met a foreigner before, never mind talked to a tall, handsome, blond American. She knew nothing of Washington, politics, Kathmandu or bureaucrats. It was forbidden for Nepali girls to associate with strange men. Still, she sat quietly and enjoyed the moment for what it was, an exciting minute that would never be repeated as long as she lived.

Far up the valley there was a distant rumble, then a boom like an explosion — not rolling thunder from the clouds above but a roar like that of an enormous tiger let out of its cage. Both Will and Sumita jumped up. From the direction of Tsho Rolpo Lake a siren began to shriek a loud, pulsating, high-pitched wail, like a giant car alarm gone crazy. From the direction of Beding another siren sounded, then another, until the entire valley resounded with shrieking.

"My God, it's actually happened," said Will. "I can't believe it! The lake has blown its banks."

With that, he grabbed Sumita's hand and began to run uphill.

"Let's go, girl," he panted. "Run like hell."

44 / When it rains, it pours

A decade ago, environmental researcher Norman Myers began trying to add up the number of humans at risk of losing their homes from global warming. He looked at all the obvious places — coastal China, India, Bangladesh, the tiny island states in the Pacific and Indian oceans, the Nile Delta, Mozambique — and predicted that by 2020, 150 million people could be environmental refugees. Major portions of Louisiana and Florida will be flooded within the century, and low-lying coastal cities like Houston might be destroyed. Ten million people will be displaced in Egypt, 100 million in Bangladesh, and 260 million globally.

~ Intergovernmental Panel on Climate Change

Kathmandu, Nepal, June 8, 2010

Lieutenant Colonel Katri Chetra of the Nepalese air force had the B2 Squirrel helicopter in the air and flying through a downpour five minutes after getting the call. Neither of his boots was laced, he hadn't shaved, and his sweater was thrown on hastily at the last moment, his ski jacket tossed in the backseat by an alert co-pilot. The chopper had been unloaded of any unnecessary equipment in under a minute, and the co-pilot jumped off, waving Chetra to go.

It was just under 45 minutes as the crow flies from Kathmandu to Tsho Rolpa Lake via helicopter, a place in the Himalayas where Chetra had never been before. He had a chart in his lap, with coordinates showing Beding and the Rolwaring River. He got the bird in the air heading north, and as soon as he was on course he glanced down at his charts. Beding was over 12,000 feet, not too high for the bird to fly, although he sincerely hoped it was not snowing at that elevation, which would severely limit visibility.

His mission was simple: Rescue an important person, perhaps a couple of people, famous Americans apparently, from the banks of the Rolwaring River at the upper end of the Rolwaring Valley, which was for some strange reason expected to be under a raging torrent, possibly from the monsoon forcing the collapse of a dam upstream.

"All in a day's work," thought Chetra, as the peaks of the Himalayas filled the windscreen of the craft, and his wipers madly thrashed against the storm. The reward money of $25,000 was a very tasty incentive to get there immediately and find the person or persons needing rescue, and to do whatever was necessary to pick them up.

"I wonder what the son of the U.S. President looks like?" he thought. "They say he is very tall. I wonder if he is an asshole, like his father?"

∩ew York City, June 8, 2010

During the 20th century, water use increased at double the rate of population growth; while the global population tripled, water use per capita increased by six times.

~ National Rivers System

Janet Spalding turned her right cheek to the camera, her best profile. Behind her a map of the world filled the TV screen, with blinking lights indicating the location of her various network reporters.

"Good evening. I'm Janet Spalding. Tonight we are pleased to bring you a special network presentation about climate change. How our ever-increasing air temperature is causing a major meltdown of the world's glaciers and polar ice caps, how our precious freshwater supply is at risk. We'll show you what warming of the air and oceans means to humanity. We'll explain how droughts will be part of a much hotter future. With me in the studio you'll meet several experts on these topics. We have a dozen environmental reporters scattered around the entire planet, to show you just what is happening to our warming world."

Spalding turned to her left.

"First of all, in the studio we have Dr. Carl Thomas, director of the National Climate Data Bank," she said, "with some news that no American has ever heard before. 'Hundred-year storms,' as meteorologists have called the greatest storms of the century, storms that break all records and become the benchmarks for our weather, are becoming more and more frequent. This is just what climate change researchers told us 20 years ago would happen. Dr. Thomas, what's the first evidence of these 100-year storms being eclipsed by even greater storms?"

"Well, Janet, global warming has produced an increase in precipitation during the last decade, mostly in the form of heavy rainstorms," said Dr. Thomas, an elderly bald man looking every inch the scientist in thick glasses, a cheap blue suit and mismatched tie. "These haven't been the moderate, beneficial rainstorms mixed in with occasional storms that we've always seen in the past. In recent decades there has been a 20 percent increase in blizzards and heavy rainstorms in the U.S."

"I understand," said Spalding, "that as far back as 1999, Great Britain's Meteorological Office warned that flooding in places like Southeast Asia would increase nearly tenfold over the coming decades. Tenfold. Are those predictions already becoming a reality?"

"Yes," replied Dr. Thomas, "we see that floods are already increasing, not only in Southeast Asia, but worldwide. For instance, rising seas have already inundated Pate and Ndau, two small islands near the Indian Ocean resort island of Lamu. Parts of Micronesia, mainly the smaller atolls, have already been abandoned due to rising seas. On the other hand, drought is also on the rise in many parts of the world. Australia, for instance, has been hit with both major droughts and floods, one after the other."

"We go now to our first on-location report of the evening," said Spalding, "To Josh Beringer in Canberra, Australia, who tells us that it's not rising seas threatening that country, but rather the lack of water. Australia is facing the worst drought crisis of its history, in what is feared will turn into a permanent drought."

Beringer stood in front of the capital building in Canberra. He was dressed in army fatigues and a bush hat, the overall affect of which was to make him look like he was on safari. He also looked very hot.

"Yes, thank you, Janet. Here in the Australian capital, government officials with whom we have spoken are quite alarmed about a new meteorological development, a phenomenon that threatens to permanently disrupt part of the country's meager rainfall. Spinning faster and tighter, the 100-mile-per-hour jet stream across the southern Pacific is pulling

•

climate bands south. It is dragging any rain that might fall on Australia down into the Southern Ocean. Scientists attribute this development to the depletion of the ozone layer over Antarctica, caused by man-made gases in the atmosphere."

Beringer turned and walked across the lush lawn of the capital grounds, his TV crew following.

"Scientists are calling this phenomenon the Antarctic Vortex. Focusing on the vortex for only the past few years, they have quantified increased velocity of the wind spin by measuring pressure differences between high latitudes over the Antarctic continent and mid latitudes in the Southern Ocean near Australia. Australia's 2003 drought was the worst in 100 years, and this drought is predicted to be worse. Scientists say a longstanding drought in the southwest corner of Western Australia State could be a foretaste of more extensive drought yet to come all across Australia, and perhaps even to become permanent."

Over 90 percent of the world's supply of fresh water is located in Antarctica.

~ National Rivers System

Berkeley, California, 2006

Class, all semester we have been talking about climate change as it relates to water. Yesterday one of you was kind enough to point out that there are still some skeptics who think that the warming the planet is currently experiencing is merely part of an ongoing, endless, natural cycle and has nothing to do with the damage that we humans are currently inflicting on the planet, such as emitting fossil fuels and gases into the atmosphere in vast amounts.

I am willing to concede that climate changes have occurred many times in the past, and well before homo sapiens became the dominant life force on the planet. For instance, we still don't know what caused the dinosaurs to disappear. Some say it was a gigantic meteorite that hit the planet, and they point to a gigantic underwater crater just off the Yucatan Peninsula in Mexico as proof. They speculate that vast amounts of dust were released into the atmosphere when the meteorite struck with the force of a thousand atomic bombs. I don't know, no scientists can say with certainty what happened in that instance, but I concede that the planet has gone through many cycles, both cold and hot, in its long history.

Those of you who were in attendance last month will remember that I told you about research on the rings of ancient trees found drowned in the bottom of California lakes, that California has suffered some major droughts in the past, most particularly a 200-year drought that occurred back in medieval times. Carbon dating of the tree rings showed exactly when there were droughts, and when California hit its zenith of moisture in the 1800s. So that research shows that, yes indeed, there are weather cycles that swing back and forth.

Recently the University of Bern, in Switzerland, released a report showing the various levels of carbon dioxide present in the atmosphere over the last 600,000 years. How did they do such an amazing thing? Simple; they went to Antarctica and drilled deep holes into the ancient ice.

Many other studies have shown that the level of carbon dioxide has risen from 280 parts per million two centuries ago, to 380 ppm today. So, yes, there are still some skeptics who claim the increase in greenhouse gases to be part of a naturally fluctuating cycle, but this new report from the University of Bern provides definitive evidence showing the contrary.

Researchers drilled holes nearly two miles deep in a remote part of east Antarctica called Dome C and secured ice samples that had not seen the light of day for many millennia. Deep Antarctic ice encases tiny bubbles of air formed from snowflakes falling over the course of several hundred thousand years. Previous ice core samples had traced greenhouse gases, such as carbon dioxide, back about 440,000 years. This new drilling brought back samples from 210,000 years further in the past.

Their report shows that today's levels of carbon dioxide in the atmosphere are 27 percent higher than at any time in the past 600,000 years. The speed at which the increase is occurring is 100 times faster than anything that happens naturally.

The research team did find eight naturally occurring cycles, of ice ages and warmer periods, and varying cycles of gas levels over that 600,000 year period. They also found a stable pattern; there were lower levels of gases during cold periods, and much higher levels of gas during warmer periods.

The facts are simple and from them we learn that there is a strong relationship between greenhouse gases and air temperature. Scientists are now trying to find ice samples going back over a million years. When their research is complete, we'll have a better understanding of when mankind started influencing our environment, and also what the future of the planet may look like. But any way you look at it, thanks to the amounts of greenhouse gases we are emitting into the air, the planet is going to get warmer. Many glaciers are going to melt, the seas are going to rise, and great climatic changes are going to occur. And, no, this is not a naturally occurring event; this is a disaster we are creating ourselves.

Marin County, June 7, 1977

Eighty percent of the fresh water we use in the U.S. is for irrigating crops and generating thermoelectric power.

~ National Rivers System

When the wheel was turned in the pump house on the east side of the San Rafael Bridge, water that emanated from the Sacramento Delta and flowed through Contra Costa County and through the East Bay Municipal Utilities District piping system, burst into the pipeline immediately, Marin-bound, and surged forward like a snake. It joined the Marin County underground piping system at the Rod and Gun Club, where half of the water flowed north toward San Rafael, while the rest was diverted south toward San Quentin prison, Larkspur, Corte Madera and points south.

At San Quentin prison, where the showers had been turned off for the duration of the drought thanks to a voluntary agreement by the prisoners (prior to the drought, they had been kept running all the time), a signal was given to guards. At the shower rooms in cell block 16, the word was passed on the prisoners. A lineup of men, waiting for their turn for their quick, three-minute "Navy-style" drought-inflicted showers, jumped back as all the showerheads in the cell block suddenly surged to life.

A cheer went up: "Yea!"

In schools, hospitals, residential homes, gyms and office buildings, water came back to full power. Countywide rationing was still in force, of course, but now a steady supply of water — hooked into the state water system, at last — meant that the crisis was over.

In the industrial area just south of the Canal District in San Rafael, a coupling on a newly installed section of pipe broke as the water hit, and a thin geyser of water shot 60 feet in the air. Workmen were on the spot within minutes, but in the interim, several men from a nearby auto repair shop came over to stare at the sight.

"Water, water everywhere, and ne'er a drop to drink," said William Busby, a car dealer from a shop just around the corner, to a local reporter. "Here we are, 10 seconds after finally getting our water turned on, pissing it away into the air."

Nepal, June 8, 2010

By three methods we may learn wisdom; first, by reflection, which is noblest; second, by imitation, which is easiest, and third by experience, which is the bitterest.

~ Confucius

Within minutes of the monsoon bursting over Tsho Rolpa, water from the steep sides of the mountain ran off the glacier and the lake began to swell. A chunk of the Trakarding Glacier about twenty yards in diameter, melted by the heat of the day before and inundated with heavy rainfall from the monsoon, slowly broke off and slid down the ice face, dropping into the far northern section of the lake with a plop. A huge wave spread across the lake like a miniature tsunami, hitting the sluice gate at the other end of the lake near the research center with a speed of about 10 feet per second. The gate slowed the tsunami for a second, but the wave, facing an obstacle in its path, merely rose up a few feet in the air and dropped over the edge of the moraine.

A second wave hit the moraine wall a few seconds later, then a third, each breaching the containment wall and flowing down the other side, sweeping rocks and debris along with it. Within a minute the loose wall of moraine began to crumble, then a small hole appeared in it.

Within seconds, the weight of 70 million square meters of water surged forward through the hole, bowing to the law of gravity. The wall of loose moraine gave way slowly, and then it suddenly exploded into a giant cloud of rocks and boulders as the weight of the tons of water bore down upon it. A hundred millions gallons of water surged forward, thirsting for its natural home down in the great oceans far away.

Walsh and Moore weren't far from Beding when the rain began to fall in a torrential downpour, but they trudged onward, heading for shelter. When the first siren went off, Moore jumped about a foot into the air at the sound.

"What the hell is that?" he shouted. "Who the hell is playing games? Those sirens aren't supposed to go off."

"What are you talking about?" said Walsh, dropping his pack to the ground, turning around and staring up the valley toward the eerie sound. "What the hell is with these sirens?"

"Those are the stinking emergency warning sirens!" yelled Moore, standing on his toes, trying to see what was happening up at the end of the valley. "They go off when the lake breaches its banks! Either somebody set them off on purpose, or the dam has blown, and the whole valley is gonna flood. All hell is going to break loose. We gotta run."

"What?" screamed Walsh. "What the hell is going on, man?"

"Where the heck is Will?" yelled back Moore. "We gotta get him!"

"We got two seconds to make up our minds," screamed Walsh, "because in about 60 seconds this whole valley is going to be under 50 feet of water going 100 miles an hour."

Walsh turned and started running fast uphill, leaving the trail to Beding and heading straight up the side of the valley like a jackrabbit. Moore turned away from the river and started to run after Walsh.

"This is it," he thought, "it's actually happening. I told everyone this was gonna happen, and now look. Will is a dead man and I am going to be a dead man too when his father finds out."

The distant sound of rushing water became an overwhelming roar, like a runaway freight train trapped in a small tunnel. Down the valley swept a hundred million tons of fluid death, a wall of water ripping all vegetation from the banks, swallowing huge chunks of land, gobbling up boulders the size of houses, and creating an instant vortex of destruction.

Walsh panted in the thin air, his strong mountain climber's legs propelling his body up the steep hill as fast as they could carry him, while he desperately grabbed handfuls of grass and rock to propel himself even faster. He ascended a hundred feet in less than a minute, as the roar of the advancing wall of water and debris thundered in his ears. The heavens continued to drop several months of precipitation on his head. His skin stung, his head hurt and his lungs screamed for mercy, yet he kept climbing.

Moore was right behind Walsh, scrambling at any foothold he could find. His heart pounded so hard he could barely speak, but he kept yelling to Walsh to run. He ventured a peek over his shoulder at the flood, and the sight stopped him in his tracks.

"Oh my God, look at that."

No more than 100 feet below, the first wall of water arrived with a thunderous rage, flinging boulders the size of houses into the air, sucking at the sides of the valley, grinding everything in its path into oblivion, a black nightmare of fluid energy and endless power. Within seconds the first wave passed below them and struck the stone huts of lower Beding, tearing them down like children's playthings while surging rapidly forward toward the lower Rolwaring Valley. The sirens continued to scream. For 50 miles downstream, in over a dozen villages, people heard the sirens and started running uphill for their lives.

Moore and Walsh stood above the flood and stared in horror at the deluge surging beneath them.

"I can't believe this, it's actually happening," said Moore. "I told you what was going to happen. Nobody would listen. The President is going to be very angry. I phoned and told him what could happen, I told you and I told Will, and now look at this."

"What do you mean you phoned the President?" said Walsh, turning and facing Moore. "What the hell is going on?"

"Come on," said Moore, heading up the side of the valley for another trail, "we gotta go find Will. With any luck the chopper ought to be here soon."

"A chopper?" yelled Walsh, following. "Will somebody tell me what is going on?"

Berkeley, California, 2006

In January 2006, the state of California updated its Water Plan, a document that had not been revised since 1998. The plan looked ahead for 25 years and confidently predicted that the state was in good shape with its water, and shouldn't anticipate any shortages, even though its previous plan predicted major water shortages as the population grows to 48 million by 2030.

The reason for the contradiction, according to engineers who worked on the plan for the State Department of Water Resources, is that new technology and new efficiencies will result in Big Agriculture using far less water. In fact, the new report estimates that the state will be using the same amount of water as it currently does, · 25 years from now, even with 12 million more people.

The report found that corporate agriculture, which currently uses 80 percent of the state's water, will use less water as new housing development — presumably built on farmland — reduces the amount of irrigated land by approximately 10 percent. The plan said that water-efficient products and technology have helped major metropolitan areas like San Francisco and Los Angeles keep their water consumption down, using no more water today than they did 20 years ago.

The water plan is the state's main planning tool for predicting water usage, and should be referred to as the "bible" for water planners across the state. However, reading the small print, one finds a shocking revelation hidden inside the plan. Nowhere is there any mention of what will happen to the state's water supply if there is an earthquake or drought.

Given that the state's own experts have long said that the state — the Bay Area, in particular — is long overdue for a killer quake, and several state departments have described what will happen to the levee system in the delta if and when an earthquake occurs, this report doesn't seem to be worth the paper it is written on.

Even worse, predicting that the state will not undergo a drought in the next 25 seems to be the epitome of optimism. As the effects of global warming increase, environmentalists around the world have warned about droughts and floods occurring more frequently and with deeper impact than ever before. Drought may not be our biggest worry; flooding may be of greater concern.

Even if there is no drought, one effect of global warming in California will likely be rain falling in lieu of snow at higher elevations in the Sierra. Rainfall through-out the winter — perhaps in bigger storms that we have experienced before — means heavier spring floods, rais-ing the possibility of a breach in the levee system. Heavy floods in the spring mean that reservoirs will overflow, leading to lower water levels in the late summer and fall months, when the water is most needed.

Those of you who plan to be engineers should be cautioned that good engineers plan to err on the side of caution, and take into account all relevant factors. Living in the state of California, the person who ignores earthquakes is a fool.

New York City, June 8, 2010

There are two big forces at work, external and internal. We have very little control over external forces such as tornadoes, earthquakes, floods, disasters, illness and pain. What really matters is the internal force. How do I respond to these disasters? Over that I have complete control.

~ Leo Buscaglia, author and educator

"We turn now to Frank Silverman, our correspondent in Dacca, Bangladesh," said Janet Spalding, "where the annual monsoon has arrived very early this year and flooding is drastically affecting the entire country. "

"Hello Janet. I'm here in Dacca, Bangladesh, which used to be known as East Pakistan," said Silverman, standing waist-deep in water in what appeared to be a river but was actually a city street. "Bangladesh is known as the 'land of rivers,' and you can see why."

Behind Silverman, several local residents floated by in small rowboats, a visual effect put together by his camera crew to emphasize the obvious; torrential rain was coming down, and the city was completely flooded.

"There are three major rivers here in Bangladesh — the Ganges, the Brahmaputra and the Padma — which flow together into the Bay of Bengal. The combined catchment area of these three rivers is a mind-boggling one million square miles. This is a very flat country, and it doesn't take much to flood it. Soil washed down from the Himalayas is adding to the flood damage. At the same time, the seas are rising, due to global climate change. At high tide, there is a grave danger that the entire country could be underwater in just a few years."

Silverman turned and pointed at the street behind him that had become a river. He pointed at an apartment building in front of him, in which residents were peering out the windows.

"Experts at the flood forecasting center here in Dacca," said Silverman, "say that most of the 150 rivers that criss-cross Bangladesh are now flowing close to their danger marks. Major rivers like Jamuna and Padma could overflow at any time within the next day or so, if the heavy rainfall continues."

"What we are talking about, Janet, is the future of an entire nation of 145 million people," said Silverman. "When the tsunami hit the Maldive Islands in 2004, there was great speculation about the future existence of that island state. The Maldives only has a population of 349,000 people. What are you going to do when 150 million people's lives are at stake, as they are here in Bangladesh? There is no way to stop the flooding or rising sea level, and nobody is doing anything about climate change either."

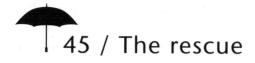

45 / The rescue

We must become the change we want to see in the world.

~ Mahatma Ghandi

Пepal, June 8, 2010

The helicopter flew low over the Rolwaring River, a raging torrent as far as the eye could see. Lieutenant Colonel Chetra had one eye on the river, and the other eye scanning the riverbanks for survivors. Near what he took to be the village of Beding, dozens of people were jumping up and down, waving their arms, trying to catch his attention. Chetra pulled out his binoculars and surveyed the survivors for any sign of the Americans.

Seeing no sign of any trekkers at the village, Chetra slowly worked his way north up the valley. Within a minute he spotted two figures on the west side of the valley, waving their arms. Looking for a place to set the chopper down, Chetra found a boulder the size of a house, about 100 yards north of where Moore and Walsh were waving their arms. Keeping the craft in a hover, he waited above the rock field for the two to appear.

Moore and Walsh soon showed up, panting from the exertion. Chetra brought the chopper close enough to have one leg touch down on the rock, while the other drifted free in the air. Walsh grabbed the leg and dragged himself aboard the craft.

"One only," said Chetra. "You help. Where is boy?"

"Will?" said Walsh. "I haven't seen him. Last I saw him, he was going down to the river with a girl. Up there, a mile or so."

Chetra and Walsh both looked down at the swollen, crashing river below. There was no way anybody could ever have survived in it for more than a few seconds.

"You come, we look," said Chetra. "He looks here."

Walsh shouted down to Moore, who had a telephone of some sort in his hands and was trying to talk on it above the whup whup of the chopper's rotor blades. Moore waved and kept talking, so Chetra pulled the craft off the rocks and started flying slowly north, following the river up toward the tiny encampment of Na. There was no sign of any life anywhere, just the raging river tearing at the banks and swallowing everything in its path. Holding his head in his hands, Walsh started to cry.

Berkeley, California, 2006

Class, this concludes our semester and I need to inform you that next week we will be holding exams on all the topics we've covered to date. I must tell you in advance if you come to the exams holding the conviction that there is no such thing as climate change, and are so bold as to put that opinion down on paper unsupported by fact, you will be respected for your individuality and your freedom of opinion, and you will automatically receive an F for the course.

Thank you to those who have acted as skeptics and have voiced their questions about the science

presented in this course. I hope you have learned something that has helped to change your mind. Many others
have asked what they can do to make a difference in this
warming world of ours, and somehow do something to
lessen the impact of climate change, and slow down the
warming that is so drastically affecting the world's water.
I am sorry to say there isn't much we can do to change
the world, but I am pleased to report that there are many
positive things you can do as individuals, and maybe
together we'll all have a collective impact.

You can take personal action, or you can encourage community action, or you can try to influence
politicians at all levels. You can set an example by using
less gas or natural gas, oil, and electricity in your daily
life. The most important energy decision you can make is
about transportation. If you buy a car, get a hybrid. Every
gallon of gas puts 20 pounds of carbon dioxide into the
atmosphere. Hey, forget a car, and buy a bike, or join a
carpool, or take mass transit, or walk.

The next time you buy an appliance, purchase
a highly efficient model. Phone your local electric or gas
utility and ask them to perform an energy audit of your
house or apartment. Reduce your daily electricity use
around your home. Work in your community to promote
energy efficiency and use of clean energy. Put pressure on
local politicians to make sure that public buildings are
models of energy efficiency. Encourage the incorporation
of passive-solar techniques in community construction or
remodeling projects.

Why not try to get your local library, businesses,
and church or synagogue to install bike racks? We can

work to create the construction of bike lanes, and change local zoning ordinances that involve excess energy use.

There is nothing stopping you from writing a letter to your local newspaper about issues pertaining to climate change. Keep a file on your newspaper's coverage of weather and water-related issues and send in responses to any stories or letters that dismiss global warming as fiction.

You can talk to your congressional representative and senators to encourage them to support actions to address the root causes of global warming, which are of course the emission of heat-trapping gases. Ask them to promote the development of clean, renewable sources of energy such as solar and wind power. Tell them that we need to reduce carbon emissions as much and as quickly as possible.

Of course you don't need to do any of these things, and when you graduate you can get your parents to go buy you a Hummer and you can go buy shares in coal companies too, if you want. But let me remind you of one last thing: This is your own world that you are building. The water you save is the water you will be drinking yourselves. You kids are the people who will have to live in the world of tomorrow. The politicians of today will be gone when the water is gone. A lot of them don't seem to care too much about the future. Do you? Do nothing if you like. The choice is yours to make.

Washington D.C., June 8, 2010

Nearly all men can stand adversity, but if you want to test a man's character, give him power.

~ Abraham Lincoln

President William White picked up the phone.

"Get me Spalding on that TV show that's on right now," he said to his aide. "The one she was bugging me about last week. I have an announcement I want to make."

The connection was quickly made, and the phone in his office rang again.

"Hello, Mr. President? This is Janet Spalding. We are live on national television. How are you tonight, sir?"

"Not well, Janet, I'm afraid. Not well at all."

"I'm sorry to hear that, sir. What is the problem?"

"I have just received some very bad news, I'm afraid. My son, as you may know, is an avid hiker and environmentalist, like a lot of kids these days. He has been on a trek in the high Himalayas. Will was trying to find out about the effect of global warming on mountain glaciers. Evidently he thought that global warming is causing glaciers to melt. Evidently, according to the news I have just received, my son has gone missing in an avalanche."

"Sir, I am extremely sorry to hear that. My sincere sympathies to you and your family," said Spalding, facing the camera directly with a look of sorrow on her face. "Thank you for sharing this news, as dreadful as it is, with us and our viewers."

"That's not why I called, Janet."

"Sir?"

"You asked me last week to come on this show, and I refused. I said the timing wasn't right. I said 'no' because I had some good news I wanted to save for a major announcement in the next week or so. Well, I want to make that announcement now."

"Please do, Mr. President."

"For a long time my administration has dodged the subject of global warming. Of course global warming is real. Even school kids know that. The CEOs of major oil companies all know about global warming. I do, you do, we all do. We all talk about it, but it just has not been politically or economically expedient for our administration to admit it publicly," said White. "What I am saying, right now and right here, is that the United States is going to commit itself, finally, to doing something about global warming. We are going to follow a new course of action. My office has delayed making any announcements because the votes have not been there. Well, we will be making an announcement tomorrow, at the White House, with all the details."

"Has something happened to change the government's position on this issue, Mr. President?"

"Yes, of course, something has happened. My son is missing, that's what has happened. I want him back. I want people at certain corporations, and in Congress, to realize that this is not a game we are playing. Global warming is real. If we had admitted that by now, my son wouldn't have gone on this stupid expedition, trying to prove to his father something I already knew. I want the nation to pray with me tonight for his safe return."

"Our hearts and prayers are with you, Mr. President. Thank you for taking this moment to share your thoughts with us. We will be praying with you tonight. I'm sure the entire nation will send out their thoughts as well. "

Nepal, June 8, 2010

It is strange how a heart must be broken before the years can make it wise.

~ Sara Teasdale, Amerian poet

Sumita passed Will a cup of hot tea. Both she and Will were soaked to the skin, sitting around a fire in the hut, trying to dry and get warmer. Down the hill they could hear the roar of the GLOF as it thrashed its savage way down the Rolwaring River, ripping its banks to bits. The sirens continued to wail faintly in the distance, down near Beding, but in the hut the main sound was the fire crackling.

"Well, that was a close call," said Will to Sumita. She said nothing, but smiled back and sipped her own cup of tea. "I hope that the other guys are OK. I bet they are safe in Beding, wondering what happened to us."

Sumita went to the corner of the hut and gathered up a yak wool blanket. She sat next to Will and wrapped herself in it. He leaned over, took the blanket, and wrapped it about both of them. She smiled and looked up at him.

"You know, I think we are both going to catch our death of cold," said Will. "May be a good idea to get rid of these wet clothes, let them dry by the fire. We don't want to get sick, on top of everything else."

The fire crackled, and the kettle started to boil again. Outside in the distance, above the faint sounds of the sirens and the roar of the river, Will could hear the faint thump thump of helicopter blades cutting through the air.

"Well, whaddya know," he said, pulling the blanket closer round them both, "it's too bad, but I think I hear the cavalry coming to the rescue."

46 / After the flood

Marin County, June 8, 1977

Percy sat on his back porch, his head in his hands, staring out at his backyard. A layer of white powder several inches thick covered his rose bushes, his garden and his lawn. A breeze had blown much of the powder into his swimming pool, half full with stolen water, on which it formed a layer of crud. The trees in the yard were covered in white powder as high as their lower branches.

"Roscoe," said Percy, patting his faithful mutt on the head, "I fear that we have been the victim of an elaborate joke. It may very well be that it is time to call a truce. One has to know when it is the proper time to beat a strategic retreat. In fact, I believe I will contact that real estate agent who has been prowling around the neighborhood. What do you think?"

Roscoe raised his head and woofed. His coat was covered in a fine layer of powder as well. From next door came the sounds of an automobile racing up the block, stereo blasting, and a man's voice soaring above the music. The car pulled up with a shriek of brakes.

"Watch out for that white powder," sang Billy, at the top of his lungs. "It'll get ya every time. Take you down and shake you, white powder wins this time."

Percy ambled over to the driveway to greet his neighbor.

"Nice day if it doesn't rain," he said. "By the way, good joke with the talcum powder."

"Whaddya mean?" said Billy, climbing out of the Tiger and opening the passenger door, where a tall, willowy, blond babe sat smiling in the passenger seat. "What talcum powder ya talking about?"

"I believe you know what I mean," said Percy, nodding toward his yard. "Isn't that the powder to which you refer in that godawful song you were just attempting to sing?"

"Hell, no, Perce," said Billy, putting his arm around his neighbor, and walking with him back to the yard. Both men stood and stared at the lawn, bushes and pool, all covered in white. "I think you forgot to read the instructions."

"What, pray, instructions were those?"

"Why, it says right on the package: Just add water and stir."

Marin County, June 8, 2010

In times of change, learners inherit the earth, while the learned find themselves beautifully equipped to deal with a world that no longer exists.

~ Eric Hoffer, writer and social commentator

"And everybody lived happily in the end."

"Grandpa, that was a very nice story," said Megan, yawning. "Are there going to be more droughts in Marin, like when you were young? Will we need to ration water this summer?"

"No, sweetheart, there is no rationing these days," said Diet. "We have enough water for everybody, but you never know what will happen in the future."

The other two little girls were already asleep on the couch. He walked Megan back to her bedroom.

"Grandpa," said Megan. "we drove over the bridge today, and we didn't see the pipeline. Did they take it away?"

"Yes, sweetheart, it's gone," said Diet, standing in the doorway. "They took it away."

"Why, Grandpa?" she said. "After you tried so hard to build it, and it saved everybody?"

"You know, sweet thing, that's another story completely," he said, turning out the light and turning away. "You go to sleep and I'll tell you that story another time."

Back in the living room, he settled down to watch TV. Janet Spalding was talking now to a reporter in Australia, and the reporter was talking about the prospect of endless drought, how scientists were saying that it might never rain again in parts of Australia. Without rain, hundreds of thousands of people were at risk of losing their property, crops and animals were dying, school yards were turning to dust, and water might have to be imported at great cost over long distances, although the government had no idea how water might be paid for, or how it could be transported over the distance required.

Reaching over to the side table, Diet picked up an old photo he kept there as a reminder, of the days when he was manager of the water district and it seemed it would never rain in beautiful Marin County ever again. It was a picture of a dead fish, impaled on a stick, found at the bottom of the Nicasio Reservoir at the end of the Great Marin Drought of 1977, the mud of the reservoir cracked and broken like the lines of an old man's face.

"When will we learn?" he said to himself. "What's that old saying? Those who ignore the mistakes of the past are doomed to repeat them? Something like that."

And he turned back to the TV screen, where Janet Spalding was talking to a man who appeared to be standing in the middle of a river while holding a microphone.

"We interrupt this show to take you from Dacca to Kathmandu, Nepal," said Spalding, "live by satellite, where Nepalese TV is presenting us with these pictures."

A helicopter was touching down on a landing pad, and the pilot was waving to the camera, and people on the ground were cheering. A big crowd was quickly forming, airport ground workers dressed in overalls and a small group of white men in businesses suits. It had been raining, as the puddles on the ground showed, but a rainbow was forming in the sky above the copter. In the background gleamed the mighty peaks of the Himalayas, capped with snow and dazzling white in the late afternoon sun.

Four people climbed out, smiling and waving. Diet recognized the tall man with blond hair and a beard as the President's son. He was holding the hand of a beautiful Nepalese girl, who was wrapped in a blanket and looking very confused. Behind her two other men were standing with their fists thrust in the air, waving to the crowd and pounding each other on their backs.

"Now what the heck is that all about?" Diet wondered, and settled in to watch.

EPILOGUE

In November of 1977 the heavens opened and it finally started to rain, coming down in buckets for a grand total of 9.49 inches that month. December was also very wet, with 11.01 inches of rain, followed by an even wetter 16.79 inches in January. After 25 months, the Great Marin Drought was officially over.

In June of 1980, J. Dietrich Stroeh tendered his resignation to the Marin Municipal Water District Board of Directors. The district was in good shape, and there were no interesting emergencies or disasters with which to deal. Looking for more challenges, Diet established Stuber Stroeh Engineering, which today is known as CSW/Stuber-Stroeh Engineering Group, located in downtown Novato.

The stresses and tensions of the drought led to constant absences from home for meetings and planning sessions, and in the early 1980s Marcia and Dietrich Stroeh agreed to a separation. Eventually, Dietrich married Marge, who had been his secretary at the water district.

Use of the San Rafael-Richmond Bridge pipeline was halted in January 1978 because of the heavy rainfall in late 1977 and early 1978. The pipeline was removed from the bridge in the early 1980s, and sold to balance the MMWD budget, even though at the time MMWD had an agreement with the L.A. Metropolitan water authorities, through the State of California, for 10,000-acre feet of water per year for Marin County.

"All we had to do was move the pipeline over the side of the bridge and it could have been kept there forever as an emergency backup," says Diet, "but the General Manager sold it for scrap. In retrospect, I think it was an unfortunate decision."

In the early 1990s, Marin residents got yet another scare, when a five-year "minor drought" afflicted the county. A voluntary rationing system was established, affecting savings of approximately 10 percent. Concerned residents immediately starting talking again about a desalination plant, an idea that originally surfaced in the 1980s but was shelved due to cost.

In 2005, a test desalination plant was constructed next to the Marin Rod and Gun Club on the shores of San Pablo Bay, not far from Point San Quentin. The costs of desalinated water were not immediately established, but estimates ranged from 4 to 6 times the cost of water currently obtained from Marin reservoirs.

This book is dedicated to William Seeger, a visionary water industry expert and my mentor and good friend.

AFTERWORD

By J. Dietrich Stroeh

The book was written to entertain and also to provide insight into an actual historical event, a severe drought that changed people's lives. This book also raises the question: "How will mankind survive with less available water, given the increase in the world's population and the resulting competition for water?"

The answer may not lie only with technology, such as desalination plants. There must be a paradigm shift in society's thinking from the current belief that "I've got mine; it's your problem" to an understanding that all available water must be shared and controlled by a single entity responsible to everyone. No one can live without water.

The lesson of the Great California Drought of 1976-77 is that there is a huge need for somebody to be in charge of each state's water supply, coordinating all water agencies and private companies. Under the present at-large system, no agency has any incentive to work with any other agency. In fact, most municipalities will fight each other rather than work together toward a solution.

When water runs short, it is also important to learn which public policies are effective, and which are resisted. Generally speaking, forced rationing is not popular, but an "allotment" program in which each person or household is allowed a certain amount — and must decide what to do with it — is accepted more readily by the public.

As water supplies become stretched, it will be necessary for all those involved in the issue of water — water districts, environmentalists, farmers, industry, fisheries, government, lumber companies, recreational interests and the general public — to develop a comprehensive plan for water supply survival. A "water master" may be necessary to coordinate all these different parties and make binding decisions according to well-defined guidelines.

Existing water supply systems must be integrated to achieve the most efficient and intelligent approach, balancing the available water supplies with the needs of a growing population.

The efficient use of water may require some of the following policies: adopting stricter conservation guidelines; more wastewater reclamation; better watershed efficiency; inter-basin watershed transfers; more efficient farming methods; elimination of water-intensive, low-profit crops; a return to landscaping that promotes native trees and plants; and new sources of water such as desalination. As supplies dwindle and the population increases, water will become dirtier and more difficult to treat; therefore it will be more expensive.

We must all work together to assure our future water needs are met. Droughts will come and go, but certainly the population will increase. With many more people and any extended drought, we will have an environmental disaster. It is an eventuality for which we must be prepared.

Novato, California, 2006

Diet Stroeh, an expert on water issues and a founding partner of CSW/ Stuber Stroeh Engineering Group, spent 20 years with the Marin Municipal Water district, the last 6 years as the General Manager who solved the 25-month Marin drought of 1976-77. He is available to speak at conferences, association meetings and other public appearances. Please contact him at: themanwhomadeitrain@sbcglobal.net

ACKNOWLEDGMENTS

This book would not have been possible without the ideas and energy of two key people, whose love and appreciation for Marin County shines every day like a ray of sunlight. I thank Dietrich Stroeh and Suzanne Dunwell for their endless energy and enthusiasm for this unique project.

Special appreciation goes to Diet for access to all his files, clippings, letters, photos and memorabilia from 1974-80, when he was General Manager of the Marin Municipal Water District, plus all the countless hours he spent with me recounting his adventures during that difficult period when it just wouldn't rain. For many years Diet has wanted to share with other people the harsh lessons that Marin learned during the drought years. As the saying goes, "Those who ignore history are doomed to repeat it." Diet is a man well ahead of his time, but soon we will all learn that earth's resources are not endless, and no resource is more essential to life than clean water.

Project Manager Suzanne Dunwell should be credited with the idea of this book in the first place. Suzanne somehow managed to keep this project on track during the many months of research, changes in style and format, roadblocks in the form of missing newspaper files, and all the other difficulties inherent in any book project. Suzanne, thanks to her unique skills and business experience, also coordinated many other aspects of this book such as editing, production, publicity and marketing. This book would not have been possible without her expert direction and guidance.

Many thanks to Joel Bartlett, meteorologist for KGO-TV in San Francisco, for his assistance in explaining various meteorological terms, his donation of books and pamphlets and other resource material relating to Pacific Coast and California weather, and for his behind-the-scenes tour of a modern television newsroom. Joel's patience, 40 years of meteorological experience, and kind assistance was also valuable during both the research and the editing process, when I struggled to learn the intricacies of global weather patterns such as the jet stream and the origins of the Madden-Julian Oscillation Effect, better known to Californians as the Pineapple Express.

Content editor Michael Harkins did a masterful job of working with a journalist who suddenly found his book was evolving into a new genre, a hybrid of history and fiction. Michael deserves thanks for his patience and explanations of how editing works, and why words need to be cut even though they have become dear friends of the writer who can't stand to lose any of them. Copy editor Laura Merlo searched out an amazing number of grammatical inconsistencies lurking in the original text.

The design and production team of Focus Design, Brian Jacobsen and Laurence Polikoff, took one look at the original layout of the book and calmly urged a more traditional design, one that people could read and actually understand. Given that there are several time periods and multiple voices represented, I thank them both for finding a way to make the book readable.

Thanks go to certain real-life characters in the book, such as engineer Ron Theisen, who took the time to explain his role in the events that transpired during the drought. Thanks also to members of Diet's family who reached back into their memories to relive the tension and frustration of the times, and to Marcia McGillis for her description of life at the Stroeh house back in 1977.

Appreciation goes to Diet's staff at CSW/Stuber-Stroeh Engineering Group who helped with charts, photos and research, including Dianne Hammerstrom, Vicki Jimenez, Helen Coale, Annette Johnson, Rebecca Walters, Rick Citti, Tom Proulx, Paul Anderson, Judy Arnold, Margie Goodman and Eric McGuire.

Finally, I'd like to thank my wife, Nancy Kirkpatrick, for allowing me to sit in an upstairs room all this time, quietly tap tap tapping away on this mysterious book of mine, when I should have been out looking for a real job, or at least scrubbing the dishes. Infinite patience is a virtue, and now that the book is a reality she can see how valuable this work is to the future of the world, or at least understand why the dishes never get done.

THE MAN WHO MADE IT RAIN   ORDER FORM

Name:	
Address:	
City:	
State:	
ZIP:	
Phone:	
Email:	

Books	Quantity	Cost Each	Amount
		$24.95	
		Subtotal:	$
		Calif. Sales Tax 7.75%	$ 2.32
		Shipping:	$ 5.00
		Grand Total	

Please make check payable to:

Public Ink

314 Sandpiper Court

Novato, CA 94949

Order online at: www.themanwhomadeitrain.com

The Man Who Made It Rain by Michael McCarthy

ISBN: 0-9772371-052495

ATTENTION CORPORATIONS, UNIVERSITIES, COLLEGES, AND PROFESSIONAL ORGIANIZATIONS: Quantity discounts are available on bulk purchases of this book for educational, gift purposes or as a premium. For information contact Public Ink, 314 Sandpiper Court, Novato, CA 94949 or send us an e-mail at: themanwho madeitrain@sbcglobal.net